THE PORTAL

Craig Conrad

Order this book online at www.trafford.com/06-1314
or email orders@trafford.com

Most Trafford titles are also available at major online book retailers.

Note for Librarians: A cataloguing record for this book is available from Library and Archives Canada at www.collectionscanada.ca/amicus/index-e.html

ISBN: 978-1-4251-8774-3

We at Trafford believe that it is the responsibility of us all, as both individuals and corporations, to make choices that are environmentally and socially sound. You, in turn, are supporting this responsible conduct each time you purchase a Trafford book, or make use of our publishing services. To find out how you are helping, please visit www.trafford.com/responsiblepublishing.html

Our mission is to efficiently provide the world's finest, most comprehensive book publishing service, enabling every author to experience success. To find out how to publish your book, your way, and have it available worldwide, visit us online at www.trafford.com/10510

www.trafford.com

North America & international
toll-free: 1 888 232 4444 (USA & Canada)
phone: 250 383 6864 • fax: 250 383 6804
email: info@trafford.com

The United Kingdom & Europe
phone: +44 (0)1865 722 113 • local rate: 0845 230 9601
facsimile: +44 (0)1865 722 868 • email: info.uk@trafford.com

20 19 18 17 16 15 14 13 12 11

LANARK, WISCONSIN
1969

PROLOGUE

Let them curse it that curse the day,
who are skillful to rouse Leviathan.

Job 3:8

Once, early in the morning,
Beelzebub arose,
With care his sweet person adorning,
He put on his Sunday clothes.

P.B. Shelley

1

THE TALL MAN HUNG BACK IN THE SHADOWS of the big maple tree, his scraggly head swiveling up one side of the dark street and down the other, until he was certain no one was about. Then he dashed from his concealment and quickly dropped the letter he had been carrying into the corner mailbox. Again his head shot darting looks along the street, making sure no one had seen him. He relaxed. No one had. The street was still empty.

A small trickle of drool leaked from the corner of his mouth as he pulled his lips back into a tight smile. Still safe, he thought to himself and, of course, to *them*. Maybe his disappearance hadn't been discovered yet.

No! the warning exploded in his brain. HE'S LOOKING!

The tall man acknowledged the information with a grunt as the smile slipped from his face. Then, he shrugged. It wouldn't matter. Let the fool look for all the good it would do him. Did his brother really think he could keep him locked up forever, separating him from his own? The trouble with James was that he always underestimated their power. After all these years, you'd think he'd know better. They are the powers that be, dear brother. The powers that be.

A car turned into the street, its headlights sweeping the trunk of the big tree before settling back on the road. The tall man quickly stepped back into the shadows. Perspiration rolled down his face, over the plastic-looking skin from under a hairline that stood out in tufts and swirls like a decaying bird's nest. He was certain no one could see him. The night held a moon, but the deep shadow of the huge, old tree provided him with perfect concealment. Still, he waited until the car's taillights disappeared in the distance. Then, he walked slowly out into the open.

The air was warm and sticky and motionless; a typical July evening in Wisconsin. There would be people outside tonight, trying to beat the heat of the indoors. Many people to choose from. He started walking.

Ten minutes of stealthy travel brought him to Fowler Street where, halfway down the block he ducked into an alley. There, under the dim illumination of a streetlight, he took a crumpled piece of paper from his pants pocket and checked the coordinates he had jotted down earlier from memory. He held the paper so close that it brushed the tip of his nose.

It had to be as exact as he could manage. That was essential. He studied the paper a moment longer, rechecking every detail, and when he was satisfied, returned the paper to his pocket. There was a short distance to go.

After three more blocks, the tall man found himself in another alley, this time between Bishop Street and Elm Boulevard. Again he checked his paper, then put it away. This is where it had to be done.

He walked back to the alley entrance at Bishop Street and stopped, tilting his head as if listening to some invisible companion.

He nodded, answering in thought-form. *Yes, this will do fine. Yes. I have it.* His thin fingers reached under his shirt and touched the knife. It was long and sharp and had a wooden handle. He listened again, then walked up Bishop Street, almost to the corner and waited.

2

TEN-YEAR-OLD DENNIS EVERS was returning home from an evening swim in Lake Michigan at the public beach in Thackeray Park. He had his wet swimsuit rolled up in a towel and tucked under his arm; his light blond hair, the same color as his mother's, was still damp from the water.

The lake had been cool and refreshing in the night heat, but the sun had set well over an hour ago and the heat still lingered. Dennis started to feel sticky again. Maybe he'd walk down to old man Jenkin's Frozen Dip for a vanilla ice cream cone before returning home.

He dug a hand into his jeans and brought out a fistful of change, mostly pennies, that he counted under the bright Texaco sign of Jake Eller's service station. Yeah, he'd just make it. But that was all right. Tomorrow he'd receive his allowance again and still be able to take in a movie over the weekend. That is, if his dad would let him.

Dennis shoved the money back into his jeans and continued down the street, his tennis shoes falling softly on the hot sidewalks, as he thought about the old Laurel and Hardy movie showing at the Pix, one of Lanark's three theaters.

His dad said all their movies were classics. He wasn't sure what that meant exactly. Unless it meant that something old was still good. He just knew he liked them. They were neat. The skinny guy always made Dennis break out in a fit of laughter whenever he started to cry.

He didn't see the tall man until he turned off Chestnut Street and started down Bishop. Then, as he got closer, he could see from the glow of the streetlight, that the man didn't look right. There was definitely something creepy about him: his hair was messed up and sticking out all over the place and he had a dopey smile on his face.

Still, he wasn't really frightened. If the guy was a pervert or something and tried anything funny, he'd just kick him between the legs and run like blazes.

Dennis tried to be nonchalant and continue on his way, but he couldn't help feeling a knot of ice forming in his stomach. Maybe he'd better cross the street so he wouldn't have to pass the guy. Just to play it safe.

Dennis crossed the street and when he couldn't resist the temptation any longer, looked back. The creepy guy was crossing over, too!

Pulling the rolled towel from under his arm and holding it firmly in his hand, Dennis took a half dozen more steps, then broke into a run. He ran halfway down the street, recrossed Bishop again and darted into the alley. Then he started to slow down. The guy was probably a mile behind him trying to catch his breath. Dennis turned his head to check the success of his escape but didn't finish the movement. A hand grabbed him by the back of his T-shirt and pulled him to a stop.

He thought about screaming but then felt something sharp scratch his throat, and the thought was never passed on to his vocal cords to be acted upon. The towel fell from his hand.

3

The tall man supervised his work. Everything seemed to be in order. Yes, it was all right. They will be pleased. Now, he must find the rest to make it complete. He would have to hurry. There was much to do before the night was over.

As he rose from the body, something dropped around his neck. He didn't have to look at it to know what it was. The pain was immediate.

"Take it off!" the tall man hissed, spinning around to face his tormentor. "Take it off!"

The man standing behind the tall man bore a striking resemblance to him. The only difference was in the appearance and the eyes. The second man was well-groomed, and his eyes lacked the other's burning intensity.

"I thought I'd find you here," the second man said. "You forgot that I have your book and I know what you're trying to do."

The tall man sank to his knees, his face a kaleidoscope of pain. He felt his body being pressed down into this ridiculous position by the mere weight of the crucifix that dangled from his neck.

"It burns!" he screamed. "Take it off!"

The second man did not answer. Instead, he moved to the small, still form sprawled grotesquely in the alley. The sight sickened him and he quickly turned away before the nausea climbed into his throat. He came at the tall man in a rage.

"You bastard! Look what you've done!"

The tall man eyed him contemptuously. "If you don't take it off, they'll get you. They know what you're doing and they'll get you for it."

The second man clenched his fists. "As God is my witness, you'll never use that damnable book again. I'm going to put an end to this madness."

He jerked the tall man to his feet and took the knife away from him. Then he dragged him out of the alley to an old, dark limousine parked in the street. He shoved him inside, got in himself, and drove away. He didn't turn on the headlights until he was a safe distance from the alley.

A block away, somewhere on Chestnut Street, a woman was calling her child in for the night. "Bil-ly! Bil-ly! Billy Herald! If you don't come in this instant, the bogeyman's going to get you!"

MILWAUKEE, WISCONSIN
1978

PART ONE

Stirrings

Awake, ye powers of Hell!

Aeschylus

But evil things, in robes of sorrow,
Assailed the monarch's high estate;
(Ah, let us mourn! – for never morrow
Shall dawn upon him, desolate!)
And round about his home the glory
That blushed and bloomed
Is but a dim-remembered story
Of the old time entombed

E. A. Poe

The

Portal

16

1

PAUL RICE STOOD BY HIS BEDROOM WINDOW and watched the rain splatter against the pane and slide in long, clear streaks down the glass. Lightning lit up the night sky and thunder rumbled threateningly close.

He looked at his watch. 2:01 a.m. He couldn't sleep. His pet demon wouldn't let him. It had been gnawing inside his head and doing somersaults in his stomach all day long; the way it had in Nam. And how many years ago had that been? Sometimes it seemed like a hundred, sometimes like only yesterday.

He turned away from the window and glanced down at the bed. Linda was still resting, her green eyes closed in sleep, her long, auburn hair draped slightly over one breast that peeked pertly over the blanket at him. The room held the unmistakable odor of sex in it.

Paul leaned over and kissed her lightly on the exposed breast, then pulled the covers up to just under her chin. She stirred, making a small throat sound, and turned over on her side, showing a length of bare shoulder and back. Paul recovered her and stepped back from the bed. He didn't want to wake her. At least one of them should get some sleep, but he was surprised at her deep slumber now, recalling earlier how keyed up she had been about the trip.

He still didn't really want to go, and a wave of apprehension washed over him that he tried to shrug off with cold logic. There was nothing to it really. Nothing to get nervous about. He was just going to meet her family – one father, one mother, one sister, one brother. Hello and goodbye. Then it would be over.

No, it wouldn't. There was more to it than that. He had promised Linda a week up there beginning tomorrow – no, today. It was already morning. It would probably be a week of observation, then cross-examination, and, of course, intentions on his part toward Linda and God knows what else. He was sorry that he had let her talk him into the trip.

Paul felt a sharp pain stab him behind his eyes, and he pinched the bridge of his nose until the throbbing subsided. Christ, he needed a drink.

Crossing the dark bedroom, he paused at the door before closing it, looking back at Linda's sleeping form once more. He closed the door softly behind him.

In the living room, he turned on the lights and headed straight for the bar. He uncorked the cognac decanter and poured a generous amount of the Courvoisier into a snifter.

He lifted the glass to his lips and took a long swallow, feeling the cognac hit his stomach and rebound with a warm glow back up to his brain. Maybe he could get the damned thing drunk enough to let him sleep.

Paul finished the drink and poured another.

Night sounds filled the room: the ticking of the mantel clock, the whoosh of the gas furnace kicking in, filling the room with blasts of warm air, and the rain drumming quietly against the house.

Paul liked the rain. He had met Linda in the rain at a concert at the Performing Arts Center. It had been good between them ever since, but now this trouble was back, tormenting him again.

Another drink.

One week wouldn't be bad. He'd go for Linda's sake. Afterward, they'd have a second week to themselves down here in Milwaukee. There would be concerts to attend, movies to see, horses to ride, and time to make love. One week wouldn't be bad at all.

When the pain came again, it hit him in the stomach, causing him to clench his teeth. He closed his eyes and hung onto the edge of the bar.

Dear God…not any more…please…I don't want this feeling…I don't want any more people to die…

The nausea passed. He opened his eyes and let go of the bar. Then he finished his drink and poured another.

2

THE GRAY CONCRETE EXPANSE OF HIGHWAY curved into a resurfaced stretch of blacktop as Linda Eastman watched Paul turn the Pontiac into the curve. The car responded to his hands with ease and grace. When the road straightened and the car came around, she looked at the countryside slide past her window again. She breathed the blowing air in deeply.

Linda loved this weather. Although some people would call it a gloomy day with only short periods of sunlight and a definite sting to the air, she thought it was beautiful. There was a serenity about autumn that summer never knew. All the kids had returned to school, and there was an absence of yelling and screaming and plastic Big Wheels racketing back and forth over the sidewalks. People no longer sat in front of their homes, or in their backyards like sunning frogs. The sudden chill of fall air drove them inside before the Wisconsin winter came with its freezing rattle. You had autumn all to yourself. There weren't many people outside to spoil it for you.

She rolled down the car window another inch, letting the wind wash across her face and stir her hair.

Paul sniffled.

"If you don't stop doing that," Linda said jokingly, "I'm going to hit you. You've been sniffling ever since we left. Didn't you take your pills?"

"I took two before we left the house," Paul said. Autumn was his favorite season, too, but it always played hell with his sinuses. Consequently, he came prepared for any emergency, stuffing his jacket pockets with bottles of Coricidin and Excedrin before leaving.

"It doesn't seem to be helping."

"Sorry, I just won't breathe anymore."

Linda smiled and pinched him lightly on the thigh.

"Ow!" Paul yelled with mock injury. "You're getting stronger."

Linda flexed her biceps. "That's from lifting all those heavy brushes and palettes. Really does wonders for a girl's arms."

Paul was still surprised that she was an artist, and a rather successful one at that, her "rainy-day-people" were really catching on. The first time he saw her, he would have bet money that she was a model. He glanced appreciatively at her breasts pushing out against the black turtleneck sweater she was wearing, then down at the stockinged thighs exposed by the pull of the car seat against her skirt. He savored the thought of last night when she was pressed beneath him, those long, good legs encircling his waist.

"You're leering," she said.

"I know. I was just thinking that lifting those brushes doesn't hurt your chest either."

She pinched him again, harder. "You're terrible."

"I know. A dirty old man at thirty-three."

"A dirty young man."

Paul smiled. Some people definitely looked better with their clothes on. Linda was one of the rare ones who had the natural beauty to walk around naked.

Linda caught his smile as he turned away. "Now what?"

"Oh, just leering again," Paul said, "and taking in how great you look."

She held her head off to the side, her green eyes flashed at him. "Why, thank you, sir."

"Pay me," Paul said, holding out his hand for compensation.

Linda slapped his hand away playfully, and then grabbed it as he tried to pull it back and held it on her lap. She noticed a slight tremor pulsing through his fingers. He was probably anxious about meeting her family, she thought. But he needn't be. They'll love him – or most of them will. She couldn't say about her father. He could be trouble. Sometimes he could get rather difficult, remembering how he found fault with every boy she had ever brought home. Pick. Pick. Pick – until he drove them away and they never came back.

But Paul was different. He wouldn't let her father browbeat him. He'd stand up for himself. If only he wouldn't keep things from her. She looked over at him and watched the wind move his black hair. Something was still bothering him, but she attributed that to the fact that he hadn't really gotten over the war yet. God, she hoped it would be soon.

About the only thing she had been able to get him to open up about was the light. He had gotten over that now, but at first, when she started spending her nights with him, he would always have to sleep with a light on. Her immediate thought had been that it was just some silly, little-boy thing that he had never outgrown – until she got him to talk about it. It seemed that ever since he had been wounded in a night ambush in Vietnam, he had this fear about sleeping in the dark. He had been afraid that his life-force or soul would leave his body and he would die.

She remembered reading something, somewhere about a similar incident. Was it Hemingway or one of his characters who couldn't sleep in the dark? She couldn't recall exactly. Anyway, Paul was over that phobia now, and in a way, she liked to think that she helped him. Maybe in time he'd be able to tell her what was still bothering him, or at least tell her that he loved her without her having to drag it out of him. She was certain he did love her. It was just that he never came right out and said it. In fact, he seemed to avoid the very words.

Linda pushed the problems from her thoughts, shelving them for another time when she would drag them out again for another look.

She squeezed his hand.

Paul turned and smiled at her. "How much longer?"

"Not long. About an hour." She closed the slightly open window. The air had become cold. "You and my brother should hit it off. You both like books so much."

"That would be Dwayne. He's what, fifteen? Sixteen?"

"Sixteen," Linda said, "and an insatiable bookworm."

"Then there's Christine."

"Chrissie."

"She's the youngest," Paul said, remembering what Linda had told him about her family.

"Fourteen – the baby."

Paul nodded and concentrated on the road ahead.

Linda fell silent, too, watching the scenery dash past the car window again: cows and horses cropping grass in pastures near small, warm-looking farms; cornstalks standing bent and brown in the wind; trees spotlighted by the sun, when it managed to poke through the clouds, highlighting the golds and reds of softly turning leaves; and pumpkins, with Halloween a few days off, lining the fields with long streaks of orange.

"Beautiful, isn't it?" Paul said, taking her out of her reverie.

Linda smiled. "I love autumn most of all. It makes you feel so good just to be alive."

Paul sniffled again.

They both laughed.

Nothing could spoil this day – not even her father. She wouldn't let him.

3

HELEN EASTMAN HAD ALWAYS WANTED a big house with large grounds and servants. Although the Fitgeralds weren't exactly her idea of old family retainers, she still considered herself lucky to have them the way people in town felt about the house. And Alison was good in the kitchen and with the housework, though she leaned on the melancholy side of life most of the time and her superstitions were enough to make a person supplicate to the heavens for relief. God, the woman had one for every occasion.

Alison's husband, Claude, on the other hand, was more down to earth; and judging from his appearance, he seemed to spend most of his time wallowing in it. He did, however, manage to keep the grounds immaculate despite his careless concern about himself.

So, looking on the plus side, Helen Eastman was satisfied with the both of them, and certainly with the house, even though Chrissie thought the Fitgeralds were creepy, and Dwayne thought something was wrong with the whole house. He and his father had been arguing again this morning about just that very thing. But then Dwayne had always been the most sensitive one of the family, seeing and feeling things that were beyond the rest of them, like the time her mother died. He knew before the phone call came. Still she couldn't help feel that he was just too wrapped up in the stories about this place. After all, it was just a house; and it was her house now. It wasn't as if it were alive or anything.

And her dear husband was only being himself this morning when he told Dwayne much the same thing, only in much stronger language – but then, anger was always John's best emotion. She sometimes felt it was his only one, especially toward Dwayne.

Ten years ago, she had had enough of his hollering and bellowing around the house and was ready to walk out. But the children were still small, and she had to think of them. They were her life. The only good things that had come out of her marriage. So she played her part, kept things amiable, and the family together. Linda was out of it now. She would wait until Dwayne and Chrissie were old enough, then she'd see.

Sometimes, when she thought about it, she guessed she had never really loved John. It was just that all her friends were getting married at the time. Everyone except her – and he was always hanging around. So, when he asked her, she accepted, resigned to the fact that she would never meet anyone else.

Not that John had not done well by her. He had. He was a good provider. His plumbing business and investments had become very successful. The house was just one of the benefits reaped. There had been others over the years: traveling, clothes, jewelry, their house in Milwaukee, their cabin in Wyoming, and their townhouse in Florida. But this house was what she always wanted. It was elegant with an old family tradition, sprawling grounds, and Lake Michigan pounding like the sea just outside her bedroom window. She would enjoy it as long as she could. Then, she would see.

Helen put down the book she hadn't really been reading, got up from her chair, and went to the bank of French doors that overlooked the driveway from the living room. She had thought she heard a car coming. Drawing the curtain aside, she looked out. Maybe it was Linda. No, just Claude and his old pickup, heading for the tool shed.

She looked out a moment longer. The front grounds were a splash of colors: red, gold, green, and brown. Some of the leaves were falling, seesawing down in long, lazy glides that ended on the lawn or the driveway. Others, already days on the ground, had dried and curled into crisp, brown shells that cracked underfoot. The sun was bright for the moment, but its warmth was false in the cool autumn air. The days would be shorter now, the nights longer. It was nature's final splurge before the bleakness of winter.

Letting the curtain drop, she turned from the glass panels, deciding to make a last minute inspection of the two guest rooms before her company arrived. She wanted everything to be perfect for Linda and her young man – was it Paul? Yes, Linda had told her his name was Paul Rice.

She started up the stairs. Early this morning, she had told Alison to dust the rooms, change all the bedding, and see to it that they were ready for occupancy.

Upstairs, she checked Linda's room first, then went down the hall to Paul's. Both rooms had been prepared according to her instructions. They smelled clean and fresh. Satisfied, she started for the stairs, then hesitated at the entrance to her son's bedroom. She paused in the doorway and sniffed the air. Nothing. She entered the room, examining the walls – decorated with several movie posters and pennants from Lanark High School and the Green Bay Packers – then the bed, the desk, and the rest of the furniture. Everything seemed natural. She tested the air again, then walked over to the closet, opened the door, smelled inside. Still nothing. No odor anywhere. Dwayne was just letting his imagination carry him away. There was nothing wrong with this room or with the closet.

The large, nautical wall clock in the upper hall struck two bells. A few seconds later, the grandfather clock in the downstairs foyer chimed the hour. It was one o'clock already. The morning had gone by fast enough and now the afternoon was flying. Helen moved to the bedroom windows, which overlooked the driveway. The drive was empty. They should be here soon. And what was keeping the rest of her family? She and the Fitgeralds were the only ones here.

Leaving Dwayne's room she walked to the head of the stairs, started down, and heard the front door open and close.

"Is that you, John?" she called down.

“It’s me, Mom.”

“Chrissie.” Helen came into the foyer. “Chrissie, have you seen your brother?”

Christine Eastman was a pretty, fourteen-year-old brunette with coquettish, gray-green eyes and a smile that would steal your heart. She was tall and slender like her mother and older sister.

“No, Mom,” she said, hanging her coat in the foyer closet. “But he said he might stop at school and see Miss Holmes about an English assignment.”

“Today? I specifically told him to stay around the house. Doesn’t he get enough school during the week?”

“Don’t worry, Mom. Dwayne knows Linda’s coming home today.”

“Your father’s been gone for over an hour, too. And I wanted everyone here when Linda arrived.”

Christine lifted her long hair up off her neck, then let it fall nonchalantly across her back again. “Well, Dad likes to look around the stores sometimes, but he’ll be here for the inspection.”

Mrs. Eastman moved to one of the two narrow windows that flanked the front door, started to look out at the driveway again, and then turned quickly back to her daughter. “Inspection?”

“Well, he always does, doesn’t he?”

“Christine, your father merely wants to make sure that the young men his daughters bring home are right for them.”

“You mean scare them off if he can.”

“Christine, what’s getting into you these days?” Mrs. Eastman said through a slight frown.

Chrissie gave a pout. Every time her mother wanted to be firm or make a point, she called her Christine. “Well, it’s true. You know how he was with Linda’s boyfriends and the way he is with Tommy. Tommy just sets foot inside the house and Daddy’s asking him if it isn’t time for him to be home.”

Helen Eastman knew her daughter was right, but would never mention John’s faults in front of the children. Besides, Chrissie had always been his favorite.

"Teenagers shouldn't be out till all hours of the night," Helen said.

"M-o-t-h-e-r, nine-thirty isn't all hours of the night. Besides, Daddy does that when Tommy's here during the day, too."

The foyer clock struck the quarter hour.

"One-fifteen," Mrs. Eastman said. "What's keeping everyone?" Then she walked over to her daughter, turned her around and pointed her toward the stairs. "Now, not another word, young lady. Go upstairs and change into a dress."

"Oh, Mom, do I gotta?" Chrissie was dressed in a big, baggy sweater and jeans.

"Yes, you gotta," Helen said, parroting her daughter's patois and sending her off with a slap on the rump.

"Ohhh." Chrissie looked back at her mother and twisted her face in a distasteful expression.

"And stop making that horrid face before your face freezes that way permanently."

Chrissie twisted her face even more and hunched over like Quasimodo.

Her mother made a threatening gesture to hit her again, and Chrissie deftly skipped away, running up the stairs. Halfway up, she stopped, turned around, and leaned on the banister. "What do you think he looks like?"

"Who, for goodness sake?"

"Linda's beau. I bet he's nice."

Mrs. Eastman raised her eyebrows in thought. "He's probably very nice if she's bringing him home. Now stop dallying and change into that dress." She lowered her voice. "They'll be here soon and I still have to light a fire under Alison so that everything is ready."

"You'd better light one under Claude, too. He was leaning on his rake as I walked up the drive, ogling me as usual." She made her Quasimodo face again.

"Christine…"

"I'm going, I'm going." She turned and darted up the stairs. Mrs. Eastman sighed, then went into the kitchen to check on Alison.

4

THE SIGHT OF TWO LONG-HAIRED BOYS walking across the Westover parking lot, one of Lanark's new shopping centers, made John Eastman physically ill. He watched them as one would observe some grotesque life form parade by his Cadillac, stringy hair blowing in the October wind, slopping along on platform shoes.

Christ. They always reminded Eastman of something out of a sideshow. If Dwayne dressed like that or kept his hair that long, he'd take the strap to him, even though he was sixteen years old. Eastman's father wouldn't have done less.

He watched the boys a moment longer, then got out of his car and went into Westover's enclosed mall, shaking his head in disgust. Eastman sported a crew cut himself, and his brown and gray hair stood up like bristles on a stiff brush. He was just a notch under six feet – everyone on his side of the family was tall – and his brown eyes always gave the impression that they disapproved of most of what they saw.

Like his father, he wore no facial hair and didn't much care for those who did. There were some men, even a few working for him at his own plumbing company, who had so much hair on their faces they looked like Hollywood monsters. It was a strain not to tell them how ridiculous they looked, but, according to the new, pinko laws, he couldn't discriminate against an employee's appearance. Eastman wondered what his father would've thought about this brave, new world if he was alive today.

Hamner's was at the far end of the mall. The store was crowded and Eastman shouldered his way through the people, heading for the catalog pickup department at the rear of the store. He frowned at the activity of store personnel putting up Christmas displays throughout the store. Garland was being strung, shelves stocked with tree lights and ornaments and tinsel, and in the middle of the floor, a Christmas tree was being trimmed. Eastman shook his head. Here it was only October – not even Halloween yet – and they were shoving Christmas at you already. Next they'd be commercializing it in July.

When he reached the pickup department, there was a bevy of women waiting at the counter. Sighing in disgust, he took a plastic card, number 25, off the counter hook and checked it against the last number called hanging from another hook on the wall behind the counter. Number 15. Goddamn. There were ten ahead of him. He looked at his watch, swore under his breath, glared at all the people milling around, and stepped back, waiting his turn.

A middle-aged woman with red hair, standing next to him, gave him a pleasant smile. Eastman didn't smile back. He was in an irritable mood. The argument he had had with his son early this morning still bothered him. There had been arguments before, but lately, it was always about the same thing. Why a grown boy had to sleep with the lights on in his room every night was beyond him. Eastman just could not understand why his son was afraid of the dark – or the closet – or whatever the hell he was afraid of. Dwayne hadn't done anything like that since he was small – and only then because he was frightened he would suffocate if the lights were out. Now, ever since they had moved into the new house, he started again.

"Number twenty," one of the girls behind the counter called out. Five to go. There were three women waiting on customers: one, tall and skinny with pimple breasts; another, short and as wide as she was high; the last, young, with stringy hair and too much eye makeup.

Eastman had tried to understand Dwayne's objections to the house, but no one else ever heard any noises, smelled any strong odor, or felt unnaturally cold in any of the rooms.

"Number twenty-three," stringy-hair said.

So if you didn't believe in ghosts or the supernatural or any of this mumbo jumbo that was sweeping across the country – and he certainly didn't – what was one to think? A phobia of some sort?

"You don't have to take a number if you only want a catalog, sir," pimple-breasts said to a new arrival.

Then there was this business about Holly. Eastman assumed that the dog had merely run off for a while, although she had never done so before, but Dwayne tried to read something else into it, connecting it in some way with his obsession about the closet. But how in the hell could a closet cause Holly's disappearance?

"Number twenty-four," five-by-five said.

And now Linda was coming home, dragging her latest boyfriend along. He wondered what this one was like, and then pushed it from his mind. He did not look forward to the prospect of meeting anyone new much less putting up with them for a week (his wife's idea). It was bad enough stumbling over Tommy Burham every day or whomever else Chrissie brought into the house.

"Number twenty-five," pimple-breasts said.

"Here," Eastman said, holding up his card and forcing his way to the counter.

Pimple-breasts smiled and took his number. "Your last name and the last two digits of your phone number."

"Eastman." He paused, thinking. "Four, two."

Still smiling, she hung his number card up, looked over a pigeonholed section of the wall that was labeled numerically in two digit numbers, selected a folder, and thumbed through its orders.

"That's John Eastman, 866 Blackmoor Road?" she asked, pulling an order from the folder.

Eastman nodded.

The woman replaced the folder and disappeared through an open doorway into the back of the department. She reappeared a minute later with a large brown package and plopped it on the counter in front of Eastman. "Will that be cash or charge, Mr. Eastman?"

"Charge." Eastman handed her his charge plate and eyed the bulk of the package. It was the fur bedspread that he and his wife had ordered for Chrissie's birthday early next month.

"That comes to one hundred and three dollars even," pimple-breasts said, ringing up the sale on a computerized cash register. Then she handed him his charge plate, the sales slip, and a pen. "Sign at the bottom, please."

Eastman signed, and as she was stapling his copies of the sale together, she stopped and looked at the order form.

"866 Blackmoor Road," she said, "isn't that…the Durie house?"

Suddenly all the conversation stopped around him; and every head at the counter turned in his direction. It was as if she had just said something not meant to be spoken aloud.

"It used to be," Eastman said, tossing the pen on the counter. "It's the Eastman house now."

"Oh, yes," pimple-breasts said and forced a smile. "Have a nice day."

Eastman scowled at her and at all the faces still turned toward him. He grabbed his package and stormed out of the store to his car. First it was the priest. Now this. The whole town was nuts.

5

"YOU SCREW ME GOOD," she said.

Dwayne Eastman smiled. Her obscenities no longer bothered him. At first, when they started having an affair, her sudden change in character startled him. How the prissy and prudish Miss Barbara Homes could turn into a passionate, demanding, and vulgar person whenever she got into bed with him was beyond his comprehension. He was not able to understand her metamorphosis. It was like being with another person. But after weeks of lovemaking, he now found her vulgarity more stimulating than shocking.

"I mean it, Dwayne," she said. "You give it to me good."

"You're a good teacher."

They both laughed.

But it was the truth. He had been a virgin when he climbed into her bed. She had encouraged him, taught him control, and did not laugh at his lack of finesse.

"You're a very promising student."

That brought on another spasm of laughter.

They were in Barbara's house, lying in her bed, spent from their previous lovemaking. This was their idyll. Their in-between time to relax and talk before Barbara would become passionate again, vulgar again, and Dwayne tumescent.

Barbara noticed that Dwayne was lost in his thoughts. He had drifted away from her again. It was becoming a habit. One she disliked. She snuggled closer and ran a seductive finger down his chest.

"A penny for your thoughts," she said. "Or has inflation spiraled the thought market, too?"

"For you, no charge," Dwayne said and kissed her gently on the lips.

He had been thinking about the closet, but he would never tell Barbara about it lest she would think him a coward or too juvenile. He feared someday she would wake up from her enchantment and send him away. Dwayne still could not believe he had actually become her lover. When he thought about it, he guessed she had really seduced him. At first, she was just friendly. Later, she started helping him with his themes for her English class and encouraged him to join her drama group. Eventually, she invited him to her house after school, then into her bed.

Dwayne would never have dreamed trying anything with her on his own, not that she wasn't an attractive woman. He liked the way she wore her long brown hair, parted in the middle, and her face never needed any makeup to give it beauty. He would never have dared simply because she was his teacher, older and more mature, and he respected her – loved her.

"Is something bothering you?" she persisted.

"Nothing. Just thinking."

"About Holly again?"

"No, not really."

"But you are worried about her, aren't you?"

Dwayne nodded. "She's been gone for two days."

Barbara nibbled his ear. "Please don't feel bad. I don't like it when you feel bad. Your dog will probably show up in a few days. Maybe she just wandered off in search of a little romance. Every girl needs a little romance in her life."

Dwayne smiled.

"That's better. That's much better."

She reached over and kissed him hard, her tongue exploring his mouth, her breasts pressing into his chest. She could feel him swell into life.

"Screw me again," she said.

The idyll was over.

6

WHEN HELEN EASTMAN WALKED into the kitchen, Alison Fitgerald was slicing carrots on the wooden cutting block. She was a large, big-boned woman in her mid-fifties with graying blond hair and muscled arms and legs. Her face, at an earlier time in life, had been quite handsome, but had now swollen into fat. She stared morosely out the kitchen window, watching her husband rake leaves in the back grounds, her big arms working the large knife in a perfunctory manner, but each cut was very smooth, very precise.

Like her parents, the only work Alison knew was how to do for others. Her mother and father were middle-aged and retired when she came along, but they did the best they could for her. She always had a roof over her head, enough food to eat, adequate clothes to wear, and their love.

Money was always hard to come by. The big check that came from out of state every month helped, but as she grew older, that soon dwindled. The checks became smaller, coming less frequently, and then they stopped completely. The little money her parents had managed to save over the years was not nearly enough to give her a college education. And so they taught her the only thing they knew – how to be a servant.

When Claude came along, she was thirty, still living at home, and had just about accepted the fact that she would be an old maid. That was twenty-five years ago. It had been good between them from the start, especially the lovemaking, but now everything they ever had together was wasting away. Not on her part, but on Claude's. He seemed to have lost his feeling for her.

"All the rooms look very nice, Alison," Helen Eastman said, standing beside her.

Alison turned away from the window. "It isn't every day that Miss Linda comes home."

"No, it isn't," Mrs. Eastman said. "The last time was about six months ago, and she only stayed a few days. This time it's something special. And it's for a whole week."

Alison finished the last of the carrots, put the knife down, and wiped her hands on her apron. "That 'something special' would be the young man she's bringing home." She sighed. "Young love. That's the best time. It was for Mr. Fitgerald and me. Now look at us."

"Why, Alison, you're never too old to love."

"It's fine to think that way, but the body gets old even though you have young ideas. It would be nice to stay young forever. Ah, but there is no way to do that."

Her gaze shifted out the kitchen window again at the figure of her husband.

"Take Mr. Fitgerald, there," Alison said. "He was quite the figure of a man when he was younger. Now he's old and shapeless like me. But he still fancies himself a ladies' man. He has an eye for the young ones."

Mrs. Eastman was awkwardly silent, embarrassed. It was the first time she had ever heard Alison talk this way. In fact, it was the longest string of words she had ever heard her put together. Helen patted her arm. "All men look at women, Alison. It's just part of their nature."

Alison nodded somberly, accepting the nature of man with the heavy weight of the inevitable truth, but did not like it one bit.

"Ah, the pies!" Alison said, slipping around Mrs. Eastman to the built-in oven which she opened with an apron-covered hand.

Helen moved in behind her. "They look beautiful."

"Just a little longer yet," she said, closing the oven door. "What time will they be here?"

"Any minute, I hope."

Something banged against the outside of the house.

Helen turned, looking at the door. "What was that?"

"Sounded like someone at the back door. Maybe it's Claude."

They moved to the door together, but Alison opened it. There was no one there. She started to close the door, and then she saw the broken body of a bird lying on the stoop.

"What is it?" Mrs. Eastman asked.

"Nothing," she said. "Just a bird. Must have lost its way. I'll tell Claude to take it away."

It was a sign, but she would not tell Mrs. Eastman what it meant. She did not want to spoil her day. Alison closed the door and returned to her duties. Mrs. Eastman left the kitchen.

Poor thing, Alison thought. The signs were always there for you to see, all around you, telling you what to expect, what to do. It was just a matter of reading their meaning. This was a bad one.

Someone in this house would die.

And soon.

7

THE REFLECTORIZED GREEN SIGN with white lettering read: LANARK.

The exit came up on Paul's right. He took it, turned off the expressway onto County Trunk Q, then followed several miles of winding highway into town.

After making the last curve into the city limits, the first part of Lanark that you saw was the ninety-foot bell tower of St. Casmir's. The Roman Catholic Church was a Gothic structure of quiet strength. Its pointed arches, stained glass windows, and weathered granite sat impressively among verdant lawns and decorative gardens.

Paul and Linda passed the church slowly, taking in all of its grandeur. They did not see the old priest standing in the churchyard watching them with worried eyes as they passed.

Beyond St. Casmir's, large expensive homes on spacious lots dotted the landscape. Ahead, another church came into view, looking like a ski lodge. This one was St. Andrew's Episcopal. Then brick condominiums appeared; and after that, more homes, but smaller and closer together with businesses cropping up among them. The stoplights increased in number until there was one on every corner. Traffic picked up. More people could be seen walking along the streets. Business places became wall-to-wall, dominating the area.

"You turn right at the next stoplight," Linda said, directing Paul.

He made the turn, passing an old World War II howitzer anchored to the ground in front of the gray stone, Roman columned building of Lanark's courthouse and jail. After a while, the business section began to fade and housing started up again. Paul could see the lake straight ahead and beautiful homes, secluded behind sprawling, wooded lands.

Paul whistled. "Pretty exclusive neighborhood."

"Wait till you see the house," Linda said. "You turn left at the end of the block – Blackmoor Road."

Paul swung the Pontiac up Blackmoor Road's sloping incline. There were not many homes along this stretch of the road; and soon there were none at all, just dark patches of close standing trees. Then the trees thinned out off to the left, and the land slanted down into well manicured acres of grass, sandy beaches, and the lake.

"Is that a park down there?" Paul asked.

"Thackeray Park," Linda said. "We're on the peninsula now. The house isn't far. There, on the right."

Paul slowed the car. A break in the woods revealed the start of a driveway.

"Here," Linda said.

Paul turned. Trees lined the drive on both sides, throwing it in shadow. Gradually, the trees fell back, leaving a clearing of lush, green lawn that led to the house.

It was a brooding, rectangular house, a fortress of light brown stone. French doors decorated its face like rows of teeth, and a tiled terrace enclosed it on three sides. A stone balustrade bordered the terrace. Six stone steps led up to the heavy wooden front door.

Paul stopped the car. The circular drive curved back to meet the road.

"What do you think?" Linda asked as they stood next to the car.

Paul smiled. "Where's the moat and drawbridge?"

Linda laughed. "Silly." She took his hand. "Come on."

As they climbed the terrace steps, Linda gave Paul an unnoticed inspection. She was certain her father would look at him up and down and inside out. Her eyes could find no fault with him. She loved his deep gray eyes, his tall, slender body, his rugged good looks, his hands. She loved everything about him – even the small scar that curved above his right eye – a souvenir from Vietnam. He had other scars. Some he still carried inside.

If anything, her father would be critical of Paul's mustache. Linda didn't care. This was going to be the man she would marry; the father of her children – even though Paul didn't know it yet.

Linda started to feel nervous. She fought if off.

Sometimes she felt that her father had never fulfilled his true calling in life. He should have been a professional critic. Linda often wondered how her mother had managed to put up with him all these years without getting a divorce. She would never have blamed her for walking out. It wasn't that Linda didn't love him. She did. He was her father, but it was embarrassing the way he acted most of the time.

Paul looked at her. "Is something wrong?"

"No," Linda said. "What could be wrong?" She rang the bell.

Alison answered on the second ring.

Paul saw a heavily powdered face cracked with age stare at them. It did not smile.

"Hello, Alison," Linda said. "Remember me?"

"Yes, Miss Linda," she said, her face never changing expression. "Come in. I'll tell your mother that you're here." She closed the door behind them, padded across the parquetry floor, and disappeared into the back of the house, leaving them alone in the entrance hall.

"Who's that?" Paul whispered.

"That," Linda said, whispering back with a smile, "is Alison."

"I gathered as much. But what is she?"

"She's the woman my mother and dad hired to help with the house. Her husband does the grounds. You should see him."

"I can hardly wait. Doesn't she ever smile?"

"If she does, I've never seen her."

The large foyer branched off into wings on both sides of the entrance. Straight ahead, a sweeping staircase rose gracefully into the upper part of the house.

"Big, isn't it?" Linda said, watching Paul look around.

"I'll say."

"It has twelve rooms. My father had some of the rooms made smaller, especially upstairs."

"Your parents must like big houses."

"They do. They've always wanted a big house, especially my mother. Come on. I'll show you around."

Linda led Paul to the first room off to the right and opened its wide double doors. The room was large. Paul was certain that the entire first floor of his house would have fit in it easily. It was furnished with dark leather couches and chairs, heavy tables, a bar, and big brass table lamps. Ceiling-to-floor bookshelves of black walnut covered most of three walls. A pair of French doors, opening onto the terrace, faced the driveway; and a portable TV set, in a wheeled cart, rested in front of them. There was a fireplace, built of large stone blocks and as wide as a one car garage, that dominated one wall, and there were books – books everywhere – bound in matching leather sets lining every shelf.

"This is the library," Linda said, watching Paul savor the room.

"Very nice," Paul said. It reminded him of a private men's club.

"I thought you'd like it."

"Like it? I think it's great."

"So, that's where you disappeared to," Linda's mother said, entering the library. The two women embraced, kissing one another on the cheek.

When Paul saw Mrs. Eastman, it was easy for him to tell where Linda got her good looks. She was shorter than Linda, but the features were the same. They could have passed for sisters.

Linda made the introduction, and Mrs. Eastman offered Paul her hand. Her grasp was warm and friendly.

"Where are your things?" Mrs. Eastman asked.

"They're still out in the car," Paul said.

“Why don’t you bring them in? Linda can show you your room and the rest of the house, if you like.”

“I like. I’ll go get our luggage.” Paul smiled and left the room.

“We put Paul in the room next to Dwayne, and you’re down the hall where you stayed the last time,” Helen Eastman said, then gave her daughter a sideways look. “Is it serious?”

“Very serious. He doesn’t know it yet, but I’m going to marry him.”

“Good. He doesn’t have to know. Men are always the last to know anyway.”

They both laughed like a couple of schoolgirls.

“I just hope Dad doesn’t start giving him the third degree.”

“Oh, you know your father. Just don’t pay any attention to what he says. I never do.”

They laughed again.

“Where is Dad, by the way?”

“He’s in town running a few errands and picking up Chrissie’s birthday present. He’ll be back shortly.” She squeezed Linda’s hand. “I’m happy for you. Very happy. Now, when Paul gets back, why don’t you show him around? I have to finish a few things in the dining room and get Alison straightened out. She seems to be upset about a bird hitting the back door. You know how she is. She tries to keep it from you, but I know when something upsets her.”

“Another omen?”

Mrs. Eastman smiled and nodded. “Honestly, lately she’s becoming as bad as your brother.”

“Dwayne? Why? What do you mean?”

They stepped out into the foyer.

“Oh, it’s just the way he’s been acting since we moved in,” Mrs. Eastman continued. “It’s nothing, really. I’m sure he’ll get over it. We’ll talk later.”

Paul bumped his way through the door that he had left slightly open, carrying four suitcases like a redcap, then set them down and closed the door.

“I’m glad your daughter didn’t bring any more clothes, Mrs.

Eastman," Paul said. "Otherwise, I'd have had to wear all of mine."

Linda looked at him with mock anger. "Well, you don't expect me to wear the same clothes every day, do you?"

Helen Eastman laughed and patted her daughter's arm. "Show Paul the rest of the house. I have to get back to Alison for a minute." Then to Paul she said, "Women's work."

After her mother left, Linda gave Paul a tour of the downstairs rooms: the dining room with its long mahogany table and chairs was set for dinner; then the living room with its soft velvet furniture; and the game room with matching pool and card tables that even boasted a table tennis setup.

Linda only indicated the direction of the kitchen in the rear of the house, feeling the time was not right to show Alison's domain when she was in a cooking frenzy – and in one of her soothsaying moods.

They went upstairs. A wide, carpeted corridor branched off left and right, its walls decorated with paintings of the Impressionists: Monet, Pissarro, Manet, Degas, Cezanne, Van Gogh, and others that Paul wasn't familiar with. Straight ahead, a large ship's-wheel clock dominated the wall space opposite the stairs.

"It looks like the Louvre," Paul said. "Is there a Prado section?"

Linda smiled. "Dad doesn't like Goya or El Greco."

"I'm impressed with what he has. Are all of them originals?"

"Some of them. A few he managed to pry away from private collectors."

"Does he have any others?"

"In the den. Winslow Homer and Montague Dawson. You want to see them?"

"Later. I'd like to get settled first. Are all the rooms up here bedrooms?"

"No. There's a sort of sewing room my mother uses, a bath, and the den that I just mentioned. You haven't been paying attention to your tour guide. The other five rooms are bedrooms."

"Sorry, tour guide. How come I don't see anything of yours hanging on the walls?"

“I’m afraid my father hasn’t quite gotten used to the fact that I want to paint instead of play the piano.”

“But you do both beautifully.”

“Liar. I flounder about at the keyboard.”

“I didn’t see a piano downstairs unless there’s one up.”

“My father sold it when I started painting.”

“Hey, is this a private conversation or can anyone join in?”

Paul turned to see a pretty teenage girl come strolling down the hall in a short, blue dress, then watched as she and Linda hugged each other with obvious affection, bombarding each other with rapid-fire questions and answers.

“Oh, Chrissie,” Linda said, finally turning to Paul. “I want you to meet Paul Rice. Paul, this is my sister, Chrissie – the baby of the family.”

Chrissie wrinkled up her nose at her sister. “Everyone always says that when they introduce me. It’s like I had two heads or something.”

Paul laughed. “Hello, Chrissie.” Then to Linda he said, “She’s even prettier than you described her.”

Chrissie smiled, obviously pleased. “Oh, Linda, I like him.” She offered her hand. “Hello, Paul Rice. How do you like the museum?”

Paul took it and smiled. “It swallows you up.”

Chrissie laughed. “It is kinda big – and sorta creepy at times. But that’s Dwayne’s department. I’m sure you’ll hear all about it soon enough, if you haven’t already.”

Paul and Linda exchanged glances.

Chrissie looked at Linda. “You mean Mom and Dad didn’t mention it in their letters?”

“No,” Linda said. Her face took on a troubled look. “Not a word. Mom did mention something vague about Dwayne a little while ago, but she didn’t go into details.”

“I’m surprised. That’s all Dad’s been hollering about lately. It’s like he’s—”

“Chrissieeee!”

Chrissie turned and yelled down the stairs. "Yes, mother?"

"Come down and help me with the table," Mrs. Eastman said. "Your father and brother should be home any moment."

Chrissie grimaced. "Yes, Mother. I'll be right down." She turned back to Linda and Paul. "I have to go. My master's voice, you know."

She kissed Linda quickly on the cheek. "It's good having you home again." Then bounded down the stairs with a wave. "See you later at the muster. Nice meeting you, Paul Rice."

"Her, I like," Paul said, after she disappeared down the stairs. "What did she mean by 'the muster'?"

"She means meeting my father," Linda said, giving him a little smile. "Come on. I'll show you to your room."

8

AFTER AN UNENTHUSIASTIC INTRODUCTION, a cold handshake, and an even colder stare – like Paul was a bug under a slide – John Eastman ushered Paul and Linda into the library.

"So, what do you do?" Eastman asked Paul.

Paul hated when people asked him that, like he was expected to either perform or apologize if his chosen field of work was not acceptable. He always had the urge to say he was a shepherd, but said, "I work for the government."

"Paul's with the post office, Dad," Linda added.

"Oh?" Eastman said.

Paul could see he wasn't overly thrilled at the answer. His stomach began to bother him.

"And just what do you do in the post office?" Eastman asked, taking a cigar from a walnut humidor.

"I'm in management, a supervisor." Maybe he wanted him to say that he licked stamps and put them on envelopes.

Eastman lit his cigar, blowing out clouds of pungent smoke. "Seems to me the service is getting worse right along. You fellows keep raising the postage but give piss poor service in return."

"Dad!" Linda said. "Paul isn't responsible…"

"Write your congressman, Mr. Eastman," Paul said. "Ask them to increase the postal subsidy so we can give the people better service instead of cutting it like some politicians are trying to do." Christ, he could use a drink. Why is it that every time people find out you work for the post office, they have to start complaining about the service?

Helen Eastman came into the room, breaking the awkward silence. "Well, how is everyone getting along? I suppose you men are swapping war stories already."

"Yeah," Eastman said coldly.

Paul knew he hadn't scored any points. Eastman seemed to be the type that wanted to assert his dominance over you the minute you walked in the door. He seemed to enjoy – and was used to – having the upper hand.

Linda gave Paul a warning look. He tried another approach. "What did you do in the war, Mr. Eastman?"

"Don't get him started on that, Paul," Helen Eastman said, sitting down on the couch next to Linda. "He'll bore you with all the missions he flew over Germany."

"Oh, you were a bomber pilot?" Paul asked.

Eastman tapped his cigar ash into an ashtray. "I flew a few missions."

"He flew twenty-five and didn't get a scratch, I'm happy to say," Mrs. Eastman added.

"B-17's?" Paul asked.

Eastman nodded.

"Paul was in Vietnam," Linda said.

Eastman looked at his daughter and then at Paul. "See any action over there?"

"A little."

"Seems like most of the young men went to Canada rather than fight."

"It was a dirty war."

"All of them are, but men don't run away and hide like cowards. They face their fears."

Paul let it drop. He didn't want to get involved in the pros and cons of Vietnam. He had enough nightmares already. He could still use a drink, but no offer seemed to be forthcoming.

Alison entered the library and announced that dinner was ready. Everyone went into the dining room.

"Well, we've waited long enough for my wandering son," Mrs. Eastman said, rearranging a bowl of broccoli on the table.

Chrissie came in from the kitchen and stood next to her mother.

"Everyone sit, please," Mrs. Eastman said. "Chrissie, over there next to your father." Eastman was already sitting. "Paul, Linda, on this side."

The table was crowded with food. Steamy aromas of meat, potatoes, and a variety of vegetables filled the room. Desserts of pumpkin and apple pies and servings of fruit-filled Jell-O waited their turn at the sideboard. Crystal goblets glittered with water, and wineglasses sparkled with Beaujolais.

Paul drank half of his wine and fought the temptation to finish all of it.

Eastman eyed him coldly.

"I hope you like filet mignon, Paul," Mrs. Eastman said. "I had a terrible time deciding what to make, but Linda said you liked steak."

"Love it," Paul said.

"You have a very appreciative guest, Mother," Linda said. "He lives on TV dinners."

Mrs. Eastman smiled. "Does anyone want their coffee now?"

No one did.

"Oh, Chrissie, the carrots aren't out," Mrs. Eastman said. "Would you please bring them in, dear?"

Chrissie pushed her chair back and got up as if she had just been asked to carry the world on her shoulders. "Yes, Mother, but I don't know where you're going to put them. There's hardly any room on the table now."

"We'll find room."

"As usual, your mother created another Henry the Eighth dinner," Eastman said as Chrissie went into the kitchen. "We'll be eating leftovers for a month."

Paul smiled. "My dad used to say what we didn't eat, we'd have to wear."

The women responded with smiles, but Eastman ignored him. A hard man to know, Paul thought.

"Where's your father now?" Mrs. Eastman asked, checking over the table for the fifth time.

"He's dead," Paul replied, a twinge of guilt ebbing in him. "And my mother."

"Oh, I'm sorry."

Chrissie came back into the room. "Well, here I am, the carrot queen. Now, where are you going to put it?"

"Here, I'll move the gravy," Linda said, starting to slide the bowl to another spot. "Ouch! That's hot!" She fanned her hand in the air.

"It won't be if we wait much longer," Eastman said, looking out the dining room windows.

The front door suddenly opened and closed and there were approaching footsteps in the foyer.

"Dwayne Eastman!" his mother said as he entered the room. "Where in the world have you been? We've been delaying dinner for an hour."

"Sorry, Mom," he said. "I was looking for Holly. I guess I just lost track of the time."

"Holly's Dwayne's dog," Linda explained to Paul.

Mrs. Eastman introduced them. Paul got up from the table. They shook hands.

"Did you find her?" Paul asked, reseating himself.

Dwayne shook his head. "I looked all over. It isn't like her to just run off."

"I'm sure you'll find her, dear," Mrs. Eastman said, smoothing down his hair. "Now, sit and eat."

"Christ, yes," Eastman said, picking up the bowl of mashed potatoes. "Before he starts talking about his closet."

Chrissie snickered.

“Now, Chrissie, don’t make fun of your brother,” Mrs. Eastman said, seating herself at the end of the table. “Dwayne, sit down.”

Dwayne slumped into a seat next to his mother, opposite Paul, his face colored with embarrassment. He gave Paul a quick look, their eyes holding for a second, then turned away.

Paul thought he saw something of himself in those eyes. They knew the same lonely places, had the same bad dreams.

“If you ask me,” Chrissie said, “the only spooky thing we have around here is Alison.”

“Shhhhh. She’ll hear you.”

“No, she won’t, Mother, she’s outside talking to Claude.”

“Well, it isn’t nice. She’s just a little superstitious. Paul, take some more filet. Don’t be afraid to eat.”

“Don’t worry, Mother,” Linda said. “You won’t have to tell him twice. He’s got two hollow legs and he never gains an ounce. I hate him.”

Paul looked at Linda and made a Cheshire-cat smile.

“I like a man that eats well,” Mrs. Eastman said.

“If you think Alison is so spooky,” Eastman asked Chrissie, “how come you’re not wearing garlic around your neck?”

“Oh, Daddy, you know what I mean.”

“John, don’t encourage her. Alison is just…well, different. I mean, she has her own ways. Dwayne, please don’t pick at your food.”

“I’m not very hungry.”

“Now what’s the matter?” Eastman asked his son.

Dwayne didn’t answer. He looked down at his plate.

“Dwayne, I’m talking to you.”

“May I be excused?” Dwayne said, putting his fork down. “I’m really not hungry.”

“No, you may not be excused, young man.”

“John, please.”

“Helen, I just asked him a question. Don’t baby him. It’s bad enough that a boy his age still has to sleep with the lights on.”

Paul and Linda exchanged glances. She shook her head not to interfere.

"Well, Dwayne. I'm waiting for an answer."

Dwayne shrugged. "About what?"

Eastman became annoyed. "Are you still thinking about that foolishness?"

"I guess so," Dwayne said in a small voice.

"This thing's getting out of hand. You're just letting your imagination control you."

"It's not my imagination."

"Then, what is it? No one else in the house sees anything. You're the only one who seems to think something is wrong."

"I never said I saw anything."

"I know. That's just the trouble."

"John," Mrs. Eastman interceded. "We have guests."

Eastman flashed her a pair of hard eyes, then waved his fork at his son. "There's nothing wrong with that closet. I want you to stop talking about it, and I want you to stop thinking about it, and I want you to act like a man and stop sleeping with the lights on."

Dwayne left the table and the room. He went upstairs.

Eastman was about to call after him, but caught his wife's reproachful stare.

This is going to be one hell of a week, Paul thought.

The rest of the meal was finished with forced conversation.

9

AFTER DINNER, EASTMAN LEFT THE TABLE without a word and came directly into the library. His face still slightly red, his anger still fired but under control, he sank into the soft leather chair by the French doors and looked out through the glass, watching the wind stir the big trees on the front lawn. Twilight colored the sky gray.

He could hear Chrissie and Linda and Paul go into the game room, their voices drifting across the hall, and start playing pool. Helen was probably still in the dining room helping Alison clear the table and load the dishwasher, even though he had told her time and again that is what he paid the help to do. Dwayne was still upstairs. Sulking, most likely.

Eastman pulled a cigar from the nearby humidor and stoked it up, his head disappearing in heavy billows of smoke. He shook the match out and threw it savagely into the ashtray. He just could not reach that boy anymore. It was as if a wall had grown between them over the years, blocking out all communication, all understanding. Dwayne seemed to be on a different wavelength these days.

Now, this damn silly business about his closet.

If Eastman had ever told his father such foolishness, he knew what he would have gotten. The bite of his father's belt across his ass, that's what. Eastman's father would never have tolerated such nonsense. He was a hardworking, God-fearing man, who looked life's fears right in the eye and taught his son to do the same.

Eastman could remember his first lesson as if it happened yesterday instead of almost fifty years ago. He had been nine at the time and was playing hide-and-seek in the alley in back of his parent's flat. It was late, an hour after his allotted check-in time, and dark. He and Roger Quintas and Bobby Peterson were hiding from fat Freddy Williams.

He had ducked behind some garbage cans next to an ash box three doors down from his house, and Freddy, stumbling into everything he came in contact with, was looking for them. Eastman was in stitches watching Freddy and had to restrain himself from laughing too loud and giving his hiding place away. But then his muffled laughter died in his throat, changing to stark fear when he felt something run up his leg under his pants.

It was a rat.

Instinctively, he clutched at his trouser leg and caught the rat by its head as it crawled above his knee. He screamed and jumped up, knocking over the garbage cans but still held the rat, through the pants material, by the back of its head. The rat dug in its hind claws, and Eastman let out another scream and grabbed the rat's rump with his other hand, immobilizing it for the time being.

Then he started to run and scream and cry, tearing past fat Freddy Williams, whom he had nearly scared to death, and past Roger and Bobby, who had now revealed themselves and were standing next to Freddy, the same deathly shade of white across their faces. He dashed through his backyard and stumbled into the house, jolting his mother out of a living room chair and his father away from the evening newspaper. Eastman's eyes were wide with terror and his body shook with palsied sobs as he tried to get the words out of his mouth.

His mother became pale and faint-looking and started screaming at his father to do something. Eastman's father got up quickly, took him by the shoulder and led him through the kitchen to the basement door.

In the basement, under the anemic glow of a low watt light bulb, Eastman stood, crying, paralyzed with fear, holding on to the rat.

His father opened the door of the old coal furnace and started to cut off the trousers with a pair of tin snips, then he took the pants, rat and all, and threw them into the fire. The rat hit the flames with a screech and began to scamper about in a frenzy. Eastman's father banged the metal furnace door shut.

Then, stern-faced and hard-eyed as usual, his father unbuckled his belt, slid it free of his trouser loops, and started to beat him across the buttocks with it.

"Eastmans don't cry," his father said.

The belt whacked against his flesh, leaving a welt.

"They don't let others see their fear."

The belt whacked.

"They face their fears like a man and lick 'em."

The belt whacked.

"I'm gonna teach you like my father taught me."

The belt whacked.

"Eastmans don't cry."

It was only later, after the shock had worn off and he was alone in his bedroom, that Eastman realized why his father had beaten him. It was not because he had stayed out too late or because he had played in the alley where he was forbidden to play, but because he had acted like a sissy.

He vowed never to cry or show fear again.

During his early years, he had many occasions to break that vow, but he never did. Not even for new lessons learned in the basement. And there were many things to learn besides acting like a man. Not even in Catholic school, where like his father before him, his character and values were forged on the anvil of hard discipline, the iron mistress of Catholic teaching. There, every priest had a leather strap and every nun a hard ruler. They did not hesitate to use them.

Eastman learned responsibility.

After school, he was taught the plumbing trade. In those days, the Eastman Plumbing Company was run by his father and uncle. They were like oil and water, as opposite as sunshine and rain. His father, always the hard taskmaster even to his own brother, would storm about, his face red with anger, hollering and raising his hands in the air when anything went wrong.

Uncle Norman would just go about his work, smiling and whistling, as if Eastman's father wasn't even there. Then, he'd wink at him and say, "Johnny, you've got to relax. You're too tense. Don't force your way through life like a man with his short hair caught in a zipper. Learn to enjoy things."

Eastman would start to laugh and his father would turn and glare at him until he stopped.

His uncle was always that way. He never argued back with his brother, never let the smile fade from his face, or the twinkle from his eyes. And, he was always fond of telling the story of how, when he was a boy in Catholic school, he had gone from classroom to classroom collecting all the leather straps from the priests. He told them that Father Riley, the school principal, had sent him to fetch them. Later, he took all the straps down to the school basement and threw them in the furnace.

Then he would laugh and say, "I surely caught hell when the priests found out. I couldn't sit down for a week."

Years later, on his deathbed, dying of cancer of the rectum, the smile, not as broad, and the twinkle, somewhat faded, were still there. When he saw Eastman, he winked, "Johnny, my boy, you look tense. You've got to learn how to relax and take it easy." Then, to his brother, he said, "Joe, do you suppose Father Riley is still sore about those straps?"

His uncle died in that white room with the white bedcovers as his father stood dry-eyed near the bed, and his mother twisted the rosary in her hands, and the priest prayed.

Eastman wanted to cry, but he didn't.

When they left the hospital, his father said, "Norman never took life seriously. Everything was fun. He lived like a man tasting a new wine every day. God have mercy on him." And he never mentioned his brother's name again.

Well, his uncle was long gone now and so were his parents. He still had the plumbing company. It prospered under his guidance. Eastman sinks, tubs, toilets, and fixtures were the best selling in the Midwest. The money poured in and life should have been easy, but it wasn't.

Eastman never shared his uncle's enjoyment of the life around him or his ease with people. He was his father's son through and through, and, like his father, he always felt threatened by the presence of others. Not so much by women – he didn't care whether they liked him or not or what they said or did – but by other men. Not that he worried about their friendship either, but rather that they were trying to undermine him, to make him look the fool, especially in the eyes of his family. This was a thought he could not bear.

In the heat of an argument, Dwayne had once told him that his anger was just a cover-up for his inferiority complex. His own son said that to him. Eastman struck him across the face. If he had ever dared to say such a thing to his father, Eastman was sure that he would have been killed on the spot.

Eastman ran a hand over his brow and wiped away the cold sweat that formed there. His shirt stuck damply to his back and chest.

The trouble was that the children were growing away from him. Not so much Chrissie – he still had time with her – but Linda and Dwayne.

Night had passed over the sky and had thrown the room into darkness, the only light coming from the glowing end of his cigar. He crushed it out in the ashtray. A black despair fell over him.

And, then for some reason, he thought of that crazy old priest again.

10

"WE'RE HOME!" Chrissie called. "In case anybody cares."

"We're in the game room, Chrissie," Mrs. Eastman called back.

Chrissie took off her coat and hung it in the hall closet.

"Maybe I should go," Tommy Burham whispered.

"Don't be silly," Chrissie said. "It's still early. I'll make us some hot cocoa."

"Yeah, but your father...."

"He won't mind."

She pulled off his jacket and put it in the closet. "Come on," she said, taking him by the hand and dragging him into the game room.

The five of them, the Eastmans, Linda, Paul, and Dwayne, were playing sheepshead on the felt and wood card table under twin pools of light from a hanging lamp shaped like a pair of dice.

"Dwayne," Eastman said, "whose side are you on? If they get another trick, we're going under."

"Sorry, Dad." Dwayne fidgeted in his chair. He hated to play cards with his father because it was like a game of war with him. He only went along with it this time because of Linda and Paul.

Chrissie and Tommy acted as spectators.

"How was the movie?" Mrs. Eastman asked, overtrumping Dwayne's ten of diamonds with the ace.

"Creepy," Chrissie said.

"What did you kids see?" Paul asked.

"The Exorcist," Tommy said. He was a good-looking boy with wavy blond hair and a pleasant smile whom Paul had met earlier when he picked up Chrissie for their date.

"Your play, Linda," Paul said.

"God, it's been so long since I've played this game, I don't remember what's high anymore," Linda said.

"I thought you saw that garbage the last time around?" Eastman said to Chrissie.

"She wanted to see the parts she missed when she had her eyes closed," Tommy said.

"Did she?" Paul asked, smiling.

"No, she closed them again."

Chrissie punched Tommy playfully on the arm.

Eastman threw his cards down in disgust. "Well, that's it. That's game for them. Some partner. Did we get Schneider?"

"You called me, remember?" Dwayne said. He counted their tricks. "We made Schneider."

"Well, that's something anyway." Eastman reached out and grabbed Chrissie around the waist, pulling her to him. "So, young lady, you spent the evening among the ghouls, huh?"

"Demons," Chrissie corrected. "Devils of the dark."

"I remember when Paul and I saw that," Linda said, smiling at him. "It took me about a month to get over it."

"She kept hearing Mercedes McCambridge's voice behind her," Paul said.

"The book was supposed to be based on a true experience. Only it happened to a boy instead of a girl," Tommy said.

"An hallucination would be more like it," Eastman said.

Chrissie looked around the room. Only the leg of the nearby pool table could be seen just outside the overlapping circles of light from the overhead dice lamp. She moved farther into the light.

"Do you think there's anything really like that…evil things that try to get at you?" Chrissie said.

Mrs. Eastman looked at her. "What makes you ask that?"

"I don't know. I just wondered."

"Just worry about the living and forget about nonsense like that," Eastman said. "Next thing you know, you'll be acting like your brother."

"John." Mrs. Eastman slapped him on the arm. "Be nice."

"So, what did I say?"

"You know what you said."

If Dwayne heard his father, he made no reply. He picked up the cards and started shuffling them, glancing over at Paul. "What do you think, Paul? Is evil a force to be reckoned with? Is it an entity in its own right?"

Paul suddenly realized that everyone was quiet, waiting for his answer. All he could manage was, "I don't know. I've seen evil in men, but whether it's a force – an entity, acting to corrupt – that's more of a question for a theologian. I really couldn't say."

Eastman seemed dissatisfied with Paul's answer. He made a sour face, then looked at Tommy Burham. "Isn't it getting late? What time is it?"

"It's only nine-thirty," Linda said, checking her watch.

The foyer clock struck the half-hour, confirming the time.

"I promised Tommy a cup of hot cocoa," Chrissie said. "It's cold outside and we need something to warm us up."

"Okay," Eastman said. "One hot cocoa. Then to bed, young lady."

Paul studied Tommy's reaction. The boy stood there and looked down at his shoes. Eastman had the knack of making you feel as welcome as a bastard in his house.

Chrissie pulled away from her father. "Come on, Tommy. One hot cocoa coming up."

"Whose deal is it?" Eastman asked.

11

PAUL WAS RESTIVE.

He thrashed about in the big bed like a wounded animal seeking refuge, his mind jumping between the ebb and flow of his thoughts. The refuge he sought was sleep, but it eluded him, always dancing just beyond his fingertips, slipping away in the darkness to laugh, then returning just long enough to taunt him again.

His thoughts wandered over last night's drinking spree, when the pain came again after all that time and he needed alcohol to smother it; and this morning, feeling shaky and a little hung over but still under control, then almost losing it in the library with Eastman and again at the dinner table; and he thought about Linda, knowing that she was the reason the pain had come back, but she would never know, he would never tell her, not like with Carrol. He had told Carrol, and then she was dead, like all the rest of them, like his mother and father...

You could never let yourself feel...never...

Then sleep finally came, and brought the dream, he had thought he was rid of along with it.

Paul had not had the death dream as he called it, for over a year now, but something must have stirred that dark part of his mind where he kept it buried and dredged it to the surface with all its grisly details.

It was always the same. He was back in Vietnam again, at Langvie. The North Vietnamese were attacking the outpost, taking it with grenades and mortars and heavy small arms fire. It was a bloodbath. The men he knew – yes, even loved – were dying in front of him, being blown to pieces or burned to a crisp or ripped open by incoming rounds. Rademaker, Phillips, Thornton, Weiss, Braddock – dead, all dead, except him.

In the dream, their bodies were always piled on top of him; he could hear the blood dripping from their wounds, see their dead eyes accusing him. Carrol was there, too, her correspondent's identification tags sewn on her fatigues that she proudly wore for the guys. Paul knew she didn't die at Langvie, that happened earlier on a street in Saigon, and yet she was always in the dream. Lately, he began seeing his mother and father on the pile as well, their eyes burning through him like hot coals.

He had loved them, all of them, and now they were dead. His fault... his fault. He was sorry. He didn't want any of them to die. So sorry... so very sorry. He tried to tell them, but he never could. The North Vietnamese were coming for him, moving through the camp, finishing off the wounded as they came, getting closer with every shot.

Paul struggled to free himself, but could not move. The weight of the others held him down. Then the firing stopped and someone was standing over him, smiling. He could never see the whole face clearly, only that the head seemed to disappear into a pointed blur and the eyes were yellow slits of light, but that sickly smile was always clear. It grinned down at him with malefic intent, like a reptile that knows it has an easy kill. Then the form bent over, and the smile came closer.

The dream always ended then, and Paul always woke up bathed in a cold sweat, his heart racing, his mind disoriented. For a moment, he could not remember where he was, the time, or day. He seemed to be drowning in a darkness that covered him like the depths of some unknown sea.

His hand reached out, like a faltering swimmer trying to find something to hold onto. He found the nightstand and the nearby lamp. He turned it on.

Paul sat up in bed, shaken, trying to slow his accelerated heart.

He felt a chill that had nothing to do with the coldness of the room. He pushed himself farther up in the bed and reached for his cigarettes, lighting one and looking at his watch. It was 3:25 a.m. Paul glanced casually around the room, pushing his damp hair back off his forehead, blowing out shapeless clouds of smoke. After he finished the cigarette, he felt the urge to empty his bladder. He swung his body out of bed.

He noticed the smell then.

It was faint, but definitely there. It was a smell that men in war never forgot. The rotting of flesh. Something needed burying.

Paul threw on his shirt, stepped into his pants and slippers, and walked around the room, trying to trace the source of the smell. He opened the door and stepped out into the hall. The odor was stronger out there.

Dwayne's room was next door. His door was open and the light was on. Paul looked in. Dwayne was sitting up in bed, his face pallid, staring at the opposite wall. Paul rapped lightly on the doorjam and walked in.

Dwayne jumped, his eyes going wide.

"Sorry," Paul said. "I didn't mean to startle you. I couldn't sleep. Thought I smelled something."

"Can you really smell it?" Dwayne asked excitedly, throwing back the covers and getting up. He was dressed in a pair of pajamas that were too short for his long legs.

"What does it smell like to you?" Dwayne asked, coming up to him.

"Like something rotting."

"But you can smell it?"

"Yes."

"You know, you're the only one besides me who can. Everyone keeps telling me I'm imagining things." Dwayne paused, then gestured toward the closet with his head and whispered, "It comes from there."

Paul looked at him. "The closet?"

Dwayne nodded. "It started again tonight."

Paul stepped over to the closet door. The odor was unmistakably there, strong and fetid. His hand instinctively reached for the doorknob.

"Don't," Dwayne warned. "It's not safe at night."

"Oh?" Paul dropped his hand and gave Dwayne a sidelong glance. "What is it?"

"I don't know. It always comes back at night. It's like there's... well, like there's something on the other side of the door."

"Did you ever look?"

"Yes, but not at night. Only during the daytime. There's just a faint smell then, but it's always cold."

Paul's brow furrowed slightly. "You mean the temperature in there is different than the rest of the house?"

"I'd say by at least forty degrees. It's like a refrigerator inside. And yet whenever I check the temperature with a gauge, the reading doesn't vary from the rest of the house."

"That's unusual."

"I know, but I always get the same results. My father says it's because of the lake – a subterranean draft or something. But why doesn't it show on the temperature gauge?"

Paul shook his head. "I don't know." Then paused and said, "Is that why you sleep with the light on?"

"Yes, I guess so. Maybe I'm being silly, but I just feel that if I didn't keep the light on at night, it would come out."

Paul studied Dwayne's eyes, searching for a trace of melodrama. He didn't like the fear he saw there.

"Do you think that's funny?" Dwayne asked.

"No."

"Everyone else does. My father, Chrissie. Linda and my mother, well, they just humor me. You're the only one who takes me seriously. There are times – and I've never told this to anyone else – that I feel there isn't just one thing behind that door, but a lot of things, waiting to get out."

"And having the light on stops them from...coming out."

"It seems to. At least for the time being."

The drift of the conversation was beginning to give Paul gooseflesh.

"I know I sound like some kind of a nut," Dwayne went on, "but I can't shake the feeling that I have. Something's wrong, and whatever it is, it isn't very good."

"How can you sleep in here?"

"I can't. Not very well anyway. Some nights it gets so bad that I have to sleep in another room." Dwayne looked down at his bare feet. "My father thinks I'm just being a coward."

Paul remembered the conversation at the dinner table only too well.

"Dad thinks everything is tangible, and if it isn't, then it just doesn't exist. But there are some things – things you can't see or touch, but are there just the same." Dwayne shrugged. "I guess I'm just more sensitive than the rest of the family. No one else has ever noticed anything strange about this house. And I've had bad feelings about it ever since we moved in."

"What about your dog? How did it react to the house?"

"Now that you mention it, she didn't like this room very much, and she was terrified of the closet. She'd always bark and growl at the door, then turn away whining and crawl under the bed."

"How did you lose her?"

"I just let her out one night as usual, and she didn't come back. I've been looking everywhere for her."

Paul put a reassuring hand on the back of Dwayne's neck. "Want some help? We can look again tomorrow, if you like."

Dwayne smiled up at him. "I'd really appreciate it."

"Then, it's settled. We'll check out this closet, too, and see what we can find. But right now we'd better get back to bed."

Paul turned to go, and then stopped in the doorway. "Dwayne, do you want to bunk in with me tonight?"

"I'd like to, but I'll have to be back by morning. Dad always checks to see where I'm sleeping."

Dwayne followed Paul out of the room. He left the bedroom light on.

12

GRACELAND, THE BIGGEST AND OLDEST nondenominational cemetery in Lanark, rested quietly under a shroud of cloud cover. The closely trimmed lawns and stately trees of its peaceful grounds were still wrapped in early-morning darkness, waiting for a dawn three hours away. Occasionally, the moon broke through the clouds, causing shadows to slither and creep with the cold autumn wind.

One shadow, unlike the rest, which depended on the wind, moved among the headstones of its own will. The beam of light it carried settled first in one direction, then another, playing briefly over marble monuments, carved cherubs, and praying stone angels.

Finally, the shadow became still, the light resting on a large crypt that stood under the quiet scrutiny of an old, gnarled maple tree. The inscription chiseled above the door read: DURIE. The light dropped, illuminating the entrance. Two stone angels, their faces worn away by time, flanked the iron gate and heavy wooden door of the tomb.

A crowbar was positioned between the outer gate and the stone of the crypt, breaking the gate lock with a metal snap. The door gave much the same way, only the scream of its wood was more pronounced, more alive.

The shadow slipped inside the crypt and merged with the syrupy darkness, the eldritch light probing the way, then steadying on a nearby sarcophagus, where a spider legged its way across the top. A patina of dust covered the bronze plate on the coffin. A gloved hand emerged into the beam of light and brushed the dust away. The name read: ANGUS DURIE.

The light moved on to the next stone coffin, and the next, and the next, until the plate read: JAMES DURIE. The shadow leaned against the stone foundation of this sarcophagus and pushed. The stone moved with a grating sound, revealing a small compartment in the floor of the crypt.

The light searched the space of the cavity. A book with old and worn leather binding rested there. The gloved hand picked it up. A slight tremor shook the crypt, as if something buried had been disturbed and the bowels of the earth had suddenly turned.

The foundation of the coffin was swung back into place, and the wooden door and iron gate of the tomb were closed.

The book was carried off into the night.

13

AT 4:30 A.M., A SEISMOGRAM was made at the University of Wisconsin in Madison, of a seismic disturbance measuring 2.5 on the Richter scale. This same disturbance was recorded at Golden, Colorado, and at other monitoring stations all over the world.

14

FATHER JUSTIN XAVIER KERRY woke with a start.

Something had moved.

The room.

Something.

What?

He clutched at the bedcovers with one hand and immediately felt for the crucifix around his neck with the other. He did not move at first, just sat there in his dark bedroom and searched the depths of the shadows for anything that did not belong.

But then they are part of the shadows…the darkness…aren't they?

Father Kerry reached over and switched on the bed lamp. He examined the room again. Nothing was changed. Nothing was moved. The dresser was still in place, as was the chair and night table. The bed was all right. Nothing funny there. He sniffed the air several times. There was no odor. Then he leaned his small body over the edge of the bed and looked under it. Nothing. Just the carpet. Dust.

The closet. What about the closet?

He reached for the bigger crucifix that was lying on the night table, pushed back the covers, and got up. Holding the crucifix out in front of him like a shield, he stalked over to the closet. He jerked the door open, still keeping the body of Jesus well in front of him, and searched it thoroughly. When he was satisfied, he closed the closet door and went back and sat on the bed.

How many times had he done this? How many nights in the past nine years had he been startled out of sleep, disturbed by threatening noises? Too many. He ran a trembling hand through his close-cut gray hair. He searched his room by rote now. It was always the same procedure. First, the furniture, then the air for an odor, then the bed, and last, the closet.

He stiffened.

Had he heard a whisper of a laugh?

That same gurgling laugh…that he could not forget after all these years.

What had awakened him? Had he screamed himself out of a nightmare? No. RCA would have heard him and would have come in to check on him. Having him stay at the rectory was some comfort. At least he wasn't alone, and RCA was his sacristan. He depended upon him. RCA was – who was he kidding – he was his crutch, his bodyguard. A priest with a bodyguard. Ah, what faith.

Father Kerry looked at the peeling face of the old electric clock on the nightstand. 4:45 a.m. He would never be able to go back to sleep now. Not without help, anyway. But then there was still part of his nightly routine left.

He padded over to the dresser, set the large crucifix he had been holding down on the dresser top, next to another crucifix lying there, and opened the bottle of brandy. He poured a stiff drink into one of the paper cups, stacked there for just that purpose, and took a healthy swallow.

This was beginning to be his faith.

He turned and looked around the room. Why does everything always look so threatening in the night? Cup in hand, he walked over to the window and peered out. The uniform darkness of Grant Street was broken only by the pools of light from the streetlights.

Father Kerry sat down on the bed again and took another swallow. Thank God, you can't see that house from here. That's all he would need – having Durie House staring at him through his bedroom window.

He got up and poured himself another drink, returning to the bed to finish it, then waited for the brandy to do its short-circuiting.

Half an hour later, he was able to sleep again.

15

A STIFF EARLY MORNING BREEZE stirred the lock of white hair that hung out beneath the black skullcap Pete Jacobs wore, summer or winter, rain or shine. He stuck a wizened hand out the window of his battered old VW to signal a left turn (his directional lights had long since given up the ghost to rust) and swung the bug off the highway onto Sumac Road.

Now he was out of the traffic that had been building into the start of another working day. Five more minutes and he would be away from all the noise, alone in his own world of peace and quiet. A lot of the people in Lanark would say he was in his own little world all the time, whether he worked in the cemetery of not.

But Pete did not care what they said about him. Not everyone was suited to work in a cemetery. For Pete, who had been alone most of his life and preferred the quiet of the dead to the noise of the living, taking care of the grounds at Graceland was ideal.

The dead never bothered you, he would say philosophically. Least ways, if you did not bother them. More than likely it was the living you had to worry about. They were the troublemakers.

And it was the troublemakers that Pete immediately thought of when he pulled up in front of the big iron gate of the cemetery and saw that the locking chain and padlock had been cut with bolt cutters.

Leaves blew across the black face of the driveway, crunching under the feet of his short, stubby body as he stormed toward the gate like an irate rabbi. He picked up the cut length of chain and dropped it in disgust. It rattled back against the wrought iron gate.

"Son of a bitch! Goddam kids!" Pete swore.

Like most people alone a great deal of the time, Pete talked to himself. When called on it by other people, he would say simply that he liked intelligent conversation and talking to himself was the best he could get.

"No respect for anything anymore."

Pete's first thought was vandals. Several months ago, shortly after Memorial Day, some kids had broken in and knocked over gravestones, took flags off veterans' graves, and broke some of the stone statues near the old crypts.

"I'd better check the crypt area first," Pete said. "No tellin' what the little monsters did over there. Goddam. If I had my way, I'd shoot the little bastards right through the head. One shot. Pow!"

Pete always carried a small .25 caliber automatic in the car with him. You had to, he reasoned. You never knew what the hell was gonna happen. And, by the time the cops got there, you'd be lyin' toes up and playin' a three string harp.

He pushed open the gate and climbed back into his VW, gunning the engine. The car belched into the cemetery grounds, emitting a number of shrieks and rattles and whines and farts of blue smoke. He jockeyed the Volkswagen across the narrow bridge that spanned the railroad tracks seventy feet below and separated the old and new sections of the cemetery. Most of the crypts were in the old section

The engine dropped into a lower whine as Pete let up on the gas pedal and cast a suspicious eye at the passing statues and crypts. All the monuments seemed intact, but one of the large crypts caught his attention. He slammed on the brakes and the VW shuddered to a shaky stop.

Pete got out and walked to within ten feet of the crypt and stopped. He could see that its iron gate and wooden door were both slightly open, and he didn't have to read the name cut into the stone to know what crypt it was.

This was the only place in the cemetery that made him feel uneasy. There was no way in hell he was going in there alone or any farther than where he now stood. Pete felt a chill spider across his groin as the old rhyme he knew as a boy whispered through his head:

Don't let the night find you at Durie House,
Or the waxing of the moon.
Unless you've a mind to spend your days there forever,
Crazy as a loon.

Pete crossed his fingers, spit three times, and swore. "Son of a bitch." It was something his mother had taught him to do whenever he had to pass Durie House.

It wasn't night and the moon wasn't out, but he certainly wasn't going to take any chances by even coming in contact with anything Durie – especially their dead. His mother didn't raise any stupid children.

Pete hurried back to his car. He'd call Chief Thayer and let him handle it. That's what he got paid for.

16

RUTH HANSON, STILL IN BATHROBE AND SLIPPERS, sat in her sunny kitchen with her daughter eyeing the jelly preserves on the table with a deep longing. She would have loved to spread some on the plain toast that she and Jennifer were munching between sips of black coffee, but Jennifer was on one of her diets again and was after her to do the same, so she would probably frown, as she always did, at her mother's hunger for sweets.

It was ridiculous the way her daughter was always dieting, taking off a pound here, or a pound there. She certainly didn't have to. Neither one of them was fat. And a little sweet now and then didn't hurt anyone. Besides, it gave you energy.

She tried to take her mind off the jelly. "Did you watch the Neil Thomas show last Friday?" she asked. Neil Thomas was to Milwaukee what Johnny Carson had been to New York.

Before Jennifer could respond, her mother answered for her. "He had on Stella Rawlings. Stella looked beautiful. She's so pretty, don't you think? Frank Roberts was on, too. He's the one that wrote that dreadful book about people's sex habits. It was filth. Just pure filth." She paused, taking a sip of her coffee. "Billy Allen was on."

Jennifer often wondered why all evangelists were called Billy.

"The poor man," Ruth went on. "It must have been awfully embarrassing being on the same program with Frank Roberts. I just love to listen to

Billy talk, don't you? Although, why in the world they had him on with the likes of Frank Roberts, I'll just never know."

Jennifer watched her mother's eyes light up whenever she mentioned Billy Allen. She was sure her mother had a thing for ministers; they seemed to turn her on.

"Maybe the TV programmers thought Allen could pick up a few pointers on sex," Jennifer said dryly.

Ruth stopped drinking her coffee and stared at her daughter, returning the cup to the table. "My, my, aren't we clever this morning?" Then remembering an old wound. "By the way, I saw Paul Rice yesterday afternoon."

Jennifer started to look surprised, caught herself, and then feigned disinterest. "Oh? Where was that?"

Her mother knew she had touched a sore and pressed her advantage. She reached for the jelly and spread some on her toast. If Jennifer noticed, she didn't say anything.

Ruth bit into the toast, savoring the sweet taste of the preserves and the salt of the barb she had just thrown at her daughter. She added more salt to the wound. "He was with Linda Eastman. You know, the Linda Eastman you went to school with at Juilliard? I was outside the store talking to Mrs. Robbins – the one that has one leg shorter than the other, poor thing – and Paul was stopped at the corner, waiting for the light."

Jennifer put down her toast. "Has she changed much?"

"Well, I only met her that once, when you were both home from school and we ran into her at Frenchy's, but you know me, I never forget a face."

Or rest until you've got the complete rundown on someone, Jennifer added silently. It was not a malicious thought, for she had the same compulsion. Paul used to tell her that she was just nosey.

"I would say Linda is still very attractive," Ruth said.

"What would they be doing here in Lanark?"

Ruth stared at her daughter in disbelief. "Honestly, Jennifer, sometimes I don't think you listen to a word I say. I told you over a year ago that the Eastmans bought the old Durie place."

“I don’t remember you telling me that.”

“Well, I did, and they’re all very nice. Helen Eastman seems like a very pleasant person.” Ruth envied her big house and her servants. “And there are the children. Chrissie’s the youngest, then Dwayne, and, of course, Linda. I’ve never met Mr. Eastman,” she said with some regret. “Although, I’ve seen him in town, he’s never been in the store.” Her voice had a tone of disappointment.

“You seem very well acquainted.” Jennifer got up and poured the both of them another cup of coffee.

“Thank you, dear. Too bad Paul didn’t have any money. I rather liked him. Not that you didn’t do the right thing. Aaron is a very good catch. A doctor is a very sound profession. He’s a good provider and you have security with him.”

Jennifer was silent. Although it had been over with Paul for three years now, and she was married, she felt an instant dislike for Linda Eastman. Sure, they had gone to the same school, but they were never that chummy to be real friends.

“Still, Paul had a way with him.”

“Mother, do you mind not mentioning Paul?”

“Well, of course not, dear, if it bothers you.”

“It doesn’t bother me, but it’s in the past. I want to forget it.”

“Certainly. I didn’t know it would upset you.”

“Mother, it doesn’t upset me. It’s just that I’m married now and I’m not interested in what Paul Rice is doing, or who he’s doing it with.”

“Of course.” Ruth had finished the last of her jelly toast and glanced cattily at her daughter. She wondered abstractly if Jennifer had ever gone to bed with Paul, then decided that she must have. Jennifer took after her father in that respect. He never seemed to get enough. Thank God, she finally had the good sense to get rid of him, even if it was after twenty years of marriage.

She had faked so many climaxes with that man that she could have won an Oscar for best actress. Ruth did not particularly enjoy sex. She had never experienced a climax in all her fifty-one years of life.

Pretending to like it had been a game with her. She did it for his sake. Men were so vain. It seemed to mean a great deal to him. So, she moaned and groaned and twisted in ecstasy, or at least what she thought sexual ecstasy would feel like at his determined thrusting, until he came and grew limp and rolled off, asking the standard male question, "Was it good?" She would always answer with a breathless yes, and wait for him to fall asleep so she could get up and douche his sperm out of her.

Gordon, her ex, had been a big disappointment. Destined never to be a success, he was content to do the mundane, satisfied, for life, with his job of department store repairman. God knows, she had tried to be a good wife to him, had tried to straighten him out, had tried to fire his ambition. She had performed her wifely duties on a regular enough basis in hope that he would want to make something more of himself for her sake. But nothing worked. Gordon had no intention of ever changing. He would always be a repairman.

After the divorce, it was like a gigantic weight had been lifted from her shoulders. Gordon, the stone, was gone and she was free – completely free.

She wanted the house and got it. What money there was in the bank, she told Gordon to keep. She didn't need it. For the last ten years of her marriage, she had worked at Feminique, a women's apparel shop in Lanark, and had successfully maneuvered herself up to manger (by going to bed with the owner) and secretly putting most of her money away.

The years following the divorce she devoted to travel. First, it had been Spain—Madrid, the Prado, the tomb of El Cid in Burges, the Alhambra, the San Fermin festival in Pamplona (a la Hemingway), and a bullfight (which made her ill), then a short jaunt to Morocco with its bad water and bad plumbing. Three years later, it had been Japan. Fujiyama, Asakusa, a walk in the rain down the Ginza, and the Great Buddha at Kamakura. Two years ago, Scandinavia. Ice blue fjords, sauna baths, and smorgasbord. Next, she hoped to see some more of Europe.

Ruth loved to talk about her trips and the things she had seen to friends and acquaintances – even customers. She never mentioned them to Jennifer, though. The information would have fallen on deaf ears. Aaron, Jennifer's husband, had practically taken her on a world tour for their honeymoon.

"Did you say something, dear?" Ruth said, pulling herself away from her thoughts.

"I asked if you have been cutting your hair." Jennifer looked strangely at her mother.

Ruth instinctively lifted a hand to her hair. "Heavens, no. Why?"

"It looks like a piece of it was cut off."

"For God's sake, where?"

"Right in front. No, more to the left. There."

"I'll have to look in the mirror." Ruth ran into the bathroom, then returned a few minutes later, a puzzled expression on her face. "Now, how in the world did that happen?"

17

"MIND YOU," ALISON FITGERALD SAID to her husband, "you're to clean the path down to the beach."

"What's wrong with the path, woman?" Claude asked, leaning on his rake and looking at his wife, reflecting sadly at her form and how she had grown into what looked like the other half of Tweedledum.

"Mrs. Eastman says it has grown over with weeds so as you can hardly walk on it. You're to clean it straightaway."

"Straightaway, am I?" Claude said, straightening up to his full five foot, five inch height – three inches shorter than his wife. "And why didn't Mr. Eastman tell me himself?"

"Because Mrs. Eastman told me, that's why," Alison said, arms akimbo, speaking down at him. "Besides, how's a body supposed to tell you anything when they can't find you half the time?"

"He could've come out here and told me." Claude didn't like taking orders from women, especially his wife, who never seemed to run out of things for him to do.

"Well, I'm tellin' you. So, consider yourself told."

Claude stared at her chest and at the sagging breasts that he knew hung like deflated balloons under her housedress.

"All right, all right," he said, hitching up his pants and scratching his crotch in the process. "Clean the path. So, you told me." There were many times that he would have liked to belt her, but he was afraid she would hit him back.

"Well, see that you do it instead of gawkin' at all the women around here."

"Who's gawkin'?" Claude defended his innocence.

Alison just fixed him with a stare and didn't say another word. She turned and marched off to the house on her large, muscular legs; the afternoon sun glistening motes of sunlight off her silver hair.

"Who's gawkin'?" Claude asked again and spit.

Alison didn't acknowledge him. She went into the house.

"Cow," Claude said under his breath, giving his pants another hitch, then raking the grass he missed catching after this morning's cutting.

I can gawk if I want to, Claude thought. A man needs something nice to look at. Better yet, to lie down with. Going to bed with his wife was like crawlin' in next to another man. Like scalin' a mountain of flesh and muscle, then stickin' your thing out the window.

He stopped raking and looked back at the house to see if she was watching him. She was nowhere in sight. He leaned on his rake and spit. It sure would be nice to have somethin' nice to stick it in before his pecker shriveled up and wasn't good for anything but pissin'. Like that tight-ass bitch Chrissie Eastman or her sister. She was a real looker, too. He wouldn't mind pokin' old lady Eastman either.

The thought spread a warm glow through his groin. He scratched his crotch, then turned suddenly and checked the house again, in case his wife decided to come back and intrude upon his fantasies.

Alison watched him through the kitchen window. Look at the little worm, she thought. Thinks he's a regular Don Juan. And who would want him except someone like me?

She let the curtain drop and turned back to the sink, returning her soapy hands to the dishwater. She was doing the remainder of the breakfast dishes, those she couldn't stack into the dishwasher, scrubbing them with more force than necessary, pretending it was her husband's thoughts she was cleaning.

Alison knew he was off in one of his dreams again. Must be getting feebleminded. He does more dreaming than work these days. And he was surely no prize. Combing those few long hairs he had left on the side of his head over his bald top like some Beau Brummell. As if that made him look any better. Then gawking at all the women with obvious intent behind those rheumy eyes of his.

Alison sighed. Still, she loved him. She had known no other man. God knows, he was far from being an ideal husband or even coming close to resembling a good provider, but he was her man.

She took another peek at Claude and was satisfied to see that his daydream was over and he was working again. He was a good worker once he put his mind to the job. The trouble was getting him to do it. Maybe she would start daydreaming and gawking. See how he liked it. She couldn't imagine what he had to dream about. He couldn't even fill her needs, let alone another woman's.

She shook her head in disgust and tried to concentrate on her dishes.

18

THE LAST OF THE CLASS LEFT ENGLISH IV, filtering through the door as Jimmy Gillispie slouched at his desk and awaited Miss Homes' wrath. Gillispie was a tall, angular boy with long black hair and hard brown eyes.

Barbara Homes stood in front of her desk and watched the last student close the classroom door before she permitted herself to face the Gillispie boy. She folded her arms and gave him a stern look, then walked slowly down the aisle to his desk.

Jimmy watched her come. He liked how her knit beige dress clung to her thighs as she walked. He wondered if she had cobwebs on her bush, or if Dwayne Eastman was really dipping his wick in her like some of the kids thought.

She stopped in front of his desk and looked down at him.

Jimmy didn't look up. Instead, he fixed his eyes on the front of her dress where her vagina would be.

Barbara read his eyes. She didn't like what she found there. They were cruel, sarcastic eyes; eyes that would mock and jeer and laugh at other people's pain. They would probably enjoy that pain, too.

"Well, young man," Barbara said. "Do you have any explanation for your vulgar behavior?"

Jimmy shrugged, but did not remove his eyes from the spot. "She was buggin' me."

“Whether she was bugging you or not is no excuse for your behavior in this classroom. Gentlemen do not say such things to ladies and I will not stand for it.” She followed his gaze and pulled in her stomach. It was a defensive twinge. His eyes felt like they were entering her. She moved off to the side.

Jimmy knew he had gotten to her. He met her eyes and gave her a knowing smile. Maybe she's got more than cobwebs covering the thing, Jimmy thought. Maybe she even wears a goddamn chastity belt so no one can get at it.

“Well, I'm waiting,” Barbara said.

“Huh?” Jimmy didn't know what the hell she was talking about. All this fuss just because he told that dumb tit, Debbie Ralston, to go fuck herself. She was a big pain in the ass. The way she struts around, you'd think she had gold between her legs or something.

“If you have no explanation for your rude outburst, I have no alternative but to suspend you.”

Jimmy shrugged again. “She was buggin' me so I told her off.” He dropped his eyes to that sensitive spot on her dress. Dumb cunt. She's just as bad as that Ralston broad. If he had his knife on them, they'd be whistling a different tune. The thought gave him an erection. He shifted in his seat.

Barbara watched him. She began to feel uncomfortable alone in the room with him. She would have liked to slap that perpetual smirk off his face. “All right,” she said. “You're suspended.” She dropped her arms and walked back to her desk.

Jimmy watched her ass as she moved away from him. Two good handfuls. Maybe he'd carve his initials on them – one on each cheek. He smiled inwardly, got up from his desk and picked up his books. “Do I come to school tomorrow or what?”

Barbara turned to face him. She had been gathering up her papers from her desk. “What did you say?” she snapped.

Jimmy sighed and rolled his eyes as if dealing with a retarded person. “Do I come to school tomorrow?”

“Yes.”

“When does my suspension start?”

"I'll let you know tomorrow. I'll have to talk to Mr. Kitterick before I leave today and work out the details."

Great. The fucking principal hated his guts already.

"You can go home now," Barbara said. "Of course, you realize that your parents will be informed about this."

"You're going to tell my dad?" Jimmy was surprised. He hadn't expected that.

"Yes," she said and almost smiled. Maybe his father could straighten him out. "Your parents have to know."

Jimmy shuffled to the door and stopped. He gave her a long, hard look and then stepped out into the hall.

Barbara watched the door close behind him. And for some reason that only her subconscious knew, her hand lifted defensively to her throat.

19

PAUL CALLED DWAYNE OVER to examine the tracks he had found. They started their search for Holly along the beach area that ran below the bluff of the house and beyond the concrete wall and iron gate that sealed off the sloping grounds of the Eastman estate from the pounding waves of Lake Michigan.

There were dog tracks all along the wet sand.

"They're too big," Dwayne said, joining Paul. "Holly's a lot smaller than that. She's just a cocker spaniel." He paused and his face took on a concerned expression. "Funny thing. I've noticed big tracks like these around the house, too. Since yesterday."

Paul smiled and whispered in a conspiratorial voice. "The Hound of the Baskervilles."

"The Hound of the Eastmans," Dwayne corrected, going along with Paul's mood.

They both laughed.

Dwayne lifted his head and his glance fell on the house. The second floor windows were just visible over the hill and the twisting path that led down to the beach. He felt the house was watching them. His mood changed. He stopped laughing.

Paul followed his gaze. "You don't care for that house too much, do you?"

Dwayne lowered his eyes. "No, not really. Mom says I'm just too sensitive about things. I think about them too much until they become obsessive. And Dad, well, you have a pretty good idea what he thinks."

"Maybe you're just fey," Paul said.

"What?"

"You're able to sense things that others can't – ESP."

"Well, I've sure been picking up a lot of bad vibrations about this place, if that's the same thing."

Paul nodded.

"So have you. You smelled it last night. You know that I'm not making it up …or just afraid of the dark."

Paul put a reassuring hand on his shoulder. "There was something there."

The sun was dropping below the roof of the house, throwing the beach into lengthening shadows. The sky was filled with thin wisps of fast-moving clouds.

"Come on," Paul said. "Let's get back to the house and check out that closet."

Dwayne felt somewhat better knowing that Paul believed him. "Let's go."

"I told you the gauge wouldn't show any change in temperature," Dwayne said. "It never does. I've tried it dozens of times and the results are always the same."

They were standing in Dwayne's closet. As closets go, it was just an ordinary walk-in type, five feet wide by six deep with a double set of wood crossbars to hang clothes.

The temperature gauge read sixty-seven degrees, but their breath came out in cold white puffs.

"It has to be at least below freezing in here," Paul said, holding the gauge and trying to get a different reading.

"I know. You can feel it. You can even see your breath, but the reading won't change. Dad keeps saying it has something to do with the lake."

Paul felt the closet walls. They were normal, not cold at all.

"Let's see," Paul said. "My room's next door and below this is the living room, but they aren't cold." He looked at Dwayne for verification.

"Right. Just the closet. My room isn't even cold." Dwayne paused. "It's funny in a way. This closet wasn't even here before."

"What do you mean?"

"Well, there was a fire. One of the Duries – James – I guess he was the last one – tried to burn the house down. He wasn't very successful though. Dad says that the house was hardly damaged at all. Anyway, when Dad bought the place, he made some changes. Most of the second floor was one big room. He had it made into three smaller ones: this one, plus the closet, the one you're staying in, and the room Linda has. So, the closet wasn't even here until after we moved in."

Paul felt his sinuses reacting to the cold air. "Let's get out of here before we turn into icicles." They stepped into the bedroom, and Paul closed the closet door. "What else do you know about the Duries?"

"Not much," Dwayne said, flopping down on his bed. "Just what a few kids told me at school. I guess they heard it from their parents, but to hear them tell it, you'd think this house was Frankenstein's castle or something. The Duries were kind of weird."

"Nothing else? Just town superstition?"

Dwayne thought for a moment, his hair dangling down over one eye. "There was one thing. Last fall I had to have some reference books for a school paper, and I ended up going to the Milwaukee Public Library because the one here didn't have what I needed. So, when I finished getting the books for school, I was a little curious about Allan Durie."

"Who's he?"

"James' brother."

"He lived here also?"

"Yeah, only no one's seen him for the last twenty years. He married some woman from the old country – Scotland – I think. Anyway, no one's seen her for even longer."

Paul moved to the bed and squatted down in front of Dwayne. Weak, gray light filtered through the window. Night was coming.

"Dwayne, where did you get this information? From the library?" Paul asked him.

"Yes, but mostly from the kids at school. The people in Lanark don't like to talk about the Duries."

"So, what happened at the library?" Paul prompted. "You said you were curious about Allan Durie."

"Yeah, he's the one all the kids mention. He was some sort of magician or sorcerer, like Cagliostro. You know what I mean?"

Paul nodded. "Go on."

"So, when I was at the library, I looked him up in the card catalog to see if they had any information on him."

"Was there?"

"There were all kinds of listings for him."

"Did you manage to look at any of the books?"

Dwayne shook his head disgustedly. "No. Dad brought me down and he was in a hurry to get back. I couldn't tell him what I wanted to do."

"Too bad."

"Yeah. I know." Then his spirits brightened. "But we could always take a drive and check it out – that is, if you want to."

Paul smiled. "We'll have to do that." Then he stood up and slapped Dwayne playfully on the leg. "We'd better go downstairs. Everyone will be wondering what happened to us."

20

AT NINE MINUTES AFTER SEVEN, Kenneth Sollis parked his sporty red Corvette in front of his place of business in the heart of Lanark's downtown section. He had just finished supper at Mariner's, Lanark's most fashionable restaurant, and felt slightly bloated from the filet of sole and Chablis.

The night air had turned cold enough to put a flush to his cheeks and turn his nose red. He drew his suit coat in tighter to help against the wind.

There are some people in the world who bring on the most negative reactions from their fellow humans. Their aura or magnetism is warped or bent, and even before a person is introduced to them, before one word is spoken, there is an overwhelming feeling of dislike.

Kenneth Sollis was one of those people.

Surprisingly enough, he was extremely successful in business. His store, The Coven, which specialized in the occult and the outré, was doing very well. This enabled him to dress well, own his own bachelor residence, drive an expensive car, and enjoy a lifestyle of freedom and privacy that kept him away from the gray-death security of a time-clock job.

Sollis' love life was not legend, but there were some women – not many – who sought his bed in equal proportion to his bank account. He did not delude himself into thinking that women were ever attracted to him because of his good looks, for Sollis, although he possessed a rather continental charm, looked like a fish.

His thick lips and facial bone structure resembled a large Muskie about to hit a lure. And many a morning he would arrive at his store to find "fish face" chalked on his sidewalk or spray-painted on his windows by the little monsters that had been conceived under the pretext of love and marriage and turned loose to torment mankind.

Sollis hated kids.

In his opinion, there were far too many of them walking around. They learned to swear and give you the finger before they were even toilet trained, and they did not respect property or older people at all. There was a certain destructive savagery about them that gave him the shivers. He never knew what to expect from them.

No, Sollis did not like kids.

But young girls were something else entirely.

He watched the girl enter his store, the saucy sway of her hips as she walked down the aisles and browsed. He was sure it was Debbie Ralston. She had been in the store before and was one of the prettiest girls in town.

He entered the store seconds later, brushing back his blond hair with his fingers and straightening his suit coat. The store was empty except for Debbie and his salesgirl, Marge, a tall, mousey-haired girl with slightly crossed eyes and a hawk nose.

"Did you enjoy your supper, Mr. Sollis?" Marge asked, drifting toward him.

Sollis nodded, blinking back the tears from the recent sting of cold wind. "Marge," he said, "why don't you go on home? It's been rather slow this evening. I'll close it up myself."

Marge hesitated. She really didn't want to go, but knew that she had just been dismissed. "Well, if you think you can manage."

Sollis smiled. "It's always difficult without you, Marge. But I think I can handle it. You just take the rest of the night off and don't worry about anything."

Marge returned his smile, obviously pleased with his compliment to her necessity and efficiency. She walked to the back office and returned with her coat. Sollis helped her on with it. Debbie Ralston wandered over to the counter at the far end of the store.

"Goodnight, Mr. Sollis," Marge said, giving him another smile.

"Goodnight, Marge."

She stepped out into the street and was gone, a blast of cold air washed over him from the closing door as he watched her go.

Poor kid, Sollis thought. He felt a certain empathy for her. She had a pretty good body, which he took advantage of whenever the mood was upon him. Her breasts were good and so were her legs. Her ass was sensational. It was just her head that was wrong. Like his own. But he never had to worry about getting women now, not anymore. He turned his attention to Debbie Ralston.

Debbie knew that he was admiring her boobs (as she called them), so she arched her back and stuck them out more, taking a deep breath at the same time. Debbie was used to being ogled. The boys at school did it all the time, and older men weren't any different. She liked the attention, and the feeling of power it gave her.

Catching the sexual nuance, Sollis smiled at her like a shark and quickly closed the distance between them. "Have you decided?" he asked.

She was standing at the glass and wood counter, trying to make up her mind about which zodiac medallion to buy. "I think the silver one," she said, putting a finger on the glass just above it.

Sollis slid open the back of the display case. "This one? The twins?"

"Yes, Gemini."

"You made a good selection," he said, placing the boxed medallion in front of her and closing the counter. "This is the series that I like the best."

"All the kids at school seem to have one. They just love them."

Sollis looked at her chest, and then raised his eyes to her face. He picked up the medallion, dangling it in front of her. "See how the light catches its beauty?"

Debbie leaned forward.

Sollis started to swing it, slowly. "Watch the medallion…see how peaceful it is…restful…you can see the ancient mysteries of the zodiac…if you look closely…even your future…look…look…"

Debbie began to feel strange, like she was drifting across the sky on a cloud…farther and farther away…

When Sollis was sure she was under hypnosis, he glanced quickly at the entrance, making certain no one was about to enter. The entrance was empty. He thought for a moment about locking the door, and then decided against it.

Sollis dropped the medallion back in its box and took out a pair of scissors from behind the counter, then quickly snipped off a lock of Debbie's hair, placing it in his pocket.

When Sollis brought her out of it, Debbie didn't remember anything of the past few minutes.

Sollis smiled at her. "Do you know what they say about Gemini?"

Debbie smiled back and shook her head.

"They have no heart," he whispered. "But I can't believe that about you. You seem to be a very warm person."

Debbie blushed, throwing back her long, blond hair, like all the pretty girls knew how to do. "Is that true? I never heard that before."

"You haven't?" He bent forward, their faces almost touching. "Maybe you'd like to take along a book on sun signs so you can read up on it."

"I don't know if I have enough." She started rummaging through her purse. "How much is the medallion?"

"Ten dollars even with the tax."

She fished out a five and five singles. "And the book?"

Sollis slipped around the counter to the appropriate bookshelf and returned with a hardbound book. "Five-ninety-five with tax."

Debbie found three more singles. "I don't think I have enough money."

"How much do you have?"

She found two quarters. "Thirteen dollars and fifty cents."

Debbie looked up at him, their eyes met. He gave her a mental thrust with a mental penis.

She responded with a wide smile. He was kind of creepy looking, she thought, but nice, in an old sort of way. She guessed his age at way over thirty.

"Sold," he said, "for thirteen-fifty."

"But..."

Sollis held up a hand. "I insist, my dear. Enjoy them both."

"Well, all right, if you insist." She handed him the money.

He rang up the sale on the cash register, put the money in the drawer, and closed it. Then he dropped the medallion and the book in a turquoise colored bag with "The Coven" printed on it in black lettering and handed it to her, his hand touching hers in the exchange.

"It's a gift," he said. "From me to you."

"Thank you," Debbie said, taking the bag. She picked up her purse, obviously flattered, but a little nonplussed at the gift. "Thank you very much, Mr. Sollis."

He waved it off. "My pleasure, my dear. Have a nice evening."

"Thank you. Goodbye."

"Goodbye."

Sollis eyed the pert sway of her derriere as she moved toward the door. He liked the short hike of her dress over her honey-colored stockinged legs. Very nice legs. And attractive sensible shoes. Not those brogan types that most girls her age clumped around in.

She looked back from the door, waved, and stepped out. The whoosh of cold air drifted back to him.

And a very nice ass. He would have to do something with that. And soon. Very soon. As soon as he finished with Ruth Hanson.

21

JIMMY GILLISPIE HAD BEEN WATCHING the school parking lot for about a half hour now. The school lights were on and threw large, rectangular checkerboards of light across the lot's black surface. Jimmy stood in the shadows of the large maple trees that bordered the parking area on the north end.

He huddled deeper into his jacket, waiting for the last arrival of students to leave their cars and enter the school building. Once inside, they would head straight for Miss Homes' Drama class and rehearsal.

Christ, he was cold. His nuts felt like they were frozen. He wished the dumb shits would hurry up and get into the building so he could get along with his business. His old man wouldn't let him have the car tonight and he had to walk here and back home again.

He bent down and rubbed his legs, trying to restore some warmth, and caught a drift of laughter from the group as they finally entered the school. It sounded like Doris Frazer's hyena laugh.

Jimmy looked at his watch. It was seven-thirty, right on the head. He'd wait another five or ten minutes in case any more latecomers showed up.

A few cars passed the entrance to the parking lot on Richmond Street, their headlights sweeping away the darkness along their path.

Jimmy looked at his watch again. Five minutes had passed. Shit, long enough, he thought. It was getting colder and he wasn't any goddam Eskimo.

The wind moved the trees and stirred the dry-shelled leaves on the ground, sailing them across the parking lot. Jimmy stepped out from the maples and made his way across the lot to the cars. When he reached the small, light green Pinto parked near the school entrance, he stopped, looked around quickly, then ducked behind the rear of the car.

He looked around again. Nothing. Just the leaves scraping along the ground. He brought the long, black-handled switchblade out of his jacket pocket and started to work on the tires.

This should fix that bitch, Homes. He only wished it was her throat.

22

"ASK IT IF THE TALBERT DEAL WILL GO THROUGH," John Eastman said, "so I know how much money I can spend on your birthday present."

"Oh, Daddy," Chrissie moaned.

They were all in the library. Chrissie, Linda, and Dwayne had a Ouija board set up on one of the cocktail tables, hands resting lightly on the felt-footed trivet. Paul stood in back of Linda and watched. Mr. and Mrs. Eastman were sitting in chairs at opposite ends of the fireplace.

Three thick logs cracked and popped with dancing flames from the grate. The foyer clock struck the quarter hour – seven-forty-five. Eastman was half reading The Milwaukee Journal, half kibitzing the Ouija board players. His wife was working on a crossword puzzle, trying to find a seven letter word for the author of Leaves of Grass.

"Let's ask it who you're going to marry," Linda said to Chrissie.

"Okay," Chrissie said. "Dwayne, you're pushing."

"I am not."

"What's it spelling?" Linda asked.

"How about Rockefeller or Getty?" Eastman suggested, looking over the top of his reading glasses.

"Tommy Burham would be nice," Mrs. Eastman said.

Chrissie turned around and gave her mother a mischievous grin.

"It's moving," Dwayne said. "K-I-N-G. King."

"You know anyone named King?" Paul asked Chrissie.

"King? No."

"Sounds like a dog's name," Eastman said.

Chrissie moaned again.

"John, you're terrible," Mrs. Eastman said, smiling at him. He seemed to be in a good mood for a change.

"It's still moving," Linda said. "K-O-N-G. Kong. King Kong?"

"Dwayne Eastman, you're horrid," Chrissie said and stuck out her tongue at him. "You were moving it the whole time. You made it spell that."

"I was not," Dwayne protested, but not very convincingly. "It's just your karma."

"You're what?" Eastman asked.

"Fate, Dad," Linda said.

Eastman made a sour face and nodded.

"Why don't you ask it who Dwayne will marry, Chrissie," Mrs. Eastman said.

"Yeah, that's a good idea. Maybe we can come up with Spider Woman or the Bride of Frankenstein," Chrissie taunted.

"Very funny," Dwayne said.

They were all resting their hands.

"What do you want to ask it now?" Linda said.

"Ask it about your marriage, Linda," Chrissie said.

"Oh, I think I already know the one," Linda said and glanced up at Paul.

Eastman caught the exchange and straightened out his newspaper with much unnecessary movement.

"Ask about Holly," Paul suggested.

Dwayne looked at him. "Yeah, let's ask it."

They put their fingertips back on the indicator.

"Where's Holly?" Dwayne asked.

"Nothing's happening," Chrissie said.

Dwayne asked the question again.

"Are you moving it, Chrissie?" Dwayne asked.

"I'm not."

“G-O…”Linda started to spell out the message. The lights in the library flickered.

“…N-E,” she continued. “Gone.”

The indicator stopped.

“Gone where?” Dwayne asked.

After a few moments pause, the trivet started moving again. GONE.

Dwayne looked up at Paul. Paul shrugged. “Evidently you’ve contacted a limited spirit.”

“That’s karma,” Eastman said, trying to be funny.

No one laughed.

“Dwayne, why don’t you ask it about your closet?” Eastman continued.

Mrs. Eastman gave her husband a sharp look.

“Well, maybe he can find out what the mystery is,” Eastman said. “Who knows? Maybe the bogeyman’s taken up residence in it.”

“Or James Durie’s ghost,” Chrissie said, trying to sound spooky.

“Very funny,” Dwayne said. “Ha ha.”

“Oh, Dwayne, don’t be such a pill,” Chrissie said. “I think that’s a keen idea. Don’t you, Linda?”

“Well, I—”

“Come on, Dwayne,” Chrissie went on. “Don’t spoil the fun. Let’s ask it about your creepy old closet.”

“Oh, all right,” Dwayne said.

They took up their positions on the trivet again.

“What’s the matter with my closet?” Dwayne asked.

Nothing happened.

“What’s the matter with my closet?” Dwayne asked again.

The lights blinked.

The indicator started to vibrate but did not move. Linda became startled and took her hands off the trivet.

“You broke the contact,” Chrissie said.

“Sorry,” Linda said. She exchanged glances with Paul.

“Maybe you’d better stop,” Paul said.

“Just once more,” Chrissie begged.

Linda reluctantly put her hands back in position.

Dwayne asked the same question again and again and again. His voice began to take on a mantra quality. Still, nothing happened.

"Ask something else," Paul said.

Helen Eastman got up and stood behind Dwayne. Her husband put down his paper.

Dwayne persisted. "What's the matter with my closet?"

The indicator trembled, then swung over slowly to the letter P and stopped.

The lights flickered.

"What the hell is wrong with these damned lights?" Eastman asked.

No one answered him.

Dwayne looked puzzled. "What is that supposed to mean?"

"Why don't you put that thing away for now?" his mother said, a slight crystallization of fear frosting her voice.

The players stared down at the Ouija board as if they were hypnotized. It was moving again.

POR.

"It stopped again," Chrissie said. "It didn't finish."

"Is it good or evil?" Dwayne asked suddenly, putting a chill in the room with his words.

No answer.

"Good or evil?"

The lights dimmed, almost going out.

The trivet began to shake violently, then suddenly flew off the board and landed on the floor.

No one said anything for a long moment. There was uneasiness in the room.

Then Chrissie looked at Dwayne and said, "You did that just to scare me."

"I didn't move it."

"Well, I know Linda wouldn't do anything like that."

"I said I didn't move it," Dwayne persisted.

"You're a big fibber." Chrissie glanced over at her father for support. "Isn't he, Daddy?"

"Maybe he was just trying a little too hard to impress everyone," Eastman said.

Dwayne turned sharply toward his father, started to say something, and then changed his mind.

"That's enough of the Ouija board for one night," Mrs. Eastman said. "Chrissie, put that thing away."

23

KENNETH SOLLIS LOCKED UP THE COVEN for the night and headed for his Corvette. The wind buffeted him around and stung his eyes, making him wish he had worn a topcoat.

The store had been closed an hour earlier than usual tonight because Feminique stayed open until nine and Sollis needed time for the preparation. He climbed behind the wheel of his car and started home, his taillights merging with the evening traffic.

Twenty minutes later, at eight-thirty, he eased the Corvette into the garage, locked up, and entered his house. He would have to work fast, but he was certain everything could be accomplished within the allotted time.

Turning on the bedroom lights, he took an envelope out of the top bureau drawer. He fingered the soft lock of dark hair inside the envelope, savoring its sensual texture. He smiled and started to hum. He would have to bathe first.

An hour later, Sollis sat in his living room and went through the motions of reading a book. He checked his watch again as he had been doing on and off for the last ten minutes when the doorbell rang. He smiled smugly, put the book away and answered the door.

Ruth Hanson stood in the doorway.

"Come in, Ruth," Sollis said and closed the door behind her.

She entered the living room, but did not look at him. Her eyes were fixed on something in the distance that only she could see.

He took her coat and purse and threw them on a nearby couch. "Come," he said, taking her by the arm and ushering her straight into the bedroom. He flicked on the lights and told her to sit on the edge of the bed. She obeyed with robotlike obedience.

Sollis looked her over. She was dressed in a smart blue suit with black hose and matching blue shoes.

"You look very lovely tonight, my dear," he said, offering her his hand. "Stand up."

She stood, and he let her hand go. "Now take off your suit and your shoes. Put the suit over there." He gestured toward a chair in the corner of the room.

He watched her disrobe and was surprised to find she wore a girdle with garters instead of pantyhose, which had become as common as a second skin these days.

Ruth folded her suit and draped it over the chair as instructed.

"Good," Sollis said. "Now the bra and panties. You can leave the rest on for now."

She took them off.

He began to examine her as if she were for sale. He was not disappointed at what he saw. Old sex, as he thought of her, still had a fine body. The breasts were large and still firm; the legs, good; the buttocks, excellent. There was only a slight bulging of flesh around the stomach and hips.

Sollis slipped out of the robe he was wearing and threw it on top of her clothes. He faced her, his penis pointing at her like a spear.

"Come here," he said. "Kneel down."

She knelt before him, eyes still focused straight ahead, her movements still automatized.

"You are going to enjoy everything that I do to you, Ruth. Do you understand?"

"Yes," she said her voice hollow and distant, like she was speaking from somewhere deep within her own body.

"Good. Now take it. It's candy." Sollis remembered Jennifer telling him about her mother's sweet tooth. "You know how much you like candy. Take it."

She did.

24

"YOU'RE THE ONLY ONE WHO UNDERSTANDS my need," Father Kerry said, talking to the bottle of brandy, which was almost empty. He picked it up and scrutinized its level with a bleary eye. He would have to lay in another supply to tide him over for the rest of the month. Of course, he would be discreet and send RCA. Can't have St. Casmir's priest stumbling in and out of liquor stores.

Kerry set the bottle back down on his desk, patting it affectionately. "You are my sleep," he smiled. "Sleep, perchance to nightmare," he misquoted. Even better: "We shall not all sleep, but we shall all be changed. First Epistle of Paul to the Corinthians. Go to the head of the class, Kerry. Go past GO, collect two hundred dollars. Go to JAIL, go directly to JAIL, go…crazy…"

Shit.

He scrubbed his face with his hand. Father Kerry, me boy, you're drunk. You're more than drunk. You're plastered.

So what?

"Fuck it."

"Sssshhhh!" Kerry pressed a finger to his lips and looked around his study to make sure no one had heard him. Naughty word. A carry-over from his army days and the Great War II. An expressive word. It covered everything, but wasn't…nice? He nodded. Nice is the word he wanted. It wasn't nice for a man of the cloth to know such a word.

He should be able to sleep soon – for a little while, anyway.

Now, that was a beautiful word: sleep. Something he had not gotten much of in the last nine years. Agonizing apprehension caused him to sleep only in little nervous snatches, with some silent part of him always watching, and waiting. After a while, he would wake up trembling in the dark, carefully studying every shadow in the room, listening to every sound of the night, waiting for the black dread to come.

He had not always been this way. Once, a million years ago, he had been a man who loved every minute of life. He had loved to laugh, to smell the flowers in his garden, to walk in the rain at night, to help people. He was not able to enjoy any of these things now.

He was suffering.

His affliction was caused by that unmentionable encounter that had left its splinter to fester in his flesh, and in his mind. He was never able to forget that grisly night. Not alone anyway, not without the brandy. It stopped those endless parades of thought that invaded his mind, reminding him of the bitter conflict between old, old enemies, and mostly…his failure.

Kerry had been to the very brink of the pit, looked into the bottom of its soulless eye and didn't have enough courage to spit in it. When he came away, he was never the same again, never whole again, never able to relate that nightmare to another human soul.

Who could he tell? A friend? A psychiatrist? They'd commit him in a minute, and most of them were worse off than he. Mother church? Maybe. They knew. They've heard it all before. But then, he'd have to tell them his part. And what proof did he have?

Shit.

How can you describe to anyone what you saw in that house? The terror you felt from that alien presence, unseen and menacing, but there nevertheless, like a hiss in the dark. A rationalizing mind would try to explain it away, but you knew with some ancient knowledge what it was.

Father Kerry shook, literally, with a fear that penetrated his body deeper than his bones. He took a long swallow of brandy.

You couldn't explain it to the average man or woman who still thought that the entire business of evil was an invention of the church. Their primitive instincts had been all but obliterated by modern technology and advanced intellect. Social evil, yes – that was acceptable – but the old evil, the diabolical kind that the ancients warned of, the kind that you faced or that whispered to you in the sweaty dead of night, that kind, they would refuse to take seriously. The world had grown up and put away all its childish fears and silly superstitions, or so it thought.

He poured himself another drink.

But why? The *why* always escaped him. All his training, his philosophy, his theology, his vows, was meshed into strands of hypocrisies by the eternal *why*. Why, why, why, why, why? Why was it so? Cause and effect? Positive and negative? Or, just plain old good and evil? Dear God, were all those stories about the rebellion in heaven, which he had never actually believed, really true?

Kerry pushed away from his desk and lurched over to the study window, taking his drink with him. Little slivers of streetlights accented the black arms of the trees that were losing their leaves to a thieving wind.

He would have liked to go to his bishop, Joe Connally, whom he had known since school days and say, "Joe, I'm scared shitless. I'm afraid to leave my church; I'm afraid to help people; I'm afraid to do anything. I'm a chicken. First class."

Damn it. Everything seems so screwed up. And the church hasn't helped either. The changes incorporated by the Second Vatican Council made him feel like he was saying an impotent mass. The gestures were empty and insipid. There was no more symbolism or mystery to the mass. The words spoken in English held no significance for him. No power. Even the Extreme Unction was now the Sacrament of the Annointing of the Sick. He wondered how many Catholics held similar conclusions on the effect of the changes.

Kerry turned away from the window and faced the room. "To the Tridentine rite." He lifted his drink in tribute and finished it, then looked at the empty glass. "Quia tu es, Deus, fortitude mea, quareme repulisti? Et quare tristis incedo dum affligit me inimicus?"

He set the glass on his desk. "Thought I wouldn't remember the Latin, huh? Fooled you. For Thou, oh God, art my strength, why has Thou cast me off? And why do I go sorrowful while the enemy afflicteth me? Amen to that. Amen. Amen. Amen."

Kerry started for the hall and his bedroom. It was past eleven o'clock. Time to sleep, or try to. He headed for the stairs.

Maybe he'd hit them with a Latin mass on Sunday. Sock it to them. Make them wake up to what's happening. He had second thoughts. Yeah, and on Monday, the Pope would drum him out of the corps.

He stumbled halfway up the stairs. "Justin Kerry, you're a drunken sot." He pulled himself up, made the landing, and bounced his way along the corridor walls to his bedroom, like a ping-pong ball.

When he finally made the bed, he stretched out and let the stupor carry him into an uneasy sleep. One hand gripped the crucifix around his neck, like it was an anchor in an unfriendly sea.

25

IN A HOUSE THAT LIES SOUTH OF DURIE HOUSE, a lone figure waited for the midnight hour to pass.

When it did, the adept, clad in a black robe, entered the nine-foot circle drawn on the floor of an empty room and carefully checked the Triangle of Art to make certain all was correct.

Inside the circle, the kabbalistic cross was formulated and the eastern, southern, and western stations purified. The northern station was left open to face Durie House. There the adept placed a black candle and burned incense, a mixture of periwinkle and rue and dried blood.

On the altar, also placed inside the circle and facing north, were the following: a replica of the famous trident of Paracelsus with the names of power engraved on it; a wand made from an oak branch, cut from a cemetery tree in the dark of night with one stroke of a knife and capped on both ends with lead; a sacrificial knife with a wooden handle; a gong, a crystal, a bell, and a small piece of black cloth, resting under a silver goblet.

Another black candle was placed in the northern station of the circle, after that, the book, taken from the Durie crypt, was put on the altar; then the black dog was carried into the circle and the circle closed, using the wand and saying the words of power.

The adept now cut the black dog's throat just as the Eastman dog's was a few days ago. After catching the blood in the goblet, the adept made another cut straight down the dog's chest and between its legs, whispering the ancient names and the names of the Six Authors of Wickedness.

Then, kneeling at the northern station, the adept whispered to the earth the sacred names, calling them out eleven times each, paying homage to the number of warriors in the Master's house. The 7,405,926. Then, after self-anointment, the adept opened the book on the altar and read aloud:

"Lord of the Flies
Rub the dust from their eyes,
For with the left hand I honor thee,
And all that is written in thy Book shall be.
From the bottomless pit they rise,
Through the portal you have devised.
Come, spirits of perdition, abandoned and defiled,
With appetites wet, with madness riled.
With the left hand I break the cross.
With the left hand I regain thy loss.
I am thy hand that wounds.
Grant me then, thy servant, thy boons.
Lord of the Beasts
I celebrate thy feasts.
Thus, I open the door to thee,
Embracing thy Dark Power for all eternity."

The adept repeated this six times, then continued reading, picking up the knife and making it worthy.

26

OFFICER WALLY SCHAEFER AND MARION KOSS were sitting on the couch in Marion's living room, watching the late, late movie on TV. They had been sitting and innocently kissing since returning from dinner and a movie.

It was time, Wally decided, to try again.

His lips brushed against Marion's ear as he reached over and started to unbutton her blouse. After three buttons, he dropped his hand in and squeezed her breast on the outside of her bra.

Marion Koss squirmed and tried to slap his hand away. "None of that stuff now. Be nice."

He rolled her bra up and dropped her breasts out like two large eggs from their containers.

"Wal-leeee," she pleaded.

Wally pushed her down on the couch, unbuttoned the remainder of her blouse and started working on her breasts with his mouth.

"Walleeee! I don't like this!"

He tried pulling down her skirt, but she held it up with a death grip. Foiled at this, he slipped his hand under her skirt and began playing with her crotch, fondling it gently through her pantyhose and panties.

Marion's body stiffened. Her head rolled from side to side as if she was trying to avoid being seen by someone else in the room. Could

Richard be watching her now? They say that the dead are all around you. The thought panicked her. She began to cry: "I don't want to! I don't want to! I don't want to!"

It became a dirge, one that finally penetrated Wally's brain, causing him to lose his desire. He eased his weight off of her and sat back on the couch. "Christ, not again."

She wiggled away, straightening her clothes, whimpering. "Please, Wally. I just don't want to."

Wally looked at her sitting there, her dress still pulled invitingly up, exposing her thighs. Wally felt weak. It was happening again. Another great night.

Wally Schaefer was a dark, good-looking man, who people often said resembled Gene Kelly, except Wally didn't dance a step. He had been on the Lanark Police Force for three years now and had been going with Marion Koss for two, meeting her, of all places, in church. He had been coerced into going to a Christmas Eve mass by a fellow officer, Barney Jensen and his wife, who introduced him to Marion. He still didn't know if the Jensens had done him a favor or not.

"Why don't you want to?" Wally asked in a disgusted voice.

Marion finished buttoning her blouse, and then pulled her skirt down. "Because it's too soon."

"For Christ's sake, Marion."

"Don't swear," she said softly, folding her hands in her lap and looking at him. "I can't help the way I feel."

"Just give me one good reason. Don't you love me?"

"You know I do."

"Then why?"

"I told you why. It's too soon."

Wally felt like tearing out his hair. "Jesus Christ, Marion, your husband's been dead for over five years. Why don't you just let him stay dead?"

"I told you I couldn't help the way I feel. I'm just not over it yet."

"My God, it's been over five years. Five years, Marion. How long is it going to take you to get over it?"

“I know. I’m just not ready yet.” How could she tell him that Richard was still too much with her? She sensed his presence in every room in the house. How could she…go to bed with another man…in Richard’s bed…with Richard watching?

“You’re a damned prude,” Wally said. “That’s the trouble. And you always will be.”

“I am not a prude.”

“Then you’re frigid or something.”

“Do I kiss you like I’m frigid?”

Wally had to admit that she didn’t. He moved closer to her and squeezed her hand. “Can’t we just try it to see how it works out? Maybe then you’ll get over this feeling. Maybe it will be good for you.”

Marion lowered her eyes and brushed some imaginary lint off her skirt. “Then you’ll have had me,” she said, her voice very low.

Wally rested an arm around her shoulders. “So?”

“It’s different with women. Men don’t care. Women have a reputation to think of.”

He kissed her cheek.

“Behave.”

“Christ!” He drew away from her, weary of the argument. It was always like this. Night after night for two years. You’d think her husband was still living with her.

He got up and started to put on his sport coat and Tyrolean hat. Shit. Might as well go home and suck on an ice cube.

“Now you’re mad,” she said.

“Why should I be mad?” he snapped. “This has only been going on for years.”

Marion came into his arms and gave him a long, pacifying kiss. “Don’t be mad. Be patient with me.”

They kissed again, longer, more passionately. “Please, Wally, stay awhile. Have another drink.”

Wally melted. He smiled and took off his hat and coat. Marion picked up his glass and disappeared into the kitchen.

Jesus, Wally thought after she left, having her for a girl was like having nobody. He was getting tired of taking cold showers and beating his meat. It was a shame. That was a lot of woman going to waste.

She returned with the drink and they sat and talked awhile longer, then Wally decided to go. Nothing had really changed.

He walked to the door and kissed her goodnight. "Be sure and lock up after me," Wally instructed. "I'll call you tomorrow."

Marion nodded and blew him a kiss, then closed the door behind him. Wally waited on the porch until he heard her lock up, and then headed for his car.

The wind had died down to a slight breeze, but the night air was still cold enough to make him shiver. Wally got in his car and drove straight ahead for three blocks until he came to old Marsh Road. Bender Street, where Marion lived, ended into Marsh as all the streets did in this ten block area.

He turned right on Marsh and lit a cigarette. When he passed the Armstrong house, a spark from his cigarette fell in his lap. Wally unintentionally stepped on the brake as he brushed the spark away, trying to prevent a burn-hole in his pants.

It was then that he caught a faint movement around the Armstrong driveway.

Wally continued on for half a block, and then stopped the car. Had he really seen someone? Or was it just a tree? Or a shadow moved by the wind? He knew that Pearl Armstrong was an old, wrinkled-up widow, and her complaints to the station of men trying to break into her house were put down as just wishful thinking. Still, he thought he saw something.

Wally turned off the ignition. He took the flashlight from the glove compartment and got out of the car, slipping the .38 from its holster on his belt.

Cutting across the lawns of the nearby houses, he edged his way to the end of the house next door to the Armstrong place. Wally waited a few moments, and then eased himself around the corner and into the shadows of the Armstrong driveway.

27

"WATCH OUT! HE'S GONNA SHOOT YOU!"

Pearl Armstrong shifted her heavy bulk uneasily in her favorite chair and took another swig from her cup of Lipton tea while she watched reruns of her favorite TV show, The Untouchables. She often got so excited during her viewing that she talked to the characters on the screen.

Pearl shook her head with concern. The situation was getting tight for Eliot Ness now. She warned him, but it looked like Frank Nitti's boys were going to get him.

"One's right behind you!" Pearl screamed at him.

Just as one of Nitti's men was about to shoot, the scene faded and the station switched to a commercial, a special offer on rock'n'roll records.

"Goddam!" Pearl swore. "They always come on with the commercials at the best times." She made this observation to no one in particular, for Pearl was alone in the house and she liked it that way. Her husband, Jack, dead these past fifteen years, was not mourned. He was not even missed. His dusting was what she missed. Jack had always dusted the house for her every week. Now, with him gone, she had to do it herself, and it wasn't easy for her to get around anymore, not at eighty-four and with bad feet.

Another commercial flashed on. This time they were selling toilet paper.

Pearl reached behind her chair, found the fifth of Old Crow wrapped in a paper bag, laced her tea, and returned the bottle to its place of solitude just in time to see Ness get the best of Nitti's hoods.

She celebrated Ness' triumph with a loud slurp of tea, moistening the dark hairs that grew above her upper lip. She dried them with a finger and returned the cup to a nearby lamp table.

Walter Winchell made a few parting comments and the episode was over. Pearl belched. Then she got out of her chair with great effort and plodded over to the TV set, changing the channel to a rerun of Perry Mason.

Returning to her chair, she tasted the tea again and settled down to enjoy another adventure in crime.

That's when she heard the noise.

At first, she thought it was coming from her TV set, but after she listened for a while and isolated it, she found the noise was coming from one of her windows on the driveway side of the house. It sounded like a window was being tampered with.

Then it stopped.

Well, we'll just see about that, she thought. Probably some piggy-man trying to bother her again, knowing that she was a widow and alone. Pearl took another sip of tea for a bracer, then got up and went into her bedroom. When she returned, she was carrying her husband's old double-barreled shotgun that she kept loaded and within easy reach of her bed.

She paused in the kitchen; her ear pressed against the back door, and listened. There was no sound outside except the wind moving against the house. The kitchen light was off, and Pearl waited in the dark. She couldn't decide whether she should unlock the door and slip out or just let the pig get in. Maybe she should call the police first, and then give whoever's out there both barrels.

Outside, Wally waited, letting his eyes adjust to the darkness. After a while, he could distinguish shapes to some degree, but for the most part, the night remained imperceptible.

He crept down the length of the adjoining house with the expertise of an Indian – or so he thought. Wally always had a vision, a sort of daydream of himself being filmed on Police Story or written about in a novel by Joseph Wambaugh. Actually, he would have settled for a good write-up in the Lanark Leader.

He stopped.

Wally, still buoyed by his dreams and a sense of insouciance, had reached what he thought was an advantageous position along the length of the neighboring yard. Now he could cross over onto the Armstrong property near its garage. He was almost there when he suddenly froze.

He could feel something – another presence – nearby in the dark, watching him. A fungoid smell drifted over to him. It seemed to be coming from the direction of the garage, just ahead of him. His eyes began to sting and water.

Slowly, Wally started to close on the garage. The smell became stronger, vile, like a charnel house. Wally had to restrain himself from vomiting.

He stepped back, away from the smell, and almost let his bladder go when he felt the hard jab of metal against his back.

"Don't move, sonny," the creaky voice said, "or I'll blow you right out of your pants."

A small startled cry escaped from Wally's lips. His legs felt like they were filled with water.

"You men are all alike," creaky voice said. "Pigs – that's what you are. I seen you come sneakin' around in my yard. Thought you could take advantage of a poor defenseless widow."

"Listen, I'm…" Wally tried to explain.

"Quiet now. You just walk straight ahead to the garage. And no funny business or your tom cattin' days are over. I've got a shotgun pressed against you."

Wally moved cautiously toward the garage, the double bores of the shotgun prompting him all the way.

The garage door was up and creaky voice told him to stop just inside of the entrance. Wally heard a light switch click on in back of him and a blaze of light startled the darkness, lighting the garage and part of the yard. Wally was still holding his .38.

“Drop the gun,” creaky voice said. “Throw it on the grass, slowly.”

Wally did as instructed.

“Good. Now let’s get a look at you before the police get here.”

“I – I am the police,” Wally managed to say.

“That’s a likely story.” The voice paused. “You got any ID?”

Wally reached into the inside pocket of his sport coat with his left hand and handed his identification back over his shoulder.

“Turn around so I can see your face.”

Wally turned and immediately recognized old Mrs. Armstrong standing there in her bathrobe holding a double-barreled shotgun in her fat arms. One heavy sausage finger was curled around both triggers.

“Walter Schaefer,” Mrs. Armstrong said, reading the name off the ID.

“Don’t you remember me, Mrs. Armstrong?” Wally asked. “I answered several of your calls here at the house in regard to prowlers.”

Pearl Armstrong squinted at him. “How come you’re dressed so funny? All in green like that? You look like the goddam tooth fairy.”

28

THEY WERE THERE AGAIN. Paul could see them clearly: Phillips, Thornton, Rademaker, Weiss, and Braddock. They were sweating, just like he was, uncomfortable and clammy, right down to their shorts and socks. The air was hot and sticky. It was hard to breathe.

Braddock turned to say something to him. He never finished. That's when they came. Everything after that was a tremendous fireworks display, bursting around him in red.

Then there was the pile of bodies on top of him, staring at him, bleeding on him. Paul couldn't move. He could hear them coming for him, as they always came for him, closer…closer.

For once, the looming face was clear and close. Paul reached for the neck and started to squeeze.

Suddenly, the dream faded and Paul was wide awake. He had his hands around Dwayne's neck. The boy was terrified, his eyes wide with fear. Paul withdrew his hands and slumped back on the bed, his body wet with a cold sweat.

"I'm sorry," Paul said. "I was having a nightmare. One I thought was over." He wiped his face with his hand.

Dwayne didn't say anything. He just stood there, fear still in his eyes, feeling his throat.

Paul eased himself up. "Did I hurt you?"

"It's okay," Dwayne managed to say. "You just scared me… reaching out like that."

"Sorry," Paul said again.

"It's okay. No harm done. I'll survive."

"Did I wake you? Did I…scream?" Paul was afraid he woke everyone in the house.

"No, you just grabbed me when I came in and turned on the light."

Paul's own throat felt raw. His sinuses were acting up again. "Is something the matter, Dwayne?"

Dwayne paused, and then looked at him. "The closet. There were noises…like voices…a lot of voices…" Dwayne looked away. "I don't know if I'm just imagining things or what…but it sort of shook me up. That's when I came in here. I thought…well, maybe I could bunk in with you again…if you don't mind."

"No, of course not." Paul smiled. "But you might be safer in there."

Dwayne returned the smile. "I'll take my chances."

Minutes later, with Dwayne bunked in beside him, Paul stared at the shadowed ceiling, wondering what kept triggering the release of that dream. And why just the dream? The stomach and head pains hadn't bothered him since he left Milwaukee. Thank God nothing has happened.

No one has died.

29

POLICE CHIEF CLIVE THAYER's big face spread into a slow grin as Wally Schaefer stood in front of his desk and explained how Pearl Armstrong got the drop on him. But Bill Jennings, the officer who answered the call at the Armstrong house, had already radioed the whole story in, including the fact that Mrs. Armstrong kept referring to Schaefer as "that goddam tooth fairy."

Wally, still dressed in his evening attire of green plaid sport coat and slacks, light green shirt with color coordinated tie, and dark green Tyrolean hat, caught Thayer's grin.

"What's the matter?" Wally asked him.

Officer Jerry Hardigan, the twelve-to-eight dispatcher, couldn't contain himself any longer and broke into a loud, booming laugh.

"Hey, Schaefer," he said. "I heard old Pearl Armstrong thought you were the tooth fairy."

"Up yours." Wally gave Hardigan the finger and looked back at Thayer, who was laughing openly now.

"Marion likes green," Wally explained to Thayer.

"Then she should just love you," Thayer said, wiping his eyes. Thayer was a tall man, just four notches over six feet, with a slightly heavy waistline and when he laughed, his belly shook the desk.

"It's not that bad," Wally said, straightening his tie. "I thought it looked rather neat."

Thayer shuffled the papers he had been putting some overtime on (actually, it was just an excuse to get out of the house) and grunted.

"In fact, you should wear more color, Chief. Instead of brown and blue all the time."

Thayer put the papers down indignantly. "I happen to like brown and blue. Besides, I'm a little too big to be walking around dressed like a damned leprechaun."

Wally reddened.

Hardigan was laughing so hard he farted.

"I still don't think it's that bad," Wally said, his voice taking on an edge.

"It's not, Wally," Thayer soothed, feeling a guilty pang for ridiculing him. "On you it looks all right. But on me, well, green isn't my color."

Thayer took a cigar out of a shirt pocket, unwrapped it, and stuck it in the corner of his mouth. He would chew it down to a butt without lighting it. That was about as far away as he could get from smoking.

"So what do you think?" Wally asked him, his face returning to its normal color.

Thayer looked up at him. "About what?"

"Mrs. Armstrong."

"Oh, it was probably just some kid that wanted to shake her up a little. Although she always thinks it's some guy trying to get at her."

"Wishful thinking. She must be ninety if she's a day."

"Older. She probably rode with the James Gang," Hardigan said.

"She probably rode with the Four Horsemen of the Apocalypse," Thayer said.

Hardigan started laughing again.

Wally smiled, relieved that he was no longer the center of attention. "Well, whoever or whatever it was sure smelled to high heaven."

“Maybe the guy’s deodorant failed,” Hardigan said.

“Naw, it was a different kind of smell.”

Thayer’s brow creased under his white mane of hair. “Different how?”

“I don’t know, like a herd of skunks with the diarrhea, or something dead that wasn’t buried.”

Thayer was lost in thought for a while. Then said, “Well, we’ll check it out again in the morning.” He yawned and looked at his watch. “God, it’s nearly four a.m.” He pushed away from his desk and stood up. He’d grab a beer when he got home and then hit the sack for a while.

As Thayer left his office, Schaefer’s words stayed with him, “Or something dead that wasn’t buried.” Now, what the hell did that mean?

30

ON THE OTHER SIDE OF TOWN, FRED OWENS creaked one blurry eye open and peered at the lighted face of the small alarm clock. Four-ten. Sunrise was exactly two hours and fifteen minutes away.

Hell, he couldn't sleep anymore, he thought. Might as well get up and start his routine. Funny how you can't sleep long when you're old. Maybe it's because the good Lord knows your time is short and doesn't want you sleeping it all away.

Owens turned the bed lamp on and swung his seventy-eight-year-old body into a sitting position, his long, bony legs touching the cold floor. He scratched his sides, shivered in the morning chill of the house, and reached for his robe at the foot of the bed. Being an old Navy man, Fred always slept in his skivvies. He'd done so for sixty years and wasn't about to stop now.

He slipped into a pair of old leather slippers (cold as ice as usual), scratched what little white hair he had on his head, and felt the urge to urinate. Shuffling down the hall to the bathroom, he flipped on the light, rocked back and forth in front of the toilet bowl, spit a few times, and waited.

That's another thing old age does for you. You can't even piss when you want to. He waited a few minutes more, then gave up. Shit. He'd piss later.

Leaving the bathroom, Fred went downstairs and turned on the kitchen lights. He made coffee, putting the pot on, then went back upstairs to his bedroom to dress.

After dressing, he stepped into the bathroom to shave, peering momentarily out the window to see if any of his little bird friends were up and about yet. The darkness was still solid even though the night was ending. Fred dropped the shade and went back to his shaving.

When he had finished, Fred checked the results in the mirror. It was always the same. He looked like he had just tried to commit suicide with his safety razor. Small nicks and gashes were bleeding all over his face and neck. He slapped on the aftershave lotion, swearing at each stinging application.

When he was satisfied he wouldn't bleed to death, he started for the kitchen and his coffee, then stopped a few steps out of the bathroom. The running water had made him want to piss again. He unzipped his fly and waited. And waited. Nothing.

Disgusted, he went down to the kitchen and poured himself a cup of coffee, then turned on the radio. Sitting down at the table, Fred slurped his coffee and stared at the bird food and sunflower seeds that he had carried in from outside on his shoes and ground into his living room rug. He'd have to vacuum today, or else his daughter would be on his back again when she dropped over with some food tomorrow.

Dad, why do you have to feed those damned birds? This place looks like a bird sanctuary. You've got bird food spilled all over, outside and inside. You're going to have rats around here. Blah, blah, blah.

Then he'd wait until she finished, look her right in the eye and say: *What else has an old fart like me got to do, Nancy? I listen to the radio, watch a little TV, go down to Booker's for a beer and to see some of the old crowd, and feed the birds. And maybe some squirrels and a rabbit or two that come around. They're my friends.*

Then his daughter would sigh and relent until the next time.

Fred had to agree with her that he wasn't living much of a life lately, but for an old codger it would have to do until he could join Martha. Ever since his wife died ten years ago, there was a void in his life that had been impossible for him to fill. So he could only wait for his time and fill in the waiting as best he could.

Fred cocked his head, listening.

Did something brush against the windows?

He looked around, slightly startled.

Nothing there.

He set his coffee cup down and lowered the volume on the radio. It was probably that Gillispie kid from next door, sneaking around killing birds or destroying property or his favorite pastime – trying to scare the hell out of somebody.

Fred wished regretfully that he wasn't thirty years younger so he could kick that son of a bitch up one side of the street and down the other. Better yet, take that punk's CB set, the one that always interferes with his TV reception, and shove it up the kid's ass with the volume turned up full. *Here's to you, good buddy.*

Fred got up and cautiously peeked out the kitchen windows. Maybe he could see the kid lurking about. The kid knew that Fred went out to feed the birds at this time every morning. Most likely he was waiting to scare him again, recalling a previous time when the kid had jumped out at him from behind the house, shouting, "Boo!" and then ran.

He just about crapped right there and then. Fred dropped his coffee tin of bird food and the bowl of nuts for the squirrels and almost dropped himself with a coronary. It took the rest of the day for him to settle his nerves down.

This time he'd fix the bastard.

Flicking on the basement lights, Fred went downstairs and returned with a ten inch pipe wrench, setting it down on the kitchen table. Next, he filled the coffee tin with bird food and put on his jacket. He picked up the coffee tin and the wrench, which he gripped like an avenging Saint Francis of Assisi, (*kill my birds, will he?*) and slipped quietly out the back door into the yard.

Outside, he walked slowly through the dewy grass toward the bird feeder located at the back end of the yard under the sheltering arms of an old box elder. He tried to tune his hearing to the sounds of the dying darkness.

There weren't any sounds. None at all.

Fred didn't quite know what to make of that. There certainly was a smell though. God, it was worse than the stockyard.

A small tingle of fear began to creep though him. Shadows shifted about the yard. The box elder loomed black and huge over the solitary standing bird feeder in a tableau of darkness and sudden foreboding.

Fred gripped the wrench tighter. He felt like turning around and going back in the house. Maybe it wasn't the Gillispie kid at all. Maybe it was…somebody else.

Something came at him from the darkness. With all the strength he could muster, Fred swung the pipe wrench at it and connected. He heard something fall to the grass.

In a whirl of terror, Fred dropped the birdseed and the wrench and ran back into the house. He locked the door and leaned shaking against it, waiting for his poor heart to stop racing so he could call the police.

Fred felt a warm liquid trickling down his leg.

Blood? Did it get him?

He looked down at the amber liquid puddling around his shoes, then at the growing spot on the front of his pants where he had just soiled himself.

PART TWO

Offerings

The awful shadow of some unseen Power
Floats through unseen among us – visiting.

P.B. Shelley

There are in every man, at every hour
Two simultaneous postulations, one towards
God, the other towards Satan.

C. Baudelaire

The

Portal

130

1

THE SUN HAD BEEN UP A GOOD THREE HOURS, trying to warm the land against a brisk lake wind that sent large waves hammering into the erosion-protecting slabs of concrete scattered along the shoreline. Spindrift rose high in the air, misting the beach like a fine rain.

Paul and Linda had thrown on some jeans and heavy sweaters after breakfast and raced down the zigzag trail to the pounding waves and wet sand below. They walked leisurely along the beach.

"Dwayne likes you," Linda said. "He's taken quite a shine to you."

"And I like him," Paul said. "He'll be a fine man."

"You two have become very secretive." Linda picked up a piece of driftwood and threw it in the face of an incoming wave.

"Secretive?" Paul asked.

"Oh, walking on the beach, talking up in his room, things like that."

"That's just man talk."

She nodded, knowing that he wouldn't tell her any more. "Chrissie likes you, too. And Mom thinks you're very attractive."

He smiled. "That's very flattering. I can't say that I made much of an impression on your father though."

Linda took his hand and squeezed it. "It takes time, Paul. Dad, well, he's rather hard to get to know at first. He can be very cold."

"I'll smother him in love and win him over to the Postal Service."

Linda laughed, then became serious. "Sometimes – well, you can be cold, too."

Paul stopped. "Me? How?"

They started walking again. A lake gull, gliding above on the wind, screeched and swooped low over the slate colored water.

"You're not so easy to know either," Linda said. "I love you, Paul. I love you very, very much, but I'm not sure you feel the same way about me."

"Don't be silly." Paul shook his head. "Cold, huh? And here I thought I had swept you off your feet with my dazzling personality."

"You did. But there's coldness under it. It says stop here. You can only come so close. I don't mean you're hard or anything like that. It's just – you don't like to share things with me. You keep a lot of things to yourself. That's where the coldness is."

Paul cocked one eye at her. "Thank you, doctor, for your analysis. Is there anything else about my schizophrenia that bothers you?"

Linda smiled. "I'm serious, Paul."

"Well, so am I."

They stopped again, and she searched his gray eyes for a reaction. If eyes were the windows of the soul, his were always shielded by an innate vigilance that prevented any further access to the inner man.

"Maybe I shouldn't say this, Paul."

"Don't stop now."

"Well, it's as if you're always holding yourself back, afraid to let yourself go."

"Afraid to love." Paul had finished it for her. He had heard it before from Jennifer Hanson.

"Yes, afraid to love."

Paul watched the lake waves build and roll and hit the concrete slabs. The lone gull was still out there, white feathers against a gray-turning sky.

"You're right," he said finally. "But there's nothing I can do about it right now. You'll just have to take me the way I am."

Well, at least he admitted it, Linda thought. It was the first time he had been that open with her since the light incident. "That's a start at least," she said and kissed him lightly on the mouth. Paul held her and kissed her again. This time, she met his tongue with hers.

"They say that doctors always fall in love with their patients," Paul said.

"You've got that the other way around."

They both laughed.

Paul looked over Linda's shoulder, up at the house that was visible above the bluff.

"Not to change the subject, doctor, but how much do you know about this house?"

They continued their walk.

"Not much. Just the town gossip – why?"

Paul paused, looking down at the sand. "Oh, just curious. What's the gossip?"

"I guess the Duries were rather eccentric. They kept pretty much to themselves, didn't mix with the townspeople. I suppose they resented it, so whenever anything bad happened around here, people blamed it on the Duries and the house."

Linda made her hand into a claw and whispered in a sinister voice, "Evil things happen at Durie House."

Paul smiled, made a claw of his own, and rested it on top of her head. "Who knows what evil lurks in Durie House?" he said in a voice like The Shadow.

"That's just about the number one song around here. They make it sound like an old Gothic horror story."

"Dwayne tells me there was a fire," Paul said.

"That was nine years ago. James Durie, the last of the line – more or less – tried to burn the place down. I guess the attempt at arson was too much for him because they found him in the house, dead from a heart attack."

"Didn't he have a brother?"

"Allan. He was the real recluse. James came into Lanark

occasionally, but Allan never did. Some of the fishermen would see him at times, walking along this very beach with that Irish Wolfhound of his, Cerberus."

Paul laughed. "Cerberus, really? This Allan Durie sounds like quite a character." Then he remembered the large dog tracks he had found on the beach during the search for Holly. "Did Allan die with his brother?"

"That's the strange part about the whole thing – aside from the fact that James tried to burn down his own house. Allan was never found or heard of. End of story. Why all the questions?"

"Dwayne told me just about the same thing."

Linda looked at him with a sideways glance. "Don't tell me Dwayne has a believer about his closet stories."

Paul didn't answer her.

"Oh, Paul, there's a basis for his fear, and it's all my fault. We were home alone one night playing games, and I hid in the closet to frighten him. I did, badly. Dwayne was only six at the time and the scare must have left a deep impression on him. That fear is surfacing again."

Paul thought of the nightmares he'd had since staying at Durie House. "Then you think it's all in Dwayne's mind?"

"Don't you?"

"I don't know."

"It's just a house. Houses don't hurt anyone. Even if it is Halloween."

"That's tomorrow. Tonight's Beggar's Night."

"Let's not talk about closets or Durie House anymore." She came into his arms. "Just hold me and tell me that you love me."

Paul started to kiss her, but she turned away. "Say it, Paul."

"You know I do."

"Then say it. Paul?"

Linda pushed away from him. The wind tugged at her hair; she held it down with her hand, tears misting in her eyes. "You can't say it, can you?"

"Linda, you don't understand. I..."

"Oh, I understand. I understand only too well." She turned and ran back along the beach toward the trail.

The wind became stronger and the gull fought against it for a while, then headed in toward land.

I do love you, Linda Eastman, Paul thought, but he didn't say it.

2

THE MORNING COLD AND OVERCAST SKY had passed without a drop of rain, changing into a warm afternoon of sunshine and balmy breezes.

It was past one by the time Claude finished cutting the weeds and tall grass that grew along the drainage ditch bordering Blackmoor Road. He had worked up a good sweat with the weeder and mower, working straight through the morning, pausing briefly now and then for a breather and once to watch a flight of late geese head for Horicon Marsh.

He ambled back to the tool shed, letting the warm wind dry him. Inside the shed, he put the weeder and mower away and picked up a battery-powered trimmer from a chest-high shelf.

He might as well start on the grounds around the house, before his wife found something more toiling for him to do.

Claude started for the house, wiping some remaining sweat off his face with his shirt sleeve and setting his baseball cap back squarely on his head.

It was then that he saw it.

The grass on the south side of the house was dead. Even the evergreens were brown and dry.

Claude circled the house, examining the grounds. It was the same all the way around. Everything – grass, shrubs, trees – that grew within ten feet of the house was dead. And whatever it was seemed to be spreading in spots.

Everything had been all right yesterday, and now this. Claude took off his cap and scratched his head, turning the problem over in his mind.

Well, he'd try and fix it. That's all he could do. He saw no need in reporting it to the Eastmans. They'd be on his ass soon enough without him telling them.

3

RALPH GORDON – RALPHIE TO HIS PARENTS and most of the kids at school (although he cringed when anyone called him that) – was hunkered down in the early evening darkness in bushes that almost enclosed Lover's Look and spied on the cars. The Look was an asphalt parking lot in Thackeray Park that overlooked the lake three miles from the Stony Point Lighthouse.

His legs, like the rest of him, were fat and began to throb from the strain of holding him in an almost motionless position for so long a time. The closest car contained Debbie Ralston and Dicky Walters. Ralphie watched enviously as they kissed and fondled each other and God knows what else.

Ralphie sighed. Walters was sure a lucky shit.

At his present age of eleven years (he would be twelve next month and was hoping for a better year than the last one) Ralphie had known no girl. Although some of his friends boasted of already having had sex with girls, he had not known such pleasure.

In the bathroom with the door locked, or in his bedroom with the door locked and a copy of Playmate magazine – stolen briefly from his father's secret collection hidden in the basement – yes, Ralphie enjoyed the girls between the pages, but the real thing – no.

His mother, a regular Barnaby Jones anyway, was suspicious and told him that masturbation was sinful and could cause him to lose his mind. So each time he indulged, he suffered through terrible anxieties.

He was afraid afterward that he would begin to rant and rave and froth at the mouth. Then his mother would know what he had done and immediately call the white-coated men to drag him off to the funny farm strapped in one of those jackets with the long sleeves that buckled in the back. They'd probably take him away in one of those panel trucks with no windows, like they did to Mr. Asher down the block the night he lost his marbles and came after his wife with a rifle.

Ralphie wondered for a time if Mr. Asher had been masturbating too much. Then he decided, after nothing happened to him, that there was nothing wrong with Mr. Asher – unless it was Mrs. Asher. He also came to the conclusion, through years of observation, that his parents didn't know anything about sex. His philosophy was based on the premise that they always acted like they never heard of it – unless, of course, it concerned him. Then they were authorities.

Sometimes he thought they were beyond sex. But then they were his mother and father, and he had been conceived – hadn't he? And he did hear their bed creak and groan through the thin walls late at night and sometimes early in the morning, and his mother telling his father to get the hell off, he was killing her. So, why did they act that way?

Parents were funny.

They bugged him about other things, too. Ralphie didn't like books or school, so his father said he was lazy and his mother said he should apply himself or he'd be sorry later.

His sister said he was a dumb turd.

But there was one thing Ralphie did like about school – writing graffiti on its walls. He prided himself on being author and wit of numerous gems written on the outside walls of Lanark High School and the inside walls of Pierce Street School's john.

Such cryptic messages as DWAYNE EASTMAN (whom he envied) IS HUMPING MISS HOMES, and ROGER KNOLL (whom he hated) SUCKS COCK, and DEBBIE RALSTON (whom he'd like to hump himself) LIKES BIG ONES.

But the one Ralphie really considered his masterpiece was: HOW DO YOU SPELL GAS RELIEF? F-A-R-T. He even caught Mr. Mitchell, his teacher, cracking a smile over that one.

There were other graffiti wits at Pierce Street School besides Ralphie. One unknown author (Ralphie was sure it was Roger Knoll) wrote: RALPHIE GORDON EATS HOMEMADE SHIT. Another (Ralphie was positive this was his sister's doing) wrote: RALPHIE GORDON IS A FAT TURD.

Ralphie's other claim to fame, besides writing and being written about, was the Thackeray Park Phantom. That's what the enraged couples in the Look called him. They called him other things, too, but generally it was just *The Phantom*. Ralphie liked that. He was just like that guy, *The Shadow*, whom he saw a couple of times on late night TV. His father told him that *The Shadow* was a popular radio program in those real old days before they had TV.

Ralphie thought that it must have been really dumb to sit there and look at the radio and not see anything.

Still, he liked the name and would have really preferred it over *The Phantom* because he felt if he was still enough, quiet enough, he'd be invisible just like the real Shadow. But unlike the real Shadow, The Phantom had a dirty mouth. He haunted couples parked at Lover's Look by hurling obscenities at them.

Like: "Hey, don't give it to her on an incline!"

Or: "Your rubber's got a leak in it!"

His favorite was: "Here comes her old man!"

Afterward, he'd run like hell.

The trauma he caused was shattering. It frightened and embarrassed the girls to the point of changing their minds about the whole thing and wanting to go home; and caused the boys, who tried desperately to get the girls back in the mood, premature ejaculations or eventual impotence or worse – left holding their own.

Many of the boys wanted to kill The Phantom. George Tanner,

who had been trying to make it for months with Sally Beck, and whose sure triumph shriveled before his own eyes after The Phantom had struck, wanted to string him up by the balls. Others, less imaginative than George, simply desired to kick his ass around the park.

They never caught him, but one night they managed to give him a good scare. The boys got together, forming a search party, and scoured the park, looking for The Phantom after one of his attacks. Ralphie became so frightened (his dumb sister told him he looked like a frozen turd when he eventually escaped and made it home) that he stayed out of the park for a month. But his passion for oratory got the better of him and The Phantom returned to Thackeray Park.

Ralphie moved one foot, ever so slightly. His legs were killing him, but he had to be careful. The least little noise could be dangerous.

He watched awhile longer. The emotions he shared with the couple in the nearby car kept him warm up to a point, but the chill autumn air started to turn him a light blue. He would have to move, and soon; otherwise, he'd be too stiff to make his getaway. Besides, Dicky and Debbie were arguing now. She probably didn't want to put out.

Gas rumbled in his stomach. He smothered a belch. Whenever his mother made hot dogs for supper, Ralphie got indigestion.

A montage of music drifted over the Look from the car radios. Ralphie looked at his Charlie Tuna watch – the one he had purchased through the mail. It was eight-sixteen. His parents would scream at him again. He'd never make it home by eight-thirty. He shrugged philosophically. They screamed at each other, too.

Shit bricks, but his legs were stiff. He wondered if he'd be able to run at all. Everything depended on his legs; once he started to move he would no longer be invisible. Well, there was only one way to find out.

The Phantom rose woodenly in the bushes. Somewhere off to the right, a bat screeched. Crickets chirped. And the Phantom farted.

Ralphie froze.

His mind panicked. God, what if they heard that? It had been as loud as a bomb and the nearest car was only ten feet away.

He waited, his heart trip-hammering with fear of discovery.

If the couple in the car, Dicky Walters and Debbie Ralston, heard Ralphie's outburst, they paid no heed, but merely went on with their argument.

Ralphie sighed with relief.

Then, a few moments later, The Phantom struck with his leaky rubber routine, and as swiftly as his fat legs could carry him, disappeared into the depths of Thackeray Park.

There was no pursuit. No one even started an engine, and, after a short sprint, The Phantom stopped running. The lagoon was up ahead and park lights reflected off its water in long, shimmering, floating lines. Maybe The Phantom would have to change his material, Ralphie thought; the old stuff didn't seem to get them anymore.

Ralphie crossed the park near the lagoon, keeping close to bushes and trees, heading for the wooded slope that topped out to Blackmoor Road. Even though the route was roundabout, he figured it was the safest way to get out of the park and home.

And then he stopped.

An uneasy feeling suddenly attacked his nerves. He felt he was no longer alone. Someone was watching him. Ralphie waited. Listened. He remembered his mother say to him, "There's nothing in the dark that isn't there in the light. There's nothing to be afraid of." Of course, she told him that when he was just a kid, but remembering it now, made him feel better and somewhat foolish. He started out for home again.

The feeling persisted, became stronger. Ralphie stopped. A hush fell over the park. Then he heard someone moving through the trees, almost stealthily. His mind raced. Maybe one of the guys followed him from the Look...or maybe it was just someone entering the park from Blackmoor Road...or maybe it was –

A knife flashed.

After a while, the crickets chirped again, and the bat resumed its flight.

4

FROM HIS SQUAD CAR, HIDDEN ON A BUSHY KNOLL overlooking Lover's Look, Wally Schaefer had an excellent vantage point for watching the night's entertainment in Thackeray Park. He picked up the Japanese binoculars from the car seat and scanned the car windows for action. Some were already steamed up. Others had heads bobbing up and down or arms locked in passionate embraces.

Some young stuff was probably getting busted tonight. The thought excited him and he straightened out the crotch of his pants. Wally sighed. Well, at least somebody was getting it. He sure as hell wasn't. Not with Marion still pining away for a dead guy that the maggots had probably eaten by now. What a waste.

Wally felt a knot of loneliness form in his stomach and dropped the binoculars back on the seat. Not much was happening down there anyway. Nothing that he could see, unless he went down and crawled into one of the cars. The thought made him chuckle.

He wondered if The Phantom had made his escape. Wally had known the true identity of The Phantom for a long time now and would have collared the fat, little punk and kicked his ass for him except that Ralphie Gordon's shenanigans gave him a good laugh now and then.

Actually, Wally had been surprised to see Ralphie. Tonight was the first night in over a month that The Phantom had been in the park.

The guys from the Look must have scared the pants off him the last time when they started searching the park for him. The entire incident had kept Wally in stitches.

Of course, if they had gotten their hands on him, Wally would have intervened, but the kids never found Ralphie. They came within inches, but never laid a glove on him. It was a good thing. Ralphie could have gotten a beating out of it.

Wally checked his watch. He had time for a smoke before he cruised the rest of the park and shagged the kids out of the Look. His dispatch radio was silent. Not much was happening. Not that anything was likely to happen here, even on Beggar's Night. Maybe a few calls would come in about kids getting out of line with their pranks; otherwise, it would be Quietville tonight.

He lit up and smoked in silence; except for the night sounds stirring around him, it was almost total. He liked the sound of the lake rolling in to meet the shoreline and the night song of the crickets.

Finishing his cigarette, Wally flipped the butt out the window and put his cap back on. He wore a service cap with the sides pulled down into wings that the Air Force boys in World War II called a *twenty-mission-crush*. They developed a crush by the weight of head-sets worn over their caps while flying. At the end of twenty missions, the cap would be neatly bent at the sides. Wally achieved the same results by bending a coat hanger into the desired shape and inserting it in his cap.

He started the engine and backed the squad car out of its concealment. With his crushed cap and mirrored sunglasses, Wally cut quite a dashing figure. The only trouble was he didn't get to wear his sunglasses that often working the four-to-twelve shift. It would have been better if he worked days.

Wally sighed. Someday, maybe. And someday he'd get Marion in the sack. He popped on his headlights. It was time to roll.

He drove slowly, turning on his spotlight, directing its pool of shocking light over the grounds. He turned onto the drive that circled the lagoon, hitting the water a few times with the spotlight to discourage any skinny dipping. Anyone who would want to, Wally mused, in this kind of weather must have a few marbles missing.

Finishing the route, Wally turned the car back on the drive and circled the lagoon in the other direction. This time the hard finger of light probed the surrounding area of trees and bushes.

Wally stopped the car halfway around and tried to get the light on something that caught his eye, but whatever it was, was just outside the direct reach of the spotlight.

Taking his flashlight with him, Wally got out of the car and started toward it. It looked like something was on the ground.

Halfway there, a sudden uneasiness laid its cold hand on the back of his neck. He stopped and looked over his shoulder. The bright, glaring eye of the spotlight looked back at him, poking through the black velvet night. Somewhere overhead a bat cruised the dark sky.

He started walking again. A faint odor came to him. It was the same one he had smelled at the Armstrong house.

Wally took his .38 out of its holster.

He held the object in the beam of his flashlight. Something was on the ground all right. It was a body.

Wally knelt beside it. "Oh, my God," he whispered, then turned away quickly, but it was too late. He started to throw up.

5

THE LIGHTED FACES OF JACK-O'-LANTERNS, in the windows and on the porches of Lanark, grinned mischievously into a cool October wind, which made some of them look like winking dismembered heads. It was Beggar's Night, and shadows danced on the wind, changing from cats to witches to werewolf claws.

By eight-fifty-five, the invading army of beggars had just about reached all their objectives and had begun to return home, booty in hand. A few diehards held out for more.

"Go on up and ring the bell," Tommy Macfarland said.

"Oh, no. I'm not gonna," Timmy Macfarland said. He was a full head shorter than his brother and, at age seven, three years younger.

"He's probably afraid old man Durie will reach out and grab him," said Russell Williams.

"I am not," Timmy insisted. He was dressed in a little devil's costume, complete with tail and horns, which his mother had made for him.

"You are, too," Russell retorted.

Timmy pushed Russell, who was Tommy's age, and knocked off his hobo hat.

Russell retaliated and Timmy bumped against his brother.

"Will you two guys knock it off," Tommy said.

Andrew Green, also age ten, just shook his head, having observed the entire shoving match, which occurred whenever Timmy was along, with distaste.

"Are we or aren't we?" Andrew asked. "Or, are we going to stand around and shove each other all night?" Andrew, considered a brain in school, was the intellectual of the group and looked rather sinister in his Count Dracula costume.

"Yeah, that's right," Tommy said. "We came out for trick or treat, so let's get with it." Tommy, who was sort of a butterball and thought of as a dullard by his teachers, was dressed in the unimaginative guise of a ghost (an old bed sheet with slits for his eyes).

"Well, he started it," Russell said. "He always starts it."

Timmy lifted his devil's mask and stuck out his tongue.

Russell made a move for him, but Tommy stopped him.

"Cut it out, you guys." Then he said to his brother. "If you're such a scaredy-cat, I'll do it."

"Well, let's do something," Andrew said, disgusted with the whole situation.

"I'm not scared," Timmy said. "I'll do it." He eyed Russell Williams coolly.

"Finally," Andrew said with mock relief. "The Duries don't even live there anymore."

Timmy switched his distasteful look to Andrew.

"Well?" Tommy said, putting his hands on his ghost-hips and looking at his brother.

"All right. I'm going." Timmy started up the longest and darkest driveway that he had ever seen in his life. He took a dozen steps, stopped and turned around. "Where will you be?"

"Right behind you, dummy!" Russell said.

"Go on!" Tommy said.

"God!" Andrew said.

Timmy shook his little fist at Russell and started up the driveway again. The night whispered secretly around him. Trees huddled in the darkness, their leafy branches stretching above him like suffocating arms. Timmy wanted to turn around to see if the others were following, but was afraid Russell would say something smart again.

Halfway there, Russell made a spooky laugh and Timmy stopped dead in his tracks and closed his eyes.

"Cut it out, Russell," Tommy said.

Timmy opened his eyes and continued up the winding drive. Russell began to make werewolf noises. Boy, Timmy thought, was he ever going to fix him.

When Timmy got to the stone steps of the terrace, he stopped and gazed, open-mouthed up at the house. Even in the dark, the house looked immense. He dropped his eyes to the shadowy front door and suddenly remembered all the spooky stories that the kids told about this place. Especially the one about old Allan Durie coming to the door on Beggar's Night, carrying his head under his arm.

Timmy tried to climb the first step, but his feet seemed to be glued to the spot.

"Are you just going to stand there?" Andrew asked. "Go up and ring the bell."

Timmy jumped. The closeness of Andrew's voice and almost-touching presence jolted Timmy up the stairs. He had forgotten that they were right behind him. Timmy turned to glare at Andrew when the front door suddenly opened and he jumped again.

"Well, what have we here?" Chrissie Eastman said, standing in the doorway. "So it was a little devil. I saw you come up the driveway."

Timmy looked up at her and almost started to cry. He wanted to run, but Russell would never let him forget it, so he just stood there, trying to hold back thc tears. Then, after a moment or two, Chrissie's smile began to melt his fear.

"Mom! Linda!" Chrissie called. "Come here a minute and see this."

Mrs. Eastman came to the door, Linda followed.

"Look," Chrissie said, "isn't he cute?"

"Oh, he's just darling," Mrs. Eastman said.

Tommy smiled. That was the reason he always made Timmy go to the door first. Everyone always fell all over him and gave away a lot more treats.

"He's even got little horns and a little tail," Linda said.

"Wouldn't you just love to pick him up and give him a big hug?" Mrs. Eastman said.

Timmy took a step backward, not quite knowing what she meant by that.

"I think we frightened him," Linda said.

"Oh, don't run away," Mrs. Eastman said. "Chrissie, go get the candy."

When the others saw that Timmy wasn't going to get eaten alive or dragged off to some slimy dungeon, they suddenly appeared behind him like a band of claim-jumpers.

"Trick or treat!" they shouted.

"Are these your friends?" Mrs. Eastman asked. "Well, we have something for them, too."

Timmy turned around and stuck his tongue out under his mask. Chrissie reappeared with a big glass bowl full of small candy bars. Each beggar was allowed one handful. Timmy, much to the dismay of the other three boys, was allowed two because his hands were smaller.

When they were back on the street, Russell turned to the others and said, "Where should we go now?"

Tommy shook his paper bag. "Let's get some more treats. Hit a few more houses."

"It's getting too late," Andrew said. "My parents told me to be in by nine."

"Dad told us to be in early, too," Timmy said.

"Dad told us to be in early, too," Russell mimicked in high falsetto. "Your brother thinks he's Cinderella," Russell said to Tommy.

Timmy made a fist at Russell.

"Now, don't you two start that again," Tommy said.

The wind had become stronger, cutting through their clothing like cold steel. Streetlights dropped pools of light along Blackmoor Road.

"I'm cold," Andrew said. "I'm going home. You guys can stay out if you want to."

"Come on, Andy," Russell pleaded. "Just a couple more."

"No." Andrew remained inflexible. "I'm going."

"I'm going, too," Timmy said. The thread that had held up his devil's tail had broken and Timmy tried to hold it up off the ground.

"You can't go home alone," Tommy said, then looked at Andrew. "How about takin' Timmy home for me?"

"He's your brother."

"Ah, come on. Be a pal. If you drop Timmy off, Russell and me can catch a few more houses."

"I still think…"

"Don't be a flake," Russell said.

"I was merely going to point out," Andrew said, "that Timmy is Tommy's responsibility."

"I can go home myself," Timmy said.

"No, you can't!" Tommy shouted. "Andy, please!"

"Oh, all right."

"Thanks," Tommy said, then turned to Timmy. "Tell Mom I'll be home in a little while."

"Finally!" Russell said with exasperation. "Let's go."

Count Dracula and the little devil watched the hobo and ghost disappear along the line of trees that hugged Blackmoor Road.

"Come on, Timmy," Andrew said. "We'd better be on our way."

Andrew started out and Timmy followed, his tail dragging behind him. They walked past Thackeray Park, where the globe-shaped park lights looked like small balloons floating in the air, then down the hill and over to Grissom Street. They could no longer see the park. The darkness and the trees blotted it out.

Thirty minutes later, they reached an alley that connected Bishop Street with Elm Boulevard (which was really a misnomer, for the elm trees had long since succumbed to Dutch elm disease and had been replaced by maples).

The walk had been chilling and numbing. Andrew could hardly wait to get home and warm up. He stopped at the alley entrance.

"All you have to do," Andrew told Timmy, "is cut through this alley to the next street, which is Elm, then walk up a few houses and you're home."

"I know," Timmy said. He used the alley all the time during the day, but at night with only one alley light, it looked spooky. He wouldn't tell that to Andrew though.

"Okay," Andrew said. "I've got a ways to go yet. Go straight home now. See you."

He started off down Bishop Street, fading into the night, then reappearing under a streetlight. He turned and waved, his words dying in the wind. "See yooouuu..." then he was gone again.

Timmy stood there and watched him go, then he looked down the alley. He started to get those creepy bumps on his arms. The only light, in the middle of the alley, looked like an island of white in a sea of darkness.

Sometimes the bigger kids would hide in an alley and grab your treat bag and run off. Timmy almost called after Andrew, but he could no longer see him, and he didn't want him to know that he was a scaredy-cat. He tightened his grip on the paper bag and entered the alley.

Leaves crunched under his feet, making a loud crispy sound in the cold night air. The wind brought a few drops of rain.

Timmy had almost reached the light when he heard something. It could have been the wind, but ever since he entered the alley, he felt he was not alone.

He stopped for an instant, then broke into a run, only to stumble over his tail. He dropped his treat bag, found it, got up, and tried to run again, tears streaming down his cheeks.

A hand caught him and choked off his scream.

The cold wind muffled his whimper.

6

NUTS.

The phone was ringing.

After making a trip to the kitchen to build a sandwich and open a bottle of beer, Police Chief Clive Thayer had just resettled himself in his leather recliner and reopened his book. He was reading Alistair MacLean's *Ice Station Zebra*, and it was getting to the point where he hated to put it down.

Reading filled a large part of his life now that Mary was gone. They had been married for over thirty years – sixty-three days over when she passed on – and then he was alone.

Thayer didn't like to think about that terrible word "alone," but it was always with him; a constant companion. He tried to keep busy, putting in long hours – unnecessary hours – at his office, but there wasn't really that much police work to do in Lanark; so he concentrated on the paperwork, which there was always plenty of and which he really didn't care for, but did to fill in the time.

And he read. It was better than falling asleep on the couch with the TV going. Mary liked to read also. Emily Dickinson and the Brownings were favorites. His taste ran mostly to adventure or spy thrillers and when he found a really good book and finished it, it was like saying goodbye to a friend.

Thayer had always been a solitary man.

He didn't mind the solitude when Mary was alive because they could share it, if that made any sense. But the way he saw it, two people who cared about each other like he and Mary did, relished their moments alone with each other. Now that she was gone, he could feel the weight of real solitude – and it was very heavy.

Thayer saddled the open book over the arm of the chair, heaved himself up, and reluctantly headed for the phone.

It was probably the station. No one else called. Maybe Pearl Armstrong was seeing men under her bed again, or Pete Jacobs spooks in his cemetery.

He answered the phone on the fifth ring.

"Yeah," Thayer said, slightly miffed at the interruption.

"Chief?" the voice said. "This is Barney." Barney Jensen was the four-to-twelve dispatcher at the station.

"Yeah, Barney, what is it?" Thayer looked longingly back at his book.

"There's been a murder near Thackeray Park Lagoon."

Thayer's attention was jarred away from the book. "What?"

"Wally just radioed it in. Christ, it must be bad. He was pukin' all the time he was talkin' to me."

"Who was it?"

"It was just a kid. Ralphie Gordon."

Thayer closed his eyes and pinched the bridge of his nose. "Christ," he said softly, then paused. "Listen, Barney, call the coroner, Dan Sunquist, and the boys from the State Crime Lab. Have them meet me out there. I'm on my way."

"Right, Chief. Will do." Then, before Thayer could hang up, "It really must be bad."

Thayer replaced the receiver, then hurried to his closet and threw on a rain-and-shine coat. He started to strap on the .357 Magnum and holster he usually wore, but halfway through the motion, changed his mind and took the snub-nosed .38 instead. Thayer slipped it into his coat pocket and went out the door. Alistair MacLean would have to wait.

It was just about the time that little Timmy MacFarland entered the alley between Elm and Bishop Streets.

There wasn't much traffic for this time of night, just the usual flow along Grand Avenue, Lanark's main street. Thayer had turned on the red flasher without the siren and now switched on the windshield wipers. A light drizzle had begun to fall, shining the streets like black glass.

After the call from Barney came in, Thayer felt the old numbness stir within him again. He had been in law enforcement all his life. Thirty years a cop in Milwaukee and ten as Lanark's Police Chief. Christ, he would be sixty in December.

People outside of police work think cops get used to violence. "They get hard," is what they say. But that's not true. You never get used to it. You learn control – to grow a hard shell over your emotions – you had to or else you'd go bananas. But you never got used to it. Not if you were any kind of a cop.

And when a kid got it, that really made it rough. It was bad enough when adults turned on one another, but when kids were the victims, it tore you in half. Thayer's only child, a girl, was stillborn, and Mary was never able to have another.

He thought about the child a lot lately.

Thayer was well into the park now. The red flasher reflected off the wet surface of the road like a long, trail of blood. He swung his car up the lagoon drive and spotted Wally's cruiser, headlights blazing, parked along the far curve of the drive.

His own headlights picked up Schaefer walking toward him in the rain. Thayer eased to a stop, cut the motor, and slipped out from behind the wheel to meet him.

"You all right?" Thayer asked. Wally looked green around the gills.

"Yeah," Wally said and avoided Thayer's eyes. "I sorta lost control of myself for a while."

"Where is he?"

"Over there." Wally pointed toward the wooded area. "Near the trees." A crowd began to gather around the police cars.

They walked through the wet grass, Wally slightly in the lead.

They stopped at the body. Wally had covered it with a tarp from his police car.

"I couldn't stand seein' him like that," Wally explained.

Thayer pulled the tarp back. "Yeah," he said, then gently recovered the body.

A few moments later, the coroner and the lab boys pulled in, red lights blinking in the rain. Thayer nodded mute greetings all around. Dan Sunquist, "Oranges" to his friends, whom Thayer knew from Milwaukee for more years than he'd care to count, stood beside him.

"Clive," Sunquist said.

"Hello, Oranges."

"What have you got?"

"A kid. He's cut up pretty bad."

Sunquist nodded, then waited wordlessly for Charlie Webber, the lab photographer, to finish taking pictures. The camera's flash attachment gave the whole scene an eerie strobe light effect. When Webber was satisfied, he said, "Okay," and Sunquist started to examine the body.

After what Thayer considered enough time for a professional like Sunquist to have finished, he said, "What else is cut off?"

Sunquist looked over his shoulder. "Have you eaten?"

Thayer waited for his old high school classmate to fill him in.

Sunquist recovered the body and stood up. He was a short, heavyset, good natured man, who resembled one of Santa's helpers more than he did country coroner.

"You got enough pictures, Charlie?" Sunquist asked.

"Yeah, I'm all set," Charlie said. Webber was a tall, cadaverous man, whom Thayer always felt should have had Oranges' job.

Sunquist signaled two assistants and the body was placed in a body bag, then strapped onto a wheeled stretcher and pushed toward the open doors of a white van.

Thayer wondered if they had taken Mary away like that. She had died nine years ago in Memorial Hospital while he was at work investigating the Dennis Evers murder.

Arteriosclerosis, the doctor had said.

Rest in peace, the priest had said.

"The throat was cut," Sunquist told him. "But there isn't much blood."

"Huh?" Thayer turned back to him, pulled away from painful memories. "What about blood?"

"There isn't enough to account for the wounds," Sunquist repeated. "His throat was cut – almost in two. His penis was severed and he was eviscerated."

"He was what?"

"Disemboweled."

Thayer frowned. Oranges liked to spring those medical terms on you. "What happened to the blood?"

"I don't know. I'll know more when I get him on the table."

"What about the penis? Did you find it?"

"No. And it wasn't under the body."

"Then the killer probably took it with him." Thayer turned and called Wally Schaefer, who was leaning against his cruiser, his face colored by the revolving red light on top of the ambulance van where they had placed Ralphie Gordon.

"Yeah, Chief," he said as he joined them, his face still pale.

"Did you pick anything up?" Thayer asked.

"Like what?" Wally said, furrows lining his brow.

"You know what."

"Jesus Christ, no!" Wally said after the realization struck him. "I wouldn't pick that up even if I saw it."

"Check with the lab boys and see if they turned up anything."

As Schaefer moved off, Sunquist said, "Looks like you've got some nut on your hands, Clive."

"Looks like," Thayer said. "How long has the boy been dead?"

"Not long. An hour or so."

They stood there for a long moment without saying anything, and then Sunquist broke the spell of silence. "Well, if you don't need me anymore, I'll be getting back." He patted Thayer on the arm and started walking back to his car.

"Yeah, sure," Thayer said. "I'll talk to you later."

Thayer stood on the wet grass with his hands in the pockets of his rain-and-shine coat, like an overweight version of Columbo, and watched Sunquist leave. Someone gave the ambulance siren a short blast, an eerie lament for the dead.

The drizzle turned into a steady rain. Soon the snow would come, Thayer thought. Christmas would be a somber event this year in the Gordon household.

Wally Schaefer came up to him. "The lab boys didn't find anything."

Thayer nodded.

"This rain doesn't help."

"Call the dispatcher," Thayer said. "Tell Barney to send another car out. I want you back at the station working on your report."

"I suppose Barney told you I…got sick," Wally said uneasily. He felt that his lack of control had somehow diminished his manhood in the eyes of his fellow officers.

"No," Thayer lied. "He didn't say a word. It happens to everyone." Then he paused. "I'll be at the Gordon house in case anything develops. It's about time they knew."

"Yeah," Wally said. His voice was almost a whisper.

Thayer had climbed back in his car and was halfway through the park when Barney's voice broke through on the radio.

"Yeah, Barney, go ahead," Thayer said, picking up the hand mike.

"Chief," Barney said. "We've got another one…"

7

AT MID-MORNING OF THE FOLLOWING DAY, Linda pushed through the glass doors of Feminique and into its hushed and carpeted interior. She wanted to kill a little time while Paul was across the street at the drugstore getting another supply of sinus tablets. He had been taking them like candy ever since they got to Lanark. Maybe he was allergic to the town…or her father.

Linda smiled inwardly at this and paused at the dress section, looking over a few of the latest styles. The store seemed to be well supplied and successful for its size, which surprised her because if Ruth Hanson was anything like her daughter, the store should have been a total flop.

She moved on, browsing here and there. The whispered, almost reverent tone of the three salesgirls waiting on customers, whose own voices were as soft and subdued, like they were all speaking in a cathedral, drifted quietly around the store. There was the smell of roses in the air.

Linda saw Ruth Hanson, standing outside one of thc fitting rooms, working on an overweight customer who was poured over-flowingly into some basic black creation.

The negligee counter caught Linda's eye and she moved over to it. She wondered if Paul would appreciate her in one, and then dismissed the idea. With Paul, she wouldn't be in it long enough to get any wear out of it. Still…they were nice.

"Are you interested in a negligee?"

"Oh," Linda said, turning around to find Ruth Hanson standing next to her. "No, not really."

"That's a shame," Ruth said. "You'd look very attractive in one."

Linda smiled. "Thank you."

Ruth smiled back. "You're Linda Eastman, aren't you?"

"Yes…" Linda looked surprised. She had only met the woman once, years ago and that was just a brief introduction by Jennifer at a restaurant.

"Oh, I never forget a face," Ruth said, reading Linda's surprise. "Especially an interesting one. You went to school with my daughter. But you were one of the older class-men – or class-women – I should say."

"As a matter of fact, Jennifer was two years ahead of me," Linda smiled back with catty satisfaction, remembering Jennifer as one of the biggest snobs at Juilliard, besides being a pill with a capital *P*.

"Oh, really?" Ruth paused, and then tried another subject. "Isn't it just terrible about those two boys last night? A lot of people just stopped in this morning to buy something to cheer them up. Everyone seems so on edge." She paused again. "Those poor boys. Can you imagine how their parents must feel?"

Linda didn't know if she was asking her a question or simply making a statement. She decided on the latter. "Yes, it's very frightening having something like that happen here in Lanark."

"It wouldn't be the first time."

Linda raised an inquiring eyebrow.

"Things like that have happened here before. People murdered and disappearing. They say that Durie House…" Ruth caught herself, suddenly remembering that the Eastmans lived there now. "Well, you've probably heard all that old talk before."

"Most old houses have stories told about them."

"Yes, they do, don't they?" Ruth smiled again. "You're sure there isn't something in the store I can help you with?"

"Well, no, I was just browsing."

Ruth patted her on the arm. "You just browse all you like. I'll certainly tell Jennifer I ran into you. Say hello to Paul from the both of us."

Linda felt a pain well up into her eyes.

"Oh, I'm sorry," Ruth said, catching Linda's reaction. "Perhaps I shouldn't have said anything. Didn't Paul tell you he knew Jennifer?"

Linda had herself under control now. "Yes," she lied. "As a matter of fact, he did mention it. I don't know what came over me just then. I guess I'm not feeling one hundred percent this morning."

One of the salesgirls interrupted. "Mrs. Hanson, would you okay this check for Mrs. Twilling?"

"Of course, Betty," Ruth said, then turned to Linda. "You just look around all you want. I'll be back if you see something you like. I hope you feel better."

Linda nodded and smiled and felt foolish because she couldn't think of anything to say. She waited until Mrs. Hanson was thoroughly occupied, then walked out quickly, still numb from the shock.

Outside, the sun met Linda with a harsh glare. She shielded her eyes and crossed the street to the car. Paul was standing on the sidewalk.

"Hello, speedy," he said. "I thought I'd have to go in and drag you out."

"I have a message from two of your admirers," Linda said caustically. "Mrs. Hanson said to tell you hello from her and Jennifer."

Paul didn't say anything. He could guess what was coming just by looking at her.

"Why didn't you tell me you knew Jennifer Hanson?" Linda asked.

"It wasn't important. It still isn't."

"Oh?" she said, still not satisfied, not ready to let it go. "Of all the people you could have gotten involved with, why Jennifer?"

"It just happened – okay? Besides you never told me about all your old beaus."

"That can be easily remedied."

Paul held up his hand in a stopping gesture. "I don't want to know."

"Then why did you bring it up? If you don't want to tell me about you and Jennifer, just say so."

"I didn't bring it up – you did." He smiled and ruffled her hair.

"Stop manhandling me!" Linda snapped at him, jerking away from his touch.

"Sorry," Paul said, taking his hand away.

"I'm *not* your pet cat or something."

He looked at her. "I said I was sorry."

Linda met his eyes and held them for a moment. She knew she had hurt him, but that was her intention; he had hurt her. She wouldn't have cared if he had bedded half the women in Lanark. Anyone but Jennifer Hanson.

Paul wanted to take her in his arms, to kiss away any hurt he had caused her, but was afraid she would turn on him again. "Linda…"

Someone poked him on the shoulder. Paul turned to see a tall, thin man with his head held at an odd angle standing next to him.

"You the fella that's stayin' with the Eastmans up at Durie House?" the man asked.

Paul looked at Linda, then back at the man. "Yes."

"The Father wants to see you," the man said.

"Who?"

"Father Kerry. He'll be waitin' over at St. Casmir's."

"He wants to see me?" Paul asked, his voice raised in surprise, then thinking: What the hell would a priest want to see him for?

"Yeah. The Father's waitin'."

"Why does he want to see me?"

"Didn't say. Just pointed you out and told me to fetch you."

Paul opened his car door.

"It ain't that far," the man said. "I'll walk you over."

Paul turned to Linda. "If I go, will you be here when I get back?"

"It's your car. You have the keys." She gave him a frosty smile.

Paul dug into his pants pocket and handed her his car keys. "Don't let that stop you."

"Thanks," Linda said, grabbing the keys and slipping behind the wheel. "I won't." She started the engine and drove off, leaving him standing with the tilted-head man.

Paul shook his head. "Women."

That brought on a wide-gapped, toothy grin from the man. "Ain't they somethin' though?" The smile vanished and the man walked up the street a few feet, then stopped and waited for Paul to follow.

Paul shrugged and fell in beside him.

8

THE LEADER, LANARK'S ONLY NEWSPAPER, did not have a morning edition, but news of last night's double slaying had spread through the community faster than a rumor. Radio and television had picked up on it as soon as they had the scent and were running the story to death every hour.

This was the biggest story to hit Lanark since the Evers' murder, nine years ago, and the subsequent arson attempt by James Durie to burn down his own house.

It was news. The kind you could sink your teeth into.

And the morning crowd of old gentlemen drinkers at Booker's Tavern, who congregated there for an early bracer to start the day, or to shake off a widower's loneliness from the night before, or just for the companionship of another human face, did just that.

Ned Booker, the proprietor, blamed the murders on TV.

Roger Hammel, age eighty-one and a retired cop, didn't agree. "Christ, there were lots of killings in the old days, too, before TV ever came along."

Rich Bottomly, three years younger than Roger, thought the courts were at fault. "It's the damned courts. They turn 'em loose faster than the cops can catch 'em."

"People have changed over the years," Fred Owens said. Fred was the group's authority on birds and small animals and second only to Tim Gorman on people. "They're gettin' nuttier every year."

Tim Gorman, Booker's resident philosopher, said, "We're to blame. All of us. Man has forgotten his brothers and will continue to kill until the stain of Cain is removed from his blood."

"Horseshit," Rich Bottomly said. "The people were just waitin' for somethin' to happen, and now they have it. Murders are interestin' to most folks – long as it doesn't happen to them."

Tim Gorman eyed him coolly. "Why were the people waiting?"

"Because of Durie House."

"Ah, you're daft, man."

"Daft is it? Durie House has stood empty for years – if, indeed, it was ever really empty – and when the Eastmans bought it, people expected somethin' to happen."

"Come on. A house is just a house."

Bottomly shrugged. "Maybe. Maybe not."

"You can't deny that the house has a sinister past," said Roger Hammel, taking Bottomly's side. "No one in town would buy it when the state tried to sell it off for back taxes. Even a buyer that came from as far away as Ohio would have no part of it."

Ned Booker poured Tim Gorman another Irish whiskey. "That's only because people like you scared them off with their crazy talk," he said.

Fred Owens nursed his beer and kummel along. "It's still a strange house."

"It's not the house," Tim Gorman said. "It's the people that lived in it."

"Then why did James Durie try to burn it down?" Fred Owens asked.

"Because he was just as nuts as the rest of the family," Gorman said.

"Horseshit," Bottomly said. "James wasn't a bad sort. And it wasn't much of a fire." Bottomly finished the last of his Pabst and pushed the empty glass toward Booker, who refilled it from the tap. "Tom Lynn was fire chief then," Bottomly went on. "He said the fire hardly caused any damage at all. In fact, it was just about out when the firemen got there."

"You're right," Hammel said, taking a sip of his wine and leaning on the bar. "James was okay in my book. From what I heard, the real son of a bitch in the family was that great-great grandfather – or whatever – Angus Durie. Anyway, he was the asshole that built the house in the first place. And it cost him a pretty penny to do it, even in those days."

"Yeah," Booker said. "A quarter of a million. Man, what I couldn't do with money like that."

"Charles Durie was a mean one," Bottomly said.

"Hell," Owens said. "Allan had his old man beat for sure meanness. When Charles looked at you, you didn't know whether to piss or run. When Allan put an eye on you, you did both."

"Ain't nobody seen Allan Durie for over twenty years," Bottomly said. "Or his wife."

"She's been gone longer than that," Booker said, taking a shot on the house. "Prob'bly both dead."

"Neither one's buried in the family crypt," Owens said.

"You should know who's there," Gorman said, "living so close to the cemetery like that."

"Pete Jacobs told me, smart ass."

"How do you know they're really dead?" Hammel asked. "Maybe they're still living somewhere in that big house."

"Yeah, and I suppose the two of 'em leave their secret room and come out at night like vampires," Gorman said.

"You can laugh if you want to," Hammel said. "But my mother taught me to cross myself every time I passed Durie House. And I still do. Even Pearl Armstrong said that house reminds her of Dracula's castle."

"She ought to know," Booker said. "She spent enough time there."

"Pearl Armstrong," Gorman said, winking at Booker. "Have you been talkin' to the Armstrong widow, Roger? You better watch your step. She could be pretty horny by now."

"Shit."

"Maybe old Pearl's a vampire," Gorman said, rising from his bar stool and covering his face with the collar of his jacket like Bela Lugosi.

Booker reached over the bar and pushed him back on the stool. "You're a vampire. Only you drink Irish whiskey instead of blood, and how you can stand the stuff is beyond me."

"Gorman don't need any blood," Bottomly said. "After drinkin' that swill for all these years, he's embalmed."

"That still makes me one of the undead. An Irish-whiskey-suckin' vampire." Gorman went into his Bela Lugosi act again, but Fred Owens, who was sitting next to him, pushed him back.

"Ned, you better cut off his supply," Owens said. "He's goin' bats."

Everyone laughed.

"Enough," Gorman said. "My throat is dry from all this talk. Ned, give everyone another drink. Put it on Bottomly's bill."

"Horseshit," Bottomly said.

9

THEY WALKED THE FOUR BLOCKS IN SILENCE.

On the way, Paul tried to guess the age of his strange new companion, fixing it somewhere in the late sixties, and couldn't help wonder what this Father Kerry wanted with him. But mostly, his thoughts were of Linda.

As St. Casmir's steeple came into view above the tree-lined streets, Paul made up his mind to leave the Eastman household and return to Milwaukee.

His guide ushered him into the rectory, then its study.

"Here he is, Father."

"Thank you, RCA," the priest said.

The man closed the door and Paul was left alone with the priest. He was short and thin with curly gray hair and glasses and maybe a few years older than the man who had brought him here.

"RCA?" Paul questioned.

"A nickname," the priest said. "Not a very complimentary one, I'm afraid. You know, the listening dog on the RCA label, with its head tilted to one side. A congenital condition. His Christian name is Jerome. He's my sacristan. My right hand."

There was a slight pause. The two men studied each other. The priest rubbed his hands together.

"You wanted to see me, Father?" Paul asked.

"Ah, yes." The priest paused again, then came up to Paul and offered his hand. "My name is Justin Kerry."

Paul shook his hand. It had a slight tremor. "Paul Rice, Father."

Father Kerry adjusted his glasses. "This is rather awkward, Mr. Rice." Another pause. "I saw you with Linda Eastman several days ago and again today while I was with RCA doing some shopping. I took the liberty of sending him for you. I do hope this isn't an inconvenience."

"Not at all."

"Good...good... Won't you sit down, Mr. Rice?" Father Kerry gestured toward a chair opposite the desk.

Paul sat down and looked around. The room held the desk, a few chairs and tables, and a number of glass-enclosed bookcases. There were several crosses hanging on the walls.

"Do you know Linda well, Father?" Paul asked.

"No, not really. I met her once – several months ago when I visited the house. She is a very lovely girl, and easy to remember."

Father Kerry moved behind his desk and looked at Paul for a long moment, studying his eyes, his face, trying to fathom the essence of the man.

Paul returned his gaze. The priest seemed nervous, like he was holding himself together with the force of his will alone.

"Father," Paul said, "is something wrong?"

He looked away. "Mr. Rice, do you have any influence with the Eastmans?"

"Well, I've only just met them. I'm afraid my influence would be rather negligible."

Father Kerry sat down behind his desk. "But you do have some over the older daughter."

"Not very much," Paul said, remembering how she drove off and left him.

"I see," Kerry said, lost in thought again, his eyes drifting up to the ceiling.

Paul shifted uncomfortably in his chair. "Father, if you'll just tell me what's wrong."

"Wrong?" Kerry dropped his eyes to meet Paul's, then pulled

them away. "This is rather delicate. Are the Eastmans still planning to live permanently at Durie House?"

"Yes. From what Linda tells me, her father is going to retire soon. He bought the house for just that purpose."

Kerry was silent again, but his face looked like he had reached some sort of decision. "Mr. Rice," he said, leaning forward. "I think it would be wise if the Eastmans didn't stay in Durie House."

Paul stared at the old priest. "Why?"

"Let's just say for their best interest and safety. Could you tell him that?"

Paul began to feel uneasy. "Knowing Mr. Eastman for only a short period of time, I would say that he wouldn't accept that as a reason to move. And coming from me, well, I'm not really the one to tell him anything."

"Still obstinate?"

"Yes, and very opinionated."

Kerry nodded. "I've talked to Mr. Eastman."

"About this same thing?"

"Yes, just after he moved in."

"And he wouldn't listen."

"He told me to leave."

"Father, excuse me, but if you would just come out and say what's troubling you," Paul said, his curiosity aroused. "Is something wrong with Durie House?"

"It has a bad reputation," Father Kerry said.

Paul remembered his first night at the house, his dreams, and his conversations with Dwayne about the closet. Suddenly, he felt a deep chill crawl up from his stomach and settle at the back of his neck.

"Father, just what is the matter with Durie House?"

Kerry was silent for a long moment, then almost whispered, "Evil, Mr. Rice. Evil." He waited for Paul's reaction. When there was none, he said, "Do you believe in evil?"

"Evil men, yes."

"As a force in itself?"

"You mean the Devil and all that?"

"Yes."

Paul could see Kerry was visibly shaken just by talking about it. "No," he said, "not as a force in the world."

"There are things, Mr. Rice, that cannot be explained," the old priest said. "But believe me, Durie House is evil. The epitome of evil."

"You told *this* to Eastman?"

"I did."

"And?"

"He told me that I had been watching too many movies like the Exorcist and had become overzealous in my profession. And that if I came out of my church once in a while and looked at the real world, I wouldn't be afraid of the bogeyman."

Paul shook his head. "That sounds like Eastman."

There was a thought pause between the two men.

Paul could see motes of sunlight dancing in through the rectory window. It seemed unnatural discussing something of this nature under the brilliance of the sun. Such things were better told on dark and stormy nights.

"If you're trying to scare me, you're doing a good job of it," Paul said finally, half-joking.

"I want to scare you," Father Kerry said. "I want to scare you enough so that you'll get that family out of that house."

"Father, you've been speaking in generalities. Can't you give me any particulars?"

The priest looked down at his hands, folded them across his lap. "I cannot," he said, his voice taking on that whispery tone again.

"I see," Paul said, but he didn't.

"Perhaps, it's already too late. After last night…I don't know…"

There was another awkward moment of silence.

Paul knew he had been dismissed. The discussion was over. Kerry was holding something back, but Paul didn't want to push him. Something he was afraid to talk about.

They said their goodbyes. It was all right. The old priest understood Paul's position. He could do nothing.

Kerry showed him out.

10

WHEN PAUL LEFT ST. CASMIR'S RECTORY, he wondered how he could ever pass on to Linda what Father Kerry had just told him without seeming like a candidate for a madhouse. Still, he felt the old priest was serious – and he was frightened of something. What? Durie House? Did Kerry's warning have anything to do with the closet in Dwayne's bedroom? Maybe he should forget about leaving and stick around for a few more days.

Paul reached the sidewalk and looked up and down the street. Linda and his car were nowhere in sight. He lit a cigarette and waited. Still no Linda. Finishing his smoke, he turned down Grant Street and started the long walk back to the house.

He got back to the drugstore intersection, where Linda had driven off, when a white Thunderbird pulled up along the curb and a voice from the past called his name. Paul walked over to the car.

"You look like you could use a ride," Jennifer Hanson said.

Paul hesitated a moment, afraid he would be adding more fuel to the recent flare-up with Linda if he got in. He looked around the intersection. Nothing. Oh, hell, he thought. She didn't even bother to come back for him. Besides, the whole argument was stupid.

He opened the car door and got in.

"Hello, Jennifer."

"Well, that's more like it," she said. "For a minute there I thought you had forgotten how to talk. Have you been stranded, or are you out for your daily constitutional?"

"A little of both," Paul said.

"I'm at your service," she said, looking into his eyes, then smiled. "Compliments of Hertz. Where can I drop you? Durie House? Or is it Eastman House now?"

Paul looked puzzled.

"My mother saw you in town with Linda Eastman," Jennifer explained. "That's how I know."

Paul nodded. "You sure it isn't out of your way?"

"Don't be silly. I'll be glad to drop you." Jennifer eased the car back into traffic. "Besides, Linda and I are old school chums."

"I didn't know you knew Linda."

"We met at Juilliard. She graduated summa cum laude, and I… well…I just graduated."

Paul smiled. She seemed to have mellowed since he last saw her. The quick temper was gone, or at least she had it under control.

She flashed her brown eyes at him. "Have I changed much in three years, Paul? Did I get fat or anything?"

"You still look good." And, she did. The same striking, black hair, the same lithe figure. "You sound like you've slowed down a little," Paul added. "Married life must agree with you. Where's your husband, by the way?"

"Aaron's still in New Orleans. He couldn't get away. His practice keeps him pretty busy, and I wanted to visit my mother awhile, so I came up alone. Are you still with the post office?"

"Oh, yes. I still have the same high paying job you liked so well."

Jennifer felt a twinge of guilt. Money had always been one of their stumbling blocks. To her, it meant a lot; to Paul it didn't seem to be that important.

She changed the subject. "How long are you staying with the Eastmans?"

"A few more days." If I don't leave sooner, Paul thought. Or, my bags aren't packed and waiting for me when I get back.

“I’m surprised the ghosts of Durie House haven’t chased you out yet. Haven’t you heard anything that goes bump in the night?”

“Durie House seems to be the major topic of conversation in this town. I was told that the people didn’t like to talk about it.”

“Don’t believe it. Everyone enjoys a good mystery, and Durie House is Lanark’s mystery castle. Every town has one.”

She turned east, away from Lanark’s business section. Soon Blackmoor Road and Durie House and she’d have to let him go. She looked at him. God, he looked good. She didn’t realize how much she had missed him, but seeing him again, being with him again, brought it all back.

“Paul, did you…miss me at all?”

“Yes…at first…then I didn’t think about it.”

Jennifer put her hand on his. “I still care for you, Paul.”

Blackmoor Road loomed ahead. He didn’t answer her, but he didn’t take his hand away either. She made the turn.

“If you want to…we could spend some time together. Your place…my mother’s …a motel. I’ll be available…if you want me.”

“What about Aaron?”

“Aaron’s a good provider, but…”

“But what?”

“I’m not in love with him.”

Paul patted her hand. “Jennifer, I appreciate the offer, but we went through this before and it didn’t work out. Besides, the last time I saw you, you told me I wasn’t any good in bed.”

“I just said that to hurt you…because you hurt me.”

Paul was quiet for a moment. “It wouldn’t work. There have been too many bedroom scenes with too many men.”

Jennifer bit her lip. “I know what I am, Paul. You don’t have to tell me. But after you left, I just didn’t care anymore…who was with me…or what I did.”

Durie House driveway was just beyond the next clump of trees.

“Better let me off here,” Paul said. “I’ll walk the rest of the way.”

Jennifer stopped the car and Paul started to get out.

“Paul.”

He turned and she kissed him on the lips.

"Will you at least think over what I said? If you change your mind, you know how to get in touch with me."

"I'll think it over," Paul said, and got out of the car. "But I don't think it would be any good...especially for you." He wanted to let her down gently. "Bye, Jennifer. Thanks for the ride." He closed the car door. "And the offer. I wish you the best."

Jennifer watched him turn and start walking up the driveway to the house. She felt down, really down. But a little sniff of coke would cheer her up. She backed into the drive, then pulled away, heading back the way she came.

11

LANARK MEMORIAL HOSPITAL, known as "the resort" to the local inhabitants, served the neighboring counties of Deer and Cath as well as Dundurn. It was a large glass and steel affair, located at the end of Bucks Road that rose ten stories above the quiet countryside in a wooded area overlooking the lake.

It was eleven-thirty when Police Chief Thayer walked into Dan Sunquist's pathology department, which also doubled as the city morgue, in the subbasement of the hospital.

The bodies of Ralphie Gordon and Timmy MacFarland lie covered on two stainless-steel tables that occupied the center of the room. A light gray tile covered all the walls from the floor to mid-wall. The top half of the walls and ceiling were finished in a slightly darker shade of the same color. Three banks of fluorescent lights lit the room. There were no windows.

Thayer waited for Sunquist to finish washing at a stainless-steel sink.

Sunquist dried his hands with paper toweling, crushed it into a tight wad, and then threw it into a metal container. He looked tired and drawn.

"Well, it isn't pretty," he said.

"I saw that last night," Thayer said.

"Yeah," Sunquist leaned back against the sink. "Well, to make it short, their throats were cut and their heads were almost completely severed from their bodies."

"How were they cut? From left to right, or right to left?"

"Both."

"Huh?"

"The angle of the wound indicates that Ralphie Gordon's throat was cut from left to right. The MacFarland boy's was just the opposite. I also found finger bruises along the lower edge of Ralphie's jaw on the left side of his face. On the other side of his face was a thumb bruise. Timmy had similar bruising. And, as I said, both throats were cut back to the spinal cord."

"Then Ralphie Gordon saw the killer before he died."

Sunquist nodded. "The killer held him with one hand, then cut his throat with the other. Timmy was taken from behind."

"A lefty," Thayer said, more to himself than Sunquist.

"Both boys were eviscerated. In each case the intestines were severed from their mesenteric attachments and laid on the ground to the left of the body. The penises were also severed. And they haven't turned up, unless your boys found them."

"No, we didn't."

"It's my guess that you won't."

"What makes you say that?"

"Just a feeling. Nothing concrete to go on. I just think the killer wanted a remembrance of the deed…a keepsake."

"Any other mutilation?"

"No."

"What about the murder weapon?" Thayer asked.

"A sharp knife, pointed, six to eight inches long. Whoever did it knew what to do. It was rather professional."

Thayer studied the tops of his shoes for a moment, storing away all the information for future reference, trying not to breathe the reek of disinfectant that saturated the room in too deeply. "How long would it take to do something like that?"

"Not long. Five or ten minutes."

"Then, in both cases, the cause of death was a cut throat."

“Loss of blood from the cut, yes. That was the first wound. The mutilations were done after, but I didn’t find much blood in either body. Both boys were missing more than I can account for.”

“You said that when we found them. What do you make of it?”

Sunquist shrugged. “It’s something I’ve never seen before, but then, you’re the detective.”

“Yeah, and I guess I better go detect.” Thayer started for the door. Sunquist’s voice stopped him.

“There was one other thing, Clive.”

Thayer turned from the door. He could hear the high pitched electrical whir of the refrigerator motors.

Sunquist removed his glasses and rubbed the bridge of his nose. “There were traces of saliva in both throat wounds. Whoever killed them,” Sunquist put his glasses back on, “drank their blood.”

“Jesus Christ.” Thayer felt a cold knot form in his stomach. He had heard or read about Eskimos and Indians drinking the blood of a fresh kill, or tearing out the liver or heart and eating it, but the kill was an animal, not another human being.

“What the hell have we got on our hands,” Thayer asked, “a vampire?”

12

THAT EVENING, FRANK BOJOLD, LIKE MOST LANARK RESIDENTS, picked up his copy of The Lanark Leader and read the grisly account of the murders under the headline JACK THE RIPPER-TYPE KILLER STALKS LANARK.

When he had finished, he switched to the evening edition of the Milwaukee paper, which he had gone out for earlier and purchased at the drugstore. Milwaukee did not headline the murders, but ran the following feature story:

TERROR IN LANARK

By Ida Caine

Lanark, Wis. The children will not go out of their homes alone any longer unless accompanied by an adult. Not at night, anyway. That is the feeling parents have in this small Wisconsin city in Dundurn County, north of Milwaukee.

Parents have become frightened since the Beggar's Night double murder here last evening of 11-year-old Ralph Gordon and 7-year-old Tim MacFarland.

The Gordon boy's body was found alongside a wooded area near the lagoon in Thackeray Park by patrolling police officer Walter Schaefer at 8:50 p.m. Tim MacFarland was discovered later, at 10:30 p.m. in an alley a block from his home by his father, Ronald MacFarland, who grew concerned after the boy did not return home from trick or treating with his brother and went out to look for him. He found his son's smashed treat bag just 50 feet from where Tim lay.

Dr. Daniel Sunquist, pathologist at Lanark Memorial Hospital, who examined the bodies, stated that both boys died in a similar manner. The throat was cut and the body mutilated. There were no marks to indicate that the boys had been bound and neither boy had been sexually abused.

Lanark's Chief of Police, Clive Thayer, said, "It's the kind of crime that gets to you. It leaves you with an empty ache inside. I feel sorry for the boys' families."

Chief Thayer also said that until further notice, all police officers in Lanark would work double shifts in an effort to beef up the law enforcement here and would press for the quick arrest of the boys' killer.

The police believe that the killer might well be someone that lives in the community. They base this on the fact that nine years ago, Dennis Evers, age 10, was found murdered in a similar manner in the same alley that claimed the MacFarland boy last night. However, the possibility that the killer was a transient is not being ruled out.

Chief Thayer told reporters, "At this stage, it could be just about anyone. The murderer could possibly live or work right here in Lanark, or in the county. It's just too early to tell."

Meanwhile, the children are being watched.

Frank put the paper down, took off his reading glasses, and headed for the hall closet, taking out his jacket.

"You can't go out," Sally Bojold told her husband.

"And why can't I?" Frank asked.

She looked at his stubborn face. "After two murders, you want to go out at night?"

"Nothing's going to happen. I'm not a kid. Besides, it's still early. Just a little after eight. Why must you always think negatively?"

"So, what are murders? Positive? Murders were committed, so I think of murders."

Mrs. Bojold was a small, exuberant woman with red hair and a chest that turned heads. People who saw her were amazed at how she defied gravity and kept her back straight.

Frank looked exasperated, like he did when he was trying to explain arithmetic to his nine-year-old son. "Nobody's going to bother me with Shane."

Shane was not a gunfighter, as Frank Bojold was fond of saying, but an eighty-pound German shepherd.

The dog sat near the door, anxiously awaiting his nightly reacquaintance with the trees, shrubs, lawns, and fire hydrants of the neighborhood.

Mrs. Bojold looked at Shane. He returned her look, cocking his head. She had to admit that Frank was probably right. No one would be likely to bother him with Shane around. But she wasn't about to tell him that.

"All right, go out and get yourself stabbed or something," she said.

Frank smiled and put the leash on Shane and threw on his jacket.

"You should put on a heavier jacket," Sally said. "It's cool outside."

"This one's warm enough."

"Okay, catch your death."

Frank smiled again. "What difference does it make? According to you, I'm going to be stabbed anyway."

Sally laughed and started to push him out the door. "Go on, get out of here."

Frank grinned lewdly and gave one of her breasts a playful squeeze. "I'll take care of you when I get back," he promised.

"Frank Bojold!" she said in mock embarrassment, pushing his hand away. "The door's wide open. What will the neighbors think?"

"Envious thoughts," he said and stared at her chest.

She laughed and pushed him out the door.

The night air was crisp and steely with a lake wind rustling through the trees. Shane fell in beside his master, giving a short woof of pleasure at the anticipation of their stroll. He stopped momentarily and sniffed at the maple tree in front of the Baldwin home next door, recalling old memories and friends.

When they reached the Owens' house, one block away, Shane began to growl.

Frank stopped, trying to pierce the darkness with his eyes. "What is it, boy? What's the matter? Is there something out there?"

Frank thought he heard footsteps behind him. Sneak-up-killer-type footsteps. He whirled around. The sidewalk was empty behind him. Leaves fell from the trees and blew in the wind like black snow.

The dog started to have a fit, growling, snarling, straining against the leash, lunging at the Owens' house.

"Shane, what the hell's the matter with you?"

Then, suddenly, the dog's attitude changed completely. He began to whimper and cower behind his master.

"Shane," Frank said, trying to control him and untangle the leash that was twisted around his legs. "What's wrong with you? What's out there?"

An outside light went on at the Owens' house and a shaky voice called, "Who's out there?"

"It's me, Fred," Frank called back. "Frank Bojold. Shane's just acting up a bit."

Fred shouted something back. Frank wasn't quite sure he heard it right. The wind seemed to have picked it up and carried it away. Then, another outside light went on and it looked like Fred was turning on every light in the house, too.

Frank looked down at Shane, still hiding behind him. He had never seen the dog act like that before.

He scanned the darkness again. Was there something out there in Fred Owens' backyard? Had he heard Fred right? It sounded like he had told him to get back home where it's safe.

Frank felt the slow rise of hair on the back of his neck. He quickly untangled the leash and hurried home.

13

DAMN! WHERE COULD SHE BE?

Jennifer's mother was late again. Maybe she had met one of her girlfriends and got into a long-winded klatch, Jennifer thought. God, that could last for hours. Jennifer crushed out her cigarette and cursed her mother's gabby tongue.

She tried to get her mind back on the TV movie she had turned on to pass the time. It was an old horror film about a werewolf or something with Lon Chaney, Jr. She found it rather inept and not to her liking. But the other channels had nothing better to offer, and she was just killing time.

God, how could she be so late? When Jennifer had called the store earlier, one of the salesgirls told her that her mother had left the Feminique almost an hour ago.

She knew that Jennifer made it a point to dine out frequently whenever she came in for a visit and there were no fashionable restaurants with even a fair cuisine in Lanark.

The Mariner's, where Paul had taken her once, served good seafood and sandwiches, but it was hardly the place you dressed for. Besides, the décolletage of her dress was much too daring for it.

Jennifer looked down at the spill of her breasts into the silver lame dress. She smiled with satisfaction. She still had good knockers. And the rest of her wasn't bad either. No, that was being modest. She had a terrific body. Even Paul said she looked good.

Paul…

He hadn't been very receptive. *Hello Jennifer. How are you? No, Jennifer, it wouldn't be good for you. I wish you the best. Bye, Jennifer.*

Shit.

Oh, he was very polite. Very courteous. Very unemotional. There had been no warmth in his voice. She had been a fool to offer herself to him like that.

He had upset her so much this morning that she had to rush home for a pick-me-up. The coke didn't help. It just made her horny. So much so that she had to use the vibrator to straighten herself out.

Paul was just like her father. He would never amount to anything. And, having a husband that worked for the post office was not her idea of social position.

Jennifer was glad her mother had finally taken the plunge and divorced her father. She was light-years above that man in personality, social bearing, and enjoyment of the affluent things in life.

How in the world her mother ever married beneath her station was beyond Jennifer's understanding. Her father's lack of interest in money, in position, in clothes and grooming was painful to bear.

God, she was glad she had seen the light. That she had the foresight to make a good marriage. Aaron was well off, very well off. And she liked him a lot. She didn't love him, but maybe that would come in time…maybe.

Anyway, his practice was still growing. Later, he'd be even more successful. And the neighborhood would stop snickering because she had married a gynecologist and would stop asking that stupid question, "Is that how you met?" which she thought was in bad taste and not funny at all.

Jennifer hadn't married Aaron just for his money, as Paul seemed to think. After all, she had contributed to the marriage, too. She couldn't make a go of it in music, but with her beauty, modeling came easy for her. She wasn't famous, not yet, but in demand.

And Aaron liked her to be glamorous. He didn't make unnecessary demands on her. She still had her career. She wasn't chained to the bed or the kitchen or the nursery. She wasn't kept barefoot and pregnant. She was her own woman, had her own identity. She was good for Aaron.

Damn.

Why was she trying to justify her marriage? Was it because she had seen Paul again and felt defensive about it?

Jennifer smiled. Her mind drifted back to their lovemaking, to the times she had spent in Paul's fucking house. Yes, that was the right word. Fucking. That's all they ever did there, or in hers.

She had to admit she had enjoyed it. Not that she ever told him he was good in bed. It didn't pay to tell a man too much. Adequate. That's what she usually told him, unless he angered her, which was most of the time. Then she'd tell him how inept he was. It must have gotten to him or else he wouldn't have mentioned it in the car today.

She smiled again. Once he told her that he was surprised she didn't give instructions to the world on how to fuck since she was such an expert at it and everything else in life.

Jennifer had only tried to toughen him up. A grown man sleeping with a light on was ridiculous. She wanted him to improve, to become better than he was, to want more, and not settle in a rut like her father.

But Paul broke it off.

She felt terrible when he left her, unwanted. Maybe that's why she drifted into bed with Kenneth Sollis. But he was too kinky. He looked harmless enough, but in the bedroom, forget it. The goddam things he wanted her to do. Him and that damn enema bag of his. Sometimes she thought he'd be happy if he could just go around sticking his syringe (he even carried his own, for Christ sakes) up every woman's ass he came in contact with.

Jennifer gave an involuntary shudder.

The humiliation of what he had done to her that final night with him weaved through her mind, leaving her with a bad taste in her mouth. Bad enough to make her cringe.

She needed a drink.

Jennifer glanced at the TV. The wolf man pounced on someone and the scene faded out with a blood sucking growl. The mantel clock showed 8:50. Had it chimed the quarter hour? She hadn't noticed.

Jennifer got up from the French provincial couch in the living room and moved to the bar. She picked up a decanter and poured a drink. After taking a sip, she made a sour face. It was cognac. Paul's drink.

Damn him to hell. Why did she follow him from the church? Why did she even bother talking to him? Him and his all-American girl. Linda Eastman, the famous artist, creator of the rainy-day-people.

Shit.

Just a lot of stupid people standing around in the rain.

Jennifer took her drink and returned to the couch and the movie. The wolf man was back to his normal Lon Chaney, Jr. self again.

She paused in her drinking. There was a strange odor in the house, like spoiled meat.

Jennifer stiffened.

She thought she heard a noise in the back room. It sounded like...someone walking. She listened, her eyes glued to the hallway entrance.

She jumped, spilling half her drink on the carpet.

Someone had screamed on TV.

God, it was probably the TV she heard right along. She was letting last night's murders work on her imagination. Next, she'd be seeing things.

Where the hell was her mother? This wasn't the first time that she was late getting home this week. Maybe she'd better call the store again. They might have heard something. But why didn't her mother at least call?

Jennifer picked up the phone.

There was no dial tone.

She jiggled it.

Dead.

She replaced the receiver. Dead phone. Dead silence.

There was even a pause on the TV. But then the wolf man moaned in agony as he changed into his hairy self under the eye of a full moon, and…

There was that smell again.

What if someone had gotten into…

Jennifer didn't complete the thought. It was too horrible, too terrifying to even think. Those things didn't happen to you. They happened to someone else. You read about them in the newspapers. You expressed your shock, your horror, your sympathy for the unfortunate victim – but it didn't happen to someone like you. You married well…you were a model…you…

Like hell it didn't.

She put her unfinished drink down on a table. Now, where was her purse? Where did she put that damned thing?

Cool. Be cool. Mustn't lose control. That could be dangerous.

She bit her knuckle and searched the room with her eyes.

Her purse was resting on a chair near the windows.

She snatched it up, tearing through it for her car keys. When she found them, she pulled the curtains aside and looked out the window. The Thunderbird was still in the driveway where she had left it earlier. It looked safe. God, did it look safe. Better than staying here… if there was someone in the house…waiting to…

Jennifer listened. Except for the TV, the house was quiet. Maybe she was just being foolish. Maybe it was nothing. She listened more intently.

A creak in the hallway. The floor always did that when someone was…walking.

Jennifer bolted for the front door, fighting the locks, swinging the door open…

On the TV, the wolf man attacked a woman and tore out her throat.

14

"THEY'RE NOT VERY BIG," Barbara said. "Are they?"

Dwayne kissed her breasts, then sat up in bed. "They're big enough for me."

She pushed him down and kissed him hard on the lips.

"I've got to go," he said. "It's getting late."

Barbara looked at the clock on the bedside table. "It's only ten after nine." She put her arms around his neck. "How about one for the road?"

Dwayne smiled. "We already did that."

She pouted. "Did we?"

He kissed her again. "Really, Barbara, I've got to go. They'll be having fits at home."

"I know," she sighed, "I just wish you could stay longer." She ruffled his hair and threw back the covers. "Well, come on, love. You'll never get ready this way."

Barbara eased into her slippers and put on her robe. "Brrrr. It's cold in here. We should have stayed under the covers."

"The last few nights have really been cold," Dwayne said, getting into his clothes. "Looks like an early winter."

"Oh, don't say that. It just makes me colder."

Barbara walked into the living room and checked the thermostat. She turned the heat up, then went back to the bedroom doorway and watched him dress. She wondered how long he would stay with her. Probably another year or two – at least until he graduated or a younger girl came along.

"Have you got time for coffee before you leave?" she asked.

"Yeah, sure. Sounds great. It'll warm me up for the walk home."

He finished dressing and joined her in the doorway. They walked into the kitchen with their arms around each other.

She poured two coffees, then set the glass pot back on the hot plate. "You should have a car," she said, handing him a cup.

"Mmmm, thanks. That looks nice and hot." He took a sip and sat down at the kitchen table. "I'll have a car next year."

Barbara took her coffee and sat down opposite him. "Maybe I'd better drive you."

"It's only a short walk. Fifteen, twenty minutes tops."

"I don't like you walking around when it's dark."

"I'll be all right."

"I'd still like to drive you," she said looking at the way his hair fell over one eye when he was just out of bed.

Dwayne reached across the table and squeezed her hand. "Really, Barbara, I'll be okay. I'm a little bigger than Ralphie Gordon or Timmy MacFarland."

"Timmy came here for trick or treat that night," she said softly. "It would only take me a minute to get dressed and I could…"

"No. I want you to stay put. I don't want you driving back alone. After I leave, lock everything up tight."

He was probably right. Besides, she had the uneasy feeling that someone had been in the house the other day. Nothing had been taken, but it looked like her drawers of undergarments – panties, bras, and stockings – had been disturbed. And there was still that unnerving incident in the school parking lot where someone slashed her tires.

She smiled at him. Dwayne was a sweet boy. And she had a penchant for boys, didn't she? That was her thing. A pedophile first class, but he would go the way of all the others. They never stayed.

She was getting old. Thirty-five next March. Well, she still had some good years left. After her looks were gone, it would be all downhill.

Fifteen years ago, she thought she would be an old married woman by now. She fell in love with a married man with three children. Old story. They had an affair. It lasted on and off for ten years.

The divorce was always soon, just around the corner, but he could never do anything just yet, because something was always happening to one child or another. She waited. She believed. She watched his children finish high school and college, then marry. The divorce was still soon, but she could no longer believe. She left.

Afterward, the men were always younger; then, finally, boys.

Barbara told people she was a widow. And, in a way, she was. The ten-year affair had been a clumsy marriage for her. Now it was dead. But maybe she was more of a survivor than anything, having almost drowned in the stormy, uncertain waters of love.

She thought of all this in the short time it took him to finish his coffee.

At the door, he kissed her with a boy's enthusiasm. "Lock up. I'll see you tomorrow."

"Tomorrow," she said, watching him leave, then disappear into the night with that boyish walk of his. She closed the door and locked it.

The figure standing in the shadows of the large willow tree in the front yard watched the lovers part. He waited for Dwayne to be well on his way before he left his cover and approached the house. It had paid off keeping an eye on the Eastman kid.

There was a knock at the door. Barbara opened it as far as the stretch of the door chain allowed. "What do you want?" she asked, clutching her robe at the throat and peering through the crack.

"I'm Claude Fitgerald," the man said.

"I know who you are," Barbara said. The whole town knew the Fitgeralds and that they worked at old Durie House. The draft of cold night air made her shiver. "What do you want? It's late."

"Business," Claude grinned. "I want to talk over some business."

"Any business you have can wait until morning. Not at this hour. I'm ready for bed."

Claude's grin widened.

Barbara drew the robe tighter. She felt like he was undressing her with his eyes. "Go away."

She started to close the door. "All right, missy," Claude said. "I'll just take my business over to that Mr. Kitterick and see what he has to say."

Barbara opened the door again. "What could you possibly want with Mr. Kitterick?"

Claude looked her up and down, grinning the whole time. "He's the principal of Lanark High School, ain't he? Maybe he'd just like to listen to what I've got? Seems to me he'd be interested in what one of his teachers is doin'."

Claude showed her the small cassette recorder he was carrying, turned it on, and adjusted the volume. It was a recording of her in bed with Dwayne.

He shut it off. "It ain't polite to discuss business through a crack in the door."

Barbara reluctantly slipped the chain off and opened the door. Claude stepped in and she closed it, backing against it.

She looked at him standing in her living room. A little, ratty old man in baggy pants and tennis shoes. There were smudges of dirt on his khaki pants near the crotch, and his baseball cap, tilted on his head at what he thought was a rakish angle, was sweat-stained and greasy. It made her skin crawl just to be in the same room with him.

Claude looked around the room – a small fireplace, a fake white bear rug in front of it, and two pillows on the floor. "A regular love nest ain't it?" he said.

Barbara moved away from the door and faced him. "What do you want, Mr. Fitgerald?"

"Well, now ain't we getting formal? You can just call me Claude." He smiled and now that he was in the light, she could see several teeth were missing.

She didn't return his smile. "What do you want, Mr. Fitgerald?" Her voice was like a slap in the face.

"Don't get sassy with me, missy. Or, I might just change my mind and go see that principal fella after all."

Barbara managed the strength to force a smile. "Where did you get that recording, Claude?"

"Now, that's better. You got something to drink? Kinda nippy outside. Need something to warm me up." He looked her over again. "Besides, I like to discuss business over a drink."

Barbara went into the kitchen and turned on the light. Claude followed close behind her. She brought out a glass and a bottle of brandy from a cabinet, poured in a generous amount, and handed him the glass.

"Now, where did you get that recording?"

Claude tossed off the brandy in one gulp and gestured for a refill.

"From right under that little bed of yours," he said. "The one with that canopy top you got on it."

Barbara almost dropped the glass. "How?"

"Oh, you'd be surprised at what a little mike like that will do if you put it in the right place. Ain't nothing to hookin' it up. A friend of mine's in the electronic business and he showed me how to do it. It ain't hard at all."

Barbara remembered the feeling she had about someone being in the house. "You broke into this house and hid a microphone. That's against the law."

He laughed and almost choked. "So's what you're doin'. Besides, if the government can do it, so can I."

Claude stared at the empty glass she was holding. He tapped it with his finger. "Come on, missy. A fella could die of thirst around here."

She poured him a drink with trembling hands. She would have liked to hit him with the bottle. "How much do you want for that recording?" She set the bottle down on the table. "I don't have much money, but…"

“Don’t want money.”

“Then, what?”

Claude grinned his jack-o’-lantern grin.

“Oh, no…” A deep intake of breath caught in her throat. “Get out!”

Claude laughed again. “I thought as long as sonny boy was pokin’ you – well, you wouldn’t mind me pokin’ you, too.”

“You’re a disgusting vulgar old man! And if you don’t leave—”

“Don’t get uppity with me,” Claude snapped. “I heard you on that there tape. You ain’t any better than me. You like to swear when you’re gettin’ it. Well, you can swear all you want with me.”

Barbara turned her back on him. She tried not to cry, but tears flooded her eyes.

Claude finished his drink and put the empty glass down on the table. He could feel an erection building under his trousers, tenting out the front of his pants. It was the first time in a year he had one that good.

“Well, if you want me to go, guess I’ll just have to see what our friend, Mr. Kitterick’s doin’.”

God, if Kitterick heard that tape, Barbara thought, she’d have to leave. Her teaching career would be over. And it was her life. The only thing she knew how to do.

Claude walked to the door.

“Don’t go,” she heard herself saying, her voice almost a whisper.

Claude stopped, looked back. “What did you say, missy? Didn’t quite hear you.”

She turned and faced him and tried to keep her voice from shaking. “Don’t go.”

He smiled and walked over to her, his tennis shoes making sucking sounds on the kitchen floor. The front of his pants bulged out like the tail of a pointer spotting game.

“That’s better,” he said. “Besides, you might like it.”

Claude pulled the cord loose on her robe and held it open. His eyes lit up with anticipation. Barbara could almost hear him smack his lips.

He cupped her breast with a grimy hand and squeezed it hard. "You might just like it a whole lot."

15

THE HOUSE WAS DARK WHEN RUTH HANSON pulled her Buick behind Jennifer's rented Thunderbird and locked the car doors. She climbed the small porch steps and unlocked the front door, determined to head straight for bed.

Inside, she locked the door again and turned on a nearby lamp, then wearily threw her purse and coat on the couch. God, she was tired, but it was a nice kind of tired. Her whole body seemed to ache all over and yet there was a warm euphoria surging through it. It was a strange feeling; something she had never experienced before.

It was as she imagined she would have felt if she ever had an orgasm. But that was ridiculous because she wasn't involved with anyone. She had only two affairs since her divorce and both turned out to be monumental flops.

The first, Jacob Behling, doctor of internal medicine, was suave and clean and clinical. He would enter her with a verve that built into a hammering frenzy, all of which lasted from one to two minutes, ending in a teeth-grinding, eye-popping ejaculation. Afterward, he'd kiss her lightly on the lips and hop out of bed before the last drop of spermatozoa ever had a chance of entering her. Ruth always felt like she had just been inoculated.

The second, Carter Ferguson, was a minister and her cousin. Ruth had always admired Carter and so, one evening, she decided to seduce him. It ended in disaster.

They were both disappointed. She had probably given the poor man a complex, besides. Somehow, she thought that doing it with a man of God would be different. Maybe she'd even have the orgasm that had so far eluded her in life.

She didn't.

Carter had been so nervous that he became impotent while trying to mount her. She had fondled him and brought him back to life only to have him ejaculate in her hand.

He had been sorry. She had been sorry. They had tried a second time without much more success. Carter had lost his erection shortly after he entered her.

In the end, they had both been glad it was over.

Carter had told her it was God's will. They weren't married. And they were related. Although, being only second cousins, he wasn't sure it was incest, but it was a sin.

Ruth sighed. Poor Carter. She wondered if he had ever gotten over his guilt. She slipped off her shoes and looked down the hall toward the bedrooms.

Jennifer must have grown tired waiting for her and gone to bed. Ruth supposed that her daughter would be slightly miffed at her in the morning for breaking their dinner engagement. Was it her fault that there was so much to do down at the store? She just couldn't get away. Although, when she thought about it, Ruth couldn't exactly remember just what had kept her.

Well, Jennifer would get over it, Ruth decided. But she still tiptoed into her bedroom to turn on the light, trying not to wake her daughter, hoping she would not have to face her until morning.

Ruth slipped out of her dress and placed it neatly over a chair. She didn't want to open any noisy closet doors. That would really wake her. And Ruth didn't feel like arguing. Not tonight, thank you.

She moved over to the bed with the intention of turning down the bedspread, but it was gone. She looked around the room. It was nowhere in sight. She wondered what in the world Jennifer could have done with it. Or had she done something with it this morning and had simply forgotten? The cleaners? Her mind was so fuzzy lately. She couldn't remember things.

Well, it wasn't important. It could wait until tomorrow. Sleep was important. Sleep now and find the bedspread tomorrow.

Ruth pulled back the rest of the covers and started to take off her jewelry. First the earrings, then the watch, then the bracelet.

She dropped an earring.

Holding the rest of her jewelry in one hand, Ruth stepped back and searched the carpet with her eyes, then with one foot.

"Now, where in the world..." Ruth said quietly. She decided that it must have bounced under the bed.

Ruth knelt down, ducked her head below the bed frame, and looked straight into Jennifer's dead face.

Ruth screamed.

She pulled away from the bed, losing the rest of her jewelry in the process, falling to her knees before she could get out of the bedroom.

She fell again in the living room, tearing her stockings. She pulled herself up and clawed at the locks on the front door, and after what seemed like an eternity with someone continuously screaming (later she would realize it had been her), she managed to throw the door open and run out into the night.

Lights were thrown on all over the neighborhood.

Ruth was still screaming when the police arrived.

16

THAYER SAT IN HIS CAR WITH THE WINDOW ROLLED DOWN and chewed on his first cigar of the morning. The day didn't seem too bad, weather-wise. Might even get up into the sixties today – or so the weatherman said on the radio, but rain tonight. Thayer checked the sky. The sun was bright and warm. Maybe, he thought, it would burn off some of the gloom in this town.

Just as Thayer was about to check the time, he saw a red Corvette dart past and pull up sharply in front of him. Kenneth Sollis climbed out, unlocked the front door of his store and disappeared inside.

Thayer decided to give him a couple of minutes. He watched the inside fluorescents flicker and form into solid bars of light; and when the CLOSED sign was taken out of the window, he got out of his car and entered the store.

Books seemed to be the biggest commodity in The Coven. They lined most of the walls and ranged on a variety of subjects. Thayer checked some of the departments that were clearly marked by orange signs with black lettering: Aura, Astrology, Clairvoyance, ESP, Hypnotism, Kabbalah, and on and on, disappearing into the back of the store, then continuing along the back wall and stopping at the display cases that bulged with everything from amulets to Zener cards.

Thayer picked up a skull leering at him from the top of a nearby counter.

"Plastic," Sollis said, walking down the other side of the counter after lighting some incense.

"Looks real enough," Thayer said, putting it down gingerly.

"It's supposed to," Sollis laughed. "That's to prevent anyone from going out and getting the real thing."

Thayer didn't join in the humor. Instead, he looked at the sign taped to the back of Sollis' cash register: HONESTY IS LIKE PREGNANCY – EITHER YOU ARE OR YOU AREN'T.

Thayer pointed to the sign. "Is that an occult saying?"

Sollis leaned over the counter to follow the line of Thayer's finger. "No," he laughed again and straightened. "Just good business."

Thayer nodded. Then in his best poker face said, "Jennifer Bernstein is dead. I guess you'd know her better as Jennifer Hanson. She was murdered last night in her mother's home." He watched Sollis' face for a reaction.

"Jennifer?" There was a slight uneasy movement of his eyes, but the face showed genuine surprise. "Oh, my God." Sollis leaned on the counter with his hands, lowered his head and stared down through the glass countertop at his merchandise, avoiding any further eye contact with Thayer.

"I understand you knew her," Thayer said. "You went together for a time."

Sollis snapped his head up. "That was several years ago."

"And you haven't been with her since, or seen her – like last night?" Thayer looked him over again. Sollis was quite the dresser: suit, vest, and tie. "This is just routine."

Sollis' thick fish features worked nervously before he managed to get the words out. "What's routine about asking where you were when a murder was committed?" He looked around to see if anyone else had entered the store. They were alone. Marge wouldn't be in until ten. "That's just like asking me if I killed her," he said.

Thayer looked at him; an almost imperceptible smile crossed his lips.

Sollis caught it. "No, I didn't kill her, goddamit. I haven't seen Jennifer in years."

“She visits her mother every year.”

“I mean as a girlfriend. Of course, I’ve seen her in town when she’s visiting up here, but so have a lot of other people.”

Sollis could remember vividly the last time Jennifer had been with him. It was in his home. They had just finished screwing. It hadn’t been lovemaking – not with Jennifer. You screwed her. You didn’t make love to her.

She was screaming and hitting him and calling him names. He had pissed in her. At the time, Sollis felt it was the least he could do to demonstrate what he thought about her goddam twisted sense of values and the boredom he began to feel with her. She had stormed out of his bed and out of his house, dripping all the way.

“So?”

“What do you mean?” Sollis said.

“So where were you last night?” Thayer said, with all the patience of a waiting spider.

Sollis looked at him and his eyes blazed. “I left the store about seven-thirty and went home. It was a slow night.”

“Anyone see you?”

“Marge saw me leave. She closed up.”

“That would be Marge Dillman.” Thayer knew the Dillman girl worked here.

Sollis nodded.

“What about at home?”

Sollis paused. He wasn’t about to tell him he was with Ruth Hanson. “I was alone.”

“All night?”

“Yes, all night. I had some supper, watched a little TV, and went to bed.”

Thayer made a pensive face.

“If I would have known that I needed an alibi, I would have made sure someone saw me.” Sollis looked thoughtful for a moment. “Why don’t you ask Paul Rice where he was last night? He’s in town you know.”

“Paul Rice?”

Sollis smiled. "Come on, you mean you didn't know that Jennifer went with Paul Rice before she went with me? Rice is in town. He's staying with the Eastmans at the old Durie House. I thought everyone in town knew that. Why don't you go over and ask him where he was last night instead of bothering me?"

"I might just do that," Thayer said and tapped the plastic skull with a finger. "Don't leave town, buddy." Then he looked at Sollis. "That goes for you, too. Check your horoscope. It'll tell you the same thing."

Sollis glared at him.

Thayer moved to the entrance, pushed open the glass door, and walked out into the bright sunlight.

After Thayer left the Sollis store, he stopped at Ruth Hanson's to talk to her again, but found that she could add little to what she had told him last night. She had worked late at the store and when she came home, she thought Jennifer had gone to bed. Being tired herself, she went straight to her bedroom. She started to undress, dropped something – an earring – bent down to pick it up and…

He didn't want to upset her anymore, so he left Mrs. Hanson to her grief and headed for his office. He chewed over last night's events as he drove. The one item that was always indigestible was the bedspread. Why was Jennifer on it? So she could be pulled under the bed? Why not leave her lay where she was murdered?

That question still nagged him when he plopped down behind his desk with a cup of coffee in an old, beat up mug. The Bernstein medical report was waiting for him on top of his desk. Dan Sunquist hadn't wasted any time getting on this one. Thayer read the report and sipped his coffee.

The autopsy showed that the Bernstein murder was almost identical to the first two killings. The throat was cut and the head was almost completely severed from the body. She was eviscerated. There were traces of saliva around the neck wound and on her face, which meant, Thayer thought, that the son of a bitch drank her blood as well as the Gordon and McFarland boys'. Her dress was ripped, and her pantyhose and panties were pulled down. But she was not raped. The only difference between this killing and the other two was the mutilation of the sexual organs. In the Gordon and McFarland cases, the penises were severed. In the Bernstein case, the clitoris was removed.

Thayer threw the report back on his desk. There were things about these murders that just didn't add up. That bedspread still bothered him. Why wasn't she just left on the bedroom floor? The bedspread was heavy. It soaked up some of the blood. There was hardly a drop on the bedroom carpet. Maybe the killer was just neat.

He shook his head. There was something else that struck him as odd. What was it now? He looked over the Bernstein report again. Maybe it was something he had seen. Then he remembered. Thayer compared the body photos of the three victims. They were the same. All three were lying on their backs with their arms and legs in a spread-out position.

They looked like five-pointed stars, Thayer thought. Yeah, whatever that means. He put the photos away and finished his coffee, then pushed away from his desk. It was going to be a long day. He still had a lot more things to check out, including Paul Rice.

Early shadows stretched across Blackmoor Road when Thayer swung his car into the Durie House driveway. On the way, he had mulled over his earlier conversation with Sollis, and although he didn't like the man, there was nothing there that pointed to him, except he did hesitate when asked if he was alone last night. Probably a woman.

Thayer stopped in front of the big house and climbed the stone steps to the terrace. After two rings on the bell, he asked Mrs. Fitgerald for Paul Rice.

When Paul came to the door, Thayer introduced himself and suggested they talk outside. Paul followed him onto the terrace.

"Have you heard about Jennifer Bernstein?" Thayer asked him, watching his face. It looked pale, haunted.

Paul was silent for a moment. "Yes, it was on TV." He shook his head. People he knew were dying again. "It's hard to believe."

"How well did you know her?"

"We went together for about a year, then broke up."

"Have a fight?"

"No, just a mutual parting."

"Were you here last night?" Thayer jerked a thumb at the house.

Paul smiled. "All night. I watched some TV with the Eastmans, then we played a cutthroat game..." he paused over his choice of words. "We played sheepshead until ten. I went to bed about a half hour later. You can check if you want."

"I will. Do you know Kenneth Sollis?"

"Just barely. Jennifer introduced us once."

"Did she ever mention anything about him to you?"

Paul shook his head. "No. Nothing."

Thayer made a sour face. "Too bad. Did she ever mention anyone else, someone she might be afraid of?"

Paul thought for a moment. "No, but Jennifer was a very attractive woman. I'm sure she must have known a lot of men."

Thayer fished a cigar out of his pocket. "You gonna be around for a while?"

"A few more days, then I planned returning to Milwaukee."

There was an uncomfortable pause between them.

"I can stick around if you want me to," Paul added.

Thayer shoved the cigar in the side of his mouth. "I think that might be a good idea. Thanks for your cooperation, Mr. Rice. I'll get back to you." He turned and started for his car.

On his way down the driveway, Thayer watched Paul reenter the house. Something was bothering that man, Thayer thought. He'd have to run a check on him with the FBI office in Milwaukee. And on Sollis.

Thayer heard a distant rumble of thunder. He looked up at the sky. Dark, heavy clouds were moving in. A few drops of rain splattered against his windshield.

Thayer hoped the rain would keep the killer off the streets tonight.

17

"YOU'D BETTER GO," BARBARA SAID.

"What's wrong?" Dwayne asked. "You've been telling me that ever since I got here."

"There's nothing wrong…I just haven't been feeling well lately."

"Maybe you'd better see a doctor."

"I will."

She got up from the couch and walked to the door, waiting in front of it nervously. "Sounds like the storm's picking up again."

They could hear the thunder roll outside the house, and the rush of rain batter against the ground. It had been raining since late afternoon.

Dwayne remained sitting next to the fireplace, savoring the warmth of the fire, his clothes still damp from his rainy walk of an hour ago. He felt reluctant to move, to leave her.

"I could stay longer," he said.

Their eyes met, but she quickly dropped hers. "No, not tonight. I feel a slight chill." She hugged her elbows for emphasis. "I'm going to mix a hot drink and go right to bed."

Dwayne got up, picked up his jacket from the back of a chair, and moved toward the door. She looked forlorn standing there in her jeans and bulky sweater, like someone without a friend in the world. He grabbed her, pulling her to him, kissing her hard on the lips.

She responded at first, making little purring sounds, exploring his mouth with her tongue. Then suddenly, she pushed him away.

"Don't." She turned her face away. "I'm not worthy of you anymore. I'm…I'm dirty."

"Don't' say that. You're the sweetest person I've ever known."

"Sweet!" She gave a shrill laugh and backed away from him. "You know what they wrote in my dear old yearbook just before I graduated from high school? 'Barbara Homes is the sweetest girl in the world,' that's what."

"They knew what they were talking about."

"You know what sweet is?" She went on as if she hadn't heard him. "It's a nothing word. It means you stand still with a dopey smile on your face while everyone and his brother tries to screw you and you just grin and bear it."

"Barbara…"

"Sweet is sick. Sweet is when you didn't do the housework properly because you had your period and it hurt like hell and you were scared because it was your first time, and your mother tries to push you down the cellar stairs as punishment, and you take it."

"Barbara, stop this."

"Sweet is when you finally meet Mr. Right, but there's a slight hitch, he's married. So he asks you to wait because he has children and you mustn't hurt the children."

"I can't stand any…"

"And when you finally can't take it anymore, you leave and pass on to better things. Like seducing young boys and letting dirty old men…"

"STOP IT!"

She looked stunned. His shouting at her had been like a slap in the face. After a moment, she came to him in a rush. "Oh, Dwayne, I'm such a bitch."

He held her against his chest. She couldn't hold the tears back any longer.

Half an hour later, Dwayne hunched down lower into his jacket, seeking a drier shelter for his neck. The slow, steady rain of earlier evening had changed into a downpour. An electrical storm had settled in, sending quick flashes of lightning and loud bursts of thunder across the night sky.

He had left Barbara's place in a murky cloud of confusion. He still didn't know what was bothering her. Her mood tonight frightened him. Something had set her off.

Barbara had changed so suddenly in the last twenty-four hours, he didn't know what to make of it. She was depressed and cried a lot. That wasn't like her. If it was something he did, she wouldn't tell him, didn't want to discuss it. "It was nothing," she said, but still she cried. He just couldn't figure out what was wrong.

Maybe he'd ask Paul how to handle a depressed girl. But, then, Paul seemed to be having his own problems with Linda. She hardly talked to him anymore, and when Paul finally got her to leave the house tonight to take in a movie, there still wasn't much communication between them.

The police chief's visit to the house didn't help much either. His father had a few comments to make about that, but then he had something to say about everything.

A car passed slowly in the rain, its headlights illuminating the explosive downpour hitting the road. Dwayne crossed the street in its wake, entering Thackeray Park.

His thoughts settled back on Barbara. He had to admit he didn't know much about women, but he'd definitely find out what was bothering her tomorrow night. Even if it meant pressing her for an answer.

He cut across the wet grass and walked toward the lagoon. His shoes and socks were getting wet in the process, but it couldn't be helped. It was a lot shorter this way. Besides, he was soaked to the skin everywhere else.

Slowing momentarily, he watched the rain erupt the dark waters of the lagoon. They found Ralphie Gordon somewhere near here, he thought. Dwayne turned and looked back over his line of travel. Nothing there but the rain and the night. He walked faster.

Up ahead, a park light stretched into a metal arm of globed light, like a white face hanging in the air, a floating white glob. For some reason, it made him think of the closet. Since the murders, the odor in the room was stronger. There was even a vibration running through the door that you could feel if you held your hand against it. There were even times he could have sworn he heard breathing behind the door.

Dwayne didn't dare tell his father that, but then there really wasn't very much he could relate to him about anyway. He'd have a fit if he ever found out about Barbara. It would be dangerous for her, too. She could probably lose her job, or worse.

No. There was no one he could discuss the closet with except Paul. No one else in the house noticed anything. It was as if they were all made out of wood, or were on another frequency. The whole family looked at him sideways whenever he mentioned the closet.

Before Paul came, he was beginning to think that maybe there was something wrong with him. But then, his dog had sensed it, too. She'd bark and whine in the middle of the night and wouldn't go anywhere near the closet. Poor Holly. He wondered where she was now.

Dwayne climbed the wooded incline that topped out on Blackmoor Road, crossing it to the driveway. The rain bounced large spears of water off the ground.

Lightning strobe-lighted the waiting house.

18

"WE'RE ONLY GOIN' TO BE GONE FOR TWO DAYS," Tommy Burham said, watching Chrissie pack for the upcoming weekend trip with him and his parents to their cabin in Upper Michigan. "You're taking enough stuff for a month."

"Well, a girl has to be prepared," Chrissie said.

"For what, for cripes sake?"

"Eventualities."

Tommy frowned. They were up in Chrissie's bedroom. Tommy was propped up on one elbow across the bed next to her suitcase and the various small piles of clothing she had stacked on the bedspread.

Lightning struck nearby and thunder cracked immediately after. Chrissie jumped. "I wish it would stop doing that."

"Why are girls always afraid of lightning and thunder?"

"Well, boys are afraid of things, too, smarty," she said and stuck out her tongue.

"Like what?"

"My brother's afraid of his closet."

Tommy laughed. "His closet?"

Chrissie dropped two sweaters into the suitcase and sat on the edge of the bed. "Promise you'll never mention this to him. My father would just kill me if he knew I told anyone."

Tommy laughed again. "Sure. I promise."

Chrissie leaned over conspiratorially. "Dwayne has this thing about the closet in his bedroom. He thinks there's something in it."

Tommy's eyes grew wide. He didn't know whether to laugh or not. "Like what?" he said, his voice starting to rise.

"Promise you'll never tell this to another soul."

"I said I promised."

"A ghost or something."

Thunder cracked again and the lights flickered.

Tommy sat up. "You're putting me on," he said with a shaky smile.

"No, I'm not. He's had this thing about that closet since we moved in here. He even has to sleep with the light on."

"Well, for cripes…"

"Shhhh."

The front door opened and closed. They heard footsteps in the foyer, then on the stairs.

"That's probably Dwayne," Chrissie whispered. "Remember what you promised."

The footsteps turned down the hall toward her bedroom. Dwayne appeared in the doorway, dripping water on the red runner that carpeted the floor.

"Dwayne Eastman," Chrissie said. "Daddy's going to have a fit if he finds out you've been walking around in this storm. You'll catch your…"

"Aren't they back yet?" Dwayne asked, looking at Tommy, who was watching him rather strangely.

"The card game must still be going on at Tommy's house," Chrissie said, getting up from the bed.

"What's it this time, sheepshead or bridge?"

"Bridge," Tommy answered. "I didn't want to be the fifth for sheepshead."

"I don't blame you," Dwayne said.

There was a long pause between the three of them that was eventually filled by the lightning and thunder. Rain stung the windows. The lights blinked. Chrissie flinched.

She watched the lights grow from anemic dimness to glowing strength, then looked at her brother. "Where have you been all this time?"

"School."

"School?"

"Yes, school. Anything wrong with that?"

"With Miss Prissy Homes, I bet."

"So? She's a fine teacher, and what I do with my time is my business."

"Well, you don't have to snap my head off."

"Sorry." Dwayne watched the lights dim again with another surge from the storm.

"Wow, that one was really close," Tommy said.

"You better get out of those wet clothes before Mom and Dad get home," Chrissie said. "Or you know what'll happen."

Dwayne looked down at the damp circle spreading around his feet. He could feel pools of water in his shoes. Even his shorts were wet.

"Guess I'd better," he said and left them, turning down the hall. He stopped at the bathroom and opened the linen closet. Taking out a towel, he threw it over his wet hair and continued on to his room. He stopped apprehensively at the doorway.

Lightning speared the night outside his windows, filling the room with shadows. He turned on the lights and walked in. Everything seemed all right. There was no odor. He felt the closet door. No vibration.

Satisfied, Dwayne toweled himself off and changed into dry clothes, but he still kept one eye on the closet.

"See how he went into his room?" Chrissie whispered.

"I didn't notice anything," Tommy said.

They were both peeking around the doorway of her bedroom. "Shhhh." Chrissie cautioned, raising a finger to her lips. "He'll hear you."

Tommy shrugged and looked at his watch, stepping back into the room. "I better get home before your dad sees me."

"But it's raining pitchforks," Chrissie protested. "Why don't you wait until it lets up?"

"The way it's coming down it could go on like that all night."

As if to justify his statement, the storm lashed against the house, rattling the windows.

"Besides," Tommy added, "I won't get wet much just from running from the house to my car. And Dwayne's home now, so you won't be alone."

"You just don't want to stay with me," she pouted.

He ran his hands through her hair and kissed her. "You know better than that."

"You older men tell that to all the girls."

Tommy smiled and kissed her again.

They went downstairs with arms intertwined around each other's waists. At the front door, Tommy threw on his jacket and dropped his driving gloves on the foyer table. He lifted her chin with a finger and gently kissed her. She opened her mouth for him, prodding his tongue with hers, and slipped her arms around his neck.

Three kisses later, Tommy zipped up his jacket and opened the front door. "See you tomorrow," he said.

One last kiss and he was out the door, running through the rain that was bouncing large pellets off the roof of his father's Mercedes. He threw up an arm to wave, then ducked into the shelter of the front seat. A few moments later, he drove off.

The driveway lit up in a brilliant flash of lightning and thunder rolled over the house. Chrissie quickly closed the door. She knew it was the lightning you were supposed to be afraid of, but it was always the thunder that frightened her.

She started to turn for the kitchen when she saw Tommy's driving gloves on the foyer table. Chrissie had bought them for him for his last birthday, two months ago, and he wore them constantly since. Sometimes, she wondered if he even wore them to bed. Well, maybe one of these days she'd find out. She smiled mischievously. If Daddy knew she had such thoughts, he'd have a fit.

With visions of a nude Tommy Burham, clad only in his driving gloves, Chrissie went into the kitchen and flipped on the overhead light. She put a kettle of water on the stove and got out the jar of Swiss Miss and two cups, deciding to make one for her grouchy brother.

The water was just about ready when the lights dimmed, almost going out. She looked up at the light. God, she wished it would stop doing that.

The doorbell rang.

Chrissie ran to the door. She knew Tommy wouldn't go home without his driving gloves. She picked up the gloves, hid them behind her back, skipped over to the door and opened it.

"Forget some—"

The hand that grabbed her chin was strong. It kept her silent and her neck straight for the knife.

19

DWAYNE FINISHED DRESSING. He had heard Tommy leave, and just now, the doorbell ring. Wondering who it was, he stepped out into the upstairs hall and listened at the top of the stairs. Still wearing the towel over his head, he dropped it around his neck and went down three steps, listening again.

He didn't hear any voices.

"Chrissie!" he called.

No answer.

"Chrissie!"

Nothing.

He went downstairs. The front door was closed and the foyer empty. There was something on the floor, near the door. He picked it up. A driving glove. It looked like one of the gloves he had helped his sister pick out for Tommy Burham's birthday.

"Chrissie!"

Dwayne checked the downstairs rooms. When he entered the kitchen, he found a jar of cocoa and two cups on the counter. Water was boiling on the stove. He turned the water off and dropped the glove on the table.

He opened the back door and looked out. Lightning snapped over the lake in long forks of blue-white light accompanied by a barrage of thunder. The rain fell in hard sheets. He tried to see into the backyard but couldn't make anything out except trees and grass, rain and darkness. He closed the door. Why would she go outside, anyway?

Walking back into the foyer, Dwayne checked all the downstairs rooms again, calling her as he did. When he returned to the foyer, his attention settled on the stairs. Could she be up there?

Dwayne went halfway up. "Chrissie!"

Then a new thought crossed his mind. Knowing the mischievous nature of his sister, it would be just like her to hide on him.

"Chrissie! If you're playing games, it isn't very funny! Chrissie!"

Damn her. He went the rest of the way up the stairs, stopping at the top and listening. The marine clock in the upper hall struck two bells, nine o'clock. Dwayne jumped at the sound.

Lightning crashed close by and thunder boomed, reverberating in the windows. The lights blinked, fluttered, and finally died, throwing the house in complete darkness.

Dwayne gripped the banister with both hands. The dark house crawled with strange shapes.

"Chrissie!"

No response.

"I'm going to leave you up here…in the dark!"

God, could she be hiding in his room? The thought made him break out in gooseflesh.

"Chrissie!" he tried again. "I'm leaving! You can just stay up there!"

The house was quiet except for the storm pounding outside and the wind keening under the eaves.

Then he thought he heard a laugh.

Dwayne froze, his right foot hanging just above the next step down. Was that Chrissie laughing? It sounded like – what? It was chambered, like someone laughing in a tomb.

Ice seemed to be forming in his veins. He never felt so cold. He turned and tried to run, then fell the last five steps to the floor, skinning his hands and knees.

He heard his name. Was the house whispering his name?

Dwayne got to his feet and raced for the front door. He yanked it open and bolted outside, straight into a pair of clutching hands.

"Let me go! Let me go!" Dwayne screamed as he fought them off.

"Dwayne! Dwayne! Goddammit, Dwayne, stop it! It's me!" his father said and shook Dwayne like a rag. "Stop it!"

Dwayne stopped struggling. He father still held his arms.

"Whatever is the matter?" Helen Eastman said, her face marked with grave concern.

Dwayne tried to back away from them. They were standing on the terrace, just beyond the eaves of the house, the rain pouring down on the three of them.

John Eastman ushered his son inside, holding him by one arm. Mrs. Eastman followed, her face still burdened with worry.

"Now, suppose you tell us what's going on," his father said.

He looked at them. He had trouble getting his tongue to form the words. The house was still dark, gray light spilled in from the open doorway. Lightning flashed, then the thunder came.

Eastman's eyes held his son's face in a vise-like stare. "What happened? Goddammit, what happened?" He shook him again.

"John, for God sakes!" Helen put a restraining hand on her husband and came between them. "You don't have to give him the third degree."

"Well, what the hell's the matter with him?"

Helen looked at her son. Even in the darkness, his face looked pale. She felt his forehead. "He's cold as ice," she said to her husband. "Dwayne, tell us what happened. Where's Chrissie?"

Dwayne started slowly, awkwardly, then the words tumbled out in a rush.

"Not that damn closet business again," Eastman said, giving his wife a sideways look.

"Dwayne, are you sure Chrissie just isn't playing a trick on you?" his mother asked. "She's probably just hiding somewhere in the house."

"But I looked everywhere…"

Eastman caught the inflection. "Did you look upstairs, in your room?"

"No…I…the lights went out."

"Just as I thought. Come on, let's go see."

Dwayne's eyes flashed to his father. He started to protest, but couldn't get it out.

"Afraid the bogeyman will get you?"

Rain blew in through the open doorway, splattering against the foyer floor. Helen wanted to close it, but it was the only light they had.

"John, you're not being fair. Anyone would be frightened under the circumstances."

"We've discussed this a hundred times before," Eastman said. "It's about time he started acting like a man. You can't go around all your life being afraid of the dark." Eastman grabbed Dwayne by the arm and pushed him toward the stairs. "Come on."

"Please, Dad…"

"Come on." Eastman's voice took on an edge.

"It's all Chrissie's fault, really," Helen said, trailing after them.

Eastman stopped on the stairs. He had become so angry about the closet that he had forgotten Chrissie's part in all this.

"Chrissie!" he yelled. Waited. "Chrissie! You come down here this instant!" He waited again. Still no response. The storm rumbled outside the house.

"John…" Helen touched her husband's arm. There was a slight uneasiness in her voice.

"It's all right," Eastman assured her. "She's probably afraid to come out now. When I get my hands on that young lady, she'll have to eat her meals standing up."

They continued up the stairs, groping their way through the dark house. Helen Eastman gave a parting glance at the open front door. It looked very inviting.

When they reached Dwayne's room, they stopped in the doorway and looked in.

"Chrissie?" Eastman said. He hesitated a moment, then pushed Dwayne ahead of him and followed close behind. They stopped in front of the closet. Mrs. Eastman remained in the doorway.

Eastman glanced at his son, then reached for the closet door.

Dwayne stiffened, his heart pounding.

Eastman pulled the door open.

Dwayne jumped, fighting back a scream.

The lights had come on.

The closet was empty.

"Well," Eastman said, closing the door, "no Chrissie – no bogeyman."

Dwayne tried to slow his racing heart.

"Where can she be?" Mrs. Eastman said, still not coming into the room.

"I don't know, but I'm going to put an end to all this foolishness once and for all. We'll find Chrissie," Eastman said to his wife, then turned to Dwayne. "You stay in this room and try to act like a man for a change."

Eastman walked to the bedroom door, removed the key from the lock and reinserted it on the outside of the door.

Dwayne looked at the closet, then back at his father.

"Dad, please don't do this."

Eastman did not respond.

"John," Mrs. Eastman interceded, "don't you think this could wait until another time?"

"No. I don't want him to grow up afraid of his own shadow."

Thunder rattled the windows.

"Dad…"

"You just stay in there, young man, and get over whatever it is that's bothering you. Chrissie's going to get hers, too. Don't worry about that."

Helen Eastman looked at her son, sensing his fear, then turned to her husband. "Don't do this. Not tonight."

Eastman gave her an icy stare.

She reached for the key, but Eastman caught her hand and pushed her back. He closed the door and locked it, putting the key in his pocket.

Dwayne wanted to run to the door and pound on it until they

let him out, but he knew it was useless. He heard their voices drift away down the hall. He looked around his room – at his bed, his dresser, and his books – but his eyes always returned to the closet.

He tried sitting on his bed. The room began to feel cold. After a while, he could see his breath blowing white with the drop in temperature. He could hear a humming sound coming from the closet. The door was vibrating with some strange power. It spread to the walls, the ceiling, and the floor. He could feel it through his shoes.

The dresser started to rock back and forth, back and forth. Long-fingered cracks appeared along the walls. The bed shook.

Dwayne jumped up and backed away from it. A cold fist of fear lodged in his throat. The bed moved violently across the room, banging into the opposite wall.

The storm cracked with explosive force, filling the room. The lights ebbed, lingered for a moment, then went out again.

In the dark, Dwayne groped for the chair, found it, and shoved it against the closet door. He stepped back and listened, trying to still the thunder of his heart.

The stench came. An overpowering, foul-smelling odor wafted through the room, permeating every corner.

Dwayne ran to the bedroom door, pounding on it with his fists, pulling on the knob with all his strength. He wanted to scream, but couldn't. Nothing came out. He could hear the faint voices of his father and mother calling Chrissie from somewhere in the house.

Dark, heavy shadows hung in the room. The dresser was still rocking. Outside, the storm lashed against the house, but there was another undercurrent of sound – the sound a doorknob makes when it is being slowly turned.

Dwayne turned and faced the closet.

He could hear the chair being pushed away from the door.

The door was opening, just as he knew it would one day.

His voice finally came to him.

He screamed.

Once.

20

PAUL LOOKED OVER AT LINDA, who was sitting uncomfortably on the car seat next to him in an obvious and exaggerated position that would avoid any chance contact with him. She had sat that way in the theater, too, throughout the entire movie.

He had not really wanted to go to the movies tonight, but he thought it would be good for both of them to get out of the house. Besides, he wanted a chance to talk to her alone. But for all the conversation he had gotten out of her, you would have thought she was a mute.

"Are you mad for life?" Paul asked.

She didn't look at him when she answered. "Maybe. I don't really know. I have to think things out."

That was the longest string of words he had gotten out of her all evening. "Linda, Jennifer's dead. Can't you forget?"

She looked down at her hands, refolding them in her lap. "I'm sorry about that...but I need time to get my head together. Things are all mixed up."

"Do you want me to leave the house?"

She turned to look at him, her jaw starting to tremble. "Where would you go? Back to Milwaukee?"

"No. I promised Chief Thayer I'd stick around for a while, but I thought...maybe another place...a motel or something. At least I'd be out of your way."

There was a pause before she answered. "You don't have to leave. Unless you want to."

Paul didn't answer. He wanted to leave Durie House and Lanark far behind him, but not for the reason she thought. The headaches and the nausea hadn't bothered him all week. Still, Jennifer was dead. Maybe if he left, the killings would stop.

He turned off Blackmoor Road and onto the driveway. Rain slanted down in front of his headlights. It was still raining, although not as hard as earlier in the evening. The headlights swept down the driveway, picking up two police cars parked in front of the house, which blazed with a light in every window.

"Oh, my God," Linda said. "What could have happened?"

Paul pulled up in back of one of the police cars. Linda jumped out of the car and ran up the steps and into the house. A minute later, Paul found Chief Thayer standing in the middle of the front hall with Mr. and Mrs. Eastman, Linda, and another police officer.

"So, after you couldn't find your daughter," Thayer said, "you went back to let your son out of his room and he was gone. Is that right?"

"Yes," Eastman said. His eyes and face were haggard beyond belief.

Linda came over to Paul. "Chrissie and Dwayne are missing," she said, her voice quiet but choked with emotion.

"I told you not to put him in there," Helen Eastman said to her husband, "but you wouldn't listen. Now he's missing, too." She was still wearing her raincoat, as was her husband. Her eyes were red, like she had been crying for some time. Paul didn't like what he saw in them.

"Why did you lock him in there in the first place?" Wally Schaefer asked. He was standing next to Thayer and holding a flashlight.

"Look, we've been over that," Eastman said, getting annoyed. "It was a disciplinary measure – that's all."

Thayer noticed Paul for the first time and acknowledged him with a nod.

"God, what could have happened to them?" Mrs. Eastman cried.

She was sobbing uncontrollably now into an already overworked handkerchief.

Eastman tried to put a comforting arm around her, but she pulled away from him, her accusing eyes hardening behind her tears.

"Linda," Eastman said, "take your mother upstairs to her room. I think she's rather tired."

"I don't want to go," Mrs. Eastman said. "I want to find them."

"Why don't you rest a little, Mrs. Eastman?" Thayer said. He almost reached out for her arm, but thought better of it, not wanting to provoke the anger she just showed toward her husband. "It will be all right. We'll find your children for you."

"Come on, Mom," Linda said, putting an arm around her. "I'll take you up."

She hesitated, then let her daughter lead her slowly toward the stairs. Her head hurt and her eyes were sore and she couldn't think straight anymore. She turned to look at Thayer. "Please find them," she said. "Please find my children."

"We will, Mrs. Eastman," Thayer reassured her. "I promise you."

Linda took her upstairs.

"Now what?" Eastman said, his hands thrust into his raincoat pockets, the sting of his wife's rejection chiseled into his face.

"We'll search the house again," Thayer said. "Then the grounds. Wally, take the upstairs. Mr. Eastman, the downstairs. Mr. Rice, you want to help me with the basement?"

Paul nodded. When the others left, he said to Thayer, "Did Eastman lock both kids up in that room?"

"No, just the boy. We checked the room out and the windows were locked from the inside. And there aren't any other ways out of there except the door and the windows. So, unless the kid had another key, or is some kind of an escape artist, or there are secret passages in this house – I don't know how the hell he got out of that room."

Paul was hoping he didn't know either.

Several hours later, they found Chrissie Eastman's body. Paul just about stumbled over her. She was lying on the grass near the end of the Eastman property in back of the tool shed. She was face up and Paul could see that she was dead. Her throat had been cut and her body mutilated.

For one long moment, Paul was back in Saigon with Carrol. She was dead, face up, stretched out in the street. A fatal round, fired from a passing motor scooter, exploded in her brain.

He started to shake. An old nausea, festered in the Vietnam war, spread through him.

After a while, he called the others.

Small knots of men stood on the grass in the rain. The heavy storm had passed, leaving behind a light drizzle. Flashlights probed the area like eyes. Two men took Chrissie's body away on a stretcher. They headed toward the driveway, which was jammed with police and emergency vehicles.

Paul came out of the house and walked over to the tool shed. He stopped a short distance away and lit a cigarette, watching Thayer talk to a smaller man with a doctor's bag. After a short conversation, Thayer joined him.

"Where are the Eastmans?" Thayer asked.

"In the house. Mrs. Eastman's resting. Linda called a local doctor and he gave her a sedative. Linda's still with her. Eastman's sitting alone in the library getting stoned. He looks like the house fell on him."

"Yeah, I can imagine."

"Was she…was she like the others?" Paul asked, the rain wetting down his hair.

"Looks that way. We'll know more after the autopsy. But I'm willing to bet on it."

Thayer threw the cigar away that he had chewed down to a stub and put a fresh one in his mouth. He stared off into the distance, toward Thackeray Park.

Paul looked at him inquiringly. "Something on your mind?"

"Just thinking about the Gordon boy. We found him down there, in the park."

"Was he the first?"

"Yeah. Now here we are four murders later."

"You still haven't found Dwayne Eastman."

Thayer turned toward Paul. "You make that sound like you don't think we'll find him."

Paul took one last drag on his cigarette and flipped it away. "I don't."

"Would you care to elaborate on that?"

Paul hesitated, knowing what Thayer's reaction would be, then told him about Dwayne's fear of the closet.

After he finished, Thayer looked at him strangely. "You think a spook did away with Dwayne Eastman?"

"I knew you'd think I had a few pieces missing upstairs."

Thayer paused. "What makes you so sure he's dead?"

"Just a feeling."

"You get many of these feelings?"

"Look, I know what I've just told you makes me out like some kind of nut," Paul said defensively, "but the fact remains that Dwayne was afraid of this house – especially that closet of his. Tonight his father locked him up alone in that room and now he's missing. Don't you think that's a bit odd?"

"I don't believe in spooks."

"I didn't say I did, but what happened to Dwayne?"

"Whoever killed his sister came back and got him."

"How? Eastman locked the door and you said the windows were still locked from the inside."

"It's an old house. There's probably another way in and out of that room – or the house, for that matter."

"We didn't find any."

"It doesn't mean there isn't one. No, somebody got into that room. Somebody that knows this house. Somebody that's good with a knife." Thayer watched Paul closely. "You were with Special Forces, weren't you?"

Paul looked at him coldly, knowing what he was leading up to.

"Proficient in killing with your hands or with weapons," Thayer continued. "Knife included. Skilled with both hands."

Paul got angry. "I happen to have liked the Eastman kids. I didn't kill them. And I didn't kill Jennifer. Or anybody else."

"Take it easy. I never said you did."

Paul got himself under control.

"You don't look so good," Thayer said, examining him casually.

"I don't feel so good. I'm wet and I'm tired and I'm sick of people dying around me."

Thayer paused, then came out with it. "Like your friends in Vietnam? Or your mother and father right after you got back?"

Paul looked at him sharply. "You've been busy."

"I checked you out, sure. It's part of the job. And I saw your service record. It's a good one. Distinguished Service Cross, Silver Star, Bronze Star, Purple Heart…"

"You forgot the breakdown and mental therapy. I suppose that makes the closet story seem even more ridiculous – coming from a certified nut. But then that's what you're looking for, isn't it? A nut?"

"You're building quite a case against yourself."

"Are you going to arrest me?"

"No. I'll build my own case."

"Going to give me a little more rope, Chief?"

Thayer changed the subject. "I'm going to form a search party to look for Dwayne Eastman tomorrow. You want to come?"

"Yes. I'd like to."

"You better go back in the house. You're beginning to look like a drowned cat."

Paul ran a hand through his wet hair. "Thanks. I like you, too."

Humor sprang into Thayer's eyes. He started to laugh. "Is there any coffee in the house?"

"Linda put a pot on."

"Let's go in. My cigar's getting wet."

21

PAUL HELPED SEARCH FOR DWAYNE EASTMAN all of the next day. The search party covered miles of shoreline and wooded areas and every inch of Thackeray Park, even dragging the lagoon. They didn't find him. Paul didn't think they would. All he got for his trouble was wet feet and a sinus attack. It had rained on and off all day, and the weatherman said the rain would continue for at least another forty-eight hours.

It was early evening when Paul finally left Thayer and returned to Durie House. Linda let him in. She looked at him hopefully.

Paul shook his head. "Nothing." He saw her hope die and unshed tears burn her eyes for release, but she didn't cry. Not last night either. She was keeping it all inside.

"You better get out of those wet things," she said finally. "You look terrible."

"Thanks," he said, giving her the heavy rain slicker that Thayer had loaned him. "You and Chief Thayer seem to have the same opinion."

She put the slicker away in the foyer closet, and then turned. "What?"

He waved it off. "Nothing. How's your mother?" He didn't ask about Eastman, who hadn't even joined the search for his son.

"She's been sleeping most of the day. The doctor said it's the best thing for her. Dad's in the library. He's just succeeded in drinking himself to sleep again. He's been in there since last night."

"Oh," Paul said, not really caring if Eastman ever came out.

They walked into the kitchen. The house was quiet except for the chiming of the hall clocks. It was six-thirty.

"Are you hungry?" Linda asked. "I'll fix you something."

"No, I grabbed a couple of hamburgers with Thayer. I could use a hot cup of coffee, though."

She poured him a cup and handed it to him.

"Thanks." He leaned back wearily against the kitchen counter, sipped the coffee, and sniffled. "Sorry," he said looking at her.

She gave him a weak smile. "Sounds like you've got your sinus trouble again. You better get out of those clothes and go straight to bed."

"I intend to. Just as soon as I finish this coffee." He took another sip. "Have the Fitgeralds been around? I thought I saw Claude this morning with one of the search parties."

"Alison was here, but I sent her home. There wasn't much she could do…things being the way they are."

Paul nodded and finished his coffee, setting the cup down on the counter. "Well, I'm going to hit the sack. I feel beat." He started to leave.

Her voice stopped him. "Paul. Arrangements have to be made for Chrissie. I don't think Mom and Dad will be much help. Would you…help me?"

Paul could feel her pain. He walked over to her and put his hands on her shoulders. "Sure," he said and kissed her lightly on the lips. She didn't come into his arms. Jennifer was still between them. "Just let me get a little sleep."

He left her standing in the kitchen and walked slowly up the stairs to his bedroom. Once there, he quickly undressed and went straight to bed. His mind wandered dreamily over the day's events, especially the conversation he had with Thayer at the hamburger joint.

Somehow the talk had drifted around to Vietnam, and he remembered Thayer saying unexpectedly: "I think you're being too hard on yourself. You weren't responsible for your friends dying. Or your parents either. And, as for the breakdown, so what? A lot of people have them. You weren't the first and you won't be the last. It's nothing to be ashamed of."

At first, Paul had resented this homespun psychoanalysis. "Sounds like you missed your calling in life."

"Naw, I'm no shrink…wouldn't care to be one. Just a student of human nature. Most cops are. Like any bartender worth his salt, or a thousand-a-night whore. I guess we're somewhere in the mix."

Paul smiled and drifted off to sleep.

He slept badly; his mind haunted by a disturbing nightmare. This time it was not the war dream, but a nightmare of another shade. There were eyes everywhere. Nothing else. Just eyes. The longer he looked at them, the more he realized that they hated him. He screamed at them and told them to go away, but the eyes only mocked him and danced wildly around the room.

Then he felt something touch him. He couldn't see anything, just the eyes, but it seemed like hands were trying to pull him out of bed and drag him off to God knows where. He hung on to the bed. His body felt like a thousand maggots were crawling over it. Yelpings and howlings that no human could reproduce drilled through his ears. The room trembled and he could feel himself slipping off the bed.

When Paul woke up, he was still holding on to the bed, his body dangling precariously over its edge. The eyes were gone; the room enameled in darkness. He pushed himself away from the edge of the bed and sat up stiffly, his skin cold and sweaty. He ran a hand over his face to clear away the lingering cobwebs drifting through his mind.

The house was quiet except for the usual night noises. Outside, the wind and rain moved against the bedroom window. He reached for the nearby bed lamp and turned it on, then looked at his watch. It was four-twenty-three. He had slept for almost ten hours. If you could call it sleep.

The slight sinus headache he had when retiring had intensified during sleep and now raged at him full force. His mouth felt like the floor of an aviary. He got up slowly, slipped into his trousers and shoes and reached for the Excedrin and antihistamine tablets on the dresser.

Paul looked at the four tablets he had just dropped into his palm and shook his head. He was in great shape—sinus headache, a breakdown, those special forerunner-of-death pains that racked his body. He would make an interesting case for a JAMA article. He closed his hand over the tablets and stepped out into the hall, heading for the kitchen and a cold glass of water.

Dwayne's room was dark and Paul had an uneasy feeling as he passed it. Was it empty? Or was there something in the darkness, lurking behind the closet door? He dismissed the thought and turned away. A rational mind didn't accept the supernatural. And man was a rational animal. Wasn't he?

Thayer's theory about Dwayne's disappearance made sense. In fact, it made the only sense. Even though the thought that a killer could enter and roam through the house at free will was hard on the nerves. Maybe that's what the old priest was trying to tell him about the house. He still hadn't mentioned to anyone what Father Kerry had told him. Not even to Dwayne. And now it was too late.

Paul moved down the hall. There was a light coming from Mrs. Eastman's room. He stopped and looked to see if everything was all right. Mrs. Eastman slept soundly in the bed, her breathing regular and easy. Linda was asleep in a chair, covered with a blanket. He turned and went downstairs.

The foyer was dark, as were all the other rooms, but as he passed the library on his way to the kitchen, Paul noticed a faint light coming from the room. It was too weak to be coming from a lamp; it was more like a small night-light. He hesitated, then thought he had better look in on Eastman, too.

All the lights in the library were off. The glow was coming from the bookcase on the far side of the room. Paul followed the eldritch light to its source.

"It's the Bible," a voice said. "It's glowing."

Paul jumped. It was Eastman. He could just barely make him out in the glow, sitting in a chair by the cold ashes of the fireplace.

"Dwayne was right about this house," Eastman said. "There's evil here."

22

SMALL GROUPS OF MOURNERS stood or sat around the somber lighted room of Dunbar's Funeral Home. The building was new and exquisitely decorated. A thick blue pile rug covered the floor. A light blue couch faced the closed casket. Two winged chairs, also light blue, flanked the couch. Behind that were ten rows of walnut, straight-backed chairs, eight abreast.

The casket was flanked with large arrangements of pedestaled flowers that spread along the room's walls. A large fall spray of ferns and orange flowers rested on the lower portion of the bronze casket.

The wall behind the casket was also covered with ferns. A small, velvet kneeling stool for prayer faced it. Two burning candles, one on each side of the casket, enclosed in red glass, stood in black, four-foot holders. The cloying heaviness of flowers filled the room.

Whispers crawled spider-like among the mourners:

"Isn't it terrible?"

"What's happening to this town?"

"What are the police doing about it?"

"They ought to call in the National Guard."

Later that night, a nervous Father Kerry gave the vigil. At nine, the mourners left, and a short time after that, the immediate family left.

Chrissie Eastman was alone in the new and exquisitely decorated building.

At eight the following morning, they were all back. Father Kerry led them in the prayers and the blessing of the casket, and then quickly left for St. Casmir to prepare the burial mass.

Paul waited in the narrow hallway with the rest of the pallbearers. The hallway was closed off from the casket alcove by heavy, dark blue drapes, but the door at the other end of the hallway was open. He could see the back end of the hearse waiting for them.

"How old are you?" one of the pallbearers asked Paul. He was a small, skinny old man with heavy wrinkles on his face and neck; one of the two uncles on Mrs. Eastman's side of the family. There was another relative – a cousin or something – Paul couldn't remember which, also in the hall along with Bob Burham, Tommy's father, and Tommy.

"Thirty-three and holding," Paul told him.

"I'm sixty-two," the old pallbearer said, then looked at Mr. Burham. "You look good and strong, too. The two of you can handle the foot of the casket. That's the heaviest part."

Paul nodded stiffly and Burham shook his head in disbelief.

"The three of us are all old farts," the old man continued. "Sixty and over. We're the last of the relation."

Suddenly, the drapes to the alcove parted. The funeral director removed the casket spray and two of his attendants pushed the casket out of the alcove on a small wheeled cart where it came to rest between the pallbearers. They guided it on the cart, three on each side, to the end of the hallway, then lifted it and carried it to the hearse.

Paul walked over to his car. The Eastmans sat stiffly in the back, like they had turned to stone. Linda was in the front. She tried not to look at the hearse.

After the mass, the drive through the leaf-covered streets to Graceland Cemetery took twenty-five minutes. The wind picked up, whipping the magnetized funeral flags on the cars. They drove with their headlights on.

When they entered the cemetery, a bell began to toll, and the sky, which had been threatening all morning, dropped a light rain on the queue of cars moving slowly along the winding drive to the gravesite.

All the pallbearers assembled at the hearse and carried the casket over a carpeted path to the open grave. Strips of green carpet, like imitation grass, concealed the raw earth around it. Someone started to sob. The trees turned black with rain.

The casket was placed on straps that were suspended over what was to be Chrissie Eastman's final resting place. The pallbearers stepped off to one side and the rest of the mourners gathered around. The Eastmans all stood together. Linda was in the middle, anchoring her parents from total collapse.

Tommy Burham, who had successfully managed to hold back his tears earlier, was crying openly now, his body hunched over with grief, his fists clenched at his sides.

Thunder rumbled across the sky. Someone whispered that the rain was Chrissie's tears. Fingers of lightning poked down from the slate colored sky. One of the assistant funeral directors opened an umbrella and held it over Father Kerry. Kerry stared at the metal ribs of the umbrella over his head, his eyes widening as lightning flashed nearby. With a nervous smile, he quickly ducked out from under it and told the man to put it away.

Barbara Homes stood alone, in back of the Eastmans, her head bowed, her chin tucked tightly against her chest. She had come to pay her respects and to say goodbye to Dwayne. Although they hadn't found him yet, according to the newspaper, she was sure he was dead. In a way, they were burying Dwayne, too.

Father Kerry looked over the mourners. The crowd was silent except for occasional sobbing. Some people here today were burdened with grief; some came out of respect; others, present at all the murder-victim funerals, merely came to satisfy a morbid curiosity, like those that slow down to pass an accident on the road.

Kerry moved to the head of the casket and began the service, his voice rising in a shaky timbre.

"In nomine Patris, et Filii, et Spiritus Sancti. Amen."

The Catholics made the sign of the cross with the priest and looked at him curiously.

Father Kerry continued the service in Latin.

"Sancte Michael Archangele, defende nos in proelic; contra nequitiam et insidias diaboli esto praesidium. Imperet illi Deus; supplices deprecamur: tuque, Princeps militiae coelestis, Satanam aliosque spiritus malignos, qui ad perditionem animarum pervagantur in mundo, divina virtute in infernum detrude."

The old pallbearer who asked Paul his age looked stricken. Paul was standing next to him.

"What was all that about?" Paul whispered.

The old man hesitated, then whispered back. "Well, my church Latin's kinda rusty, but I think the priest just asked the Archangel Michael to protect us from the Devil. Funny kinda prayer to use for the burial." The old man shook his head. "He isn't supposed to give any service in Latin anymore either."

When Kerry finished the service, he blessed the casket with an aspergillum and then handed it to the funeral director who used it and passed it to Paul.

The aspergillum felt cold and wet in his hand. He made the sign of the cross over the casket and gave it to the next pallbearer.

Each mourner blessed the casket. And before everyone began drifting back to their cars, an assistant funeral director, the one who had tried to hold the umbrella over Father Kerry, thanked the people on behalf of the Eastmans.

Paul joined Linda as the rain started to fall harder now, and the mourners scurried for the shelter of their cars. Mrs. Eastman stepped forward and approached Father Kerry before he could leave.

"Father, I need your help," she said, putting her hand on his arm and anchoring him to the spot. "I know that I haven't been a very good Catholic over the years…not going to church or confession as often as I should. But I've never stopped believing. That should count for something…"

Kerry nodded, the rain plastering down his hair and streaking his glasses.

"My grandmother told me that the priest always came to bless her home when there was trouble."

Kerry stiffened.

"Maybe because we didn't have that done before…maybe that's why…" Her voice broke and her body started to shake.

Kerry was glad that the rain had streaked his glasses so he wouldn't have to look at her eyes. Please don't ask me, he thought. Please don't ask me.

She regained control of herself. "Please, Father, would you? Would you please, please bless our house?"

He couldn't see that she was staring right through him.

"Mrs. Eastman…" He put his head down. "I…I can't. Please don't ask."

She squeezed his arm. "Thank you, Father. I knew you'd understand. Things will be so much better, I know."

"Mrs. Eastman…"

"Perhaps even Dwayne will come back. He's gone, you know. I'll expect you tomorrow night. Thank you again, Father."

"Mrs. Eastman!"

Thunder smothered his words.

She turned and walked past Chrissie's casket that was dripping rain into the open grave, and down the slight incline to where Linda and Paul were waiting with her husband under the wet, morning sky.

Kerry tried to call after her again. This time his voice was lost in the start-up of the machine that would lower Chrissie Eastman's body into the ground.

23

1:30 P.M.

Debbie Ralston's mother was livid.

"You're getting raisins all over my kitchen floor!" She screamed from her wheelchair.

"Oh, Mother," Debbie moaned and made a face that was burdened with the pain of tolerance. She was making oatmeal with raisins and in the process of her cooking, spilled some raisins on the floor.

"Just look at this mess," Mrs. Ralston said. "I'm getting them all over my wheels."

Debbie lifted her eyes to the ceiling, beseeching God to have mercy and spare her from this. Big deal, she thought. No wonder her father had to come home drunk every night. "Really, Mother, I'll pick them all up."

Florence Ralston, whose color was coming back into her face now, (if you could call milky-white her natural color) was picking raisins off the wheels of her chair and distastefully dropping them on the floor like squashed bugs.

"Why are you making oatmeal now?" she asked. "You just finished eating lunch an hour ago."

"Because I just feel like having some oatmeal. It's no big thing."

"No, the 'big thing' is going over to Dicky Walters' again tonight. You just make sure you're home early," she said, pointing a pale finger at Debbie.

Florence Ralston was a small, delicately featured woman with honey-blond hair, who was once voted the prettiest girl in high school. She had met Arnie Ralston a year after the Korean War, and was bedded and wedded, in that order, soon afterward. She had never wanted children, but when Debbie accidentally came along, there was not much she could do about the situation.

It was after the childbearing that she decided her health had definitely begun to fail. Consequently, the lovemaking became less and less frequent (it was an endangered species, according to her husband) and finally nonexistent. The last ten years, she was in bed more than she was up (Arnie told her she'd lie down if she had a hangnail) and saw her doctor at least once a week. The wheelchair was her latest panacea; a move to conserve her energy.

"Mother, Dicky only lives a block away," Debbie said.

"I don't care. It's bad enough your father comes home late every night. I don't want to have to worry about you, too."

Debbie couldn't picture her mother worrying about anyone but herself. "It's his bowling night."

"What?" Mrs. Ralston picked off several more raisins and dropped them on the floor.

"Tonight's his bowling night. Dad's never home till late."

"Bowling." She made a distasteful face, as if she had eaten something disagreeable. "If people had any sense, they wouldn't go out at all until the police caught that lunatic."

Debbie shut off the stove and sampled the oatmeal. "People really couldn't do that, Mother. Life has to go on."

"Ha, a lot you know about life. Just make sure you pick up every one of those raisins – and be home early tonight."

"Dicky's going to call for me."

"Make sure he walks you home after. You hear me?"

"Yes, Mother," Debbie said, stabbing the oatmeal with her spoon.

Satisfied, Mrs. Ralston turned her chair, picked off another raisin and wheeled into the living room.

Debbie shook her head. She didn't understand her mother. She thought it would please her that she was doing her own cooking and didn't have to bother her for anything, but all she did was scream.

She spooned the oatmeal into a bowl and sat down at the kitchen table. In her sixteen years of her young life, she couldn't remember a time when her mother wasn't sick or complaining about something. Daddy called her Mrs. Hypochondriac. Poor Daddy, no wonder he hated to come home.

She ate her oatmeal and tried not to think about her mother. There were other, better thoughts to dwell on. For one, she was a very pretty girl and a very popular one, and she knew it. Everyone said she was the best looking girl at Lanark High School. She knew how the boys, and even some men, ogled her, always looking at her legs or at her boobs. She saw the desire in their eyes and felt their yearning.

But no one had her yet. Although, she did let Dicky Walters, the second most popular boy in school, suck her boobs and put his finger in her...thing. Since then, he's been after her to go all the way. But she remained resolute.

Being the most popular girl in school, she always felt she should save herself for the most popular boy, Dwayne Eastman. All the girls were crazy about him, but he wasn't making it with anyone. He dated, but nothing ever happened. Ruthie Beerworth said he just kissed her lightly on the mouth when he dropped her off after their date and said goodnight.

Maybe he really was sleeping with Miss Homes like they say. But for the life of her, Debbie couldn't imagine anyone ever getting close to Miss Morals, let alone in her bed. But maybe Miss Homes was different when she was alone.

She had to admit that she didn't know everything. Her mother never told her anything at all. She had to learn about menstruation and sex from her girlfriends. If it wouldn't have been for them, she probably would still think dumb stuff like you got pregnant when a boy kissed you, or that you were bleeding to death when it was actually just your time of the month.

Debbie sighed. All that was academic now. Dwayne was missing – probably dead. Just like the others.

She finished her oatmeal, rinsed the bowl out and set it on the sink. Dicky Walters came back into her thoughts. She had sort of a date with him tonight, promising to come over to his house and help him with his geometry.

Bending down resignedly, she started to pick up the raisins on the kitchen floor.

Dicky would probably try to get in her pants again tonight, like he always did.

God, she wished Dwayne Eastman was still alive.

2:20 P.M.

Thayer sat in his office going over everything in his mind again and again, and again. He had gotten into a shouting match earlier with Pat Donahue, who looked more like a bartender than he did Mayor of Lanark. Donahue was screaming for some results. He wanted this son of a bitch caught, and he wanted it done before there was another murder. Thayer informed him, in much the same language, that he wanted the same thing.

In fact, Thayer had suggested that Donahue might ask the governor to bring in the National Guard to help patrol the streets at night. His Honor said he'd think about it. But he didn't want to do that unless it was absolutely necessary. A move like that would make everyone look bad – like we couldn't handle it ourselves. Thayer knew what Donahue really meant was that it would make him look bad, and he had aspirations of becoming governor some day.

They settled on a curfew.

Thayer wanted it early, as soon as it was dark. But Donahue felt that an early curfew would be bad for the business community. He held out for ten o'clock. That way everyone would be happy. The merchants, restaurants, and other businesses wouldn't suffer a financial loss, and the public would be satisfied that something was being done.

Thayer had reminded him that all four – and possibly five –

murders took place prior to 10 p.m. But Donahue pointed out, in his own wordy way, that two of the murders happened right in the victim's own home. So what was the sense of a curfew at all? Ten o'clock would be early enough. Effective tomorrow night.

Thayer had left before he really got mad. Politicians always gave him a pain in the ass. And Donahue was the biggest ass-pain around.

2:35 P.M.

He had been good out there today.

That Latin service really zonked their minds.

Then Mrs. Eastman had to spoil it.

Shit.

It was starting again.

The fear was back.

Had it ever left?

Kerry slumped behind his old rectory desk and eased the heavy burden of the cross he carried with another brandy. Didn't that woman realize what she was asking him? Evidently not. Christ had struggled with His cross to Calvary for part of a day. He had struggled with his cross for almost ten years. There were times when he would have gladly traded places.

He sat in his chair like a shriveled, old leprechaun that had lost his magical power, staring into his drink, hoping it would restore his faith, but knowing sadly that it never would.

Things hadn't been that bad. If you overlook the fact that he had to drink himself to sleep sometimes. But now they were starting up again, and he feared that he would not be able to do anything about it. He just didn't have what it takes anymore. He could just see himself telling the Bishop that he was scared shitless.

The Bishop would just look at him with those black, piercing Welsh eyes of his and say, "Now, Justin, all you need is a little rest. Get your mind off things. Take a vacation."

Then Kerry would be shipped off to Arizona again to dry out, and, after a time, he would come back and be all right. Since the last time, he had been all right for quite a while. Then they found Ralphie Gordon cut to ribbons, and he knew it was starting again.

He took a long swallow of the brandy. He should have stayed an instructor. Things were so much simpler then. You taught others in the faith. You didn't have to practice it.

There, he could have written a paper on the lighter side of metaphysics, one he had been planning for years. Here, faced with the darker side of the coin, he wasn't able to cope. He had tried to put it all down on paper. Just as it had happened. To exorcise on paper what he couldn't with prayer. It didn't work. He took another drink. His mother had told him he'd make a fine priest. And when she died, rotting with disease, it had shaken him, jumbled his beliefs. She had been a fine woman, and he couldn't understand why God had taken her in such a way.

She hadn't been afraid to die. Father Kellog, the family priest, had told her that death was wonderful. Heaven was waiting. If people knew the truth, they would kill themselves to get there.

Kerry always had the urge to drag Father Kellog out of his safe niche in Madison and up to Durie House. Then he'd see what the good Father had to say about death.

Kellog had never seen what he had seen; never heard what he had heard.

They told him they'd get him. They'd wait, but they'd get him.

He poured another drink and tried to drown out the vivid image of that night.

3:30 P.M.

Pearl Armstrong was watching TV as usual. Only this time, her dead husband's shotgun was within the same easy reach as her whiskey bottle. If anyone came around, they'd have a hell of a time getting at her, she mused. She'd empty both barrels into the killer. She'd not be as easy a victim as the others.

A TV movie was just starting. It was a Thin Man mystery starring William Powell and Myrna Loy. Her tea, still on the table next to her, was just about the right temperature now. She reached for the Old Crow.

4:45 P.M.

Saturday's child.

That's what she must be.

Now how did that old rhyme go? Monday's child is fair of face. Tuesday's child is full of grace. Wednesday's child is full of woe. Thursday's child has far to go. Friday's child is loving and giving. Saturday's child has to work for its living. But a child that's born on the Sabbath Day is fair and wise and good and gay.

That was it. Alison Fitgerald sighed resignedly. If only she would have been born on a Sunday. A Monday would have been all right, too; although, in her younger days she hadn't been a bad looker. There were those that even told her she'd look good in a burlap sack. She looked down at her body. Not anymore, though. She looked like a sack. All bumps and lumps.

Saturday's child.

That's what she was.

And if that wasn't bad enough, she was a Capricorn. Even her horoscope said the only way she'd ever have any money is by going out and working for it. No easy rides. But doing for others is all she ever knew. Probably all she'd ever know. It was too late for her to learn anything new now. Best to stick at what she did better than most.

Of course, if the spirits helped her that would be different. And they did sometimes, if you knew how to ask. The spirits would do anything for you. They knew all there is to know. Could do all there is to do. Even though they were dead. But you could still talk to them, if you had a mind to. And they'd talk right back to you. Yes, they would. Some folks didn't believe that, but you could. Maybe she'd call on a few and change some things around here. She nodded to herself. Yes, she just might do that.

Alison sat in the living room of her small cottage with the lights off and watched the evening shadows lengthen across the carpet. The chair she sat in was her chair, the one she had picked out at Haskel's Furniture Store here in Lanark, and always fell asleep in after returning home and making do for Claude. It was soft and velvety, and easy to dream in.

In her dreams, she saw herself young again, dressed in the best clothes money could buy. She had the best of everything. All the luxuries a body could want. And all the men wanted her.

God, her feet hurt. She untied the laces of her white orthopedic shoes and eased them off. Immediate relief circulated through them. She wiggled her toes in freedom. This was the best part of the day. Or it would be if Claude would stay home.

He told her he was going out after supper, going to line up a few jobs. That was a lie. She could always tell when he was lying. He probably found some woman that he wanted to sneak a peek at. The way he does at the Eastman women. It's a wonder Mr. Eastman hasn't had a word with him about it. Not that it would do any good. Claude would just get sullen, then after a while he'd start all over again. But that's the way it was with men. Always looking for some new place to put it in.

Alison looked around the room, at the tired walls that needed painting, at the new but cheaply made furniture that reflected unfilled dreams, and last at her large, aging body with heavy arms and sore feet. She put her hands to her face and traced the wrinkled and loose skin that had set in. She felt her arms. They were a man's arms. Claude called her muscle-bound. She let them drop to the chair and started to cry.

It was terrible to grow old and be alone. Claude hadn't touched her in months. Said he had trouble getting it up now. Probably didn't have any trouble getting it up for anyone else.

She tried to wipe away the tears with the back of her hand, but they kept coming. She reached over to her purse, on a nearby lamp table, fished out some tissue and blew her nose.

She wished she was young again, with a body that would laugh at age and a soul that would not know loneliness or indifference. She didn't know which of the three was worst.

Together, they formed the unholy three. A three pronged spear of pestilence. That was the pale horse. Not death, but old age, loneliness, and indifference. Yes, that was true. They rode together.

Alison blew her nose again. There must be something she could do about it. Something she must do about it.

The house grew dark and creaked and moaned, like an old man with painful joints, feeling the cold night air settle deep into its bones. Alison continued to cry. She didn't turn on a light. The darkness was soothing. She could no longer see herself.

5:30 P.M.

Fred Owens checked the doors and windows for the third time in the last half hour. Satisfied that everything was secure, he returned to his chair in the living room.

There had been no strange noises around his house this evening. Only the rain tapping against the side of the house and drumming on the roof. And that's the way he wanted to keep it. He had on every light in the house, including the outside lights.

There was plenty of coffee on the stove, and the TV programming would run late into the morning. If need be, he had a few books he could read to tide him over until dawn. He was ready for his vigil.

Fred didn't sleep at night anymore. Not since the early morning encounter in his backyard and the strange murders taking place in Lanark. He was sure, with a certainty that he could almost touch, that someone was stalking him, trying to get in the house and kill him like the others. He shivered at the thought.

The house creaked. He snapped his head around and tried to locate the source. It was just the house settling.

After his heart climbed back down into his chest, he thought seriously about going over to Webb Miller's gun shop tomorrow and buying a gun.

Tim Gorman, feeling his whiskey and trying to be funny, told Fred, down at Booker's this morning, that the rain and the killings would continue for forty days and forty nights.

Remembering it now, Fred still didn't think it was funny.

6:10 P.M.

Shane sat by the front door and looked imploringly at his master.

"No walk tonight, Shane," Frank Bojold said. "It's raining. You'll just have to be satisfied with a romp in the backyard."

He took the big shepherd by the collar and led him to the back door, then opened it. The dog hesitated in the doorway.

"Go on. Do your duty and hurry back in. And don't go where the grass is dying. It looks bad enough the way it is."

Shane looked back at him and then went out.

Bojold closed the door behind him. The rain was as good an excuse as any. Actually, he hadn't taken the dog out for an evening walk since the night Fred Owens told him to go home, and he wasn't about to go out again until the streets were safe.

Sally Bojold joined her husband in the kitchen. They waited in silence for Shane to come back in, so they could lock the door securely again.

After a while, Sally broke the silence. "Why is everything dying in this town? People…trees…grass…"

Frank shook his head. He didn't know, and he wasn't sure he wanted to.

7:20 P.M.

Ruth Hanson looked at the store clock. The way the time was dragging, she thought her watch had stopped. Thank God her day was almost over. In less than two hours she could go home and try to sleep in that house. She probably wouldn't make it. Not without help. Not without the sleeping pills.

But she wouldn't take those until she talked to Aaron. Her son-in-law called every night now since returning to New Orleans. He had come to Lanark to bury Jennifer, then quickly left on the next plane out.

Ruth would listen to him.

She would be sympathetic.

And after a while, they would both cry.

7:45 A.M.

"That was pretty good, missy," Claude said.

He had just ejaculated and was resting his full weight on Barbara Homes, wishing he could get another erection so he could indulge himself again.

Barbara grimaced under him and turned her head away.

This was pretty good stuff, Claude thought. Better than screwin' his muscle-bound wife – that was like doin' it with a man. He shook his head. He couldn't imagine how he had stood it all these years.

He sighed philosophically. No erection was forthcoming. Hell, he might as well get up. He disengaged himself and stood at the side of the bed, looking down at her.

"Still not talkin', missy?" Claude asked.

Barbara never talked to him. Never acknowledged his presence when he was with her. She just let him in, gave him a drink when he asked for one (most of the time he just helped himself), went into the bedroom, took off her clothes, and laid passively on the bed until he left.

Bitch, Claude thought. Couldn't even tell if she liked gettin' it or not. Just lays there like a goddamn piece of wood. Christ, it had to be better than that little peanut of a thing the Eastman kid probably had to stick in her. She didn't say nothin' about her little boyfriend being gone now either. Missing and presumed dead, like they say in the army.

Hell, he didn't care if she talked or not. She could be deaf and dumb for all that it mattered.

After he had dressed, Claude stopped in the bedroom doorway and looked back at her. She was still on the bed. She hadn't moved, except to cover herself.

"See you in a couple of days, missy," Claude said. "Or maybe sooner if I get the urge."

Barbara waited until she heard the front door close before she dragged herself up. She'd take a shower as she always did after he left and try to wash some of the filth off of her.

She walked into the bathroom, flipped on the lights, and started to run the shower. A few moments later, she began to cry.

God, she hated that vile old man.

She'd like to cut his throat.

8:05 P.M.

Outside, the rain fell in fine, straight lines that seemed to be slackening. Claude pulled up his jacket collar and stepped off the porch. His old Chevy pickup was parked down the road, about a block from the house. He looked around, then headed for it. The rain felt cold against his face.

Halfway to his truck he stopped and looked around again. He had the strange feeling that someone was close by, watching him. The road was empty. There was nothing but the night and the rain. But he was sure someone was near. He kept on walking.

When he reached the pickup, he paused again, taking another look around. Thunder grumbled distantly over the lake. He opened the cab door and stepped into a puddle. The water rose over the top of his tennis shoe and soaked his foot.

"Son of a bitch." Claude pulled his foot out quickly and tried to shake it dry, then stopped. The feeling of being watched was still with him. Stronger than before. Someone was nearby. Closer than before.

He pulled his baseball cap down tighter on his head and sloshed over to the pickup, getting in quickly. The engine roared into life and the truck rattled down the road.

A pair of white orthopedic shoes stepped out into the road and watched the pickup's taillights disappear in the rain.

8:30 P.M.

Linda looked in on her mother. She was asleep on the top of the bed, still wearing her clothes from the funeral. Linda tiptoed in and covered her with a robe that was laying across one of the bedroom chairs. She stood and watched her for a while before turning off all but one of the lamps and tiptoeing out again.

Her mother was sedated most of the time now and that was probably best. She had taken it hard, but then, so had her father. Both of them had nearly collapsed on her at the funeral, and she was sure they hadn't spoken a word to each other since this nightmare started.

Thinking of her father, Linda suddenly wondered where he was now. She hadn't seen him since he was downstairs – and that was over an hour ago. On impulse, she stopped at Dwayne's room and looked in. She could just make out his image from the glow of the hall light. He was sitting in the dark.

"Dad," Linda called softly from the doorway. "Dad, are you all right?"

He didn't answer.

She entered the room and turned on the lamp next to him on the night table. "Dad." She shook him gently on the shoulder. "Dad."

He just sat in the chair, staring at the closet.

She shook him a little harder. "Dad."

"Huh?" He blinked at her. His mind seemed to be fighting its way back from very far away. He managed to focus in on her. "I'm sorry…did you say something?"

"I just asked if you were all right."

"All right? Yes…of course…I'm fine."

Linda folded her arms for warmth. The room was cold and damp.

"Dad, it's freezing in here. Why don't you come downstairs? I'll make a fire in the library and you can sit in your chair and have a nice warm brandy. It will make you feel better. Dad…?"

His eyes had turned back to the closet. "I want to stay here for a while."

He looked rather pale and Linda felt his forehead. It was like ice. "Dad, you'll catch a cold sitting up here. Come downstairs."

He didn't answer her.

She relented. "All right. But only for a little while. Then come down to the library. Okay?"

He nodded slowly. "Okay."

She kissed him gently on the forehead and left the room with one last backward glance. She wished he'd come with her instead of sitting in here like that.

When he heard her on the stairs, Eastman reached over and turned off the lamp. Then he brought out the small .380 Llama automatic from his trouser pocket and held it on his lap. If there was something in this room, he wanted to face it head on.

Paul had just finished building a fire in the massive fireplace and pouring two brandies when Linda entered the library.

"Oh, good," Linda said. "You made a fire. It makes the house more pleasant."

"I thought it was getting too Gothic around here." He handed her a brandy. "Here, take this. You look like you could use it." She looked weary and cold. "Where is everybody?"

Linda took the glass and managed a small sip. "Mom's asleep. I gave her two of those pills the doctor prescribed. She dropped off right away. And Dad's sitting up in Dwayne's room. I don't know how he can stand it. It's freezing up there."

Paul turned toward the foyer, his eyes resting on the stairs.

Linda shivered and moved closer to the fire. "Can't say much for the rest of the house either." She hugged herself for warmth. "God, it gets cold in here lately. But maybe I'm just tired." She turned back to face him.

Paul was still at the bar, looking out into the hall.

"Paul, is something wrong?"

He turned to her. "What?"

"Is something wrong?"

"I don't know. I was just thinking about your father – upstairs in that room."

"I asked him to come down, but he said he wanted to stay there for a while. I think he's taking it worse than my mother."

Paul took a drink of his brandy. "Yeah, I guess he would."

Their eyes met and Paul looked away.

"You mean because he locked Dwayne in that room?" Linda said.

Paul didn't answer.

"I know what you're thinking. That Dwayne would still be here if Dad hadn't locked him up in there. Dad was just trying to help Dwayne in his own way. He thought –"

"I know what he thought," Paul said. Right now Eastman wasn't one of his favorite people. He wasn't sure he even liked the man.

"You can't blame him, really. Dwayne must have gotten out some way and met…" Her voice faltered. "Anyway, I don't believe there's anything wrong with that closet. Things don't just pop out of closets and carry you off somewhere."

"Dwayne's missing. And the police have been all over the house and still haven't found any secret passageways."

Her eyes flashed with anger. "I suppose you're an authority on closets."

"Everyone has a closet in their life. Some fear they'd rather not face."

"Paul Rice, philosopher." Her voice had an edge to it.

"You're getting angry at me again."

She turned and stared into the flames. "I suppose I am. It's just that so much has happened. And you make me mad sometimes. I wanted this visit to be so good. I wanted everything to be..." Her voice started to break.

Paul moved over to her and took her in his arms. She pressed her face into his chest. "Oh, Paul, I'm sorry. I'm sorry about Jennifer, too. I guess I was just jealous and didn't know what to do about it and now Dwayne's missing and Chrissie's dead. God, why is all this happening?"

Paul held her tightly and kissed her hair. He wished he could give her an answer, but anything he could say would be inadequate.

She looked up at him. "I love you, Paul. I love you more than anything in this world."

He kissed her. It seemed like years since she was last in his arms.

"I don't know what I would have done if you hadn't been here." Her eyes misted over. She started to cry, her body shook with sobs.

"Cry it all out," Paul said, holding her as she buried her face against him. She was quite a girl, he thought. She had expressed an unspoken grief through this whole rotten mess, never once breaking down – until now.

He held her until she stopped. There wasn't much more he could do. Words were so weak at times. And this was the first time he had seen her cry. It made him feel empty inside.

He took their brandy glasses and set them on the mantel. "Come on, I've got some coffee on in the kitchen." He gave her his handkerchief. "The coffee will taste good after the brandy."

She dried her eyes and blew her nose. "Did Alison leave yet?"

"Hours ago. She made up some sandwiches before she left."

"I'm not very hungry. Maybe just coffee."

"Okay, one cup of coffee and..."

"And what?" She looked at him suspiciously.

"And you can watch me eat."

She laughed and he took her hand and led her into the foyer.

The red light of the coffeemaker glared at them from the dark kitchen until Paul switched on the overhead light. He poured the coffee as Linda sat down at the kitchen table.

Paul handed her a cup and sat down opposite her with a cup of his own.

"Thank you," Linda said. "You'll make some woman a fine husband."

"You think so, huh?"

"I know so."

Paul glanced up at the window over the sink. A black patch of darkness hung there like a picture. He dropped his eyes to Linda. "I think it would be a good idea if we got your father out of that room."

Linda sipped her coffee and frowned. She put her cup down. "Why?"

"Let's just say I think he shouldn't be up there alone."

"You're beginning to sound like..." her voice almost broke "...my brother. It's just a house, Paul. Just a room – stone and wood and plaster. What phantoms can be conjured out of that?"

He paused with thought and looked into his cup of coffee. What could he tell her? That the chemistry of the house felt bad, or that the malevolent ghost of some Durie stalked the rooms. He didn't actually believe in ghosts, and yet he could have sworn that he saw his father appear before him on the night he was buried.

Paul shrugged. "What can I say?"

"Do you really think there's something wrong with this house?"

"Dwayne thought so."

"I'm not asking about my brother. I know how he felt. I want to know what you think. A simple yes or no answer."

Paul paused again. "Yes. I think there's something wrong with this house." Then he told her what Father Kerry wanted with him that day at his rectory.

Afterward, Linda sat quietly and drank her coffee. The idea was absurd. She didn't believe in haunted houses. Paul and Father Kerry were just embellishing Dwayne's obsession with Durie House. There was no doubt in her mind that they would find a simple, logical explanation for her brother's disappearance eventually.

Perhaps Paul was just upset over the recent killings. God, they all were. But she didn't think he was really over Vietnam yet. Maybe Father Kerry triggered his imagination into believing in ghosts and goblins. If he would just calm himself and reason things out, she was sure he could exorcise all his suspicions about the house.

"Paul," she said finally, "Father Kerry told my father the same thing. He's just an old man. Maybe too old."

Paul held up his hand to stop her. "Okay, so we're both senile, but just to humor me, let's get your father out of that room."

She set her coffee cup down and studied his face. Was the strain of the last few days affecting him, too? Now he was beginning to jump at shadows and back away from half-open doors. She pushed away from the table and got up. "All right. Just to humor you. But I still think you're being silly."

After his daughter had gone downstairs, Eastman flicked off the Llama's safety and chambered a cartridge. He was probably being stupid, he thought, sitting here in the dark, waiting for God knows what to come out of a closet, of all places. He did not believe in phantoms of evil, but he did believe in the flesh and blood variety. And yet he still couldn't explain to himself with any satisfaction why the Bible in the library was glowing, or his reaction to it at the time.

But this was an old house and maybe, just maybe, there was some sort of passageway that led from the outside to this room or from another secret room inside the house. Dwayne had suspected something of the sort, and, God forgive him, he hadn't believed him. If only he would have listened. If. A big word. A very big word. Filled with endless possibilities.

Well, he would see. They say that criminals always return to the scene of the crime. If that was true, this one would be in for a big surprise, for Eastman half believed, with a feeling that was rapidly growing into conviction, that whoever was killing people in this town had somehow gotten into this house – this room – and dragged his son off. Either that or the stories about Allan Durie still being alive and in this house were true.

But he had to do something. He was sure his wife, who had pointedly avoided him since their tragic loss of the children, hated him now; the distance between them growing steadily wider for the unforgivable thing she felt he had done. So he had to redeem himself in her eyes. He had never thought to ask her forgiveness. The loss of his son and daughter was bad enough, but he still felt he had done nothing wrong as far as Dwayne was concerned. To ask her pardon would have been too much to bear.

When a woman married, she became one with her husband. His thoughts were her thoughts. His way was her way. His decisions were her decisions. There was no arguing, no difference of opinion. That's the way it always had been with the Eastman women.

But Helen had hurt him deeply. Her reaction had been uncalled for. She had shamed him in front of strangers, made him look inadequate and –

Suddenly Eastman thought he heard the tingling of bells from a long way off. He strained to listen. There was a faint babble of voices, like a crowd of people all talking at the same time. It was probably coming from downstairs. Maybe some people had dropped in.

He kept listening. No, this wasn't coming from downstairs. It was coming from the closet. It seemed to be getting louder now, and he could hear something else. A sloshing sound. Like someone was walking in shoes filled with water.

He became rigid. The noises were building. They were right inside his head now. He heard his name being called over and over. And then, the sadness came. He had never felt such utter despair well up in him before. So much so, that he wanted to cry out the loneliness and sorrow that was now flooding through him in an overwhelming tide.

Eastman covered his ears with his hands, but it was no use. The voices were inside him now. They were part of him.

And the door. Was it opening, ever so slowly, or was that just a trick of his eyes, of the darkness that enveloped him? No. It was moving. He tried to bring his hands down, away from his ears, and pick up the automatic, but he could move them no farther than the arms of the chair. The door was tantalizing him into paralysis. It was like watching a snake slither closer and closer, numbing every nerve of his body with its creeping movement.

It was the rat crawling up his leg all over again, inch by inch, but this time he couldn't run home; he couldn't even move. What he felt now was beyond comprehension – beyond sanity.

He tried to scream, but the words for help never left his throat. They were frozen, as was his mind and heart. Everything was locked inside him now, petrified into a solid fear, an endless nightmare of insanity locked within.

The voices hissed in his brain.

The door opened.

Eastman felt a stab of pain in his chest, like a cold hand squeezing his heart.

His eyes went wide, his mouth opened slightly in a silent scream, but the only form of protest that he could manage against what was invading him was to slump forward and fall on the floor.

Ten minutes later, that's how Linda and Paul found him.

Only Paul noticed the smell.

9:01 P.M.

"I thought you needed help with your geometry?" Debbie Ralston said. "Not with your sex life."

“Well, I could use some help along those lines, too,” Dicky Walters grinned. He was a good-looking boy with flashy white teeth, a cocky smile, and the easy grace of a natural athlete.

“Just relax. Here, have another toke.” He handed her the reefer.

She pushed it away. “One was enough.”

“It’s good stuff. Mexican.” He shoved it at her again.

“I don’t want anymore. I don’t want to get high.”

They were sitting on the couch in the Walters’ spacious living room. Dicky had all the lights turned off except a small amber base light of a lamp.

Dicky took another toke.

“Your parents are gonna smell that stuff when they get home,” Debbie warned.

“Naw, I’ve done this lots of times. They never say anything. I think they smoke a little themselves.”

All the same, Debbie noticed that he pinched out the marijuana and put the butt in his shirt pocket, then got up and opened a window.

“Now where were we?” he said, sliding up next to her and resting a hand on her thigh.

“Look, Dicky, just because I let you touch me once doesn’t mean I want you putting your fingers in me all the time.”

In a moment of passion last summer, she had let him finger her while on a date at a drive-in movie. When he tried to use something else, she stubbornly refused and he took her home in a huff.

“I don’t want to put my finger in you,” he said, putting his arm around her and flashing his bedroom, brown eyes.

Debbie moved away from him, sliding farther down the long, white couch. “Get your geometry book.”

Dicky reacted, closing the distance between them with a quickness of movement that would have brought a smile to the lips of his football coach.

Her eyes shifted down to the huge bulge in the front of his pants and she thought of what Doris Carr, who had done it with Dicky, told her: “He’s got the biggest, hairiest thing you ever saw.” And Sue Watts, who also had the pleasure: “God, I thought it was comin’ out the other end."

"Come on," he said, looking into her eyes, then down at her breasts. "I know you like me."

"I like you," Debbie said, pushing his hand away as it started to cup her breast. "But that doesn't mean I want to go hopping off to bed with you."

She really didn't know why she said that. Actually, she wouldn't mind doing it with him. Maybe, she tried to convince herself, it was the pain involved with the first time that frightened her.

Doris Carr had told her: "Honest, Debbie, it just hurts a little when they bust your cherry. But after that, boy, oh boy, oh boy!"

But did she want to suffer that pain with Dicky Walters? He seemed rather insensitive most of the time. And besides, she had always secretly hoped that Dwayne Eastman would be the one that would do it.

She heard Doris Carr's voice again: "If you're waiting for Dwayne Eastman to break it for you, you'll be old and gray, and have cobwebs on it. Besides, he's probably all cut up and dead by now."

Dicky ignored her last rebuff and kissed her neck.

"Your mom and dad will be home soon," she said.

"They won't be back for a while yet," he assured her between kisses. "I told you they're bowling down at Reynolds' Lanes. We've got plenty of time."

He pulled her to him and kissed her hard, forcing his tongue into her mouth.

Debbie gagged and shoved him away.

Dicky sat back and looked at her. His eyes were hard.

"What the hell's the matter with you? When we're around other kids, you flounce around and act like we're makin' it together, but when we're alone, it's this hands off shit. Some of the other guys say the same thing. In front of an audience you're Miss Warmth, but alone with a guy you're nothin' but a cold fish."

Silence spread between them. His face flushed with anger.

He turned on her again. "You know what you are? You're nothin' but a goddamn prick tease! You get your jollies off by gettin' a guy all hot and bothered!"

Tears stung her eyes. "I am not," she cried. "I am not a prick... what you said."

"You're a prick tease!" he shouted. "You're the biggest goddamn prick tease in Lanark High School! Probably the biggest in the whole world!"

Debbie cried openly now. "Dicky Walters, you take that back!"

"Shit!"

"If you don't take that back, I'll never speak to you again as long as I live."

"Who cares. You only talk about dumb stuff, anyway."

She jumped up from the couch. "I'm going home."

He got up quickly and indicated the door with a jerk of his thumb. "Good, there's the door."

She stormed toward the door, then stopped and turned back to him. "Where's my coat?"

He stomped into his bedroom, came out with her coat, and threw it at her. "Here!"

She put it on quickly, not bothering to button it, then fumbled with the door and ran out.

Dicky almost called her back, but he fought down the impulse and closed the door.

Outside, the hard rain had turned into a fine mist. Debbie walked with her head down, tears rolled down her cheeks. Wet leaves, pressed into the sidewalk like dead flowers, stuck to her shoes. A slight wind blew rain from the trees.

She only had a short distance to go now, about half a block, and she'd be home. But she couldn't stop crying. She wiped at her eyes with the back of her hand. One day she'd make him pay, she thought. He'd be sorry. She'd make him crawl for all those hateful things he said to her.

As she neared the thick bushes that crowded the sidewalk from the Palmer's lawn, she heard someone in back of her. She knew Dicky would come after her, but it was too late. As far as she was concerned, she would have nothing more to do with him.

She whirled around to face him. "Dicky Walters, you can just go right back—"

A strong hand clamped across her mouth. She was lifted off her feet and carried silently between two houses, two doors away from her home.

9:25 P.M.

Sollis locked all the doors.

He had followed the necessary fasting during the last three days and was ready to start the ceremony. He went into his bedroom and turned on the light, removed all his clothes, then padded barefoot into the shower and washed thoroughly.

Stepping out of the shower, he grabbed a large bath towel and dried himself off. Once he had begun, he didn't have to worry about being interrupted, because no one came over unless invited. He knew that the slightest interruption in the ceremony could be dangerous.

He went back into his bedroom and reached into the back recesses of his closet, bringing out the black, silk ritual robe with an inverted pentagram embroidered over the breast. He put it on. Then he brought out the black sandals and put those on. Next, he took an envelope out of his top bureau drawer and carried it into the kitchen. He turned on the basement lights and unlocked the basement door.

After going down the stairs, he moved toward the door of the special room he had built five years ago. He unlocked the door and stepped in, then struck a match and lit the black candles on a nearby table, for the room contained no electric lighting.

Picking up the candelabrum, he approached the altar, which stood in the middle of a nine foot circle. Everything on the altar was ready, as it always was for the next ceremony. Sollis started with the preliminaries, making all the movements counterclockwise.

Outside the circle, the forces waited. Inside the circle, which Sollis had closed with his ritual stick after stepping through, he took the lock of hair from the envelope, cupped it to his chest with both hands, and started the summoning.

"My purpose is to enslave a partner," Sollis began.

“I wish to make Debbie Ralston a slave to my commands, obedient to my wishes, and willing to submit to all my desires. Bring her forth now.”

He repeated this eleven times, then knelt and whispered to the earth the name of an evil one suited for this purpose.

Afterward, he finished with the dismissing part of the ritual, thanking and ordering all forces back to where they belong. Then he waited, trying to detect any force that had not obeyed his dismissal and might be waiting for him outside the circle. Feeling none, he opened the circle and stepped out. It was safe.

Extinguishing all the candles and locking the door behind him, Sollis went upstairs to prepare himself for Debbie Ralston.

9:55 P.M.

Arnie Ralston, Debbie’s father, and Lester Heywood were leaving Smokey’s Lounge in a huff – mainly because Smokey refused to serve them any more drinks.

“You’re no gentleman,” Arnie shouted to Smokey from the door, being careful to pronounce every word correctly as further proof of his sobriety. “And not a very good innkeeper either.”

Lester tried to parrot Arnie’s indignation by standing on his tiptoes and glaring at Smokey over Arnie’s shoulder, but the height was too much for him and he fell against Arnie. The two of them almost fell down, but somehow managed to get their legs going in the right direction and kept their balance.

Smokey cocked a baleful eye at them from behind the knotty pine décor of his bar. Hunting and fishing trophies decorated all the walls.

“Out!” Smokey bellowed. He glued his eyes on them like the twin barrels of one of his shotguns. “Go home and sleep it off! And don’t drive!”

Arnie and Lester tried to match his stare, putting on a show of being highly insulted.

Even though there was still a killer running loose in Lanark, the bar was crowded. It was bowling night, and Smokey’s was an habitual stopping off spot for a sandwich and nightcap before heading home.

Besides, many people felt there was safety in numbers.

"Close the damn door!" One of the patrons shouted from the bar. "It's cold outside."

"Yeah," another added. "Go home and sober up."

Arnie and Lester, each in turn, broke off their staring duel with Smokey like men suddenly coming out of a deep coma. Then, each in turn again straightened his clothes and left, letting the door swing shut behind them.

"Where'd ya put yer car?" Arnie asked Lester once they were outside.

Lester furrowed his brow and tried to look thoughtful, but his eyes lacked the concentration. "I dunno," he said finally.

"Must be in the back," Arnie suggested.

"Must be."

They staggered around the corner of the building to the parking lot, inseparable in their stupors as when they were sober. Arnie and Lester had grown up together, gone to the same schools, served with the same outfit in Korea, married their respective girls in the same year, settled down, and lived one block from each other on Cornet Drive.

They were known as the Mutt and Jeff of the bowling team that was sponsored by Smokey's Lounge. Whereas Arnie was tall and angular, Lester was short and square. They would have made an excellent Leo Gorcey and Huntz Hall, except Arnie had a perfectly straight nose and both wore glasses.

They stopped at a new Buick, wet and glistening under the evening mist. Arnie tried the door. It was locked. "You got the key?"

Lester fumbled in his pockets, spilling change on the wet blacktop of the parking lot. He finally succeeded in cupping everything in his hands and then very carefully peeked through his thumbs at the assortment. "Can't seem to find 'em," he mumbled.

"Look in yer back pockets," Arnie said, leaning against the Buick.

Lester tried holding everything with one hand, spilling more change, and searched his back pockets with his free hand. He was about to tell Arnie that he must have lost them when he suddenly stopped his search and got a funny look on his face, like he had just remembered something important.

He swayed closer to the car, leaning over at a precarious angle, and stared at it myopically. The angle proved to be critical, and he lost his balance, lost the rest of his change, and slid down the length of the car before he stopped himself by grabbing the CB trunk antenna.

Arnie looked at him disgustedly. "Yer drunk, Lester."

Lester got to his feet with much difficulty, moved over to the passenger side of the car where Arnie was resting, and, in a hoarse voice, said, "It's yer car, Arnie."

"It ain't." Arnie put his hands in his pockets and brought out the car keys. "Sheeeeiiiit. So 'tis." He broke into a short laugh that brought on a coughing fit. Between coughs and five attempts with the car key, he finally got the car door open.

Lester waited patiently at his side. When the door swung open, he fell into the car and landed in a heap across the front seat.

Arnie's entrance was more dignified. With three tries this time, he opened the other door, got in, pushed Lester up into a sitting position, and slammed the door on his leg.

"Son of a bitch! Goddamn fucking door!" Swearing seemed to dull the pain. "Shit!"

"Yer not gonna drive are we?" Lester asked. "Smokey told us—"

"Fuck Smokey," Arnie said, rubbing his leg. "Sure'n hell ain't gonna walk. What's Smokey know. He's just a innkeeper. A mere innkeeper. And a lousy one at that."

Arnie closed his door and started the engine, turning on the lights and backing out of the parking space with a series of jerks. Narrowly missing two cars in the process, he stopped suddenly and switched on the wipers. The night mist was heavy enough to foul the windshield. Then with stuttering starts and stops, moved the Buick out of the lot and onto Decker Street.

He glanced over at Lester who was slouched brokenly against the door with his eyes closed. Arnie gave him a rough shake. "Hey!

You asleep?"

Lester blinked back into consciousness and sat up. "No. No. I'm not sleepin'."

Arnie eyed him suspiciously and turned on the CB radio, which was his pride and joy, and which his wife hated with a passion. Maybe that's why he liked it so much. Anyway, he was in no hurry to get home and listen to more of her goddamn aches and pains.

As sure as snow comes in the winter, she'd be on him as soon as he came in the door. It hurts here. It hurts there. It hurts everywhere. Christ, it was like livin' with a professional patient.

The CB cracked into life. "Breaker. Breaker," the voice on the band said. "Quack, quack, quack."

"Sounds like a zoo," Lester laughed.

Arnie tried to get the voice in clearer.

"Woof, woof, woof."

"Must be that wiseass kid again," Arnie said. "Thinks he's a comed…thinks he's funny."

"Polly want a cracker? Polly want a cracker?" the voice said.

"He must be mobile," Arnie said. "Let's see if we can catch the prick. I'll drive around and you watch the poundage. Tell me when it increases."

Lester leaned forward and focused on the radio.

"What's it say now?"

"Ninety-three," Lester said.

"Ninety-three? There ain't no such poundage." He took his eyes off the road and looked at the set, just missing an oncoming car that blared its horn at him.

"Asshole!" Arnie yelled back, then leaned over at the set again. "Damn it, Lester. You're lookin' at the FM dial."

"Oh."

"Pay attention. We'll get this jerk."

"Chirp, chirp, chirp," the voice went on.

When Arnie turned down Archer Street, some three blocks from where Kenneth Sollis lived, his headlights picked up someone crossing the street in the middle of the block. Even through his whiskey haze, Arnie could tell that something was not right. Especially the walk. It wasn't a normal person's walk. It was more like something that comes after you in your nightmares – dragging, halting, and grinning. The car moved closer, and he saw the torn flesh and the blood and the face…

Arnie hit the brakes hard, swerving the car. Lester looked up. A parked car loomed ahead, and the Buick plowed into it. Lester hit his head on the dash, unconsciousness flooded over him, but Arnie was conscious, sober, his jaws working like a fish out of water.

The thing smiled at him, then disappeared down the street and into the darkness, moving with that same terrible walk, like death coming to call.

Arnie sat there unable to move except for the shaking of his body.

Christ, the thing looked just like Debbie.

10:20 P.M.

The pounding on the front door was as loud as thunder.

Sollis got up nonchalantly from his easy chair, made his face into what he thought was a charming smile, and opened the door. His fish smile twisted into a contortion of horror.

It was Debbie.

She gave him a smile, which Sollis didn't see, not right away, not at first glance, nor did he see the large slash across her throat that looked like another mouth. His eyes were riveted to the evisceration that had been done to her.

He backed away, unable to believe what stood before him.

She raised her arms to embrace him, all the time smiling, coming to him. Her clothing was ripped open and her breasts hung like two decaying melons above her torn flesh. Wet and snarled hair hung above her eyes. She looked like she had just crawled out of some watery grave.

"Keep away from me!" Sollis screamed, retreating farther into the house. "Keep away from me!"

Debbie kept smiling, arms outstretched. Her advance was inexorable, like the passing of time, like death.

"Go back! Damn it go back! I command you to go back!"

Sollis fell over a table and struck his head. He quickly scrambled to his feet, but his vision was blurred and there was blood on his forehead.

He tried to steel himself. He pointed to the open door. "In the name of the Power that brought you here, I command you to leave!"

Debbie smiled her frozen smile. Her feral eyes blazed. She dragged one foot forward, then the other.

Sollis was losing control now. "Get out! Please get out!"

He backed against the living room wall. She was closing in on him, almost touching him. He closed his eyes and grimaced in horror, then slid down the wall and twisted away from her, backing into the kitchen and stumbling into the table.

"Debbie, go back!" he screamed. "Go back!"

She moved closer, smiling her sick smile, that grotesque second mouth gaping at him.

"Go back, Debbie! You're dead!"

Debbie just looked at him with an of-course-I'm-dead gleam in her eyes.

Sollis moved around the kitchen table and when the opportunity was available, sprang to the basement door. He unlocked it quickly and flung it open, bolting down the stairs, then faltered and tumbled down the steps to the basement floor.

He got to his feet slowly, swayed and almost fell again, but managed to catch the stair railing for support. His head was swimming, but he could hear her coming down the basement stairs. One step. Then another. And another…

He staggered to his ritual room and fumbled the keys out of his pocket. They fell on the floor. Luckily, he snatched them up again, then tried to find the lock in the darkness. He couldn't hear her on the stairs anymore, but he knew she was back there somewhere, close behind him.

After what seemed like an eternity, the key slid home and the door opened. Sollis jumped inside, slammed the door shut and locked it. He held his breath. The doorknob turned. A moment later, chambered pounding started. Over and over again. Incessantly.

He would have to dismiss her. Burn the lock of hair and send her back…to where she came from.

With trembling hands, Sollis picked up the matches off the table and began lighting the candles.

The pounding continued.

He started the ritual.

10:40 P.M.

Just when Marion Koss thought she would scream, the penetration stopped and she felt something rake across her breast, like a hand with very long fingernails.

Did a person change that much on the other side?

The thrusting started with jackhammer force, driving through her like a gouge, ripping, tearing. Tears came to her eyes. It had never been like this before.

"It hurts!" she wailed.

The thrusting increased.

"Please stop!"

It became harder. More punishing.

"Please, Richard!"

The pain became unbearable and her screams mounted in crescendo, then finally died on her trembling lips as she passed out.

She was in her bedroom, naked on the bed, alone, except for that presence which had come to her in a dream. The one she thought was her dead husband.

11:06 P.M.

Linda and her mother were upstairs. Mrs. Eastman was still sedated, unaware that her husband had died tonight. Linda tossed and turned in her bedroom, fighting for sleep that would not come.

Paul sat in the library, having a brandy, watching the fire die. He felt uneasy about Eastman's death. The paramedic had told him it was a heart attack. But a nagging question still haunted him—what caused it?

Skeptical that he would find anything, but still not wanting to overlook the possibility that someone had gotten into the house, he had searched the outside grounds after Linda had gone upstairs.

There was no trace of entry, none that he could detect anyway, but he did find tracks in the soft ground near the house – and always near a window.

They were the tracks of a large dog.

Didn't Linda tell him that Allan Durie had owned an Irish Wolfhound?

11:59 P.M.

The phone rang for the third time.

Just before the fourth ring the receiver was picked up.

"Hello," the voice said.

"This is Sollis." His voice trembled.

There was silence on the other end.

"I'd like to know," Sollis said, looking quickly over his shoulder, then continuing in a whisper, "just what in the hell you think you're doing?"

"What do you mean?" the voice said.

"You know damn well what I mean."

"Don't play games. I haven't got the time."

"Listen, I didn't instruct you in the Power so you could go out and kill people. What's the matter with you? Are you going crazy?"

A short pause and then, "I don't know what you're talkin' about."

This time it was Sollis who reflected for a moment. "You found the book didn't you? Durie's book. The one I told you about."

"I didn't find any book. Listen, I don't have time to talk now."

"You listen," Sollis said quickly. "I want to see you. I want to talk about that book…"

The phone went dead on the other end.

"...Right away," Sollis finished. He held the receiver for a long moment before he hung it up.

Minutes later, he rechecked the entire house to make sure Debbie Ralston was really gone.

PART THREE

The Pale Door

And Travellers, now, within that valley,
Through the red-litten windows see
Vast forms that move fantastically
To a discordant melody:
While, like a ghastly rapid river,
Through the pale door
A hideous throng rush out forever,
And laugh, but smile no more.

E. A. Poe

1

THE RAIN HAD STOPPED, but the late-morning sun was obscured by a lingering cold breath of night fog, which still rose from the lows and hollows of the earth, giving Lanark and the surrounding countryside an eerie, foreboding appearance. Paul drove as fast as the fog would allow, swinging his Pontiac into the fast lane of the highway and heading for Milwaukee. He had had a busy morning.

Earlier he had gone to see Father Kerry, to find out once and for all what the old priest really knew about Durie House, but he never got past the front door of the rectory. RCA told him Kerry was feeling poorly and couldn't see anyone. Maybe another time.

He left reluctantly. As he walked back to his car, he remembered something Dwayne had told him: there were some books written about the Duries. He stopped at the Lanark Library.

The library's section on the occult had been rather anemic. They didn't have anything that could help him. In fact, none of the books even mentioned the Duries, so he started to check old newspaper stories.

Using the reading machine because the actual newspapers were on spools of microfilm, he found out that there had been three newspapers in Lanark's history: The Lanark Bugle went bust and later emerged, after new money and new owners, as The Lanark Times. Then, years later, the Times followed the same fate as The Bugle. The Lanark Leader was born from the ashes.

According to the newspapers, murders and disappearances were not uncommon in Lanark. The earliest he found went back to 1866, when Shawn Kilpatrick, age 9, was found murdered and mutilated in a place called Benson's Woods. The following years were spotted with similar stories, and Paul decided to make some notes.

Mandy Hamm, age 8, murdered and mutilated, Benson's Woods; Tom Macarthur, age 20, murdered and mutilated, opposite Handy's Marsh; Virginia Bork, age 35, murdered and mutilated, near Graceland Cemetery on Richmond Street; Collin Freeman, age 18, murdered and mutilated, near Handy's Marsh; Jill Nickel, age 11, murdered and mutilated, alley between Court and Elm Streets; Agnes Potts, age 51, murdered and mutilated, near Graceland Cemetery; Dennis Evers, age 10, murdered and mutilated, in alley between Bishop and Elm Streets.

There were dozens of disappearances, too – but not like Dwayne's – so he decided to overlook them and just concentrate on the murders. If there was a pattern to it all, he reasoned it would be in the way the victims were all killed and that in some areas the murderer struck more than once, but he readily dismissed the thought that the same person was still killing after all these years.

After two hours, he left the Lanark Library in a daze. What he was thinking was whacky. It just couldn't be. Maybe he just had a bad case of occult-itis that seemed to be sweeping the country. It was nonsense. Beyond nature. Beyond reason.

And yet –

He knew it was there, just as Dwayne had known. The murders. The house. It was all an ominous jigsaw puzzle that he couldn't quite fit together.

From the library, he had gone straight to Thayer's office. Paul told him where he was going and asked him to keep an eye on Linda and her mother while he was gone because, even with her father dying the way he did in Dwayne's room, he couldn't persuade her to leave the house. She still insisted everything was normal. Her father just died of a heart attack. The past few days had simply been too much for him. His heart failed and he died. A perfectly natural cause.

Now, thinking about it in the car, Paul knew better. The effect – a heart attack – may be perfectly normal, but, with a reluctant acceptance that was steadily creeping into icy realization, he felt the cause was anything but normal.

And why the gun?

Linda felt her father probably had thoughts about taking his life. Paul disagreed. Eastman wasn't the suicide type, but then, he never thought that about himself either. How many times had he taken his own gun out of the drawer and contemplated its blue, shiny death appeal?

No, Eastman was shaken, but he wouldn't kill himself. The gun was for protection and whatever he saw in that room frightened him to death before he could use it.

Paul hadn't told Thayer that or about the newspaper stories, and he was glad Thayer hadn't questioned him about going to Milwaukee. In fact, after another killing last night, he was surprised Thayer let him go.

If he was still a suspect, the police were letting him run. Maybe they thought if they gave him enough rope, he'd hang himself.

Paul looked at his watch. It was almost noon. He increased his pressure on the gas pedal. He wanted to be back before nightfall. Before things started happening again at Durie House.

The main branch of the Milwaukee Library was located in the downtown area of the city, housed under the rotunda dome and cartouche carvings of an old building that was once the museum. Inside its entrance loggia, at the main desk, Paul asked a woman librarian about the books he wanted to see. He was directed to another floor where a younger woman, whose pretty smile became uneasy when Paul told her what he wanted, ushered him through the hushed silence of the large room to the occult section.

"If you need any help, I'll be at the desk," she said, forcing a smile.

Paul smiled back in rote pleasantness, and after she left, he began searching along the rows of books. Pulling several books from the shelves, he carried them to a nearby table and sat down under a bank of overhead fluorescent lights. An old man who looked like a paper-bag wino dozed in a nearby chair.

Paul picked up the first book, *Devil Worship* by C.B. Aubrey, and started reading. After several minutes of scanning, he found a slight mention of Charles Durie, Allan's father:

Many students of the occult now agree that Charles Durie carried out the Durie tradition by continuing to search for the fabled door to the underworld itself. Whether or not such a door actually exists is open to much debate. Many so-called masters (if anyone really masters the occult) hold this theory in ridicule.

Paul found much the same account in the next three books: *The Occult And The Outre. Strange Beliefs*, and *The Necromancers*. He scanned through more of the books, references of the Duries being rather brief in all of them.

In the last book, *The Black Arts* by Kelly Williams, Paul read a chapter on the sacrifices of animals – black animals. He immediately thought of Holly, Dwayne's missing dog. Hadn't Dwayne told him that the dog was black? He'd have to ask Linda when he got back to Lanark. He looked over more of the pages, then found a paragraph of interest:

Although it is easy to say that the Door to Hell Theory is just wishful thinking on the part of devil worshipers on the whole, there has been, through the ages, references to just such a door. If this portal exists, one can only speculate on the evil and destruction that would be unleashed upon mankind if it is ever opened.

Paul returned the books to the shelves and started to hunt for more, then changed his mind, deciding that looking through them this way would take up too much time. He was about to go to the card index to look up the Duries when a book title caught his eye. It was *Allen Durie, The Devil's Adept* by Philip Deering. He took the book back to the table.

The sun was below the trees and the overhead fluorescent tubing began to take on a more noticeable glow when Paul finally turned the last page. He sat there for a moment, trying to digest everything he had just read, then checked to see when the book was printed. It was dated three years ago. He turned to the short paragraph about the author on the back of the book's paper jacket. One sentence caught his interest: Philip Deering made his home in Milwaukee, Wisconsin.

After returning the book, Paul hurried down the escalator to the public telephones near the entrance. There were five Philip Deerings listed in the directory. He dug in his pockets for change and started dialing.

On the fourth try he was successful, but the voice on the other end of the line became hesitant.

"Yes, I wrote the book. Why?"

"Mr. Deering, you don't know me. My name is Paul Rice. I just read your book and I've got to talk to you."

"Why?" Deering asked flatly.

Paul tried to decide if the voice sounded old or young. Old, he guessed.

"The book certainly wasn't a best seller," Deering said. "I appreciate your interest, but I'm rather busy. I haven't the time to see people. I'm sorry."

"Please, Mr. Deering. I won't take up much of your time. If I could just talk to you for a few minutes."

"Really, Mr. – is it – Rice?"

"Yes."

"I just don't have any spare—"

"It's about Durie House. I've just come from there."

There was silence on the other end.

"Mr. Deering, are you there?"

"Yes. Yes. I'm here. Is there…something happening out there?"

"Yes. All hell is breaking loose."

"I've read about those murders in the paper," Deering said. "All right. I'll spare you a little time. But you better come out here. I don't want to discuss this on the phone. Have you paper and pencil handy? I'll give you my address."

"I've got your address from the phone book," Paul said.

"Oh. Yes, of course. Do you know how to get here?"

"I can find it."

"All right then, Mr. Rice. I'll be expecting you."

"Thank you. I'll be right over." Paul hung up and hurried to his car.

The Westminster chime of the railroad station clock struck four times in the distance.

It would be dark soon.

2

THE DEERING HOME WAS LOCATED on a slight bluff that overlooked the cold waters of Lake Michigan. Paul swung his car up the drive. In the distance, he could see a white cabin cruiser tied to a slip bobbing peacefully in the twilight. The house and grounds reminded him somewhat of the Durie place. He parked under a port cochere and got out.

Paul rang the bell and got an immediate response. A tall, slender man with a bush of white hair and piercing blue eyes, whom Paul guessed to be in his sixties, stood in the doorway.

"Mr. Rice?"

"Yes."

"I'm Philip Deering."

They shook hands. Deering's grip was firm and surprisingly strong.

"I saw you drive up. Come in."

Paul stepped into a cool, dark foyer that contained an expansive staircase. There was a pungent, overpowering smell in the room.

"I hope you don't mind the incense, Mr. Rice. I find that it relaxes me."

"No, of course not," Paul lied. It was strong enough to make his eyes water.

"This way," Deering said, closing the door and leading Paul to the left of the foyer and into a paneled room of old wood, leather chairs, walls of books, and more incense.

"Please sit down," Deering gestured to one of two leather chairs that flanked a slow burning fire in the fireplace. The room was dark, except for the fire and a lamp, which threw a puddle of light across the massive desk that was littered with a typewriter and several piles of paper.

Paul sat down, and Deering took the opposite chair.

"Now, Mr. Rice," he said, picking up an unlit pipe from a nearby table and sticking it in his mouth. "Tell me about Durie House."

Paul told him about the murders in Lanark, then he told him about Dwayne and his own connection with the Eastman family. He mentioned the closet and Dwayne's disappearance and Eastman's death last.

After Paul had finished, Deering sat back in his chair and sucked thoughtfully on his pipe for a few moments. Then he got up and went to the desk, filling the pipe with tobacco from a humidor.

"I gather," Deering said, "that you think there's some connection between the murders and Durie House."

Paul looked at him. "Don't you?"

"Maybe." Deering clamped his jaw down on the pipe and put a match to it, his face disappearing in a cloud of smoke. "And maybe not. It could be just a psychopath. Someone that likes to kill for his – or her – own perverted reasons."

Paul leaned forward in his chair. "But what if there is a connection? What if these killings are…well, sort of a sacrifice? What would the killer hope to gain?"

Deering walked slowly back to his chair and threw the match into the fire. "If the killer is dealing in the Black Arts," he said, "and if the killings are sacrifices, then the answer to your questions is simple. Power. To win the services of the Evil Old Ones. To gain favor with the Master Of Darkness, himself."

Paul looked down at the carpet, then up at the old man. "I found several books at the library that mention the Durie family was preoccupied with finding some sort of portal."

"Hadin's Portal. The door to the nether world; gateway to Hell."

"Who is Hadin?"

"Hadin was a disciple of Apollonius. He was supposedly credited with opening the portal; however, he did something wrong and the portal closed. His failure caused the Devil so much displeasure that he drove Hadin mad. Some scholars give the honors to Eve. If she didn't open the door completely, she at least left it slightly ajar. Others credit Pandora. You know the story of Pandora?"

"A little," Paul said. "I was interested in Greek and Roman mythology in school. She opened a box and flooded the world with evil and pestilence."

Deering nodded. "She was the first mortal woman. On orders from Zeus, Hephaestus molded her into creation with clay and water to bring misery on the human race. Zeus gave her a box – it was actually a jar – and forbade her to open it. Of course, he knew she wouldn't listen, and she didn't. Poor thing couldn't resist opening it."

"Then there actually is a portal. Or is that just a myth, too?"

Deering checked the bowl of his pipe, then put it back in his mouth. "My father thought so. Charles Durie and later his son, Allan, and my father were colleagues of a sort – until the Duries completely veered off on the darker side of things. The portal interested my father purely as a means of establishing contact with another world. To the Duries, it meant something else entirely.

"Anyway, Allan told my father that he had succeeded in creating a portal. That he had corrected Hadin's error and had perfected a grimoire – a book of magic – with the precise instructions and rituals necessary in bringing these creatures from the bowels of time and space into our plane of existence."

"Did your father ever see this grimoire?" Paul asked.

Deering relit his pipe. "No. But by that time, he no longer cared one way or the other. He had enough of the Duries and their Ritual Magic. His association with them had almost ruined him. He died a sick, broken, and disillusioned man."

"You don't believe in the portal, then. That's why you played it down in your book."

"No, I don't. If you came here tonight for another answer, I'm sorry, but I can't give you one. It's hard to believe in something like the portal. Things like that belong in the dark pages of history when man was at his worst. In the cold and sobering light of science and computers, it just can't be."

Paul didn't blame him for his skepticism. He had felt the same way. The whole thing was like some old B-movie horror story where you called out the armed forces to bomb the house or something. It all sounded so foolish. And yet it nagged at him.

"But if the portal did exist," Paul persisted, "what would it be like? Could it be anywhere?"

Deering smiled. "If it exists, and I stress the word 'if,' it could be any point of space on our plane. It would be a cold spot. There would be a temperature drop of freezing proportion, so much so, that you would immediately feel it were you to come in contact. And, of course, there would be a malodor. Probably a burny putrescence."

The closet, Paul thought and felt a slight prickling at the back of his neck.

Then Deering leaned forward and almost whispered: "As long as we're dealing in the realms of if, Mr. Rice, and if there is a portal in Durie House, then you would be in grave danger. There would be malevolent forces at work that would stop at nothing until the portal had been opened. You'd be dealing with the worst kind of evil, an evil that would consume you and everyone else in its path."

Paul looked shaken. He rubbed the back of his neck. The fire bounced shadows around the room.

"I'm sorry," Deering said, seeing Paul's reaction. "Remember, I said 'if.'"

Paul turned toward the curtained windows of Deering's study and watched the darkness build outside. He thought of Dwayne and his abhorrence of the closet.

"You look like you could use a drink," Deering said.

"Yes, I guess I could."

Deering walked over to a small cabinet-bar and poured a good four-fingers of brandy into a glass. "Here you are," he said. "This should fix you up."

“Thank you.” Paul finished off half of it.

“Better?”

“Better.”

Deering relit his pipe again and shuffled over to the fire, watching the flames dance and play around the logs.

Paul watched him for a moment, then came out with something that had been on his mind for quite a while: “Could Allan Durie be putting his theory into practice now?”

Deering turned around and slowly took his pipe from his mouth. “You think Allan Durie is still alive?”

“Yes.” Paul watched the old man chew the thought over in his mind.

Deering shrugged. “It could be. The authorities only found one body in the house after the fire.”

“They found his brother, James.”

“That could account for the recent killings in Lanark.”

“You think Allan Durie is capable of murder?”

“I think Allan Durie is capable of anything.”

“But you said the portal doesn’t exist.”

“It doesn’t matter if it exists or not,” Deering said. “If someone believes in the portal, and if that someone is Allan Durie, then everyone at Durie House is in peril.”

The room became silent.

Paul finished his drink and set the glass on the lamp table.

“Mr. Deering,” he said, “I wonder if I might impose on you further? Could I use your telephone?”

“Of course. You want to call someone at Durie House?”

Paul nodded. “Yes.”

“The phone’s out in the hall near the stairs. Here, I’ll show you.” Deering turned on the hall light and led Paul to the phone.

Paul dialed the number and listened to the phone ring on the other end. Three, four rings. Come on, answer it. Five, six –

“Hello.”

“Linda, this is Paul.”

“Paul, where are you? When are you coming back?”

"I'm still in Milwaukee. Linda, listen to me. How's your mother? Is she still asleep?"

"No, she's up. We were just going to wash her hair. I thought that might make her feel better."

Paul paused, unsure of how to proceed. "Look, I know we've been over this all before, but this time for God's sake, please don't argue. Take your mother and get out of that house."

"But why? Where will we go?"

"Please listen to me. I'll explain later. Go to Chief Thayer's office. I'll meet you there. But get out of that house, now."

"Paul, I can't drag Mother around in her condition. I told you that this morning. Besides, Father Kerry's supposed to come here tonight."

Paul didn't think Kerry would leave his church to come to Durie House tonight or any other night, but said, "Okay, just call him and tell him not to come. Then get out of there. I don't want to frighten you, but you and your mother are in danger every minute you're in that house."

"Oh, Paul, I don't know. Like you said, we've been over this before, and I still think you're being foolish. Besides, what will I tell Mother? She doesn't even realize Dad is dead."

"I don't know. Tell her anything. Tell her you're taking her shopping. Just get out of there." Paul hesitated for a moment, then plunged ahead. "Linda, from what I've learned today, there's reason to believe that Allan Durie's alive and most likely responsible for the killings in Lanark. There's already been two – possibly three – deaths in that house – his house. Do you want to take an unnecessary chance and stay there just to prove I'm being foolish? What if I'm not?"

She was silent for a moment. Paul hoped he had frightened her enough to leave.

"All right," she said. "We'll go."

"Good. Now please…"

"I know. I'll get Mother and we'll leave right away."

"Good girl. I'll see you at Thayer's."

"Hurry back."

"I'm on my way." A thought sprang at him from the back of his mind. "Oh, Linda, one more thing. Holly was black, wasn't she?"

"Dwayne's dog? Yes. What on earth does that mean?"

"Maybe something, maybe nothing."

"I know, you'll tell me later."

"Get going. I'll see you soon."

Paul hung up just as Deering walked back into the hall.

"I'd better get back," Paul said.

Deering nodded. "I'm sorry I couldn't have been more help. If the boy's disappearance still troubles you – I mean if you feel convinced there's something…well, unnatural going on at Durie House – I have some friends at the university you could talk to. They work in the Department of Parapsychology."

"I'm afraid there isn't time right now."

"Well, perhaps I'll find something if I go over my father's notes. Is there somewhere I can reach you?"

"Call the police in Lanark. Ask for Chief Thayer. T-H-A-Y-E-R. He'll know where I am."

"I'll do that."

Paul started to leave, then noticed several pictures hanging on the wall above the telephone. One was a photograph of Durie House; the others were of men.

"The man with the gray hair," Paul said. "Is that your father?"

"No. That's Allan Durie."

Paul nodded. They walked to the door. He thanked Deering for his time. They shook hands again. The old man opened the door for him.

"Watch yourself, Mr. Rice. Allan Durie is an evil man."

"I'll do that."

Deering closed the door. Paul stood there for a moment, under the port cochere, his mind reeling around with a carousel of thoughts, none of which made any sense.

He headed for his car.

3

HELEN EASTMAN LOOKED AT HER HAIR in the upstairs bathroom mirror. It was terrible, she thought. It was dirty and made her scalp itch. She hadn't washed it since that day she went to the cemetery. She couldn't remember why she went, but there seemed to be a lot of other people there, too.

The image in the mirror looked haunted. She raised a thin hand to her face. Her eyes were two dark wounds; her skin was pasty-white. She didn't know why she was so tired lately. It seemed like all she was doing was sleeping. Probably caught some kind of flu-bug. Well, there was nothing she could do about that. It would work itself out in time.

She heard the downstairs phone ring several times, and then Linda answered it. Probably John calling, telling them he was on his way home from the office. He was working too many hours as usual. She would be glad when he retired. He could do it now if he wanted to, but John liked to keep active.

That meant supper would be late. Dwayne and Chrissie would be hungry. They hadn't eaten anything all day. They shouldn't have skipped breakfast and left the house like that. John, too, for that matter. She'd have to talk to him about that. It was up to him to set a good example for the children.

She looked at her watch. It was getting late. She wondered why the children weren't home from school yet. And John. What could be keeping him so long? Linda had told her something about him this morning. Now what was it? She couldn't remember. She'd have to ask Linda about it later.

God, why had she slept so long? She felt like she was drugged or something. She hoped Alison had prepared supper before she left. It would be a struggle if she had to manage it by herself tonight.

The lights dimmed. A few moments later, a breath of cold stench drifted into the bathroom from the hall.

Mrs. Eastman shivered. She pulled her bathrobe around her tighter. Funny. She was never cold in this house before. Only Dwayne felt the cold. She would have to tell him that she was beginning to feel it. Maybe that would cheer him up.

But first she had to do something about her hair. She'd give it a quick wash and then…what? Oh, yes. She'd get dressed. Maybe then she wouldn't feel so drowsy. She always felt better when her hair was clean.

She opened the linen closet and took out a towel, then ran water into the basin, testing it with her hand until she found the right temperature. She closed the basin and filled it three-quarters full.

For a moment, just as she unscrewed the cap from the shampoo bottle, she thought she saw something in the mirror. But when she looked again, there was nothing there. She lowered her head to the water and began to wet her hair.

Suddenly, her head was shoved under the water. She felt pressure on her head and shoulders, like a pair of hands holding her down. She tried to scream, but only succeeded in swallowing a lot of water. Then just as she was about to lose consciousness, her head was jerked up by the hair, and she was slammed against the bathroom tiles.

Downstairs, Linda had finished talking to Paul and had tried several times to reach Father Kerry, but his line stayed busy. When she finally did get through, there was no answer. She hung up the phone and started upstairs to get her mother. She would try again before they left.

Then she heard her mother screaming.

My God, what could be wrong, she thought. She raced up the stairs. Maybe the realization finally hit her mother that Dad was gone now, too. She had told her this morning, but there was no response. It was as if she had told her that there was no mail today. The reaction had been the same.

As Linda neared the top of the stairs, she heard pounding, like something was being thrown against the walls. When she reached the upstairs hall, she saw what that something was. Her mother was no longer screaming. She was being bounced off the hallway walls, like a rubber ball, by some invisible force.

The pounding grew louder. Mrs. Eastman was thrown against the walls with increasing violence – first one and then the other. And whatever was doing it was moving down the hall with her.

"Mother!" Linda screamed. She tried to go to her, but couldn't. It was like she was moving through molasses. She could only stand there and watch in horror as her mother was picked up and thrown – over and over and over again.

"MOTHER! MOTHER!" Linda was screaming and crying at the same time.

There were splotches of blood along the walls. Paintings exploded in their frames and shattered like glass. Her mother continued the macabre dance down the hallway.

"NO, OH NO, OH NOOOOO!" Panic grew in Linda. God, it was true. It was all true. Paul was right. And Dwayne. Why didn't she listen? Why didn't they all leave this morning when Paul suggested it?

The hallway took on an eerie, blue-green glow. The ceiling and walls shivered, then bulged in and out, like they were breathing. The cold stench became overpowering.

Linda sobbed helplessly, in fear and frustration. Nausea rolled up from her stomach. She felt as if her sanity was being slowly sucked away. She had never known such fear, not like this.

Her mother was within reach now. Linda grabbed for her as she was hurled past, momentarily getting her arm, but unable to hold on. Mrs. Eastman hit the banister with such force that she smashed through it, falling to the hall floor below.

Linda backed against the wall, her face twisted with unbelieving terror, her skin cold and clammy. She jerked her hands up to her face and screamed. The sound died somewhere in her throat.

The coldness enveloped her. It was like she was suspended in a frozen world. Malevolent faces and eyes formed around her, then evaporated into nothing. Demented voices battered her eardrums. She felt cold, freezing hands touch her body, her face. Her hair stood on end.

Something grabbed her by the hair and slammed her head back against the wall. Pain exploded behind her eyes. She slid down the wall and tumbled to the bottom of the stairs, rolling across the foyer floor and bumping against her mother's body.

Linda sat up slowly, stunned. She touched her mother. She was dead. She knew she was dead. Linda pushed herself away, getting up on rubbery legs. Her head swam in a myriad of colors.

The floor shook. Something moved above her. She looked up slowly. The heavy foyer chandelier was swaying as if caught in a stiff wind, then its crystal exploded, showering the hall with a fine snow.

Linda jerked her head toward the staircase. A loud booming noise had started in the upstairs hall, like someone pounding on the walls with the metal ball of a wrecking crew. The sound moved down the stairs.

She backed away, spinning around and running for the front door. It was locked. She opened the bolts, but the door wouldn't budge. Other doors, off the foyer, began opening and closing. Loud, bubbly laughter swirled around her.

Oh God. Dear God. Tears rolled down her cheeks. The booming was coming toward her, pounding along the walls with pile-driving force. She could feel its malevolence being directed against her. Something alien had taken over the house.

She ran for the kitchen, trying for the back door, but was picked up and thrown into the library. The booming was all around her now, louder, more intense. She got to her feet. Lamps danced madly in the air, leather chairs split down the middle, the walls and ceiling cracked.

Linda tried to run out of the room, but was thrown back. Books began flying off the shelves, sailing across the room with tremendous force. One hit her. Then another. And another. She ran toward the French doors, shielding her head with her arms.

The booming was deafening now. More books sailed past her head. Shadows moved everywhere. She felt her body rise off the floor, then hurl through the air.

She hit the French doors backwards, smashing through the glass, cutting her scalp and hands and arms, landing on the cold tile of the terrace. Dazed, she rolled to her feet slowly. Pieces of broken glass cracked under her shoes. A vague recollection drifted through her mind: Her mother was still in the house.

But she was dead. Wasn't she?

Linda whimpered. God, she couldn't. God forgive her, but she couldn't go back. She'd never go back.

She turned and ran into the fog.

4

NOT AGAIN, PAUL THOUGHT.

The car sputtered, then stopped completely. He tried to restart it, but it wouldn't turn over. Damn. He hit the steering wheel with the palm of his hand. This was getting to be ridiculous.

He sighed and got out of the car. Thick spiderwebs of fog clung to the trees and road. He could hear the foghorn droning in the distance off Rocky Point. Lanark wasn't far. If he could only get there.

This was the fourth time the car had mysteriously stalled-out on him since he left the main highway and got on the county trunk road. Each time he had checked under the hood he could find nothing wrong. Then just as mysteriously, he was able to start it again.

Paul lifted the hood and checked the spark plugs and distributor cap. Everything looked all right, as it always did. He took off the air filter and examined the carburetor. Nothing there. He put the filter back, dropped the hood, and got back in the car. He turned the key. The engine caught. He shook his head in disbelief. This was the damnedest thing he ever saw.

A mile later, the engine faltered once more, and Paul coasted to a stop on the shoulder of the road. He got out disgustedly and looked under the hood again. Still nothing wrong. He went back behind the wheel and tried it. The engine roared into life. He put the car in gear and moved off the gravel shoulder. The car started to sputter, then died.

For Christ sake. Paul couldn't understand what was wrong. This time he didn't get out. He waited for a minute, then tried to restart it. Nothing.

He hated to get out and look at the engine. He knew he wouldn't find anything wrong. But he just couldn't sit there in the middle of the road, especially with the fog as thick as it was. Someone might come along and rear-end him. Besides, he was anxious to get back to Lanark.

Damn. Paul gave in and reached for the door. It wouldn't open. He tried again, harder. It wouldn't budge. A whisper of a laugh slithered through the car. He turned quickly and looked in the backseat. It was empty. But the air inside the car became fetid.

Fear started to creep up his spine. He pulled on the door again. It still wouldn't open. Then a sick, whispering laugh. He thought he saw something in the backseat, reflected in the rearview mirror. He spun around. Nothing there. He slid across to the passenger-side door, tried it. It held fast.

A weakness began to seep into his legs, and goose bumps pricked across his skin. The car became cold. Paul could see his breath drifting out in small white clouds from his mouth. The smell was stronger, making him want to vomit. He fought off the urge.

Paul thought he heard something. A wheezing. Like someone breathing in the seat behind him. He strained to listen. Nothing. He held his breath. It had stopped. Whatever it was, was listening, too.

"What the hell do you want?" Paul shouted, his voice rising to a high pitch. "Leave me alone! Go back where you came from!"

Silence.

Then a gurgling laugh that was filled with vicious amusement.

Paul crossed himself. He didn't know if that would do any good, but he felt better after he did it.

The laughing continued.

"You son of a bitch!" Paul shouted. "Leave me alone! Leave us all alone! Go back to hell, you bastard!"

The laughter stopped.

This time Paul did see something in the mirror – two yellow eyes and the vague outline of a head.

It took every nerve in his body to turn his head. But when he did, he saw a hand with clawlike fingers resting on top of the front seat. It stayed there for a moment, then disappeared into the darkness of the back of the car.

The car began to sway.

It rocked slowly, gradually increasing in speed. The side window closest to Paul cracked and starred. Then the others, one by one, all around the car, until the last window – the windshield – exploded into a web of cracks in front of him.

"Jesus, Mary, and Joseph," Paul whispered.

The car kept rocking back and forth, as if a large hand was moving it.

Paul became angry. He didn't like being this helpless. He was still scared silly, but if this godless thing was going to do him in, or drag him off to hell or wherever, then the son of a bitch would have a fight on its hands.

He brought his feet up, knees against his chest, and smashed them against the windshield. Again and again he struck the starred glass until the opening was large enough for him to squeeze through.

The car was still shaking violently, but Paul pulled himself through the opening and onto the hood of the car before he was thrown to the ground.

He got to his feet quickly and started running down the road. He didn't look back. He just ran until he thought his heart would burst.

But it was his lungs that began to sear with pain. Paul slowed to a wheezing lope, then a staggering walk, lurching down the middle of the road like a drunk.

A silly thought passed through his mind. He used to run home from the movies like this when he was a kid – after seeing Frankenstein or Dracula or whatever monster happened to be playing. In those days, he believed in monsters. Somewhere along the line, he had forgotten.

He faltered, falling to the road, scraping his hands as he tried to break his fall. Getting to his knees, he rested there momentarily and waited to catch his breath. The road ahead was shrouded in fog.

Breathing was painful. God, he was in great shape. A little running and he was ready for an iron lung. He got up and started walking slowly, turning around occasionally toward the car and listening to the night.

Fog swirled eerily around him. He felt shut off from the outside world. This was like another planet – forbidden and menacing. Reality, as he knew it, had ceased to exist. It had been replaced by nightmarish creatures and insane fear.

A slight breeze moved among the trees at his side. The deep hum of the foghorn drifted through the night in intermittent bursts. The wind became stronger. Dead leaves flew through the air like bats. Trees swayed, rustled, creaked, but the fog remained thick and ominous.

Then he heard it.

Something was running through the woods, coming from the direction of the car. He could hear it smashing through the underbrush, snapping twigs and branches as it came after him.

Paul started to run again. His legs felt leaden, his body numb with fatigue. Fear urged him on.

It seemed to be getting closer and Paul was certain he was the target. Whatever was out there was after him.

He stumbled and almost fell again, but caught his balance at the last moment and lunged crazily forward. He mustn't fall now, he thought. The town couldn't be too far away. Just a little farther. He had to keep going.

The road twisted off to the left and disappeared in a heavy bank of fog. The leaves on the road were slippery under his feet. Paul hesitated for a fraction of a second as he neared the curve, then plunged ahead.

Once the bend straightened out, he remembered that St. Casmir's wasn't far off. He could see the iron fence of the churchyard between patches of fog. He followed the fence until he found the gate. The woods still exploded with the sounds of pursuit.

Paul fumbled with the gate latch.

Then he paused, listening.

The woods were quiet. He couldn't hear it anymore.

But there was something…a clicking…like…like the sound a dog's nails make when it runs on pavement.

It was running on the road now.

Paul turned his attention back to the gate. The latch refused to respond to his hand. The running grew nearer. He had a vision of himself being torn to shreds by those clawlike hands he saw in the car. He attacked the latch with both hands.

"Come on! Come on, damn it!"

How close was it now?

"Jesus…"

Perspiration poured down his face and stung his eyes.

"…Christ."

The gate swung open.

He dashed through and headed for the church. Something turned into the yard behind him as he raced up the steps, taking them three at a time. Almost falling, he staggered up to the entrance and pulled on the heavy, wooden door.

Panic seized him for an instant. Christ, what if it's locked? But his doubt was quickly flooded with relief as the church door opened.

Paul threw himself inside and swung the door shut behind him, just as something smashed against it, sending shocks of vibration through his hands and arms before falling away. He locked the door, then waited for his heart to stop its trip-hammer strokes, before putting an ear up to the wood. He couldn't hear anything. Just the mournful cry of the foghorn.

Several minutes passed. Still nothing. Finally, he turned into the vestibule, then through that to the interior of the church, and collapsed in the nearest pew, his mouth frozen in a rictus of fear.

Paul closed his eyes and tried to relax. Perspiration dampened his hair, rolled down his body under his clothes, sticking them to his skin, but he still felt cold.

The church was quiet. Soothing. Peaceful. Paul felt some of the weariness leave him. He had never been in a church alone like this before. He could almost hear the votive candles in their cups of red glass burning on both sides of the altar. The smell of hot wax drifted across the pews.

Painted statues of the Stations of the Cross stood along both walls, their eyes fixed on the chancel and the sanctuary lamp, hanging above the tabernacle. A nimbus seemed to dance around it. Paul watched the lamp for a long time. He felt strengthened by it.

Images of his mother came to him. He remembered her telling him about the lamp when he was a boy.

"It honors the Divine Presence," she had told him. "It means Christ is here. This is His house."

Paul would strain his eyes looking. "In the lamp?"

"Yes. He's in the lamp. He's everywhere."

"But I don't see Him. Just the lamp."

"He's there, none the less."

Then Paul would be quiet and nod, feigning understanding, but still straining to see Him.

After a while, he almost dozed, but caught himself drifting off. Paul shook himself awake. No time for sleep now. He had to get going again. He couldn't stay in the church and hide like Father Kerry. Paul wondered where the priest was now. He had to find him and talk to him, and Linda. God, he hoped she got out of the house all right. This thing, this evil didn't seem to be confined to Durie House any longer. It was spreading over the whole town.

Paul got up and went back to the door. He listened, but couldn't detect anything. The foghorn was still moaning its repetitive syllabic call into the night. He unlocked the door, easing it open a crack and peeked out.

The churchyard was empty, but Paul felt that whatever had chased him was probably still out there in the fog, waiting. He closed the door and relocked it. He'd have to leave another way. If only he had a weapon of some sort, but what do you use against something like this?

He walked back into the body of the church, started down the aisle, then stopped and turned around. He looked at the holy water fonts at the aisle entrance. Maybe he had found his weapon. He walked back to the fonts. Now if only he had something to put it in.

Searching his jacket pockets, Paul found a half-filled bottle of Coricidin and another of Excedrin. They were small, but they were all he had. He emptied the tablets into his pocket and filled each bottle with holy water from the fonts. For the first time in his life, his sinus trouble might prove helpful.

He capped the bottles and went down the aisle toward the altar, then behind that to the back of the church where he found a door off to one side that led to the churchyard.

He unlocked it. Then he placed one of the bottles in his pocket and uncapped the other. Taking a deep breath, he opened the door slowly, and stepped out.

Paul slid off to the side of the door, pressing his back against the cold stone of the church, and listening for what the darkness held. He peered into the fog and tried to detect anything that might be lurking under its protective cover.

Nothing.

Just fog, rolling over the grounds in thick, heavy layers.

Placing his thumb over the top of the bottle so he wouldn't spill any of the holy water, Paul started to move along the side of the building, toward the rear of the church. His breathing seemed abnormally loud to him. He wondered if anyone else could hear it.

Paul froze.

His skin turned to gooseflesh.

He knew he wasn't alone.

Something was moving through the fog, stalking him across the churchyard.

Paul picked up a rush of movement out of the corner of his eye.

A dark figure sprang at him with a snarl, jaws open, eyes feral. It was some kind of a dog. A big dog. He threw the holy water.

The dog missed this throat, but hit him in the chest, knocking him down. The water landed on the animal with a hiss, like water thrown on a fire. It backed away.

Paul scrambled to his feet and watched the dog roll on the ground, snapping at itself with an unearthly whine, smoke smoldering from its fur like it was on fire. Then, a minute later, the dog got up with a snarl and turned its attention back to Paul.

Paul thrust his hand in his jacket pocket and got out the second bottle and uncapped it. As the dog came closer, he could see that the water had caught the animal across the snout and part of the body. The wounds looked like they had been made by a hot branding iron.

Deliberately slow, inching forward, red eyes blazing, its muzzle curled back above long, deadly yellow teeth, the dog came for him. Paul stepped back, his shoulder blades brushing against the church building. He felt his testicles draw up. Pretty soon they would be in his throat. He wished he had a bucket of holy water instead of this dinky bottle.

The dog kept coming, watching his hand, the one he held the bottle in. Paul caught the direction of its eyes. The son of a bitch knew. He'd have to be careful. He'd have to catch him across the eyes.

Paul tried to press himself into the stone behind him. This wasn't any good. The bastard will just keep coming. The dog was so close now that Paul could smell the reeking stink that emanated from it.

He watched the dog's eyes, and began to bring his left hand up slowly, ever so slowly, to meet his right, which was bent at the elbow in front of his body, holding the bottle. Then just as slowly, he made the transfer, concealing the exchange as best he could. The dog's attention stayed riveted to his right hand.

Barely breathing now, Paul steeled himself for what was to come. He had to make some kind of a move, before the dog was on him. He feinted with his right hand, pretending to throw the water. Taking the feint, the dog lunged, hitting Paul with the full force of its body. Paul felt teeth sink into his right arm with eye-tearing pain. He threw the holy water with his other hand.

There was a terrible hiss. Smoke poured from the dog's eyes. It dropped Paul's arm and fell back, howling in pain, snapping blindly in every direction.

Paul stood rooted to the spot, watching the dog wither in agony, trying to decide what to do next if it came for him again. Then he sensed something. Another presence. Out there in the fog.

He lifted his eyes from the dog and looked directly behind the animal.

Someone was standing there.

Paul could only make out a shape. It looked like a man, wearing a hat and a long overcoat. He stood motionless, watching. The fog moving around him. There was something definitely alien and inimical about him.

Paul started to move away.

"See you again."

Paul heard the words more inside his own head than actually coming form the figure standing in front of him. It made Paul feel uneasy, like something had just crawled out of the dark passages of his mind.

Then suddenly, the man was gone. And the dog, too. Paul was stunned. He had been looking right at them, then, an instant later, they had both disappeared.

Was he going crazy? Maybe Linda was right, and he was letting himself get caught up in Dwayne's influence. His imagination was skyrocketing to the point where he was actually seeing things that weren't there. Things that were only subliminal images projected on his mind's eye by an overactive subconscious. A subconscious keyed by...fear.

Paul looked at his arm, examining the punctures in his flesh through the torn sleeve of his jacket. Was he imagining this, too? He touched the wound and grimaced in pain. For something that wasn't there, it felt very real.

Just as real as the hand he now felt on his shoulder.

5

THAYER LEFT THE POLICE BUILDING and got into his car. The fog didn't show any signs of lifting. If anything, it looked like it was getting thicker. He shook his head in disgust. That's all he needed. First rain, now fog. Everyone was working double shifts the way it was, and this damn stuff wouldn't make it any easier.

He pulled away from the curb and drove slowly through the streets, chewing absently on a fresh cigar. This case was giving him fits. And if that wasn't enough, the area newspapers were getting to be a bigger pain in the ass than the mayor. They were milking the murders for every drop of blood they could get. Anything for that great god circulation. It was the kind of newspaper hokum that made Thayer's blood boil.

Fuck 'em. Thayer rolled down the car window and spit. No need to get worked up over those hairpins. Whoever was cutting up people in this town was doing a good enough job of getting under his skin. But he'd get the bastard if it was the last thing he did.

The only trouble was nothing about these killings made any sense. He was still on square one. Every suspected drug user, sex offender, and vagrant in the area had been pulled in and questioned over and over again until he finally had to let them go, leaving him right where he started from – without a suspect.

Sure, dozens were busted for drug possession, including many students from the high schools and nearby Mather University. The arrests turned up ample supplies of pot and pills, even some acid and mescaline, and, for a while, a handful of promising suspects. But their alibis eventually checked out, and they were cleared of any suspicion and released.

Thayer really didn't think an addict was involved anyway. There had never been much of a dope problem in Lanark. Some marijuana smokers and pill takers, yes, but not much of the hard stuff, nothing that would freak a kid out so he'd butcher someone during a bad trip. Thayer conceded that it could have happened once – but five or six times?

Dan Sunquist thought the killings were some sort of cult mumbo jumbo. Something in the line of the Manson Family. God knows there were enough cults spread around the country, and more than enough people of this bewildered generation eager to join.

But there weren't any nomad families of bent kids around here. There was Durie House, of course, which people blamed just about everything on, even the bad weather, but every town had a Durie House and the Duries were gone now. Or were they?

Thayer felt discouraged. There was something gnawing at him, inside out. It was more than an itch he couldn't reach. It was one he couldn't even find. Who the hell was he looking for anyway? It could be anybody. Resident, nonresident. Young, old. Male, female. White, black, red, brown, yellow, orange. Thayer laughed inwardly. If the killer was orange, he should be able to find him easy enough.

No such luck. This one wasn't orange, but the mind was sick. That was evident enough by the mutilations, but what the hell happened to the parts of the body they didn't find? Did the murderer keep them as grisly souvenirs or was that just a red herring, something to throw them off the trail?

And why were all the bodies always found the same way? Was their positioning important? Or the direction they faced? What was to the north?

Shit. He had a hell of a lot more questions than answers.

The fog crept silently through the night. The streets were

becoming wet with its mist. He could hear the foghorn booming off Stony Point.

Dwayne Eastman's disappearance bothered him, too. How do you just vanish from a locked room? At least in the Hanson house they found a forced window.

He was getting a headache. He hadn't slept for over thirty-six hours. Last night had been a real bummer. First, Eastman dies of a heart attack, and then Debbie Ralston is murdered just like the others. And to top it all off, Arnie Ralston smashes up his car and insists he saw his daughter walking around twelve blocks from where they found her body.

Lester Heywood was with him, but he was knocked silly when Arnie cracked up the car. Thayer shook his head. Who knows what they saw. They were both plastered out of their skulls. They could have seen anything. Pink elephants in polka dot bikinis.

Ralston was getting as bad as Rice. Yeah, and where the hell was Rice? He had left for Milwaukee early this morning and promised to check in with him as soon as he got back. Thayer hoped he hadn't been foolish to let him go. Maybe he skipped. No. Rice wasn't the type. He had a gut feeling about Rice, and those feelings had never let him down yet.

Thayer drove past Thackeray Park, then turned around and came back. He had come this way to check on the Eastman women, but might as well take a turn of the park first.

The park looked bad, even in the fog. The blight or whatever it was that started at Durie House had spread through the park, killing off all the trees and shrubs and grass that got in its way. The infestation had spread all the way down to the Marsh Road area.

Thayer swung into Lover's Look. There was a car parked near the water, barely noticeable in the fog. He looked at his watch. It was ten after ten. Now who the hell could that be?

He stopped the car and slid his bulk out from behind the wheel. Flashlight in hand, he approached the car. His other hand rested on the butt of his .357 Magnum.

His line of travel brought him to the passenger-side door. The car looked empty. He looked in the open window and turned on the flashlight. A face popped up and stared straight at him. It startled him for an instant. His revolver was halfway out of its holster before he recognized a wide-eyed Sally Walenski. Bobby Perkins was in the car with her.

"What are you doin' out here?" Thayer barked, hitting their faces with the light. "It's ten minutes past curfew."

"Sorry, sir," Bobby said. Bobby was a thin, acne-faced kid, who was trying, without much success, to grow a mustache.

"We just forgot about the time," Sally said, then smiled. "We didn't mean to do anything wrong."

She had a smile that could melt ice, but Thayer didn't soften.

"Your folks are probably worried sick about you. Don't you know what happened in this park? What's happening all over town?"

Thayer watched their faces for the effect. He wanted to make sure the warning had sunken in.

"Well, do you?"

"Yes, sir," they said in tandem.

"Good. Keep it in mind." He leaned on the car door and stuck his face through the window. "Bobby, I want you to take this young lady directly home. Then go home yourself. And I don't want to see you – either of you – breaking curfew again. You got that?"

They both nodded, bobbing their heads like two frightened birds.

"Then get out of here."

Bobby backed the car up and immediately stalled out. He started it again, drove forward in a jerky motion, and pulled out of the lot.

Thayer shook his head. Damn fool kids. People getting murdered left and right, and they're out romancin'. It was going to be rough on all the kids' love lives with the curfew on, but they'd just have to be satisfied with holding hands at school for the present.

He smiled. It had been a long time since his Mary had those two youngsters as pupils back in grade school. Yeah, a long time.

He started back to his car. The fog was so heavy over the lake that he couldn't even see the water. He could only hear it, washing softly against the concrete slabs piled up along the shoreline.

When Thayer returned to the car, he radioed in about the Perkins and Walenski kids.

"Their parents will be relieved to hear that, Chief," Barney Jensen's voice came back to him. "They've already called in to report them missing."

"You'd better call them back and let them know the kids are all right."

"Will do. Anything happening out there?"

"Nothing. Just a lot of fog."

"Yeah, Carson just called in from the south end. He said it's so bad out there that he almost hit an abandoned car some joker left on County Trunk Q."

Thayer became concerned. "Did MV make the owner?"

"Not yet. It's still in the process. Hal Klein went out with his tow truck to bring it in. Carson's standing by."

"Good. Let me know the minute you hear from the MV people."

"Right, Chief."

"Barney," Thayer paused. "Did Paul Rice come in yet?"

"No. Anything wrong?"

"I don't know. Just a feeling. You'd better get on the horn and notify those kids' parents."

"Will do."

Thayer ten-foured and drove to the lagoon.

He didn't really expect to find anything new there. They had gone over the area thoroughly before, but he wanted to take a look at the wooded side of the lagoon. The side that ran up to Blackmoor Road and beyond to Durie House.

Thayer was sure the killer had entered the park from the road. And he was just as sure that the killer knew exactly who was home in Durie House the night Chrissie Eastman was murdered and her brother disappeared.

The Eastman girl had probably opened the door for her killer.

But why was she dragged outside? Thayer knew there had to be a reason, but so far he couldn't put his finger on it.

He stopped the car and got out. Fog rolled around him in giant patches, making the grass wet. He entered the tree line.

The ground began a small, steady incline toward the road above him. The killer probably had a car parked up there, Thayer mused. Then came down and spotted Ralphie.

He walked farther into the trees. In the beam of his flashlight, the fog seemed to hang from the trees like thick cobwebs. The sound of the foghorn added an eerie cadence to the night.

Thayer stopped in his tracks.

He turned off his flashlight.

Someone was moving above him – coming down through the trees at a steady run.

The lingering fog made it almost impossible to see anything. But whoever it was, was coming right at him.

He drew the .357 Magnum from its holster.

His heart picked up an impulse from his brain and increased its beat.

He waited.

Then something ran into him, and clawed at his face.

6

HE WAITED FOR HIS HEART TO CLIMB DOWN OUT OF HIS THROAT.

"Scared ya, didn't I," RCA said.

Paul's face was ashen, and he was breathing like he couldn't get enough air.

"Christ," Paul said, waiting for the air to fill his lungs before he could continue. "Don't *ever* do that again."

RCA chuckled, exposing the wide gap between his front teeth. Then his face suddenly changed, losing its smile, as he jerked his head around awkwardly on his crooked neck, searching the night.

"Come on," he said. "We best be gettin' inside."

Paul followed him numbly, the fright and shock draining away, but his arm still registering pain. RCA led him back through the side door of the church, then into a small room, ushering him to a wooden bench and table.

Paul winced when he touched his arm.

"You got hurt, huh?"

"Yeah. A dog bit me." Paul made up his mind not to tell him anything more.

"A dog? A hound of hell would be more like it."

Paul looked at him. They exchanged a mute understanding.

"You know?"

"Same thing happened years ago. The night Father Kerry came back from *that* house."

"It happened before? At Durie House?"

"Yeah, only I don't like to talk about it. It gives me the heebie-jeebies. Just like it does the Father. That's why he ain't left the church much since."

Paul's face flinched with a stab of pain. The arm was really bothering him now.

"Let's have a look at it. Roll up your sleeve."

Paul drew the sleeve of his jacket up gingerly, then rolled back his shirtsleeve, exposing the wound on his forearm. The skin around the punctures had begun to discolor and a yellow, fetid substance oozed from the holes.

"Pretty ain't it," RCA said, examining Paul's arm. "Think I got somethin' will fix it up."

He shuffled out of the room. Paul listened to his shambling feet until the sound disappeared in the huge canyon of the church.

The room window rattled. He turned quickly and stared at it, hoping it was only the wind. He was relieved to hear RCA coming back to the room.

"I think this is just what the doctor ordered," RCA said, carrying a small bottle of clear liquid. "Hold out your arm."

"What is it?" Paul asked, lifting his arm up stiffly.

"Holy water," RCA said, and poured it on the wound.

Paul screamed, tears stinging his eyes, almost passing out, as the water cauterized the bite, then left his arm whole and unmarked.

"Don't that beat all?" RCA chuckled.

Paul couldn't believe it. He examined his arm closely where the ugly punctures had been only a moment ago. They were completely gone. The skin was smooth and clear.

"How did you know to do that?" Paul asked.

"Seen it on a spook show on late-night TV. It worked on Father Kerry when he dragged himself in here all torn and bleedin' that night. Figured it would work on you."

Flexing his arm, Paul marveled at the rapid healing. He still couldn't believe what his eyes were seeing. He rolled down his shirtsleeve and pulled his jacket sleeve down.

RCA put the empty bottle on the table. A pleased-with-myself expression spread across his face.

Paul waited, letting him savor his feelings, then said, "RCA, tell me about the night Father Kerry went to Durie House."

RCA turned and looked at him, and Paul thought he noticed a small tic of fear start to twitch on the side of his face.

"I said I ain't goin' to talk about it," he said stubbornly.

"I thought you like Father Kerry?"

"Ain't none better."

"Well, I want to help him and unless I have some idea of what I'm up against, I won't be able to."

"Nobody can help him."

"Is he home now? I want to talk to him," Paul said, giving up on RCA.

The sacristan shook his head. "Went out. That ain't like him. Not at night. I thought you was him out there in the churchyard."

Paul wondered if the old priest had actually followed up on Mrs. Eastman's request. "He might be in trouble."

"What kind of trouble?" RCA looked worried.

"I think he went to Durie House. Alone."

RCA turned pale, but his eyes still held a trace of skepticism. "He wouldn't go there."

"Mrs. Eastman asked him. At the funeral."

RCA sat down heavily across the table from Paul. He shook his head in despair. "It'll kill him this time."

Paul felt the taste of desperation well up in his mouth. "RCA, for God sakes, tell me what happened. What is Father Kerry afraid of? Is Allan Durie still alive?"

"Don't know nothin' about Allan Durie. You best be askin' Pearl Armstrong. She used to be his whore when she was younger. Wasn't a bad looker then. Had her a couple of times myself after Durie dumped her. Now she's ugly as sin."

"What about Father Kerry?"

"I don't know the whole of it," RCA said, staring up at the ceiling.

"I only know how he looked when he came back that night."

Paul leaned forward on the table. The room seemed to take on an eerie stillness.

"The Father was asked to come to Durie House that night by James Durie. By the tone of it all, I guess he wanted Father Kerry to help him in some way. Seems like there was somethin' bad goin' on for a long time.

"So the Father ups and goes. I didn't know till much later what happened up there. But that night when he got back to the church, he looked like the Devil himself was after him. His face was all dirty and bleedin', his clothes were ripped, and he was scared, really scared. He had an animal bite on his leg just like you did on your arm. So, I helped him to his room. Him not sayin' a word, and me not askin'."

RCA looked down at his hands, and then at Paul. "Later that night, after I gets him cleaned up and tucked in and all, I hear somethin' prowlin' around outside the church. So I gets me a crucifix and a big, heavy candleholder and takes me a peek.

"It was a big dog. Black as night it was. With two red glarin' eyes. It was like nothin' I ever seen before or want to see again."

Paul could feel a freezing current of blood spread through his body with icy slowness. The room window rattled again.

"It was watchin' the church," RCA went on. "Like it was waitin' for somebody to come out, or maybe lookin' for a way in. Well, I didn't waste any time out there. I got back in the church and locked all the doors. In the mornin' it was gone."

Paul thought of his own recent encounter. "You said you found out later what happened," Paul prompted.

"I did. But it was years later. After that night, Father Kerry took to the bottle. And who could blame him. Then, one night, when he was slightly under the weather, the story came spillin' out of his poor soul.

"James wanted him to chase the devils out of Durie House. He never got the chance. They turned on him. Almost killed him. Said they'd be waitin' to get him no matter how long it took.

“Well, James Durie died that night. And Father Kerry came tearin’ home, runnin’ his car just about into the gate. He ain’t hardly set a foot outside of the church since. Not at night, anyway. Can’t say as I blame him none.”

But he was out tonight, Paul thought. And might be in that damn house alone. He hoped he was wrong. He hoped Kerry was with Linda and her mother at Thayer’s office.

And he hoped they were all safe.

7

TEN MINUTES AFTER LINDA EASTMAN had made her terrified escape from Durie House, Father Kerry's Dodge pulled into its driveway.

Kerry had just spent a frantic half hour trying to reach Mrs. Eastman by phone, but the line was always busy. He remembered holding the phone away from his ear and looking at it, the busy signal droning on incessantly, hoping someone would eventually answer it. But no one did. He let the phone slip slowly from his fingers, his hope gone, and reluctantly placed it back on the cradle.

Kerry started to pace his study. Surely the woman must have understood him at the cemetery. He could not possibly come. His mind drifted back to the scene at the funeral: her standing there in the rain, holding him with an iron grip, her eyes fixed and staring, but not at him, at something only she could see.

He shook his head. No, she did not understand. It had been more of a command to come than anything else, and yet there was a desperate need behind her words.

Kerry ran a nervous hand through his hair. What to do, what to do. He had agonized over it all night and all day. Maybe if he went there, not inside, definitely not inside, but outside the front door and explained to her that he could not possibly help her.

But then what could he say? Should he tell her about the house and add to her already overburdened mind? God knows he had tried to tell them, tried to warn them. They wouldn't listen.

He stopped pacing. Maybe he could bless the house from the outside. Yes. He liked the idea. A quick, fast blessing, then back in the car and home. That might satisfy her. God, it would have to. And it would be safe.

Now, in the car, Kerry felt his resolve weakening. Why hadn't he thought of this sooner – during the day? Maybe he should wait until tomorrow when it's light. He almost stopped and turned around. No, damn it. He'd go and get it over with, otherwise it would haunt him all night, and he had enough phantoms in his dreams now.

Kerry eased the Dodge to a stop and got out. The fog horn lifted its voice over the waters of the lake as he approached the house, which stood obscurely in a bank of swirling fog. There were lights on upstairs just like there were the last time he came to this house.

He pushed the thought from his mind and trudged up the stone steps to the door, rang the bell and waited. No response. He rang again. Still no response.

Good, he thought. He could go back to the church and forget about the whole thing and tell Mrs. Eastman that he had come out to the house and no one was home. Kerry wasn't that eager to see her again anyway. The conversation with her at the cemetery still left him unnerved.

Suddenly, the door opened, swinging slowly, without even a creak. No one was there.

Fear and indecision engulfed him as he stood there staring into the black maw of the doorway. There were no lights on in the foyer. A deeper part of his mind warned him not to go in, but the warning was lost in a sudden, stronger urge to enter.

He did.

"Mrs. Eastman?" he called softly.

The door closed behind him.

The strength that had carried him into the house was gone, evaporating into the cold, fetid stillness of the room. Fear was back, howling and screaming.

Kerry sprang back to the door, but it wouldn't open. He wanted to beat on it and cry, but instead merely stepped back and reminded himself to stay under control. That was half the battle.

Standing in the dark hall, he listened to the movements of the house—a nearby clock chimed the half hour; the gas furnace kicked in with a rush of heated air, billowing a hall curtain hanging above a heating grate and startling him to the point of panic.

A moment later, when his eyes grew accustomed to the dark and he was able to see the cause, Kerry closed his eyes in relief, but only for a second. The foghorn's mournful cry drifted through the house, unsettling him.

Near the door, he felt along the wall for the light switch, found it, and flicked it on. Nothing happened. It must be a fuse, he thought. There had been lights on upstairs when he drove up.

Kerry moved to the stairs and started up. He could see a faint glow of light along the upstairs hall.

"Mrs. Eastman?" he called again.

The lights that hadn't worked minutes ago suddenly went on, throwing the foyer and all the downstairs rooms into a harsh brilliance. The library caught his eye and through its open doors he could see some of the wreckage. He moved away from the stairs and entered the library.

The room was a disaster. Books were all over the floor; chairs were overturned and torn apart; the liquor cabinet was tipped over, decanters and glasses broken, liquor staining the carpet; tables were splintered and drapes pulled free from their rods.

It was just like the last time, Kerry thought. The night the house went mad.

Out of the corner of his eye he thought he saw movement on the stairs, but when he turned to face it, there was nothing there.

Kerry tried to quiet his uneasiness, tried to control his breathing, and ease his throbbing heart.

Where was everyone? Where was Mrs. Eastman?

He shuffled back into the foyer, looking at the cracks in the walls and ceiling. The floor was slippery with powdered crystal, and near the bottom of the stairs there was a stain. It looked like blood.

Kerry felt himself losing control, felt his legs freeze solid.

The front door opened. Slowly.

Tendrils of fog drifted in across the floor.

No one entered.

On wooden legs, Kerry stumbled toward the door.

It slammed shut in his face.

A loud cackle of vicious, sardonic laughter filled the house.

And, one by one, the doors to all the rooms off the foyer banged shut.

Kerry backed into the corner near the door, fear riding him, his muscles shrinking under his skin, his mind hanging precariously over a bottomless pit, slipping inexorably into the darkness below. When it fell, he knew he would never be the same again. Never be sane again.

The laughter died away, and a whispering of voices replaced it, surrounding him with whiplashes of sound, jerking his body like blows. It sounded like one word repeated over and over again, only he couldn't quite understand it. It was like a tape played at the wrong speed.

Then the word became clear to him.

"*Sacerdos*!"

It became a chant:

"*Sacerdos! Sacerdos! Sacerdos!*"

Kerry felt himself going over the edge. He screamed at the top of his voice. "YES, A PRIEST, YOU DEVILS! DO YOUR WORST!"

The house suddenly fell into a loud silence.

Kerry could hear himself breathing.

The lights went out.

Something was coming down the stairs.

8

THE FOG WAS GRAY AND QUIET AROUND THEM. Paul and RCA moved uneasily through it, like intruders in another dimension, and even though they had fortified themselves with crucifixes and bottles of holy water stuffed in their pockets, they still stopped frequently along the way to Thayer's office to look over their shoulders.

The dog was nowhere in sight.

An hour later, they stood in front of Thayer's desk, as he sat behind it, drumming his fingers impatiently, and looking over the MV report that confirmed the abandoned car found earlier belonged to Paul.

Paul told Thayer what happened. Not everything. Paul had persuaded RCA, after leaving St. Casmir's, to let him do the talking, and he held back about what really happened to the car and about the dog attack.

He did mention going to the library and talking to Deering and that the author knew the Duries, but didn't say a word concerning the closet or anything about the supernatural. He felt Thayer might think he was having a relapse, and he didn't want to wind up in a room with soft walls. Paul finished by saying that both he and RCA believed that Father Kerry had gone to Durie House and that the priest could be in trouble.

Thayer stopped drumming on his desk. He unwrapped a cigar and stuck it in his mouth. He had a strong feeling that Rice wasn't telling him everything, and gave Paul a suspicious look.

Paul avoided his stare. "Did Linda and her mother get here all right?"

Thayer rolled the cigar around in his mouth. "Linda Eastman's in the hospital."

Paul moved closer to the desk. "What…?"

Thayer waved him off. "Take it easy. She's all right. Just a few cuts and scratches."

"What happened?"

"I don't know. She's not talking. The doctor says she's in severe shock. It will be a while before she says anything. I found her running through the woods in Thackeray Park like the Devil was after her. Poor girl was scared stiff."

Paul and RCA exchanged glances. "What about her mother?" Paul asked. "Did you find her?"

Thayer shook his head. "Nothing yet. I sent two men to check out Durie House while I took Miss Eastman to the hospital. They haven't reported. In fact, they're overdue. We haven't been able to reach them on the radio."

Thayer caught another silent exchange between Paul and RCA, noticing their nervousness. "You sure you two are telling me everything?"

"There isn't any more to tell," Paul said quickly. " I just had some car trouble."

"Funny kind of car trouble," Thayer said. "All the windows broken and the car all dented up."

"I don't know anything about that. It must have happened after I left the car."

"Why didn't you come right here instead of stopping at the church?"

Paul hesitated. "I thought Father Kerry could give me a ride."

Thayer regarded him for a moment, still not satisfied.

"Christ!" Paul exploded. "If you suspect me of anything, than lock me up!"

Thayer got up from his chair and looked like he intended to do just that. "I ought to," he said. "I ought to lock you both up, because

I still think there's a hell of a lot that the two of you aren't telling me."

"We should go to Durie House," RCA said gloomily, then looked at Thayer. "Afterwards I have a feelin' you're goin' to have a lot more questions."

Thayer looked at the both of them again.

"We're wasting time," Paul said impatiently.

Thayer grabbed his cap and jacket, and the three of them went out the door.

Outside Memorial Hospital, where Paul talked Thayer into stopping first, Thayer and RCA sat in the car, waiting uncomfortably while Paul went in and persuaded a somewhat reluctant doctor to let him see Linda for a moment.

When Paul entered her room, Linda was sleeping. She had been sedated, the doctor had told him, and was resting comfortably. She was resting, but her face looked tense to Paul, like she was still frightened, still haunted, even in her dreams. He wondered what horrors she had seen at that house.

Paul kissed her lightly on the lips and slipped one of the crucifixes RCA had given him around her neck. He would have liked to stay and hold her in his arms and tell her he loved her. That was something he had never been able to say before, but there wasn't time.

He stopped at the door and looked back at her for a moment, then stepped out of the room.

As Paul left, Linda's hands came up and clutched the crucifix. Her body relaxed. Her face took on a peaceful expression, like a great fear was suddenly gone.

Durie House looked ominous in the brooding fog. The great old trees of its grounds were black and dead; they watched inimically as the car turned up the driveway and stopped.

Father Kerry's Dodge was still parked in front of the house. Behind it was an empty squad car.

"I don't like it," RCA said. "Father Kerry should've been out of there by now."

The three of them exchanged dark glances, then got out and started for the house. Thayer led the way, his revolver in one hand, his flashlight in the other. They paused at the door. The house seemed horribly quiet. Paul and RCA each uncapped a bottle of holy water that they had brought with them.

"What the hell is that for?" Thayer asked them.

"That's just what it's for," Paul answered.

The expression mirrored on Thayer's face suggested a so-you-didn't-tell-me-everything look. "What is that stuff?" he said.

"Holy water," RCA said.

"Holy water? What do you guys expect to find in there, the Lord of the Flies?"

Paul almost told him that that's exactly what he expected to find, but let it pass. "Come on," he said. "Let's go in. We've got to find out what happened to everybody."

Thayer shook his head at their foolishness, but couldn't help feel the start of a small, clammy chill at the back of his neck by their tone.

Paul tried the door. It was locked. He was about to use force when RCA called them from farther down the terrace. They joined him in front of the French doors that Linda had been catapulted through earlier.

"What do you make of that?" RCA said.

"Looks like something was thrown right through it," Thayer said, opening the doors wider.

"Or someone," Paul added. The thought of Linda, cut and scratched in her hospital bed, formed a knot of apprehension in his stomach.

Turning on his flashlight, Thayer walked into the library and directed its long beam along the wreckage of furniture and books. Paul and RCA followed. Glass crunched under their feet. The foul, lifeless air of the house hit them like a bad taste.

"Christ, it looks like a tornado hit this place," Thayer said.

They stood in the middle of the room and looked around, their breath coming out in long, white puffs.

"Put the lights on," RCA said, his voice rising slightly.

"Where are they?" Thayer asked.

"Over there on the wall," Paul directed. "To the left of the entrance."

"Got 'em." Thayer flipped the wall switch, throwing the wall sconces into a shadowy light that was more unnerving than the dark.

They crawled about the room, stepping over the debris like survivors from an earthquake, each with his own thoughts, each with his own fears.

"Damn, it's cold enough in here to snow," Thayer said, hunching up against the chill of the house. "Can't say too much about the smell either."

"Look!" RCA flinched and pointed to a heavy lamp table that was still in one piece.

It was rocking slowly, back and forth.

"Throw some holy water on it," Paul said.

But RCA only backed away until he bumped into Thayer, who was standing near the foyer entrance with an astonished look on his face.

Paul walked over to the table and sprinkled it with holy water. There was a loud hiss as the water hit the wood. The table stopped moving.

"What in God's name…?" Thayer was at a loss for words.

RCA developed a noticeable tick on the side of his face.

"Let's check the other rooms," Paul suggested. "And get out of here."

"I'm with you," Thayer said. "Then maybe you'll tell me just what the hell is goin' on around here."

Paul didn't answer. He walked into the foyer instead, then waited for Thayer to bring the flashlight. RCA hurried after them.

Paul found the foyer lights and turned them on. An oppressive silence hung on the air that seemed charged with menace. Then they heard a low susurration of sound that gradually increased into a loud, hollow wheezing, like a broken bellows.

"It's the house," RCA said. "It's breathing."

They moved closer together. Thayer looked at Paul as if he still couldn't believe what was happening.

Panic spread into RCA's eyes. He sprang for the front door and tried to open it.

"It won't open!" He turned quickly toward Paul and Thayer. "The fuckin' thing won't open! We're trapped!"

"We can still get out the way we came in," Paul said.

RCA calmed somewhat and nodded. "Yeah, I forgot about that." He was still visibly shaken, and Paul was sorry that he had let him come along.

The breathing became louder.

RCA shouted. "Father Kerry! Father Kerry! Where are you?"

His sudden outburst startled Paul, causing his heart to jump a beat. Paul noticed that Thayer was uneasy, too.

"Christ," Thayer said to RCA. "You damn near made me piss in my pants. Get a grip on yourself."

"This is bad," RCA said, his words coming in a rush. "I didn't think it would be this bad. We've got to find Father Kerry and get out of here. Every minute we stay in this house we're in danger."

"Go outside and stay in the car," Thayer said. "Rice and me will find Father Kerry."

"I don't want to be alone," RCA said, then looked at Paul. "None of us should be alone around here. You know that."

"Okay, okay," Paul said. "We'll stay together."

"Let's look upstairs," Thayer said and started up. Paul followed, then RCA.

They were halfway up the stairs when they saw him.

It was Father Kerry. He was standing at the head of the stairs, looking down at them, his face hidden in the shadows of the hall, his arms spread as in some grotesque benediction.

"Father?" Paul said.

The priest didn't answer. He only stood there, swaying slightly.

RCA started to moan. It was a guttural, gurgling sound that bubbled saliva at the corners of his mouth.

"Jesus," Thayer whispered to Paul. "Look at his feet."

Paul dropped his eyes to Kerry's feet, which were pointing, toes down, a good two feet off the floor.

The chambered breathing of the house became deafening.

RCA, who had noticed something wrong with Father Kerry right away, became incontinent.

Thayer could feel his own bowels slipping. He had only really been frightened once before in his life, and that was when his squad car overturned while chasing a speeder, and he ended up in a drainage ditch, pinned upside down in the car while it filled slowly with water. But that was nothing like this. God, nothing like this at all.

Transfixed, his face leeched white with fear, Paul watched Father Kerry dangle in the air, his arms still spread in a grisly blessing, his shoes never touching the floor, held up on invisible strings and manipulated by some demented puppet-master. They finally got him, Paul thought. And Mrs. Eastman, and Thayer's men. How many more would they take?

They could see Kerry's face now. His eyes wide, staring into nothingness. Empty. Lifeless. His lips twisted into a malevolent grin.

RCA screamed, dropping his bottle of holy water, then ran past Paul and Thayer and tried to pull Kerry down. The priest's outstretched arms closed around him in a revolting embrace. There was a dull hum. Then RCA's body jumped as if hit with an electric current; his thin hands clawed the air under Kerry's hugging arms. A high-pitched whine came from his throat. A bacon-frying sound filled the air, mingling with the constant breathing of the house.

Paul and Thayer watched in horror, unable to move, unable to help. RCA started choking as purple bile spilled over his lips. Smoke poured from his body. His hands contorted into fists. Then there was a loud popping sound, like glass, and both bodies exploded into intense blue flames.

They stood that way for a moment, locked in death, flames consuming them, then sagged and heaved, falling to the stairs. There was another intense explosion of flames. What was once their bodies crumbled apart, breaking up into little piles of burning matter. A minute later, the fires died away, and only ashes remained.

The horror became too great. The mind boggled and could no longer grasp reality as it had been known. The body nerves became frayed and raw, unable to respond.

Paul could see Thayer's chalk-white face, his glazed eyes, his body ready to collapse. It was like looking into a mirror.

He knew the house would take them next.

9

"I'M SORRY ABOUT RCA," Paul said softly. "I shouldn't have let him come."

"It's not your fault," Thayer said. "How were you to know what would happen?"

They sat silently for several minutes in Thayer's kitchen. After the fourth drink, their hands had lost some of the tremor, and their minds, cushioned by the alcohol, were able to gain a foothold against the creeping, slimy fear that still clung to them.

Thayer shook his head, trying to physically dispel the cluster of thoughts that were jarring his mind. "I know what I saw, but I still can't believe that I actually saw it."

"It was real," Paul said. "Believe it."

"In this day and age. Something like this is happening. If we were to tell anybody, they'd lock us up in the laughing academy and throw away the key."

"I went through the same argument myself. But it's there. You saw it."

"Damn it," Thayer said, putting his glass down hard on the table. "I still don't believe it. We're just suffering from some sort of mass hallucination."

He talked with a lethargic slowness that suggested insobriety. But he was not drunk. His tongue just seemed to feel twice its size. It had been that way since he left Durie House.

He was still a little vague on how he got out. He remembered Paul dragging him down the stairs, and doors closing, doors closing everywhere so they couldn't get out; then Paul throwing something in a bottle at the front door – he guessed it was holy water – and then there was an explosion, but the way was clear, and they were running toward the car, then in it and barreling down the driveway.

"It was no hallucination," Paul said. "If it was, where are Father Kerry and RCA? No. It was real all right."

"But these things don't happen. Not now." Thayer was trying to rationalize it away. "Things like this are made up in Hollywood to give people a good shudder. You take your girl to see one so she'll snuggle close, but then you both go home and forget about it."

He was right, Paul thought, remembering movies he had seen with Linda. And once out of the theater, back in the world of reality, the movies were easily forgotten. But what they were experiencing now wasn't a movie.

"Back in your office you told me I was holding out on you," Paul said. "Well, you were right. I was. There was more to it than just car trouble."

Paul took a sip of his drink and told Thayer everything he had held back. This time he left nothing out.

When Paul had finished, Thayer drained his glass and quickly poured another. "You're doing wonders for my nerves. Right now they're just hanging together with spit and alcohol."

Paul smiled. He was beginning to like this man. There had been a camaraderie formed between them tonight that shared danger often brings.

"I'm not sure what's holding me together," Paul said. "And right now I don't think I want to know."

Thayer returned the smile. "I remember my mother telling me about good and evil, heaven and hell, God and the Devil – but just hearing it is one thing. Seeing it…well, it makes you wonder."

"You were in the house."

"I know. That's just the trouble." Thayer paused, trying to put his finger on what he wanted to say. "I've never been a religious man. No matter how many fire-and-brimstone meetings my mother dragged me to as a kid. If God existed, fine. If not, that was okay, too. I mean – to me – if you're dead, that's it. There's nothing else. The worms get you. This life is all you've got. All you're going to get."

"And now you're not so sure," Paul said.

"Yeah. So maybe there is something to this religious stuff after all."

"There had better be or we'll be sharing the same cell at the laughing academy."

Thayer broke out in a fit of laughter, infecting Paul with his glee, until they were both laughing so hard that tears began to well in their eyes.

The laughter was good for their sanity, which they were trying to preserve, trying to strengthen the weak threads that held it precariously together over the dark abyss of madness. But they knew why the laughter was so contagious. It was gallows humor. They were whistling in the dark.

Thayer stopped as abruptly as he had started. His fingers began playing with his whiskey glass, making wet concentric circles on the kitchen table. He was still having trouble explaining this nightmare to himself.

Paul watched him struggle with it, his own laughter dying on his lips.

"How do I stop it, Paul?" Thayer said, staring into his glass, as if he expected to find an answer somewhere on the bottom. "If what you think is true – and I feel that it is – then these murders are sacrifices to that…that portal up there in Durie House. And if whatever it is up there starts to spread…I mean…what do I do? What in God's name do I do? Call out the Army, Navy, and Air Force?"

"Maybe that wouldn't be such a bad idea," Paul said, remembering he had thought much the same thing earlier this evening.

"Yeah, and I'd do it in a minute if I thought anyone would believe me." He looked up from his drink. "It has to be stopped right here. In Lanark. You agree?"

Paul nodded.

"Any ideas? I'm open to suggestions."

"Well, for one thing, I don't think the portal's completely open yet. If we can stop the sacrifices, that will stop it from spreading. Then the house will have to be destroyed."

"You're beginning to sound like the Mayor. That's all he says, 'Stop the killings.' What does everyone think I've been trying to do?"

"I know you've been up against it. But at least now you know why the killings are happening. And you know who's doing them."

"Yeah. Now all I have to do is find Allan Durie."

"RCA mentioned something that happened a long time ago," Paul said. "When Durie was younger, he was involved with some woman. A Pearl something or other."

"Pearl Armstrong?"

"That's it. You know her?"

"I wish I didn't," Thayer said. "What's she got to do with Allan Durie?"

"RCA said she was his 'whore.' And probably everybody else's too after Durie dumped her."

"Maybe her sweetie's come back. We'll find out in the morning."

Thayer poured them another round. They drank and talked and waited for the dawn.

10

DAWN.

The heavy fog was gone, but frail threads of it lingered over the town under a gum-colored sky. It would be another day without sun.

Paul tiptoed into Linda's room. Thayer had dropped him off before heading over to the office. Neither one of them had gotten any sleep. The mind needs reassurance during the night.

He put a hand to her forehead; it was cool to the touch. She was holding the crucifix, he had placed around her neck last night, with one hand. She looked rested and at peace. Which was more than he could say for himself after catching a glimpse of his face in Thayer's bathroom mirror this morning. He bent over and kissed her gently on the lips.

Paul slumped into a chair near the bed and took her free hand in his. The feeble light passing through the window gave the room a milky-gray effect. He squeezed her hand slightly and wished she could talk to him. There was so much he wanted to tell her, things he never said before, things that needed saying. He had always been afraid to reveal his true feelings for her. Something always happened to the people he cared about. But not this time. He wouldn't let it. He wanted her to know.

The door opened and a nurse walked quietly into the room. She did not see Paul until she was bending over the bed to check on Linda. She moved back with a start.

"Sorry," Paul said. "I didn't mean to startle you."

"Mr. Rice?" she said, remembering him ask about Miss Eastman at the desk last night.

"Yes, I thought it would be all right if I sat with her for a little while."

"She'll be out for some time yet. She won't even know you're here."

"I'll know."

The nurse nodded and smiled. She turned and left, closing the door.

Paul looked toward the window at the weak daylight, trying to build its strength. He wondered what the day would bring...and the night.

11

PEARL ARMSTRONG SAT IN HER FAVORITE wing chair, the TV blaring with *The Price is Right*, and the announcer telling someone to "C'mon down," and observed Thayer and Paul over the rim of her teacup.

"I never did think Allan died in that fire," she said, putting her cup down. "Not him. He's too mean to die."

"Do you know where we can find him?" Thayer said, leaning forward on the couch. "Where he might be hiding?"

"No." Then she looked straight at him. "Not here if that's what you mean. I wouldn't let him in the door. Not after what he did to me."

"What was that?" Thayer said.

"That's for me to know."

"Pearl, this is a murder investigation. I have to know everything you can tell me about Allan Durie."

"What's to know. Anyone can tell you what a devil he is."

"But you probably know a great deal more than anyone else."

Pearl smiled. "Old tongues clacking again?"

"We were told you and Durie were pretty close."

She stiffened. "Who told you that? Jerome Klayman?"

Paul watched her reaction, suddenly realizing that this was the first time he had ever heard RCA's last name.

"He's a fine one to talk. Just like all the other men. Pigs. That's all they are. Pigs. Get what they want from a girl and then they don't want to bother with you anymore."

"Mrs. Armstrong," Paul said, "is there anything at all you can tell us about him? Some habit or special place he liked to go. Something that might help us find him."

She gave him a suspicious look.

A woman on the TV shrieked with glee after winning a car. Pearl turned toward the screen, ignoring her callers.

"Pearl," Thayer said. "You can either talk to us here or down at the station. But you're going to talk to us."

The wrinkled face turned back to them. "There ain't nothin' to talk about. All that happened over fifty years ago."

Thayer waited.

"Oh, fudge," Pearl said, realizing Thayer meant what he said. "I told you what he's like."

"Tell us again."

She sighed. "Allan had a way about him that women took to in those days. But he liked to hurt people. He enjoyed it when everybody was afraid of him. He liked having power over them."

"Did he deal in" – Paul searched for the right words – "any unholy practices?"

Pearl hesitated. She wished this young man Thayer brought with him would sit down instead of standing around like a doorman. He was making her nervous. She took a slug of tea.

"He had a special room," she said, "upstairs in that house. Wouldn't let anyone see it. But I did once. It was a big room with a circle on the floor, and there were markings along the circle in different languages.

"He knew all the old tongues. Latin, Celtic…Drudic?"

"Druidic?" Paul said.

"Yeah, somethin' like that. There were others, older, I don't remember anymore. He said they were tongues of the Ancient Gods. Said he could summon things to do his bidding."

"Did he?" Paul asked.

Pearl shrugged. "Most likely. He enjoyed trafficking with the unholy. The whole family was like that. Except James. James cared about people. I think Allan's wife was like that, too, before he drove her batty."

"Durie was married?" Thayer said.

"He married his cousin. Brought her here from Scotland. She was a little mousy thing with big eyes and a chest as flat as a board. He used to tie her up in a chair and make her watch while he took me to bed. Used to give her fits."

"I can imagine," Thayer said. "Where is she now?"

Pearl took another sip of her tea. "She's been in Deerford for God knows how long. Probably still there."

Paul gave Thayer a questioning look.

"Deerford's an institution for the mentally ill," Thayer told him.

"Nice guy," Paul said.

Pearl cackled and almost choked on her tea. "Oh, he was a real sweetheart. Did the same thing with his own sister."

Paul and Thayer exchanged glances. This was the first they heard of a sister.

"He drove his sister insane?" Thayer said.

"No, no" Pearl said. "Took her to bed in front of his wife. Not that he had to force her. She liked it. Mary was always moonin' after him. Besides, Mary hated his wife. Didn't like me either, or any other woman that came near him. Tried to do me in with a knife once, but James stopped her."

"What happened to this sister?" Thayer asked.

Pearl glared at him. "I was gettin' to that. You want me to talk or not?"

"Sorry." Thayer tried to look contrite. "Go on."

"She got pregnant. That's what happened to her."

Thayer was about to ask something else, then stopped himself when Pearl gave him a hard look.

"His wife was barren," she went on, "so Allan wanted the child. But things didn't work out that way. The baby died and Mary, too, birthin' it right in that house."

There was a long silence.

"Well," Pearl snapped. "You got any more questions?"

"I have one, Mrs. Armstrong," Paul said. "If Allan Durie was such a 'devil' as you put it, why did you stay with him?"

"He wasn't at first. He could be nice at times. And it was excitin' bein' with him. Besides, he gave me things. Things a poor girl couldn't afford."

"Did he ever give you a book to keep for him?" Paul asked.

"A book? No. Just things for myself."

"Why did you break up?"

"He got me just like he did Mary."

"Pregnant?"

Pearl nodded. "But that's all he cared about. The child, not me. He got some old quack that almost did me in. Gutted me up so bad that I could never have another baby." She paused. "After it was over, Allan kicked me out."

"The baby," Thayer said, "was it a boy or a girl?"

"I don't know. I never saw it. He would never let me see it. I was given money and sent away. That lasted three or four years. When I got back, the baby was gone."

"Dead?" Thayer said.

She shook her head. "Sent away. I think James did it to get it away from Allan."

"Didn't James ever tell you what the baby was? Or where he sent the child?"

"No. Never. He was afraid I would find it and use it to go back to Allan."

"Would you have?" Paul said.

"I don't know. I was pretty crazy about him at the time. Even if he was a pig."

Then she cackled again. "But I got the last laugh on both of 'em. Never told either one about it. Though, sometimes it nearly busted my gut not to."

She started laughing again. They waited for her to stop. Pearl looked at them, her eyes sparkling with glee.

"The baby," she said. "It was James'."

12

AN HOUR BEFORE NOON.

Paul sat down wearily across the desk from Thayer, nursing a cup of acid coffee from the vending machine. It was his sixth cup of the morning and his stomach and mouth were already suffering. He had just returned with Thayer from a quick breakfast at a McDonald's.

He took a small sip of his coffee, made a sour face, and set the Styrofoam cup down on Thayer's desk.

"What's the matter?" Thayer asked. "Can't you stand the local brew?"

"How can you drink that stuff?" Thayer was two cups up on him. "It tastes like Montezuma's revenge."

Thayer laughed, taking a good slug of his own coffee. "You get used to it. It'll grow hair on your chest."

"And probably in your stomach."

"It is a little hairy at that."

Yeah, let's keep the conversation light, Paul thought. Let's keep last night's fear buried. Anyone could tell by looking at them that they were in control. Some control. One good loud noise and they'd both be under the desk. He fought off the bone-heaviness of a sleepless night, and his mind went lazily over what Pearl Armstrong had told them.

"You thinking about the Duries?" Thayer asked, catching his silence.

Paul nodded. "Sort of."

"Well, if you ask me, the whole damn family's nuts from playin' musical beds, including Pearl. She fitted right in."

"What bothers me is how an old man like Allan Durie could manage to kill anyone. He must be at least ninety by now."

"What are you trying to do? Eliminate my chief suspect?"

"Well, it could be someone else. Someone who got their hands on Durie's grimoire."

"His what?"

"The book of rituals I told you about last night."

Thayer started to take another sip of coffee, then changed his mind and set the cup back down. "Maybe the missing child has something to do with all this."

Paul shrugged. "Maybe. But why? Pearl said James was the father not Allan. And he seemed to be the only one in the family that was normal."

"Like I said, the whole family seems nuts to me. Could be the kid never knew who its real father was. And Alan thought it was his. Maybe the kid's following in daddy's footsteps."

"That kid would be in its fifties by now. That is, if it's still alive, and if it's here in Lanark."

"Well, that's another road open to us if the Allan Durie thing fizzles out."

The telephone rang.

Thayer picked it up, then motioned for Paul to take it. "It's for you. Philip Deering."

Paul got up and took the phone. "Hello."

"Mr. Rice?" Deering said.

"Yes."

"I've been going through my father's notes on Allan Durie."

"Did you find anything?"

"Well, nothing that I haven't already told you. Sorry. I thought there might be something here."

Paul paused. "Mr. Deering, do you know anything about a child being at Durie House?"

"No." Deering sounded surprised. "No, I never heard anything like that. Allan's wife never had any children, and James wasn't married. There was a sister, Mary, but she died in childbearing. Got involved with some man from the town. The Durie's hushed it up. The child died as well." Deering paused. "Did Allan or James leave anything behind? Anything written down?"

"If they did, we haven't been able to find it."

"That's too bad. I thought there might be some notes or letters in the house."

"Well, Durie House isn't one of my favorite places just now."

"Oh? Something happen?"

Paul told him about last night's horrors.

Deering became silent. Paul could hear his nervous breathing.

"That's very hard to accept," Deering said finally. "Not that I don't believe you. But there has to be another explanation."

"I wish there was. Isn't there anything, some counter ceremony, that we could use to stop this thing?"

"There might be. There's a ritual that dates back to the seventeenth century that the Roman Catholics use. But it's an exorcism. Using it could be very dangerous. It could backfire."

"Well, something has to be done."

"I agree," Deering said. "But I don't think this is the right approach." He was silent for several moments. "Maybe I should come out there."

"We could use your help."

"Yes, well…you'll be at the same place…the police station?"

"If not, they'll know where to reach me." Paul started to give him directions.

"I know the way." Deering interrupted. "Don't forget my family used to live in Lanark. Until later then. I'll see you sometime today."

After Deering hung up, Paul couldn't help feel that the same miasma of fear that had hung over Father Kerry had now settled over Deering, regardless of the old man's skeptic claims about the supernatural. Paul repeated the conversation to Thayer.

"He's frightened," Paul said.

"Who isn't." Thayer took a cigar from his shirt pocket, unwrapped it, and put it in his mouth. "I felt like leavin' town this morning and not coming back."

Paul smiled, then lit up a cigarette. He held the match for Thayer. "You want a light for that thing?"

"I never light 'em. Much as I'd like to. Just suck on 'em."

Paul shook out the match. "Deering mentioned notes or letters that the Durie's might have left around."

The cigar almost fell out of Thayer's mouth. "You don't want to go back to that house to look, do you?"

"Not really."

Thayer looked relieved.

"You suppose Father Kerry wrote anything down?" Paul asked.

"Maybe he was too frightened. Hell, who wouldn't be? But there's only one way to find out. Let's go see."

13

The drive to St. Casmir's took thirty minutes. The sky was overcast with the threat of still more rain. After the last few days, Paul wondered if the sun would ever shine again.

"Have you got any keys?" he asked as Thayer parked the car.

Thayer patted his jacket pocket. "Something better."

They left the car and went through the churchyard where Paul had run for his life last night. Entering the church, they made their way to Father Kerry's office. The door was open.

When Paul walked into the room, he remembered how RCA had first summoned him to listen to the frightened priest's warning about Durie House. And how many days ago was that? It seemed like years. He wished now that he would have done what Kerry asked of him. But it was impossible at the time. Eastman would never have listened to anything he had to say.

Paul sat down in the high-backed leather chair behind the desk and started searching the drawers. If Kerry did keep notes, they could possibly help them find Allan Durie.

"What makes you think Kerry kept his notes here rather than at his house?" Thayer asked.

"If you were as frightened as Kerry, but still managed to put in writing what happened to you in that house, where would you keep it, so whatever's up there couldn't reach out and destroy it?"

Thayer thought for a moment. "Yeah, I guess a church would be the safest place."

Paul rummaged through most of the drawers, finding nothing of importance, then in the last one, he found a closed compartment under a Bible.

"This might be something," Paul said, trying to lift the panel. "It's locked."

Thayer pulled a small leather case from his jacket pocket, unzipped it, and examined the set of picklocks closely.

"Some keys," Paul said.

"These are all the keys I need," Thayer said, moving over to the drawer. He selected a pick and went to work on the lock. A moment later, he had the compartment open.

"I'm impressed," Paul said. "What did you say you did before you became a cop?"

"Never you mind. Any good cop worth his salt knows how to use these." He slipped the pick back into the case, rezipped it, and put it back in his pocket.

There was no diary, but they found a large manila envelope addressed to RCA and marked "To Be Opened After My Death." It was signed Justin Kerry.

Paul opened it as Thayer stood next to him. They read the thin, elegant handwriting together:

My Dear Friend,

In the event of my death, which most certainly has come to pass or you would not have used the key I gave to you and found this letter, I have but a few last requests.

First, and most important, is my burial. I would like my body blessed in God's church and buried in holy ground, the Ninety-first Psalm read over me, prayers said for my soul. If this is impossible, than my body should be consumed by holy fire, depriving that fiend or his legions of any use of it. If there is no body – and there might not be, for I do not know what face death will be wearing when those devils send it – I can only hope that God will take a hand, though why He would bother on my behalf I do not know. I have failed Him miserably.

I have tried to live my life as a simple man and servant of the Lord, but living in a constant stupor of alcohol these last several years, the latter has not been easy to do. You know this better than I, my friend, having to help drag this drunken hulk of a body upstairs countless times. I now realize that as a priest I have been nothing but a cipher all the years of my ministry. I taught the Gospel to others, but did not fully embrace it myself, consequently losing what little faith I had and all of God's trust in dealing with the Durie affair.

I have told you some of this, but not all. It was not easy for me to talk of my failure.

It all started innocently enough that hot and humid evening in July. I was telephoned and asked to come to Durie House by one of the remaining brothers, James, who I had met and talked to, although briefly, several times over the years in Lanark while administering to my daily needs. I considered him a pleasant enough man, although very intense and nervous.

Having never seen the man in church, I considered the phone call an excellent opportunity to bring him back to the faith that he seemed to have forsaken. Even though Durie's voice was strained and frightened over the phone, I went to see him like an unsuspecting sheep. Little did I realize how unprepared I was for what awaited me that night, or how it would change the rest of my life.

I arrived at the house shortly after ten. Durie was in a nervous frenzy. He appearance was disheveled, to say the least. His clothes were torn and covered with dirt, and he looked like he had been beaten about the face. He was very frightened and admitted me hurriedly into the house. The first thing I noticed upon entering was the deathly cold that hung about the place, even though the night was sticky with warmth. I quickly reasoned that the man must have had his air conditioning turned up to the highest setting on the dial. But then, there was the smell. The whole house was odoriferous, and the stench had me on the verge of gagging several times. It was as if the house was littered with excrement.

Durie was relieved to see me. I kept asking what had happened to him, but he kept putting me off saying, "In due time, Father. In due time." He ushered me quickly into the library and closed the doors behind us. Then in a whisper, as if he were afraid someone would overhear, begged me to listen to his confession.

I naturally complied. This made him feel somewhat better, but all the time he was talking to me he spoke in a whisper and kept looking around the room. I asked him if we were alone. "No, Father," he said. "You're never alone here. They're probably listening." He didn't elaborate on this and I didn't push him, for he kept insisting that there wasn't much time and I should hear him out.

After a nervous hesitation at some cracking noise somewhere in the house, he told me that he was afraid of losing not only his life, but his soul as well. He feared he had fallen out of grace with God, not for anything he had done, at least before tonight, but because of his family's dealings – especially his brother, Allan, who had succeeded in carrying out the Durie obsession.

He hesitated again, then continued in an even lower voice, so much so, that I could barely hear him, and what I did hear I could hardly believe.

It seems as if his brother had been trying for some time, picking up where the rest of the Durie Family had left off, to establish a link, what James called a "portal" between this plane and the inner plane of true evil, the lower world order, or what we theologians call Hell. The very pit. The storehouse of man's fears and miseries and whatever else it contained.

Twenty years ago Allan succeeded in creating a book of rituals that he thought would open this "portal."

Durie stopped to study my reaction to what he had just told me, and, I must confess, I was rather skeptical, although it sent a chill through me to hear his words. At first, I thought he was suffering from some form of dementia. As a priest, I was schooled in the existence of evil as a real force in the world, but I never gave much credence to Hell as actually existing. I now realize how wrong I was.

James begged me for my own sake, as well as his, to believe him. I said I did, but only to put his fears to rest. This seemed to satisfy him and he continued talking.

Years ago, when Allan was younger, there had been a child. But the poor thing was not conceived in marriage. Allan's wife could not give him an heir to the unholy Durie Legacy. James named Pearl Armstrong as the mother. A few years after the child was born, Allan started tutoring it (James would not tell me if the child was a boy or girl) in his ways.

This was too much for James, and he managed to get the child out of his brother's evil clutches. There were six of them in the house at that time: James, Allan, Allan's wife, the child, and two servants, Joseph and Rose Boucher, a middle-aged couple who had been with the Duries for years.

James spirited the child out of the house, sending the Bouchers, who had no children of their own, along as foster parents. They were to raise the child as their own and under no circumstances were they ever to reveal where they had gone. James would provide them with money, and he was as good as his word until the family fortune dwindled down to nothing and only the house remained.

For James, the remaining years alone with his brother in this house must have truly been a nightmare. Allan's wife was gone, locked away behind the institutionalized walls of Deerford, and James literally became his brother's keeper, locking him in at night, seeing to it that he never left the house, watching him grow more and more under the control of the evil he was trying to release.

The years began to take their toll on him. In the end, after Allan had his accursed book completed and James realized what he was doing, James had to keep him locked up day and night. He had to be forever on the alert, for not only was his own life in constant danger, but everyone else's whenever Allan managed to escape. It was like the old days all over again when Duries prowled the night, searching for victims and the right combination of gruesome handiwork that would open the way for their God of Darkness.

How many innocent people were struck down depended on how

fast James could find his brother and bring him back to the house. Why he did not turn him over to the authorities, I do not know. I can only guess that as reclusive and clannish as the Duries had always been at keeping to themselves, it must have been difficult for him to turn his own brother over to the law, which represented a town where the Duries were not liked.

On some of his escapes, Allan had mailed a letter to his child, explaining the Durie Legacy, the evil fruit of being a Durie. James managed to intercept two of these letters, but he was certain there had been others that Allan succeeded in mailing. How he had found out the child's whereabouts James did not know. Unless "they" told him. "They" being the devils that lived in him now, and in Durie House.

Finally, two days ago, things came to a head. James said his brother's condition worsened. He started in on his rituals again, intending to open the "portal," and keep it opened. James had hidden the book, but Allan knew the rituals by heart. He had to make sure Allan stayed locked up.

Tonight was worse. James said Allan became very violent, howling and carrying on like a madman. James tried to restrain him, but Allan attacked him, knocking him down and escaping into the night. James went after him, finding him in Lanark, but not soon enough. He was in an alley, bending over the body of a young boy he had just murdered. I learned later that the boy was Dennis Evers.

James subdued his brother with the aid of a crucifix and took him back to the house. When he tried to lock him in his room, Allan turned on him. The crucifix, James had slipped over Allan's head to control him, was gone. It was on the floor; its chain unbroken. "They" were at work again.

A violent struggle followed. In order to save himself, James killed his brother with the very knife Allan had used to murder the boy. Later, after he recovered from the shock of what he had done, he buried Allan in the cellar, putting the crucifix in the grave to keep him still and at peace – if that was possible.

James was repentant about his brother, but felt that it was probably better for him this way. And he was happy about the child. He knew that the Bouchers had done their best. What was important was the child had grown up in a normal home life, untouched by Allan's evil influence.

After listening to what he told me, to say it merely disturbed me would be an understatement. It troubled me deeply, stirring a fear in me that I did not know I had. I tried to tell myself that the man was out of his head and probably suffering from shock of some kind. Surely, there was a logical explanation for everything he had told me, and I did not really believe he had actually killed his brother.

With weak conviction, I started to give him absolution for sins I was sure never happened, then the house turned on me. A loud rapping echoed through the house, like a huge fist pounding on the walls, coming down the hall toward the library. The room began to tremble as the pounding reached us. A din of voices invaded my mind, calling me by name, spewing vile and evil invectives at me. Books and furniture were thrown around the room. Doors started opening and closing by themselves. My clothes began to tear, as if invisible hands were laid upon me. I was attacked by fists and teeth, and claws.

I have gone over this many times in my mind, trying to remember everything that happened, trying to put into words the naked fear that overcame me, trying to rationalize my actions. But it is no use. There was no excuse for what I had done. I was terrified to say the least. I had faced the Dark One for the first time and failed. I disgraced the cloth I wear and fell from God's grace that night.

I ran.

God help me. I just ran. I ran to my car and drove at break-neck speed all the way back to my church, leaving that poor man alone in that house. I abandoned James Durie and fled for my life, with something stalking my heels all the way.

Looking back on it now, it is still difficult to put into words the terror I felt. One must experience such an ordeal in order to understand. Not that I condone my actions. I have never forgiven myself. I never will.

I learned later, after I deserted him, that James tried to burn the house down, but managed to destroy only a small part of it. As you know, the firemen found him dead inside the house. They said it was a natural cause, heart attack, but I know what really killed him.

No one is the same after something like this. My life has been no exception. I have lived in fear these past years, jumping at any noise, wary of shadows, terrified of the night. And so, lacking in courage, I found it in a bottle – but it was not a cure. It only dulled the pain somewhat, shorting out my fears and anxieties for a time and allowing me to sleep, but it was always a muddled and terrifying sleep, filled with lurking phantoms, watching and waiting for me. And somewhere in the ancient chambers of my mind, behind a door that I dreaded to open, was the haunting thought that I would have to face the evil of Durie House again.

I have never told the police what happened that night, or of the grave in the cellar, or who killed the Evers boy, or any of it. All had remained sub rosa. No one even knows I was there that night. Except you, my friend, and you have never asked me any questions. That is why I felt you had the right to know, which brings me to my second request. I would like you to turn this letter over to the Bishop. Let him decide what to tell the police.

James Durie gave me the Boucher's address. I have enclosed it with this letter.

God forgive me.

Justin Xavier Kerry.

Paul put the letter down and looked in the envelope, taking out a small piece of paper. It read:

Mr. & Mrs. Joseph Boucher

215 Elmont Avenue

Seattle, Washington

"What do you think?" Paul asked.

Thayer shook his head. "Jesus Christ, the Evers kid, too."

"That eliminates your prime suspect."

"Yeah, and where does that leave me? Unless…" Thayer took the letter and the address, put them back in the envelope and stuck it in his pocket.

"Let's go back to the office," Thayer said. "I want to put in a call to Seattle. I've got an old buddy on the force out there. Maybe he can give us some fast information on the Bouchers."

14

ANDY KASSAVIK WAS A GOOD MAN. Thayer had partnered with him for ten years in Milwaukee until Andy got a better job offer in Seattle and moved his family out there.

Thayer told him, after some sociable conversation and promises to come out for a visit someday, what he wanted, and that he needed the information five murders ago. Andy promised he'd get back to him as soon as he had anything, but Thayer really didn't expect to hear from him until tomorrow. He'd have to sweat out tonight with what information he had.

After Thayer hung up, he felt uneasy. He always did when he had to wait on other people for anything, and the fact that Deering hadn't shown up yet didn't help. Paul had tried to call him several times, but there was no answer. So they sat around Thayer's office and brooded over it. Neither one of them wanted to put it into words, but each knew what the other was thinking. Deering might be in trouble.

So they waited. Deering might call or walk in at any moment.

Barney Jensen brought them coffee from the vending machine. He had been called in early, three hours before his shift started, because Red Engman, the eight-to-four dispatcher, went home nursing a bad cold and a high fever.

Thayer sat on the edge of his desk and looked through the medical reports for what seemed the thousandth time. Paul's stomach started to turn over and hide when Barney handed him the coffee.

Thayer blew out a long sigh of exasperation. "I've been over these things I don't know how many times and I still can't find any rhyme or reason in them. The killings took place all over town."

"The only pattern I can see," Barney said, looking over Thayer's shoulder and drinking coffee, "are the mutilations. The boys have their peckers cut off and the girls…"

"You don't have to tell me," Thayer said, throwing the reports on his desk, a feigned expression of pain on his face. "I know what was cut off."

Paul smiled, pulled out his cigarettes, and watched a folded-up square of paper fall to the floor. He picked it up and opened it.

"Maybe this is something," Paul said. "I forgot I had it." He got up from a nearby chair and handed the sheet of paper to Thayer. "I copied it from the Lanark Library. They have old newspaper stories of other murders in this area. The earliest goes back to 1866."

Paul waited for Thayer to finish reading, then said, "It seems that some of the murders occurred more than once in the same place. Places like Benson's Woods and Handy's Marsh. Mean anything to you?"

Thayer looked over the paper again. "Yeah, Benson's Woods used to be the area that's Thackeray Park now."

"And Handy's Marsh is Old Marsh Road," Barney added, leaning over Thayer's shoulder again.

"Look here," Thayer said, reading from Paul's notes. "Mandy Hamm murdered in Benson's Woods. That's where the Gordon Boy was killed. And here," Thayer's voice rising slightly with excitement. "Jill Nickel murdered in alley between Court and Elm Streets, and Dennis Evers in an alley between Bishop and Elm. Bishop is Court Street now. They changed the name a while back."

"That makes three for the alley," Barney remarked. "That's where we found the MacFarland boy."

"Yeah," Thayer said, standing up. "Three there. I thought I saw another for Thackeray Park. Oh, here, at the beginning. Shawn Kilpatrick, Benson's Woods. That's three there, but I don't see any other similarities. We haven't had any recent killings near Graceland Cemetery or Handy's March."

"Wait a minute," Paul said. "Let's pinpoint these on a map of the town."

Thayer walked to the wall behind his desk where a large, colored map of Lanark was tacked up to a corkboard. Green headed pins were sticking in various sections of the map.

"The current ones are already up here," Thayer said.

"What about Dwayne Eastman?" Barney asked. "You didn't put in any pin for him."

"I think we can omit him. What do you think, Paul?"

Paul started to take a sip of his coffee and then changed his mind. He had had so much of the stuff in the last few days he was sure his blood had turned to caffeine.

"No, not Dwayne," Paul said softly. "Chrissie Eastman's the one that fits into the pattern."

"What about Mrs. Eastman and Father Kerry and RCA?" Barney asked. "Or the two officers that went out there? You told me they were all dead, but you haven't got any bodies. You omittin' them, too?"

"Something else got to them." Thayer said. "Something in that house."

"You mean there's two killers goin' around?" Barney looked confused.

Paul and Thayer exchanged glances. The fear that had seized them last night in Durie House was held uncertainly in check by a thin protective membrane of time and distance, and daylight.

"Sort of," Paul said to Barney.

"So what have we got?" Thayer said, changing the subject, his eyes scanning the map. "Ralphie Gordon in the park, thc MacFarland boy in the Bishop-Elm alley, Jennifer Bernstein in her mother's house – that would be Raymond Street – Chrissie Eastman near Durie House, and Debbie Ralston on Cornet Drive."

Thayer rechecked the locations listed on the paper, then stuck two more pins in the map, one for Graceland Cemetery, one for Old Marsh Road.

“These two new locations cover a lot of area,” Thayer said.

Paul joined him at the map, studying it closely. He still wasn’t sure what he was looking for.

“It seems to me,” Thayer said, “that whoever gets close to this thing suddenly gets eliminated. Dwayne Eastman, maybe his father, RCA –”

“You mean whoever knows something winds up dead?” Barney asked, feeling a slight discomfort at his recent knowledge.

“That’s what I said,” Thayer told him.

“Do you have a ruler and a marking pencil?” Paul asked Thayer.

Thayer moved to his desk, rummaged through it, then returned to Paul and handed him a ruler and a liquid-tipped marker. “You got an idea?” Thayer asked him.

Paul took the ruler and marker absently, lost in his thoughts. “Huh? Oh, maybe…something I’ve read or seen recently. Let’s move these two new pins so they line up a little more with the others.”

Paul drew connecting lines between all the pins.

“Seems to box the compass,” Thayer observed. “Two east, two west, two north.”

“Just one on the south side of town though,” Barney said, picking up the train of thought.

Paul finished and stepped back from the map.

“Doesn’t look like anything to me,” Thayer said, rubbing his chin thoughtfully.

“Looks like a lot of nothing with parts missing,” Barney said.

Paul smiled. “Look, there’s only been one killing in the south section of town so far, but suppose there was another.”

Paul added another pin, then connected the remaining lines. “Now what do you see?” Paul said, stepping back.

“A cross?” Thayer said.

“Funny looking cross,” Barney said, tilting his head to one side to look at it. “It’s off kilter.”

“It’s upside down,” Paul said. “The books I looked through at the library said an upside down cross was just like an inverted pentagram…the sign of the Devil.”

"Then the victims are sacrificed to form this pattern," Thayer said, trying to make his voice sound normal and not betray the sudden coldness he felt in his throat.

"Right," Paul said, dropping the ruler and marker on Thayer's desk. "And if Allan Durie is dead, then someone else must have his book. Someone who's trying to open the portal for reasons of their own."

Barney stood with his mouth open, looking from one to the other of them, not sure he was really hearing this right.

"That's the book Father Kerry was talking about in his letter," Thayer said. "The one James Durie promised no one would ever get their hands on."

"The killings must have to form some symbolic shape in order to have an effect on the closet," Paul said. "They have to be a sign of devotion to the Dark Powers."

"Jesus Christ," Barney said. "You guys are givin' me cold flashes."

"It's my guess," Paul continued, "that when the killings have been completed – the upside down cross completed – the portal will be open."

Thayer shook his head. "God, and then what?"

"We had a taste of it last night at Durie House," Paul said. "Imagine if it were to spread…"

Paul didn't finish. Thayer knew what he meant to say. It would spread like a plague, infecting everything. He shuddered inwardly.

No one spoke. They stood there silently, feeling the room press in on them, the electric charge of the air, fear crawling up their spines on long, hairy legs.

Thayer made a sudden movement away from the wall, like he had just stepped in a nest of snakes.

"What's the matter?" Paul asked.

"Nothing. Sometimes I think…nothing…"

"You seeing things? Shadows creeping along the floor, dancing on a wall, or in a corner."

"You, too?"

Paul nodded. "Ever since last night. But I never see it head on."

"Yeah, it seems like it's always out of the corner of your eye."

"You guys aren't pullin' my leg, are you?" Barney asked. "I mean, this is all hard to believe. I never put much stock in there being a Devil."

The overhead fluorescent lights blinked, buzzing like a fly, then stayed on.

"He must have heard you," Paul said.

Barney thought he was kidding and started to smile, then knew that he wasn't and changed his mind.

Thayer turned to Paul. "You better try Deering again. He should have been here by now."

Paul picked up the telephone and dialed Deering's number. He let the phone ring for over a minute. There was no answer. He replaced the receiver.

Thayer ran a hand through his hair. "I don't like it." He glanced at his watch. "Let's take a ride out there. We can be back before it's full dark."

Paul grabbed his jacket off the back of a chair. "Let's go."

"Barney," Thayer said, walking over to him, "I want everyone working tonight, and I want them to concentrate on Old Marsh Road, Graceland Cemetery, and the south side of town." He refolded the sheet of paper Paul had given him and stuck it in his pocket. "If there's going to be any more killing, that's where they'll be. And, Barney…"

"I know," Barney said. "Don't leave the station. Grab what sleep I can down here. My old lady's really going to enjoy that."

"Sorry."

"What about Red?" Barney asked. "Should I call him in? He's probably in bed with that cold of his."

"See how Red feels," Thayer said. "If he's up to it, get him in. If not, have Jerry Hardigan spell you at the radio."

"Good," Barney said. "I don't want to be in the office alone."

15

AN HOUR AND A HALF LATER, when Thayer turned the car into the driveway and saw Deering's house for the first time, he gave Paul a long sidelong look.

"Yeah, I know," Paul said. "It looks a lot like Durie House."

"Let's hope it doesn't have the same type of entertainment," Thayer said, and stopped the car.

They got out and walked to the house. Paul rang the bell. On the third ring, a tall, attractive woman with shoulder-length honey-colored hair answered the door.

"Is Mr. Deering in?" Paul asked.

"No," she said. "I'm afraid you've just missed him."

"Did he say where he was going?" Thayer asked.

A troubled look came into her eyes when she saw Thayer's badge on his jacket. "He told me he was driving up to Lanark. He left a number where he could be reached. If you like, I'll get it for you."

She gave Paul a warm smile.

"No, that's all right," Thayer said. "It's probably the number at the station." He turned to Paul. "We must have missed him on the interstate."

The woman looked at them. "Is anything wrong?"

"No," Paul said. "Nothing. We'll catch up to him in Lanark."

She gave him another smile and started to close the door.

"Ahh, one more thing," Paul said. "Was Mr. Deering home most of the day?"

"Why, yes, as far as I know." She smiled again. She had an easy, charming smile. "I only arrived myself about three hours ago to type up his notes." She checked her watch for verification. "Yes, just about three hours ago."

"Are you his secretary?" Paul asked.

"Secretary and man Friday." She looked directly at Paul. "I've been with Mr. Deering since my husband died three years ago. My name is Lora Keys."

"Then Deering's been here since you arrived," Thayer said.

"Yes. Before that I couldn't say, although he looked like he had been working on something all morning."

"Were you inside the house all the time you've been here?" Paul asked.

She paused for a moment, gathering her thoughts. "Yes. I was typing in my office and going over some of Mr. Deering's notes with him. I haven't been outside the house since I arrived. Why?"

"We were just curious why Mr. Deering didn't answer his phone," Thayer said.

"The phone? Why there haven't been any calls here at all. Not since I've been here anyway, and the hall extension is right outside my office. I can't miss hearing it if it rings."

"Thank you," Paul said. "You've been most helpful."

She nodded, gave Paul another big smile, and slowly closed the door.

"If they were both home," Thayer said, after they had returned to the car, "why didn't they answer the phone?"

Paul shook his head. "I don't know. You had the telephone company check out the line before we left so it couldn't be phone trouble. Maybe Durie House can reach out farther than we thought and didn't want us to get through."

"Well, if Deering's in Lanark, we'll know soon enough. I told Barney to call me on the radio the minute he got to the station."

Thayer paused, then looked over at Paul. "I have a hunch we're going to have a busy night."

A hazy twilight began to fill the sky as they pulled into the street.

Night was not far behind.

16

FRED OWENS KNEW THAT SOMEONE OR something was trying to kill him.

The hard realization of his situation had hit him with an overwhelming impact early that morning in the predawn darkness of his own backyard. And whatever it was out there kept coming back. The other night Frank Bojold's dog spotted it lurking around the house, and there were times he could even sense it watching him.

Feeling his blood start to run cold, Fred went back downstairs, returning to his TV dinner. He was scaring himself again. When you're an old fart, Fred reasoned, you're cold enough the way it is without thinkin' ghoulish thoughts to freeze your bones.

Chief Thayer said he had men watching the house, didn't he? But Fred had to admit the thought wasn't very reassuring. They wouldn't be much help. What could they do really? Swing past every now and then in a car. They had the whole town to watch over.

Fred dropped into his recliner and eyed the half-eaten TV dinner on the coffee table. The Fish 'N Chips stared back at him. He had lost his appetite. Even his bird friends seemed to have lost their desire to eat. Not that he didn't see to it that they always got plenty, they just weren't eating as much lately, and he didn't venture out at four in the morning to feed them anymore. Ten o'clock was soon enough. There were plenty of people moving about then, under the good old light of day.

The night was different. He didn't go out at all when night came. He stayed inside, right in the living room, every light in the house on, watching TV, or reading, waiting for the dawn. The only time he stirred from his roost was to examine the windows and doors every half-hour to make sure they were still securely locked, or get a snack from the kitchen, or check out a noise.

There weren't many noises in this old house, thank God. She was solidly built. Not like those cardboard boxes they slap together nowadays. Hell, in some you can hear your neighbors every time they take a piss. Like his daughter's place, walls as thin as paper, just the scantiest material separating you from the elements.

But not this house. It was reasonably quiet. Christ, the whole neighborhood was quiet as far as that goes. Probably being close to the cemetery had a lot to do with it. Folks didn't want to do any sinnin' that close to eternity.

His wife had said all the sinnin' in the world was caused by the Devil. She believed in him, and in her Ouija board. She'd drag that damn thing out and consult it for everythin' under the sun, that is until one day she read somewhere that using a Ouija was just invitin' trouble. It was like askin' the Devil and his kind to step into your parlor.

Fred sighed. It was lonely without her. That made him think of the story he had heard down at Booker's. About the old gent who was so lonesome he eventually asked the Devil himself to come and pay him a visit.

The doorbell rang.

"Jesus Christ!" Fred shouted.

His heart started to hammer in his chest, and he nearly wet his pants again.

Finally, getting himself under control, he came to the door.

"Who's there?" he asked in a shaky voice.

"Wally," a voice said.

Fred peeked out the window next to the door and saw Officer Wally Schaefer, who he knew on sight, standing under the white glare of his porch light.

Fred opened the door and let him in, redoing all the locks as soon as Schaefer was inside.

"Chief Thayer told me to drop in now and then and see how you were doing," Wally said, following him into the living room, his body throwing a shadow across Fred's unfinished dinner.

"Well, I'm still alive, if that's what you mean," Fred said.

"So I see," Wally smiled. "Anything new?"

"No, but that don't mean that thing ain't still out there."

Wally nodded, looking around, still not sure the whole thing wasn't just Fred's nerves. Why would anyone single him out, and then keep coming back? All the other murder victims had been much younger.

"What are you doin' so far from home?" Fred asked. "I thought you stuck mainly to the peninsula."

"I do, but tonight we're taking in more territory. Every man has a wider beat," Wally lied. He didn't want to unnerve the old man by telling him they were expecting trouble on this side of town.

Fred eyed him suspiciously, not sure whether to believe him or not. "You talk to my neighbor, Frank Bojold?"

"No. Should I?"

"Frank was walkin' his dog a couple of nights back, and when he got in front of my place, that dog damn near had kittens."

"You've got a lot of wild animals coming in your yard, Fred. Probably the dog just spotted one. You feed practically everything around here that walks, crawls, or flies."

When Fred saw that Schaefer wasn't going to believe a word he told him, he sat down heavily in his recliner, sulking. "This wasn't any animal," he said, annoyance creeping into his voice.

"Anything else?"

Fred didn't answer him. Wally could see that the old guy was getting rattled.

"Just take it easy," Wally said. "We're cruising the area. And we'll be watching your place. If there's anybody out there, we'll get him."

Still no answer.

“Well,” Wally said, feeling uncomfortable in Fred’s stony silence. “I’d best be getting on.” Wally was anxious to stop at Marion’s. She had been acting kind of funny lately, and he wanted to see if she was all right.

“See you, Fred. Lock up after me.”

Fred snapped his dentures together with a click. “You don’t have to tell me that.”

Wally grinned and stepped out onto the porch. Fred closed the door and quickly locked it. A few minutes later, when he heard Wally’s car drive off, he started moving from room to room, checking all the windows again.

It would be a long time before dawn.

17

"BREAKER. BREAKER."

"Go ahead," Red Devil said, letting him on the channel.

"Who have I got?" the breaker said.

"This is the one Red Devil. Who am I talking to?"

"This is the one Red Devil," the breaker, Jimmy Gillispie said, mimicking the voice of Art Hammond, whose CD handle was Red Devil.

"Come again?" Red Devil said. "I didn't catch your handle."

Jimmy stifled a fit of the giggles by holding the hand mike of the Franklin CB radio against his chest.

"This is the one Red Devil," Jimmy mimicked again.

Silence on the band.

Jimmy sat in his father's car shaking with laughter, imagining the dumb look on Art's face.

"Is that really your handle?" Red Devil asked.

"Is that really your handle?" Jimmy shot back at him, unable to stop his glee from spilling over the air.

"Are you mobile?" Red Devil asked, his voice very serious now.

"Base."

"What's your 20?"

"It's 1241 Pine Crest," Jimmy said, having convulsions of laughter now. That was Red Devil's address. The dumb boob.

Silence.

"Breaker. Breaker." A new voice came on.

"Go ahead," Red Devil said.

"Red Devil, this is Wily Coyote."

"Go ahead, Wily."

"That must be that wise guy that thinks he's so funny."

Wily Coyote was Richie Douglas. Jimmy looked out the car window at the street. Richie was mobile. He'd have to be careful.

"Just ignore him guys," a new voice said. That was the beaver that Red Devil was ratchet-jawing with before Jimmy broke in. The dumb cunt that lived about three blocks from him and called herself Penelope.

"Negatory on that," Wily said. "Wise guys like that need their clocks fixed."

"Hey, Penelope," Jimmy broke in, hardly able to control the pleasure he got from his own wit. "How about if I come over to your 20 and you service my antenna? It needs some lubrication. You read that, beaver?" Actually, he had no desire for her at all. She was ugly as a toe. A tall, skinny, no-breasted, stick in the mud.

Silence.

"Why don't you do that," Penelope said finally. "I'll see if I have anything small enough for your antenna."

Red Devil and Wily Coyote started to laugh.

"That's telling him, Penelope," Wily Coyote said. "Mark one for you."

Anger flashed in Jimmy Gillispie's eyes, burning away the glee that had just danced there.

"Hey, Penelope," Jimmy said. "Why don't you go to the john. Take a 10-100 and wash your mouth out with it."

"Listen, wise ass," Wily said. "I'm gonna find out who—"

Jimmy cut him off, keying his mike and throwing a dead carrier on the air so that no one could receive or transmit on that channel. He held it there for as long as he could, as long as he thought it was safe. There'd be other mobile CB'ers out, cruising in their cars, and they'd be looking for him now.

He hated the CB'ers, with their stupid handles and dumb radio lingo. In fact, when he thought about it, there wasn't anyone he really liked. People were an annoyance. There were too damn many of them. Always getting in your way, spoiling things for you.

It was time to move. He dead-carried long enough. Hanging up the mike and shutting off the radio, he turned on the engine and started to move to another location. Maybe he'd park in front of old man Owens' house and screw up his TV reception. Or better yet, he'd get up early in the morning and wait for the old fart to feed his dumb birds, then he'd scare the old shit out of his underwear. Jimmy laughed at the recollection of the last time. Owens almost dropped a load in his pants.

Father Nature. That's what Jimmy called him, along with a few other names. Another toe. Him and those stupid birds. Jimmy hated him. Always hollering. Just because he knocked off a few birds now and then with his BB gun.

Jimmy looked at his watch. It was five minutes after seven. He still had time for a little fun before the curfew. Ever since that jerk Ralphie Gordon got himself cut up to start all the trouble, you had to be in by ten o'clock. Big deal.

Jimmy laughed again. His cousin, who works for Dunbar Funeral Home, which handled the arrangements for most of the murder victims, told him that part of the Ralston broad's cunt was cut off and so was Ralphie Gordon's dong. The thought made Jimmy break out in a new fit of laughter. Ralphie's dong. The little fat jerk wouldn't be able to beat his meat anymore.

Then for some unknown reason a totally alien feeling of sadness welled up in him. A desolation that almost brought tears to his eyes. Grief for Ralphie? Tough shit. Why should he be sad? He shook it off.

He saw several mobile CB'ers cruising around, their long antennas cutting through the night like shark fins in a black sea. Probably trying to find him, he thought. Let the fuckers look.

Jimmy checked his watch again. Seven-fifteen. He'd have to hurry if he wanted some fun, otherwise his old man would be on his back again. *Seventeen-year-old boys should be in at a respectable hour.* That was his old man's favorite bellow. That and: *Be in by eight o'clock and leave that CB radio alone. Sure, Dad. I never touch it, Dad.* And under his breath: *Fuck you, Dad.*

Leaving the downtown traffic behind, Jimmy turned down Palmer Street, dark, residential, quiet. Twenty minutes of travel brought him to Old Marsh Road, darker, one streetlight per block, and to a secret spot of his just off the road and behind some underbrush that was large enough to conceal the car.

He switched off the engine and listened to the night. It was peaceful out here. Very little traffic on this old washboard, and only a few houses. The closest was the Armstrong place. The guy's name was Jack. No shit. Jack Armstrong. What a dumbass name.

Jimmy turned on the Franklin and started to make animal noises into the mike.

Across the street, the shadow that had been slowly moving along the side of the Armstrong house stopped, watching Jimmy's car settle behind a cluster of leafless trees and shrubs, its headlights quickly blinking out.

The moon, the eye of the night, spilled its witchlight over the marsh. The figure pressed deeper into the shadows, considering the windfall. Whoever was out there in that car would serve just as well as the old hag inside the house. Of course, it would have to be done here, in the backyard.

Moonlight silvered Old Marsh Road as the figure crossed over, twenty yards behind the car.

"Breaker. Breaker," Jimmy said. "Quack, quack, quack."

His laughter rolled out of the car windows.

"Rubbadubdub. Three broads in a tub."

"Get off the air, you jerk," A radio voice answered him. That would be Little Ivy, Jimmy thought, another beaver.

"How'd you like to hold my antenna, Little Ivy?" Jimmy was beside himself with laughter now.

"Why don't you stick it in your ear," Little Ivy said.

Jimmy gave her the Bronx cheer.

His eyes drifted to the passenger-side window and the marsh beyond. It was quiet. The crickets and frogs had stopped their night calling. Suddenly, Jimmy got a creepy feeling, like the time he wandered into Graceland Cemetery when he was six and couldn't find his way out, until some people found him and took him home.

He shook it off.

"Chirp, chirp, chirp," Jimmy said.

"Why don't you go cut your throat with a dull knife?" Little Ivy said.

What was that? Jimmy turned around, listened. He thought he heard something. Naw. Nothing. For a moment he thought some CB'ers had found him. Mustn't get spooked.

"Hey, Little Ivy," Jimmy cooed, then started to make sucking noises.

Another sound.

Moonlight twinkled off the chrome ornament on the hood.

Extreme sadness racked him, like he had felt earlier this evening, only stronger, more powerful.

His laughter died, washed away in a wave of despair.

The figure closed in on him.

"Hey," Little Ivy said after a while. "That jerk finally got off the air."

"Maybe he did us all a favor and dropped dead," Wily Coyote said.

They all agreed on how great that would be.

18

SHE WAS BEGINNING TO GET TO HIM.

Wally stood in Marion's kitchen, finishing a cup of coffee and watching her go through the motions of domesticity. If you could call moving about in a somnambulistic manner that resembled a trance, household chores. She moved listlessly, trying to gather up her supper dishes and carry them to the sink. Any moment now, Wally expected her to fall flat on her face.

Marion swayed at the kitchen sink, put a hand to her brow and giggled. Wally rushed over and caught her. She fell against him.

"Are you all right?" Wally asked.

"It's nothing, really," Marion said, still giggling like a schoolgirl. "I just feel a little lightheaded."

"Why don't you sit down. You look as white as a ghost."

Marion giggled again. "Oh, it's nothing. I'll be all right." Then she moved her head close to Wally's ear and whispered, "He's listening, you know."

Wally looked at her. "Who's listening?"

"He…they…everything is heard, recorded…"

Wally felt a shiver of uneasiness pass through his body. She was giving him the creeps. Ever since he stopped in to check on her, coming right over from Fred Owens' place, she'd been acting like an escapee from a padded room, giggling, walking around zombielike, talking to herself.

Night pressed against the kitchen windows. He'd have to leave. He was supposed to be patrolling the Owens' neighborhood.

Marion stepped away from him, walking over to the kitchen table, then stopping suddenly and staring out the double windows. She stood with her back to him, watching the autumn darkness, her head tilted off to one side as if she was listening to something—or someone.

Wally moved behind her and looked over her shoulder, trying to follow her line of concentration. What the hell did she see out there? The backyard? The darkness? What?

She threw her head back suddenly and laughed, then just as suddenly stopped, turning to face him. Wally could see that the expression on her face was different now. There was a strange light playing around her eyes, a hint of a smile on her lips. Wally wasn't sure he cared for either one. Both gave her a malevolent appearance.

Marion came into his arms, pressing her lips against his, darting her tongue in his mouth like a snake, her breath had a sweet-sour taste. Wally pulled away.

She smiled at him. "How would you like to fuck me?"

Wally stared at her, puzzled, wondering if he had heard her right.

"You needn't look so confused. I thought you wanted me."

"I do, but…"

"But, what?"

"I don't think you're quite yourself tonight."

She laughed again. "I have never felt better."

"Well, I don't think you realize what you just said."

"I know exactly what I said."

Wally studied her face. Her eyes were still dancing in pools of yellow light, that smile still on her lips. He didn't know what to make of her. He'd been waiting two years for her to go to bed with him, but tonight, for some reason he couldn't explain, it didn't seem right.

"I'll put you to bed," he said.

"Good, then you can fuck me."

"Marion!" He was shocked. He had never heard her use language like that before. It was like she was a different person.

She laughed that crazy laugh again and danced away from him, then stopped halfway through a swirl, her head held off to one side, listening.

"What is it?" Wally asked. He was getting worried. Maybe she was coming down with the flu.

"Yes," Marion said. "Yes."

She straightened her head and started to unbutton her blouse. She wore no bra underneath and her breasts hung free and smooth. Cupping them with her hands, she pointed them at him, the dark brown nipples erect and firm.

"Wouldn't you like to suck on these?"

Wally didn't know what to say anymore. This wasn't Marion. At least not the Marion he knew. But his body didn't know the difference. He was getting an erection.

Her eyes caught the tentlike rise of his pants and gleamed at him. "I'll just take this off," she said, removing her blouse and dropping it on the floor. "And this." She stepped out of her skirt. "And this." She slipped off her panties.

Wally was transfixed. His body processes started to kick in, furnishing him with an erection as hard as stone. But there was something, a small voice drowning in the sudden rise of his blood, that warned him of danger.

She leered at him. "Now," she said.

She moved against him, grinding at the front of his trousers with her body, cooing at him, gurgling deep in her throat. She fumbled with his gun belt. It fell to the kitchen floor with a muffled thud. Then she unbuckled his pants and let them drop around his ankles, drawing his penis out through his shorts.

Wally was going crazy. He squeezed her breast.

"That's it, baby," she said. "Mmmmm. Momma's gonna give it to you good."

Her hand still gripping him, she led him to the kitchen table, eased her buttocks onto it, kicked off her slippers, and started to run her legs over his thighs.

Wally almost stumbled when she pulled him, and he saw those legs, the ones he had admired for so long, opening for him now.

"Come on, Wally," Marion purred, saliva trickling from the corner of her mouth. "Fuck me. Fuck me good."

Wally couldn't take any more. He plunged into her with a moan. She encircled him with her legs and started to do things he never thought possible. Christ, this was good. This was the best he ever had. But he didn't know how much longer he could last.

"Harder," Marion moaned. "Harder. That's it. Give it to me like Richard. Hard and deep. That's it, baby. Soon. Soon now."

Passion clouding his mind, Wally didn't hear her, didn't see her hand curl around the large bread knife lying on the table, didn't feel the sudden coldness of the room.

19

IT WAS A MINUTE PAST EIGHT when Thayer and Paul returned to Lanark. The town seemed quiet enough, normal enough, for the present anyway.

They stopped at the station and Barney told them Deering still hadn't shown up yet, or called, for that matter. All the officers were on duty and out on the streets. Even Red Engman was in, sitting at the radio, runny nose, watery eyes, and all. After twenty minutes of listening to him sneeze continually and contaminate the office, Thayer sent him home.

And that's where he was heading, to grab a beer and at least one hour of sleep as soon as he dropped Paul off at the hospital. Barney waved them off and asked Thayer to pick up a couple of hamburgers for him on his way back.

At home, Thayer flipped on the living room lights and closed the front door. He threw off his cap and jacket and sank into the nearest chair, kicking off his boots. God he was tired. Bone weary and ass heavy.

He sat there for a few minutes, wondering if Durie House had managed to touch anyone in town yet. He was sure it would. The weaker ones first, the susceptible, vulnerable to its dark influence. How long would it be before they started to destroy one another? People were doing a pretty good job of it now without Durie House. Maybe it was already too late. And Deering. He was sure the house had something to do with his disappearance. He had a feeling they would find him soon, only he wouldn't be among the living.

Thayer rubbed his eyes, and after a few more minutes, forced himself up. He padded out to the kitchen, turning on more lights, and checked the refrigerator. There wasn't much to choose from: Two cans of Blatz, various condiments, half a loaf of bread, and coffee. He popped open one of the beers and took a long pull, then looked in the freezer compartment, its offerings were just as meager. One chicken pot pie and a pizza.

Feeling a little hungry, he took out the pizza and prepared it for the oven. He hadn't eaten since this morning and his stomach was screaming for attention. Not that it needed any. It was getting to the point where he couldn't see his belt buckle anymore.

Thayer took his beer into the living room and flopped down in his favorite chair, feeling the weariness eat at him. He started to doze.

The telephone rang.

He got up with a grunt and picked up the receiver. "Yeah."

"That you, Chief?"

"Yeah, Barney, it's me. What's up?" His mind was still struggling back from sleep, all ten minutes of it.

"Everything," Barney said, his voice excited. "The calls have been coming in so fast I need a secretary. First off, there's been another one."

"Where?"

"South side of town. Old Marsh Road. Just like you figured. Some of the boys are out there now."

"Who was it?"

"Another kid. Jimmy Gillispie," and before Thayer could say it – "Yeah, I called the coroner's office. Sunquist's on his way."

"Who found him?"

"Pearl Armstrong. The kid was practically on her back doorstep. Mike Baker and Ross Johnson are out there now. They found the kid's car across the street behind some shrubbery. Looks like he was taken from the car and killed on the Armstrong property."

"I'm on my way," Thayer said and started to hang up.

"There's more. The boys found Deering's car. The registration was in the glove compartment."

"Was he in it?"

"No. The car was empty and all smashed up – just like Paul Rice's. In fact, they found it along the same stretch of road, only it wasn't on County Q. It was off the road about twenty yards, in the woods not far from St. Casmir's."

"Have them check out the church," Thayer said, remembering what Paul had told him about his narrow escape. "Deering may have stumbled in there. And have them search those woods." Thayer paused. "Did Kassavik call?"

"No, not yet."

"Pass the call along the moment he does. I'll be at the Armstrong place."

Thayer hung up, got out of the house fast, and hit the siren as he accelerated the car away from the curb. He was halfway to Pearl Armstrong's house, trying to remember what it was about her or her house that kept popping vaguely through his mind ever since he got in the car, when Barney hailed him on the car radio and patched through Andy Kassavik's call.

"You do fast work," Thayer said into the hand mike. "I really didn't expect to hear from you until late tomorrow."

"We lucked out on this one," Andy said. "Finding the Bouchers wasn't any problem, but they both turned up dead and the whole thing could have petered out right there. But it didn't and that's where the luck comes in. We managed to find a younger brother of Boucher who's still alive. We traced him through the cemetery records. He's a nice old gent, lives right here in the city, and he's got a trunk full of his brother's things in his attic."

"What did you find?" Thayer asked.

"Well, nothing much at first. We went through it with the old boy's permission…"

"Was the child a boy?"

“No, a girl.”

“A girl? Are you sure?” Thayer felt stunned. It couldn’t be a girl. A woman didn’t have the physical strength to pull off these killings.

“I’m sure,” Andy said. “We found pictures and a faded wedding announcement clipped from a newspaper.”

“What’s her name?”

“Elizabeth Boucher.”

“Say again.”

“Here, this is right from the clipping. I copied it with my own little hands. Elizabeth Alison Boucher. That’s the girl’s full name. She married a guy named—”

“Claude Fitgerald,” Thayer finished it for him.

There was a pause on the other end, then Andy said, “How’d you know?”

“Just a hunch. Andy, thanks a million. I owe you one, buddy.”

“Listen, don’t you want her description?”

“No.”

“Well, do you want me to check if she’s still in the state?”

“No, I know where she is. Thanks again, Andy. I’ll get back to you.”

“Just get your ass up here so we can lift a few together.”

“That’s a promise.”

Andy finished his call and Thayer got Barney back on the radio. “Barney, have Peterson meet me at the Fitgerald home right away. If I’m not there when he arrives, tell him to wait and not let anyone leave. I’m going to pick up Paul Rice.”

Thayer hung up the mike and turned the car around.

Barney didn’t have a chance to tell him Wally Schaefer was missing.

20

"HOW IS SHE?" THAYER ASKED as Paul climbed into the car in front of Memorial Hospital.

"Still sedated," Paul said. "But she seems to be resting peacefully." He turned and looked at Thayer. "What's happening? The nurse that got me wasn't exactly brimming with information."

Thayer put the car in gear and sped out of the hospital driveway. He filled Paul in as he drove.

Paul shook his head. "Alison Fitgerald?"

"Yeah, and I kept thinking it had to be a boy," Thayer said. "But Alison fits right in. She's big and strong. Christ, she's got arms on her like a man."

"All the trouble James Durie went through to get her away from Allan, and it was all for nothing. She came back anyway."

"And took up where the Duries left off. Just like I thought."

"Some of those letters must have reached her. But it took a long time for her to get back."

"The house was still waiting though."

They were both silent for a moment, watching the road ahead being picked up by the headlights, briefly revealing what the darkness held, then passing it back again.

"You really think she's responsible for all the killings?" Paul asked, breaking the silence.

“Don’t you?”

“I don’t know.”

“Look, from what we found out she must have learned – probably through those letters – that Allan Durie was her father.”

“But he wasn’t.”

“Yeah, but she didn’t know that, and neither did Allan. Nobody did except Pearl. It’s my guess that when she came back to Lanark she stayed close to the house until she found that grimoire thing. Hell, the house was empty until Eastman bought it, so she had all the time in the world to look around. Nobody ever goes up there. Then when the Eastmans started to move in, it was easy for her to get herself hired, because no one in Lanark wanted to work up there.”

“Her search for the book must have been complicated with all the Eastmans in the house,” Paul said.

“But she still managed to get her hands on it.” Thayer paused. “I don’t think the book was ever in the house. James must have hidden it somewhere else. I think it was in the Durie crypt.”

“Why? Did you find anything out there?”

“Not exactly. But it fits. When Pete Jacobs reported vandalism out at Graceland Cemetery, I naturally had it checked out. Nothing was found, except that someone had forced their way through the cemetery gates, and into the Durie crypt. The killings started right after that.”

Thayer shook his head.

Paul caught his reaction. “Yeah,” he said, “I know the feeling. It’s still unreal.”

“I told you that I’ve never been a particularly religious man, Paul. And now coming face to face with something like this…well, it just shakes the hell out of the very foundations of your life.”

Paul knew what Thayer meant. Inwardly, he felt the same way, but it didn’t change anything. It was still there, and it was real, whether they accepted it or not.

“Do you have enough to arrest her on?” Paul asked.

“No. Not really. But I’ll get it. I can take her in for questioning and scare the hell out of her for a change.”

Minutes later, Thayer stopped the car. "Here we are."

The Fitgerald house was the small, inexpensive, slapped-together type that boomed right after World War II. It was built for the returning vet, some place for him to hang his hat, other than a foxhole.

They got out of the car slowly, almost reluctantly. Even in the night they could see that the ground looked barren, the grass and trees had died, giving the house a bleak and desolate appearance.

A figure loomed up to meet them.

"Hello, John," Thayer said.

"No one's left," Peterson said.

They all looked at the house. The lights were on.

"Okay," Thayer said. "John, you stay out here in case she gets past us." Then he said to Paul, "You ready?"

Paul took a deep breath. "No."

"Neither am I."

They exchanged grim smiles.

The small porch creaked under their weight. They stood there like men on the gallows, waiting for the trap to drop. Finally, Thayer rapped on the door.

A minute later, Mrs. Fitgerald opened it and stood in the doorway, her face drawn and doughy-looking in the background lighting of the house.

She eyed them coldly and nodded. "Is there something I can do for you?"

"We'd like to ask you some questions, Mrs. Fitgerald." Thayer said.

She hesitated for a moment. "Of course. Anything I can do to help. Come in."

They entered, following her into thc living room. It was small, but neatly furnished. She turned to face them.

"We'd like you to come with us," Thayer said. "Down to police headquarters."

She gave him a weak smile. "Of course," she said, being the very picture of cooperation and congeniality. Not at all the type that would cut the throats of six people.

"It's about Claude, isn't it?" she asked.

Thayer and Paul exchanged glances.

"You know about those terrible things he's been doin'."

"That's what we want to talk to you about," Thayer lied.

"I'm glad you found out. He's turned his back on God and thrown in with the Devil." She nodded. "That's right, yes, with the Devil."

"Mrs. Fitgerald," Paul said, "why didn't you tell Chief Thayer that you were a Durie?"

"I was afraid. Besides, I always thought the Bouchers were my real parents, until those terrible letters started to come. And I didn't want you to hurt Claude."

"Did he make you come back?" Thayer asked.

Alison nodded again. "I think he had a notion that there might be some money in it for him. But there was nothin'. The Durie fortune was long gone and the state took the house for taxes owed. We didn't have much money – we never had much – not with Claude's schemes. They were supposed to make us rich, but they never did, so even if I was to tell the tax people I was a Durie, I still didn't have the money for the house. Then the Eastmans bought it."

"What did Claude have to say about that?" Thayer asked.

"He didn't like it none. Oh, I've just got to sit down. My feet are killin' me." She eased her body into the nearest chair. "Been on my feet all day. It takes a lot out of you…now what was I sayin'?"

"You were telling us about how Claude didn't like it when the Eastmans bought the house," Paul prompted her.

"Yes, Claude. Well, he fixed it with Mr. Eastman to look after the place. You know, it wasn't money he was after at all. It was that book. The one mentioned in those letters. He almost tore Durie House apart lookin' for it before Mr. Eastman came along."

"How did he find the book?" Paul asked.

"Oh, he got me to talkin' one night, and rememberin'. I didn't remember much, but now that I saw the house again and was working in it a few things came back to me. I remembered a man takin' me to one of the buildings in the cemetery when I was a little girl and puttin' something – no, like I told Claude – he was takin' something out, from underneath a stone coffin. And I think he told me – because these words have always stuck in my mind – that the best hidin' place in the world was always your own grave."

"Do you remember what it was he took out?" Thayer asked.

She paused for a moment, thinking, then said, "No, but I think it was money because he gave it to my father – I mean Mr. Boucher – and they took me away after that." She looked at Thayer. "Are we leavin' right away? If not, I'd like to slip my shoes off."

Thayer nodded. "Go ahead."

She pulled her shoes off, sighing with relief as she wiggled her stockinged feet in freedom.

"What did Claude do with the book, Mrs. Fitgerald?" Paul asked.

"I don't know. He never showed it to me and I don't know what's in it. The last letter I got said it was a book of power, but Claude kept the letter and I never saw it again. But whatever it is it's got something to do with that house up there, and it's not good."

"Mrs. Fitgerald," Thayer said, "Did Claude kill those people?"

She put her head down and examined her feet. "Yes," she said, her voice almost a whisper. "I guess he did. At first I thought he was just steppin' out on me. Claude always fancied himself a ladies' man."

"You followed him," Paul guessed, trying to imagine Claude Fitgerald as a roué.

She looked surprised. "Yes. One night I finally did. I really didn't want to. It was just that every night he was out something terrible would happen."

"Like a murder," Thayer said. He was wondering if she was telling him the truth. Could he believe her? Or was she just trying to set up old Claude? "Go on," he said, watching her eyes.

"I'd see it in the paper the next day, and I knew he must be involved in it someway. Him and that devil-lovin' friend of his, Mr. Sollis."

"Kenneth Sollis?" Thayer knew there was something about that man that he didn't like.

“The same. Fillin’ Claude’s head with all those crazy notions. They’re thicker than peas in a pod, those two. Always whisperin’ and carryin’ on.” She paused, then looked directly at Thayer. “Please don’t hurt Claude. It’s that book that’s got him crazy. He never hurt anybody before. He’s not the best man in the world, but he’s all I got.”

Paul watched her as tears started to pool in her eyes. “Mrs. Fitgerald,” he said softly, “you said you followed him once. Did you see him…kill anyone?”

She shook her head. “No. Never. The night I followed him, he took the truck and I used our old Ford. When he got to where he was goin’, I just waited around until he left.”

“Where was that?”

“He went to see that schoolteacher…Miss Homes…stayed there for quite a while.”

Thayer rubbed his jaw. Barbara Homes was something new. But he couldn’t understand why she would spend time with a man like Claude. And where was he now?

“Where’s your husband now?” Paul asked, as if he had read Thayer’s thoughts.

“Out…somewhere…I don’t know…maybe with her…”

Then Thayer whispered something that Paul just barely picked up.

“Fred Owens.”

21

AT THE SAME TIME THAT PAUL AND THAYER had been on their way to the Fitgerald home, Kenneth Sollis was nervously pacing about in his office in the back of his store. The front of the store was closed and locked up for the night, only the closing lights were on and a lamp on top of Sollis' desk.

There was a knock on the back door, the alley entrance to his office. Sollis sprang to it, quickly unlocked it, and jerked it open.

Claude Fitgerald walked in.

Sollis quickly closed the door, then turned to face him. He was furious. "What the hell's the matter with you?"

"I still don't know what you're talkin' about," Claude said.

"Do you know what you're getting yourself into? And me? I'm the one who instructed you."

"I didn't even have to use what you showed me. I found out that a tape recorder can be just as good."

Sollis took a step toward him. "What did you do with the book, Allan Durie's grimoire?"

Claude took a step backward to compensate for Sollis' advance, then pulled down his greasy baseball cap and peered out at him from under its brim. "I keep tellin' you I didn't find the book," he said. "I was lookin' for it in that damn house for five years before my old lady let it slip one night about some hidin' place her uncle showed her when she was a kid."

“Where was that?” Sollis’ face began to change from anger to interest.

“In the Durie crypt, under James Durie’s coffin.”

“And then you found the book.”

“I didn’t find nothin’. Exceptin’ that the crypt had already been broken into. The hidin’ place was empty.”

Sollis sat down, his face bleached white. “That book was the way of it all. Power. Fame. Riches. Immortality…everything you could imagine…want.” He shook his head, trying to drive away the shock of disappointment. “When you came to me and told me your wife was Allan Durie’s daughter, you wanted me to help you in certain areas of your life. I did so, more than willingly.”

“Only because you thought I was gonna give you the book.”

Sollis stared at him over the glare of the desk lamp. “You’re lying,” he said. “You have it. You just don’t want to share it with me.”

Claude took off his baseball cap and slapped it against the edge of Sollis’ desk. Sollis flinched at the impact.

“You’re goin’ squirrelly,” Claude said. “That’s what’s the matter with you. You ain’t listenin’ to what I’ve been sayin’. I don’t have the book. I never had it.”

“Well, someone must have it!” Sollis shouted at him. “Otherwise why all the sacrifices?”

“I don’t know.” Claude plopped the cap back on his head. “I was thinkin’ maybe you could answer that.”

“Me?” Sollis got to his feet. “Why me?”

Claude gave him a calculating smile. “’Cause you might just have the book.”

“You’re crazy. Would I be trying to get the book from you if I had it already?”

Claude moved over to the back door, then turned to look at Sollis. “You might,” he said. “If you was smart and didn’t want anyone to know you had it, ‘specially me. See you around, Sollis. Can’t spend time jawin’ with you all night. Got a little lady waitin’ for me. Didn’t have to conjure anythin’ up either.”

He opened the door and stepped out.

"Liar!" Sollis shouted.

Claude slammed the door and crossed the alley to where he had parked his pickup. Then got in and drove away.

Five minutes later, when he stopped for his first traffic light at Grant and Fawly streets, he was sure the car behind him was Sollis' red Corvette. The light changed and Claude made a left turn. The car followed. Claude kept watching the car in his rearview mirror as he went through a number of turns he didn't have to just to make sure the car was actually following him.

It was.

Now why the hell is that dumb fuck tailin' me? Claude scratched the back of his neck. He think I'm gonna lead him to the book? Claude shook his head. That man just ain't got no sense.

The truck sped up, taking a few more turns through the downtown area. Claude checked the mirror.

The car was still with him.

Claude turned down Grahome Street; it was narrow and tree-lined and quiet. He stopped the pickup halfway down the block, switching off the engine, cutting the headlights.

"I've had just about enough of this, Mr. Kenneth Sollis," Claude said to himself.

The car stopped twenty feet in back of his truck, turning off its lights. No one got out.

Claude climbed down from the cab and walked back to the car. He leaned over the driver's side window and said, "Now what in the hell do you think you're doin'…?"

22

FRED OWENS' HOUSE WAS DARK when the car rolled to a stop in front of it. Thayer didn't know if Alison Fitgerald was lying about her husband or not. Either way he couldn't afford to take any chances. He put her in custody and had Peterson take her down to the station, then he put out a call to have Kenneth Sollis and Claude Fitgerald picked up.

If the Fitgerald woman wasn't lying, this was one of two places left where Claude had to make a sacrifice in order to complete his devil's cross. He had tried here before and failed. That's what Thayer had been racking his brain to remember. Pearl Armstrong and Fred Owens had both complained of prowlers recently. And Owens' house was in spitting distance of Graceland Cemetery. Thayer knew Fitgerald had to return. And he wanted to be here to greet him.

Thayer cut the engine and lights, then reached into the pocket of his raincoat, lying on the seat between him and Paul, and took out the .38 Special he had brought along. He handed it to Paul.

"I take it you know how to use this," Thayer said.

Paul nodded and took the gun. It had been awhile, but the feel of it wasn't unfamiliar.

"You think he's in there?" Paul asked.

"I don't know. Every cop in town is looking for him. But he has friends in low places."

They got out of the car. A cold lake wind pulled at their clothes.

There was a moon overhead, throwing shadows along the street that leaped out at them with every gust of wind, then shambled back to hide. The dark maw of Owens' porch waited for them.

"I don't like the lights being out," Thayer said. "Ever since the old man had that scare in his backyard he's been burning all his lights till sunup."

Paul nodded. Thayer had filled him in about Fred Owens on the ride over. A draft of wind blew under his jacket, chilling him with its cold breath, but he was already cold, and it wasn't from the wind. He wondered if Thayer felt the same way.

"How are we going to work this?" Paul asked nervously. His old standbys were with him again: dry mouth, wet palms, stomach turned upside down.

Just then the backup unit Thayer had radioed for pulled up in back of his cruiser, lights off and no siren. Chris Foley, a tall, heavyset officer, much in the same mold as Thayer, joined them on the sidewalk.

"Take the rear of the house, Chris," Thayer told him. "We'll go in the front."

Foley nodded and drew his revolver, moving off quietly to the back of the house. Paul and Thayer started toward the front.

"It seems like all we're doing lately is going from one damn house to another," Thayer whispered as they climbed the porch stairs.

"Let's hope this is the last one," Paul whispered back.

Thayer reached for the door. He wasn't about to knock or ring the bell. He was sure Claude was in the house. Owens hadn't answered his phone when he called him from Alison Fitgerald's home.

The doorknob twisted slowly in his hand, but the door wouldn't budge. It was locked. Thayer stepped back and was just about to shoot his way in when Paul found a forced window at the end of the porch. It had been reclosed, but not relocked.

Paul silently motioned Thayer over as he slid the window open, revealing the vaulted darkness of the house. Thayer gave Paul a wary look, then climbed through. Paul followed.

After their eyes adjusted to the darkness, they discovered the room was a combination den and aquarium. There were several fish tanks in the room; one near the door that Thayer almost knocked over trying to get his flashlight to work. It wouldn't and Thayer jammed it back in his pocket. Paul wasn't surprised at its sudden failure. Even the tank lights were out.

The den opened into the living room where a small staircase was tucked against the wall. The whole room was a chiaroscuro of shadows, which when touched turned into chairs and tables and walls.

A board creaked somewhere in the house.

They both jumped, aging ten years apiece.

By the time this is over, Thayer thought, he'll be ready for a rocker.

They checked out the remaining rooms downstairs—the kitchen and a half-bath. Both were empty. Returning to the living room, Thayer found the stairs and started up, motioning for Paul, with a touch on his arm, to follow.

As they climbed, the upstairs seemed even darker than the ground level, as if they were descending into deep, concealing water instead of climbing a staircase in the house of a man they hoped was still alive.

A cold sweat broke out over Paul's body. He dried the palms of his hands against his jacket.

When they reached the top of the stairs, there was a quick movement off to the right, the peripheral vision picking it up first before passing it on to the rest of the eye. Then a howling scream, more like an animal than a man, paralyzed them both, freezing them to the spot where they stood.

A figure lunged forward and Paul heard Thayer cry out in pain, the knife thrust catching him in the chest, just under the heart. He fell back against Paul and they both tumbled down the stairs as the figure darted past them, jumping over the banister into the living room.

"Fitgerald!" Paul shouted and managed to snap off a shot.

The figure raced for the front door, then got delayed momentarily fumbling with the locks. Paul got to his knees, bringing the .38 up in both hands as the door jerked open. The .38 exploded again and Paul saw Fitgerald stagger in the doorway, then disappear down the porch.

Turning quickly, Paul found Thayer lying behind him on the stairs. Blood was oozing from a wound in his chest, and his breathing seemed strained.

"How are you doing?" Paul asked softly.

"Christ," Thayer wheezed, "he's fast. I didn't even have time to use my John Wayne draw." He tried to laugh and ended up coughing.

A shot exploded outside the house.

Thayer grabbed Paul's arm. "Paul, don't worry about me," he said slowly. "Just get the son of a bitch." He handed Paul his Magnum. "Take this."

Paul took it, but was reluctant to leave him.

"Go on, man. Don't let him get away. Take Foley and get him."

Paul hesitated, then turned slowly and went outside just as another gunshot ripped the cold night air. As he rounded the back of the house, Paul saw Foley jumping a neighboring fence and Fitgerald running under a streetlight just ahead of him, heading for the cemetery.

Neighboring dogs began barking as Foley cleared the last yard and Fitgerald scampered up and over the wire fence of the cemetery like a spider. Foley fired again, but Fitgerald had moved back into the cemetery grounds as Foley started to climb the fence.

Paul knew he had promised he'd get Fitgerald, but Thayer needed an ambulance, and he needed it now. Paul ran around to the front of the house, trying to get to Thayer's car and the radio when he almost knocked someone over coming up the walk.

It was Barney Jensen.

"I was just going to call you," Paul said. "Thayer's hurt. He needs a doctor."

"Is it bad?" Barney asked. He looked stricken.

"I don't know…it was dark…it's not good."

"Christ."

"Fitgerald got away. He took off across the cemetery. Foley's chasing him. I've got to get back..."

Barney grabbed his arm. "Don't go yet, Paul. Wait till I call for an ambulance. I've got something to tell you."

Barney trotted back to his cruiser parked at an angle at the curb, one door still hanging open. Paul followed reluctantly.

Another gunshot came echoing back in the night. Foley might need help, Paul thought. He wanted to take off and get over to the cemetery. He listened to Barney make the call. Jesus Christ, Barney, come on...come on...come –

Barney finished and hung up the mike. He turned to Paul. "I've been trying to get Thayer ever since he put out that APB on Claude Fitgerald. I don't know what's wrong with his radio, but I finally gave up and told Hardigan to watch the store while I grabbed his cruiser."

"Barney, what the hell are you trying to tell me?" Paul said impatiently.

"We found Claude Fitgerald's pickup parked in an alley on the west side of town. He was spread-eagled in the truck bed. Cut up just like the others."

Paul looked stunned. "You sure it was Claude?"

"Sure I'm sure. The officers on the scene made a positive ID."

"Then who the hell..." Paul looked off in the direction of the cemetery, as if waiting for some revelation to drift back to him.

"What does it all mean, Paul?" Barney asked, following his gaze. Ever since he had been in on the conversation between Thayer and Paul this afternoon at the station, he had felt uneasy. The urge to keep looking over his shoulder was always with him, like he expected something to materialize out of thin air and start sucking his blood.

"Sollis..." Paul said, not really hearing him, talking to himself as much as to Barney. "Could it be Sollis?"

"It's not Sollis."

Paul turned back to him.

"We picked him up. He's at the station now, screaming about his rights, and his stolen car. He couldn't be the one you're chasing."

Two quick shots drifted back to them.

"Barney, take care of Thayer," Paul said. "Send every man you've got to the cemetery. I'll get back to you."

"But, Paul, shouldn't you…"

Barney didn't finish. Paul had already broken into a run, heading for the cemetery.

Barney turned away and hurried into the house.

Nagging thoughts ripped through Paul's mind as he made his way to the cemetery fence. Fitgerald was dead. Sacrificed like the others. His wife was in custody. Sollis was in custody. Allan Durie was dead. Buried years ago in the cellar of Durie House.

Paul put both guns, the Magnum and the .38, on safety, tucked them behind his belt, and started up the metal rigging of the fence. Names and faces continued to cartwheel at him, faces of the dead, faces of the living, and yet there was one face he kept coming back to.

Dropping clear on the other side, Paul drew out the Magnum, took it off safety, and headed into the heart of the cemetery. He hadn't heard anything since the two shots minutes ago. Darkness hung over the markers, spotted by wispy clouds covering the moon, giving the graves a mottled appearance.

More minutes ticked by. Paul was well into the cemetery now, near the crypts. The night air was turning colder. His breath came out in ghostly threads of white vapor. Then the clouds cleared the moon and Paul saw Foley.

He was lying face down near a large marker, a Madonna supplicating to heaven with open hands. Paul turned him over gently.

Foley stared up at him. His eyes trying hard to keep their focus. There was a large amount of blood on the front of this shirt and a whistling in his voice when he struggled to speak.

"I…hit…him…" Foley said with difficulty, his voice barely audible over the wail of sirens now filling the neighborhood. "Twice…point blank…he….ran…crypts…"

“Don’t try to talk anymore,” Paul said. “Help will be here shortly.” Paul doubted whether that would be soon enough for him.

Paul stood up. The banshee-wail of the sirens died. He could see the blinking red lights become stationary in the distance. One set would be Thayer’s ambulance.

God, don’t let him die.

He turned away, walking toward the crypts. There was no movement. No sound. He wondered which crypt he had run into. If anything, he would try to get to Durie House, having failed at Fred Owens’ place. Or had he failed? They hadn’t seen Owens, and if he was dead, then the ritual was complete. The portal would be open.

His eyes fell on a broken iron gate. The name DURIE was chiseled into the stone above the entrance. All the other crypts in the area had looked secure. If Foley had hurt him, would he have sought refuge here? Maybe he was dead. Foley said he hit him twice, and Paul was certain he had hit him at least once back at the house.

Paul opened the iron gate. There was blood on it, near the broken latch. He was in there all right. Now all he had to do was flush him out…or go in after him.

All?

He could wait for help, but if Owens was dead there was no time to waste. He had to stop him…and close the portal…somehow.

His mouth dry, his heart jumping crazily in his chest, he eased the inner door of the crypt open. When it was open wide enough for him to slip through, Paul felt along the nearest inside wall with his left hand, the Magnum ready in the other. The wall was cold to the touch, clammy.

Detecting no obstacle or presence along the left side of the entrance, Paul hesitated apprehensively, then ducked in quickly, stepping off to the left, his back pressed tightly against the wall.

The inside of the crypt was as dark as a hole, as still as the death that reposed there. The gray darkness of the night spilled in weakly through the doorway, giving a little light.

Paul inched his way along the wall until he reached the corner, then hunkered down and waited, listening. He could hear his watch ticking in the silence.

A knot formed around his heart, as cold as the marble headstones that lined the cemetery. For one mad moment, Paul thought his mind would betray him, stirring up his old terror of the dark and the hysteria and gagging that always ensued. He was over that he told himself. He was no longer afraid of his life-force leaving him in inky darkness, rushing out like air escaping from a ruptured tire. He was over it, over it. And this was passing…it was getting better…better…

The panic passed. Paul's head cleared, his breathing came back to normal. He wiped a sweaty palm on his pants and gripped the Magnum again. His eyes tried to penetrate the black veil that surrounded him; his ears tried to draw the quieter sounds from the depths of the crypt.

And then—was someone—breathing?

Paul held his own breath, trying to pinpoint where the sound was coming from.

He heard it again.

The rush of air from a mouth, as someone struggled to control his breathing. It was coming from the other side of the crypt.

Paul left his own breath out slowly. He pointed the Magnum in the direction of the sound and checked the .38, taking it off safety and shoving it back in his belt.

"Why don't you give it up?" Paul asked, his voice chambered in the crypt. "It's all over, Mr. Deering."

The breathing stopped.

Then a laugh, like you would expect the Devil to laugh.

Then Deering's voice: "You're very perceptive, Mr. Rice. And to think of all the lengths I went through – even using my boat sometimes to visit all the charming people of Lanark. And now you've found me out. I should have disposed of you the night you came to my house."

"You almost did…in the car."

“Yes, that was a nice touch…pity it didn’t work. But then you managed to escape my friends in the churchyard, too, and again at the house. You’ve been very lucky, Mr. Rice. But have no fear. We’ll get you.”

Paul thought he heard some movement. Maybe Deering was moving in on him.

“How did you find me out, Mr. Rice?” Deering asked. “I’m very interested.”

“It was easy. Just a process of elimination. You faked your own disappearance along the same stretch of road where I was attacked to make it look convincing. Then you killed twice tonight. Fitgerald found the grimoire before you did, didn’t he?”

“You’re doing very well. Go on.”

Again the movement.

“My guess is that he sold it to you,” Paul went on, following the movement with the Magnum. “He probably met you through Sollis, then tried to deal on his own.”

“The little weasel caught me searching Durie House for it. Of course, that was before the Eastmans came along.” Deering’s voice sounded closer, off to the right. “We made a deal. If he found it, he’d sell it to me. He did.”

“And you paid him off in blood,” Paul said.

“Why should I pay for something that was mine. It was my father’s genius that discovered the secret of opening the portal. The Duries were bunglers. My father did all the work, took all the risks, and they stole it from him, took the credit for it. My father died a broken man.”

More movement—closer—much closer…

Paul braced the Magnum with both hands. Deering would be coming anytime now.

“I suppose,” Paul said, “that after you started butchering people, Fitgerald knew it was you and wanted more money for his silence.”

“You know the nature of the beast very well. Blackmail was his game, but then he didn’t play it very well. He should never have given me the book first, not without being paid in full. I thought I might find him with Sollis tonight. And since I needed a car…and a sacrifice…"

The movement stopped.

Paul squatted down lower, making himself as small a target as possible.

"Fitgerald got what he deserved," Deering droned on. "Just as all those who interfere do…in the end." Deering paused as another thought struck him. "You know, it's a pity, Mr. Rice, that you won't join me in this. My Master is very generous…very grateful for the services rendered in his name. Perhaps you will consider this."

Paul didn't answer. Deering was close. Paul could smell his rotting stench. It was like the one at Durie House.

"Mr. Rice?"

Paul steadied the Magnum.

"Not answering?" Deering sighed. "It's as I thought. Maybe it's just as well…but a shame. Evil is man's basic nature. Only hypocrites and fools proclaim otherwise."

Deering paused again.

"You put things together very nicely," he continued. "You have a fine mind, and most of the time you know how to use it, but sometimes you feel a little guilty, don't you? About your friends… your mother and father…your sweetheart. You've thought about joining them many times."

Deep, numbing cold worked its way up from his groin, chilling his blood. *My God, how did he know*? Paul thought.

"You can join them, you know," Deering went on. "Carrol is waiting for you. She's the one you love, not Linda. They'll all be glad to see you, and it's easy…so easy. You have a gun, don't you, Mr. Rice? Why don't you use it? You've always wanted to. Just lift the gun."

Paul's hand started to rise. The darkness was soothing him, calling him.

"Feel the coolness of the barrel against your temple…so pleasant…peaceful…like a lover's embrace…Carrol's embrace…"

Paul felt the Magnum come to rest against his head.

"Carrol's waiting, Rice. And all it takes is a little pressure on the trigger. Just a little squeeze...and all your troubles will be over. No more guilt...no more deaths. Just eternal peace and bliss."

Paul's finger tightened on the trigger.

"All you have to do is squeeze the trigger. You know how it's done. You've done it before...many times before. It's easy...do it now, Rice...Carrol's waiting...now..."

"Carrol," Paul said softly. His hand began to shake, the trigger-finger trembling between two wills, between two worlds. *Carrol was waiting, but Carrol was dead, she died in Vietnam. Linda was waiting, and she loved him, and he loved her, and she was alive, not dead, alive*. He fought his way out of the cocoon of blackness that was smothering him.

"NNNNNOOOOO!" Paul shouted, jerking the gun down.

Deering was fast, incredibly fast. He was on Paul before he knew it, slashing down with the knife where Paul's chest would have been if he was standing, striking off the wall with a shower of sparks.

Still hunkered down, Paul fired twice. Both shots exploded in flashes of light, catching Deering solidly in his chest, throwing him backwards, and knocking him down. But the man's strength was superhuman. He was on his feet quickly and closing on Paul again.

Paul rose to meet him, managing to get off another shot before he felt Deering's knife slash down, hitting the gun and knocking it loose. The Magnum fell to the floor. Deering began howling like a madman as Paul caught his left hand at the wrist before he could plunge the knife forward again. Deering hissed in Paul's face and started choking him with his other hand. His strength was incredible. Paul was beginning to wonder if he had hit him at all, or if bullets just didn't have any effect on him.

Deering's face was a mask of loathing, his lips twisted back in a doglike snarl, feral eyes blazing like twin orbs of yellow light, drool beginning to collect in the corner of his mouth. Paul was driven back against the wall. He didn't know how long he could keep

Deering's knife away from him. He already felt himself slipping under the stone-crushing grip of Deering's fingers, the vortex of unconsciousness spreading over him, taunting him with deep and final sleep.

Paul tried to break Deering's grip on his throat, but couldn't, his left hand falling away limply, brushing against the .38 still in his belt. Darkness was closing in, carrying him away on a black river of pain. Paul groped for the .38, found it, and brought it out and up, two inches away from Deering's right temple.

He pulled the trigger.

Deering's grip slackened.

Again.

His hand fell away from Paul's throat.

Again.

The knife clattered on the floor.

Again.

Deering fell, sliding off Paul's body like a snake.

Paul stepped away from him, rocking back and forth on shaky legs. His head was clearing, the cobwebs being burned off by the steady supply of oxygen to his brain. His throat felt like raw hamburger. He staggered slightly, his foot kicking something. It was the Magnum. He picked it up and walked over to Deering's body, still not certain that the man was really dead.

Deering was lying on his back, just inside the farthest edge of gray light rectangled through the doorway. His face hardening into a rictus of imminent death. Paul could hear no breathing, but he didn't want to touch him to make sure.

Then there was a wheezy whisper: "We'll get you, Rice."

Paul jumped back away from the body, terror and revulsion swept through him, and a moan, from somewhere deep within him, rushed out through his lips.

How could this thing still be alive and talking to him?

Both guns came up instinctively. The .38 clicked empty. The Magnum exploded three more rounds into Deering's body.

The last gunshot drifted away into an apprehensive silence. It was then that Paul realized that it hadn't been Deering talking at all.

The form he had seen in the swirling fog of St. Casmir's churchyard was standing in the crypt doorway.

Paul still couldn't see the face, but he was sure the thing was smiling at him again. He could feel it in his bones. It stood there for another moment, and then it was gone. Deering's familiar, or whatever manifestation from hell it was called, faded into the night.

But Paul got the message. He knew it wasn't over yet.

There was still Durie House.

23

2:41 A.M.

St. Casmir's.

Alone, tense, struggling to keep his hands steady, Paul knelt at the altar. The church was quiet, peaceful. The smell of candles filled the air, soothing him for the moment.

He had a rough idea of what he wanted to do, and to do it he would have to return to the screaming bedlam of Durie House. Whether it would work or not was another matter. He was not anxious to find out. It would take everything he had left within him, but he knew he would have to go back and put an end to it now, or never know a moment of peace.

The only thing that he had going for him was that the portal was not open. Fred Owens was alive. He had run upstairs and locked himself in the bathroom when Deering broke into the house.

Paul looked up at the large crucifix hanging at the back of the altar, at the face of Christ, his thorned head, his deep eyes. He would have to hurry, before he couldn't move at all.

Paul finished his prayer with a moment of silence, then walked up the altar to the tabernacle. Removing all of the hosts and placing them in his pockets, he then lowered the sanctuary lamp ("the Lamp of Christ," as his mother called it) and carried it to the front of the church, stopping at the holy water fonts and filling several small bottles, which he had gotten earlier from Barney Jensen when he returned with him to the police station, and put these in his pockets also.

Next, Paul sprinkled himself with the holy water, front and back, dabbing his eyes with two small cotton balls, also from Barney, and then stuffed the cotton securely in his ears.

Before going outside, Paul found a crucifix and placed it around his neck, then picked up the lamp and carried it out to Thayer's car.

Outside, the wind was stronger, colder, blowing in from off the lake, moving hard against the trees and rattling skeletal branches that were now devoid of leaves. Shadows coiled in the darkness as he walked through the iron gate to the car. Before putting the lamp inside, he sprinkled the car, inside and out, with holy water from one of the bottles, then got in and started off for Durie House.

Paul drove slowly through the streets. The curfew hour was long past, and there was no traffic. Lanark was silent; almost dead. Most of the houses were dark, a few all lit up. Streetlights, cabled between poles, dipping low over the middle of the street, swayed and danced with the wind.

When he was nearly there, he stopped the car. Taking several of the hosts from his pocket, he molded them with holy water around the lamp, which rested on the passenger-side floor of the car. After he finished, he started on his way again, fighting down his nerves, trying to control a tick that had now developed on the side of his face.

Ten minutes later, his headlights picked up the sign: Blackmoor Road. He hesitated when he turned the corner. Then increased the pressure on the gas peddle. It wouldn't be long now, he thought. The house would be waiting for him.

His senses were alerted as soon as he pulled in the driveway. The wind rose to a high pitch, shaking the trees around the house, keening over the car. He could hear the lake pounding the bluff below through the closed windows of the car. And up ahead, Durie House waited at the turn of the drive, a malign stillness behind the cold, brooding stones. The hair on the back of his neck began to rise. He crossed himself.

As soon as Paul turned off the ignition and opened the door, it was like stepping into red molasses. A red glare was all around him, pulsating, bombarding him with its flashes. He was out of the car and moving, but slowly, so very slowly, and, for an instant, his mind drifted to some far away place and he had forgotten why he had come to this house. Then he saw the lamp inside the car, and he remembered.

After he picked it up, the voices came, gibbering at him from the surrounding night. It was as if all the people in a large city were talking at once, their voices sped up in some sing-song language that he couldn't understand. A bellowing resonance that grew and grew. Jarring. Deafening. Paul's head reeled with hot pokers of pain.

Holding the lamp in his hands, Paul labored to the back of the car, tugging and twisting his way as if he were caught in glue. His neck muscles bulging with strain, his eyes wide and white, he plodded forward, one step, then another, and another. He felt as if some leviathan was hovering above him, trying to squash him with the sound of its voice. But there were many voices, all babbling, and yet, strangely enough, Paul was able to understand some of it now. They were voices of ill will, abusive, obscene, cursing, malignant.

"We've been waiting for you, filth. We're going to drag you down into the *Nothingness*. You are nothing. You puny fucker of bitches. You son of a whoring pig. You dare to stand against *us?* To challenge our *power*?"

By the time Paul reached the terrace, his vision was blurred and he almost dropped the lamp. He dabbed more holy water on his eyes and over his ears, muffling the onslaught, then threw some of it out in front of him; the drops of water glowed like tracer bullets as he flicked it ahead of him to clear the way.

Paul reached the front door. It was hanging open, resting heavily on one hinge, still shattered from the night he and Thayer had blown it open making their escape.

"You stupid cur. You think you can stop us with *fire*? You have no power. You are *nothing*. We'll squash you like the bug you are."

He faltered as he entered the house, then for some strange reason the words of a prayer formed on his tongue. As a boy he had only learned to say Hail Marys and Our Fathers, but these words came as clearly to mind as if he had known them all his life.

"He that dwelleth in the secret place of the most High shall abide under the shadow of the Almighty..."

The molasses seemed to thicken as Paul made his way through the foyer. Suddenly, the grandfather clock tore away from the wall and hurled toward him. Paul knew he could never get out of the way fast enough, so he just held the lamp out to meet it and closed his eyes. The clock struck the lamp and exploded into a million pieces, disappearing in a hiss and a puff of smoke.

"...I will say of the Lord, He is my refuge and my fortress; my God; in him will I trust..."

Paul started up the stairs. The keening voices continued, jerking him to and fro, jolting his mind with agony until he stumbled, almost dropping the lamp. He got up, fell again, got up, struggling to stay on his feet. The voices were slowly driving him mad.

"...Surely he shall deliver thee from the snare of the fowler, and from the noisome pestilence..."

"You silly fool," the voices croaked at him. "You think you can get rid of us with prayers? Killer. You killed your own mother and father...your friends...your love-bitch."

Paul straightened up, trying not to listen.

"...He shall cover thee with his feathers, and under his wings shalt thou trust; his truth shall be thy shield and buckler..."

The chants of hell subsided momentarily, and Paul made it to the top of the stairs, then started down the hall to Dwayne's room. His mouth burned with every step and his eardrums ached and his stomach continually tried to empty itself into his throat. He felt shrunken, a shadow of himself in a house of shadows, like some giant hand had reached down and compressed him.

"...Thou shalt not be afraid for the terror by night, nor the arrow that flieth by day..."

The whole house was vibrating now. The floors shook, the

ceilings cracked, the walls ballooned like grotesque pregnancies, and behind the walls scurrying movement, as if something alive was waiting—to get out.

"…Nor for the pestilence that walketh in the darkness; nor for the destruction that wasteth at noonday…"

As Paul neared Dwayne's room, he felt depressingly suicidal. He didn't know why, but he could have easily wept. He felt deprived of grace and beauty, and love. He felt useless, as if his own physical existence was a travesty. He was nothing. A non-being. A negative. Something was trying to worm its way into his mind and take control. He tried to fight it, to shake off its death-grip before it made him submit.

"…A thousand shall fall at thy side, and ten thousand at thy right hand; but it shall not come nigh thee…"

The bedroom door slammed shut in front of him. His hands moved automatically. He was unaware he had directed them, moving the lamp against the wood of the door, and blowing it open like it was struck with a battering ram.

"…Only with thine eyes shalt thou behold and see the reward of the wicked…"

The bedroom was an icehouse. He had never been so cold, and yet his clothing was plastered against his body with sweat. Breathing was difficult, and he was tired beyond belief. All he wanted to do was lie down, and go to sleep.

"…Because thou hast made the Lord, which is my refuge, even the most High, thy habitation…"

Something was in the room.

It was Deering's familiar.

The thing he had seen at the churchyard and again at the crypt was standing in front of the closet, blocking Paul's way. He couldn't see its face – nor did he want to – for it stood in deep shadow; a creature of darkness. Nevertheless, Paul knew what it would look like. He had seen it before in his dreams. It was the soldier-thing that always lurked over him just before he screamed his way back to consciousness.

"…There shall no evil befall thee, neither shall any plague come nigh thy dwelling…"

"Coming here was a mistake, Rice," the thing whispered to him. "You don't have enough power to fight us." It laughed, a gurgling kind of laugh. "You were crazy to even think so."

"…For he shall give his angels charge over thee, to keep thee in all thy ways…"

It started to move toward him.

"There are too many of us, Rice. The Cosmic God of Evil is too strong for you. Why don't you just go away…or become one of us?"

"…They shall bear thee up in their hands, lest thou dash thy foot against a stone…"

When the thing walked, it had a reptilian movement to it. The thing stopped directly in front of him, but Paul didn't look up. He kept his eyes lowered.

"…Thou shalt tread upon the lion and adder; the young lion and the dragon shalt thou trample under feet…"

The air in the room was cold and dead. The stench was worse here. Was this the smell of madness…of evil? Paul was beginning to feel sick, delirious. He had an impulse, almost sexual in nature, to throw the lamp away and jump into the closet. It would end his loneliness, his remorse, his…

If you would but worship me. I would give you all there is to have.

Paul listened to the voice crawling inside his head. The lamp began to feel heavy. *If he could just put it down…*

"…Because he hath set his love upon me, therefore will I deliver him; I will set him on high, because he hath known my name…"

"It's so easy to become one of us, Rice," the thing said. "So very easy…SSSOOOOOOOO!"

Paul was touching it with the lamp.

It started to burn like a dry tree, then reached out for him with one blazing arm.

Paul stepped back, watching the flames build into an almost blinding brilliance. It screamed one long, loud, agonizing wail. The flames began to fade as the thing dwindled in size, until there was nothing left but a small pile of smoldering ashes.

"...He shall call upon me, and I will answer him; I will be with him in trouble; I will deliver him, and honour him..."

Paul walked to the closet, taking small, halting steps. The door was open. Hideous forms paraded across his vision as he looked in. Bulbous eyes, grotesque teeth, claw-hands and claw–feet, breasts, vaginas, penises – even excrement and urine floated in front of him. Eviscerated bodies danced, and oozing eyes, like broken eggs, glared. Paul began to vomit. He felt his bladder go and warmth spread down his leg.

"...With long life will I satisfy him, and show him my salvation..."

Paul raised the lamp.

A plaintive voice rose, then fell, like a dying wind.

"We will give you anything you want."

Paul threw the lamp into the closet.

"ANYTHINIIIIinnnnggggg!"

The voices were all gibbering now, a madhouse of screams. Paul's mind cleared, and he was able to move quickly, the molasses effect dissipating as the fire roared into the bedroom in an all consuming rage.

Paul ran down the hall, taking the stairs two at a time, the fire spreading quickly behind him, engulfing the upstairs in a wall of flames. The house was burning like it was made of paper.

There was more screaming. Deep, soul-rending shouts of agony. Then it collapsed into a steady stream of unintelligible sounds as the house shook in a convulsion of pain.

Flames leaped down the staircase and the foyer ceiling fell in just as Paul darted past and out the front door. He stumbled down the terrace steps, falling away from the fire that now reached out through the downstairs windows, then pushed himself up and ran halfway down the drive before stopping and looking back at the house. It was a solid block of flames that cracked and popped like a huge bonfire.

The screams still rang in his ears. He couldn't stop shaking.

EPILOGUE

I have more memories than if I were a thousand years old.

C. Baudelaire

The

Portal

396

I

JUNE 16, 1979. 3:20 A.M. SATURDAY.

Paul watched the fog build into thick, heavy rolls and gather ominously outside his living room window. Linda was in the bedroom. Finally sleeping, thank God, Paul thought. She had had another bad night, and he had held her until she was able to sleep again. Who could blame her after what she had been through.

He took a pack of cigarettes from his robe pocket and lit one. He wasn't sleeping too well either, not after what happened. The war-dream seemed to be gone and also the pain and nausea of pursuing doom that had followed him since Vietnam, but in their place was something less tangible, less definitive in its nature. It haunted the mind. Not being able to sleep at night was just part of it; another was the feeling of being malevolently watched at odd times during the day or night by some invisible lurker. He was sure Linda felt it, too, and Thayer, though they never spoke of it.

A year had almost passed since Durie House was destroyed, completely burned, even its stones were gone, only the hole of its foundation was left. And after, Thayer laid the bones of the Lanark murders to rest, to the satisfaction of everyone concerned without disclosing the insanity of what really took place.

Everything was neatly labeled and put on display for reasonable people to look at without doubt or fear and say, "Yes, that's the way it was." Even Marion Koss was being tried in a routine manner for the murder of Officer Schaefer, even though the poor thing was surely under the influence of Durie House at the time. Paul broke into a slight ironic smile. But of course none of that will come out at the trial. And if he has his way, there will be no trial.

Just stick to the facts, ma'am, as Jack Webb would say. But what are the facts, really, Paul thought. What did they know for sure? Or was it what they didn't know that bothered him. Was the portal destroyed by the fire? Or is it still there in empty space where Durie House once stood, waiting for another Deering to come along? And what happened to Allan Durie's grimoire? The book Deering got from a foolish Claude Fitgerald. Thayer had Deering's house turned upside down and inside out, but couldn't find it. Was that part of what haunted him now?

Paul shook his head and turned away from the window. He put the cigarette out and lit another. Leave it alone, he thought. Put it behind you and try to live again. It was over. All he had to do was bury it, and help Linda do the same.

The telephone startled him, rousing him as if from a deep sleep, its ring jarring and loud, a frightening, late-night noise. He looked at it for a few seconds, then quickly picked it up so it wouldn't wake Linda. He recognized Thayer's voice immediately.

"Paul…" Thayer hesitated.

"Paul, it's starting again. There's been another murder…"